ABOUT T

R.H.Hale was born in Edinburgh, Scotland. After gaining a First Class honours degree in science at Kingston University in Surrey, she went on to explore the arts and has since worked in theatre including the Edinburgh Fringe, ghost tours, and writing. She currently resides in East Lothian.

R. H. HALE

CHURCH MOUSE

BOOK ONE

Memoir of a vampire's servant

CHIMAERA PRODUCTIONS

First published as an eBook by Help For Writers Ltd in 2017.
This paperback edition published in Great Britain by Chimaera Productions in 2018.

www.chimaeraproductions.org

ISBN: 978-1-910823-28-6

Printed and bound in Great Britain by CLOC Ltd, Tottenham N17 9QU

This publication is a work of fiction. Any resemblance to actual events or real persons, living or dead, is purely coincidental.

This book is dedicated to my parents

PROLOGUE

20th December 1998.

Children's singing voices dissolve in the church's thin air.

'In the bleak midwinter, frosty …'

My sleeve is wet. They'll see my red eyes where I crouch. Running out of time, I must stop crying or they'll see.

'… wind made moan.'

Tap-tap-tap on wood. A breath of wind.

Tap-tap.

A draught comes through the keyhole, no more than a breath, so cold it burns.

What is it you like more? Crying, or crying outside our door?

'Who's that? What are you doing in there?'

In here is far away.

'Are you a ghost?'

What's a ghost?

'A dead person, but sort of … still here, never went to heaven.'

Or hell?

'No.'

Oh. Maybe I am, then.

'They say not to believe in ghosts, that there's no such thing.'

What am I then?

'I dunno.'

What are you?

'Just a girl.'

What's that?

'I – I'm a person.'

Hehe, and what's that?

'A human.'

Oh. But what's that*?*

'A human, ya know. Teacher says we came from monkeys.'

That makes you an animal. You like animals?
'Yes. We're drawing picture projects of them in school.'
Then you know some animals eat people.
'Um, yes.'
So, what am I?
'If you're a ghost, are you the ghost of whoever's buried in there?'
I should say not, he was a bore. Blow your nose.
'Does that make you a friendly ghost?'
That depends on the friends. Where are yours?
'They went and sided with them.'
What's 'them'?
'The choir. Bullies.'
Is that what ails our recurring doorkeeper tonight?
'I didn't want to be in the church choir. They won't leave me alone.'
Are they here?
'Two of them.'
Their names.
'Definitely Naomi Brennan, she's over there. Steph–'
Shhhhh.
'Sorry. Stephanie Loutit. Jason Dawes too, same class as me.'
So if I'm a ghost and a ghost is a person and a person is a human and a human is from monkeys and that makes me an animal, that means I can eat people too if I like, doesn't it?
'No.'
But it's what you said I was! Because you're wise, aren't you? Or are you not?
I sense a trap. Budding dread tastes of metal in my saliva.
Are you not clever?
'I – I hope I am.'
So now I have to, don't I? Whom do I slice, you or someone else?

'What? No, don't! You can't.'

Ahhh, but you said I was. Plus, if I'm a ghost I can just float on through this door and get you, can't I?

'Maybe.'

By your wise analogy I need only be a 'person' to qualify. Choose. Or we decide.

I should get up and run away. Somehow I know I can't; it'll get me.

'Don't, that's scary. I don't know.'

Choose or we decide. Does your flesh cut like butter or pop like a pus head?

'No, you're fibbing. I want to go away now.'

You can't, Monkey. We're faster. And getting bored.

'Please can I go?'

Choose. Last chance.

(Say something!) 'The bullies. Take them.'

Those three unwise monkeys. Have you heard of the Three Wise Monkeys?

'Not sure. I think so.'

There were four – Is that our doorkeeper blubbering again?

Sniffing, snivelling, holding it in for all I'm worth. 'No.'

And would blabbing to everyone about closet ghosts be wise or unwise?

'Unwise.'

Why?

'They'll laugh and they won't believe me.'

Is that all?

'And … and I'll be a fourth unwise monkey?'

Clever human–person–girl. Is being Number Four what you want?

'No.'

Let's see how clever you are.

The icy draught wisps, and goes away.

'Hello?'

...

'Hello? Are you there?'

~

[Retrieved from *The Bronmeg Post* news archive]

23rd December 1998:

> Bronmeg Police are appealing for witnesses following a vicious attack on eight-year-old Naomi Brennan, found at 8:40 p.m. last night. According to a public statement issued by Detective Inspector Forbes, 'The attacker severely mauled the child's face and inflicted fatal injuries. We ask that any eyewitnesses contact their local police authority. We are following various leads ...'

27th December 1998:

> ... state that Jason Dawes is in critical condition. Police reports indicate that the victim's ears were mutilated. However, due to the nature of the attack they cannot rule out the possibility of an animal attack at this time.

2nd January 1998:

> At approximately eight o'clock on Thursday 31st December, Stephanie Loutit, aged 8, was found severely lacerated less than a mile from her home. Detective Inspector Nichols informed the Bronmeg Post that 'The manner of these recent child mutilations may be related.' In the space of a week, local children Naomi Brennan and Jason Dawes were also fatally attacked in similar circumstances.

~

I'm listening.

'C'mon, Rob, just tell us! Whaddid you hear him say?'

'I'm not supposed to tell you! I wasn't supposed to hear him. My daddy says police stuff's secret.'

'We won't tell! Honest!'

'Teachers aren't saying anything! Not fair!'

'Yeah, c'mon Rob! What happened?'

Rob is popular, the best football player in P. E. He used to brag about his policeman dad being James Bond. This is the first time I've seen him afraid.

'I don't know.' Rob shrugs.

'Tell us! G'on Rob, I got extra lunch money this week!'

'Yeah, I have too! Whaddid ya dad saaaaay?'

They all crowd around Rob at once.

'*C'mon Rob! What he say? What he say? Are any of 'em comin' back? What he say? What –*'

'*Okaaay!* He said Naomi's eyes were plucked out and Steph's tongue got bit off. I think they died like Jason. But don't tell anyone! I'll get grounded! I'll get my arse tanned!'

They're too busy gasping to hear Rob's guilty appeal.

I was only seven years old.

PART ONE

They had lived so long ago, their time was so unlike the present, their hopes and motives were so widely removed from ours, that between them and the living there seemed to stretch a gulf too wide for even a spirit to pass.

Thomas Hardy, *The Mayor of Casterbridge*

Chapter One

Do you find that in the phantasm of memory, places are larger than their physical reality? That a set of walls, columns, ceiling or windows, surface in your mind then tower over you like a Sphinx, contemplating you with entrenched superiority? History grows on places like a fungus until they have eyes of their own; a secret soul, a hidden murmur.

I can still feel the invasive pollen in my nose from the orchids in the chancel. On a bright day, the sun would turn stained glass faces, robes, angels, saints, skies and disciples of every shade and hue into a bewitching seduction. In my mind's eye, I walk slowly down the nave of my old friend, enemy and companion. As ever my tentative footsteps, light as they are, make the empty church certain to betray me; each step lets the watchful air cry out my presence, from the slow deep thud of my boot heel, to its chorus of echoes rippling like alarm bells off the aisles to the chancel, through the transept arches and back to the nave again. Funny how it always seems louder the slower you walk. It is a comforting sound, but only when you know you are alone, and always loudest when you desperately need to be invisible.

I look up. The old beams are of pale timber, like the re-vamped floor, thanks or no thanks to council-funded refurbish-

ment rather too garish for a church this age. Authentic in swerving elegance, those beams are insulted by walls of cheap white
paint, where the original Renaissance stone claws its way back
through the papery layer in grey patches and cracks, glaring at
the modern floor as if to spit on it. I take comfort in that, too.

I was a curious sort of girl, I suppose. So long as no one
watched me, this building, the stained glass and meditative
echoes, were all mine. As a child I was granted the freedom to
play solo games, imaginary adventures or hide and seek with
myself, running up and down the aisles, finding secluded shadows in and out of the transepts, usually hiding from my elderly
aunts behind the arcade pillars, my trusty allies.

Aunts Pam and Alison would spend ages at a time chatting with Minister Falkirk, complimenting his altar flowers,
where did he buy them, might they have a cutting, and so on,
incessantly tedious babble. Whereas I, from the age of three
onwards, was given free rein, a temporary window of liberty
to run around the church on their nagging condition that I stay
indoors. I soon found some favourite spots.

The pipe organ always unnerved me. Classical in appearance, oversized for the building, to me it was a gigantic overbearing leviathan; I was afraid to go near it, half-certain it
waited ready to open its mouth in some great gape of baleen
pipes and chew me, further, further in, and *gulp*. I grew bolder
with age while the organ comparatively shrank in size, until
ultimately, we reached a truce, the company of that loud beast
preferable to the two elderly ladies I was obliged to call family.

Family. Related by blood. I found it hard to believe. I saw
nothing of myself in them; they raised me on the principle
that family is a good thing, where all caring and self-sacrifice
comes from, but if I was already at odds with run-of-the-mill
normality, I was certainly at odds with *them*. Their reaction to
my perpetual indifference was to try and 'smooth out the incon-
sistencies in her character', all because normality, according to

popular opinion, is also supposed to be a good thing.

I feel it necessary to explain to you my connection with this church, so let's just clear up something important first, shall we: God, religion, prayers, Moses, the Ten so-called Commandments? It did not occur to me to care. I was taken to sermons and told to sing hymns because that is what little girls are expected to do – what they're told. While heads bowed in prayer, and Falkirk, astute and gloomy in his ministerial garb, prattled on from his lectern, I lost myself in the stained glass.

I knew every inch of these kaleidoscopic windows.

The splashes of luscious purple were my favourite – such a juicy tint that always made me thirsty – and I loved the crusading figures in armour, straining hard to see every detail on their weaponry and the haloed beings to which they played martyr, fashioning my own stories for them a thousand times over. Sadly, with age I became jaded. The windows never changed. No new stories. In the disheartening wisdom that comes with maturity, their faces became tired, their gestures lazy, their stories and adventures fading to be replaced by something blandly biblical. I could not help feeling, like a sharp snag in my side, that the glass figures had let me down, they had sided with the very normality I once used them to escape from. I grew bitter towards the glass effigies and forgot their stories; they blended into a meaningless population, like everyone else.

I achieved independent thought by way of solitude, and through this established my tolerant non-belief. From puberty onwards, my attendance at sermons became less and less, and yet you would still find me there alone on random days of the week, daydreaming or reading Dickens, Carl Sagan, the Brontës and Oscar Wilde in the pews or my habitual hideaways. There was no hypocrisy in my private detours there after school or on weekends, the church and I had a relationship: I loved the *building*. It was a simple pleasure compared to living in my aunts' house, the Christianity, hymns and psalms being immaterial.

I also had an addiction. The smell. Not the obtrusive reek of orchids, daffodils or lilies on the altar – the *real* smell of the church and its stonework. My favourite features were those small, unnoticed fingerprints of the past: old nails in the wall, so rusted and bent they appeared melted; shafts of wood in the mortar, worn down to stumps; a crooked hook, once smooth and round, now a jagged talon. I would find them in overlooked corners and then seek out more. I would touch them, running my finger slowly, almost lovingly, over the texture, taking care to do no harm, thinking all the time, *This is a piece of time travel. When hammered into the wall, this world was so different. The man standing here, the clothes he wore, the masons, the scents, the things he heard. What did the worker look like, sound like? I'm touching a piece of life from a world nobody remembers.* In this hypnotic bliss, I let the earthen scent transcend me. Old stone, like a quiet old man, immune to the fast track of unwary humanity, humbled and wizened with age – *this* was the building I knew and loved. Time leaves its breath on places, if you know where to look.

This young girl's fancy envisaged that the heart and soul of a place known to her for so long, that had absorbed revolutions, sickness, poverty and the smoke of wars, could warmly look upon her and whisper, *You and I, friend. Let them stay numb. We can smell the true essence beneath conventional niceties and flowers on Sunday. We know each other's secrets, don't we, Rona?*

Secrets.

Well, it did. It looked at me. Looked me up and down. And as if the hideousness of that organ served as a premonitory warning, indeed it came to pass that I was chewed, gulped and swallowed. By the time I reached adulthood, I still knew less of my church than I know of you, Stranger.

Part One

~

Instances from this early phase of my life bear mentioning. I have explained that there were nooks and crannies, and though to a small child that is a playground, by church standards St Patrick's was not particularly big.

You enter the front portal through a large pair of arched doors, the ceiling of a narthex passes over you. The other entrance is for staff only, an uninteresting single door hidden under the arcade in the south aisle to your right. Don't bother trying it, it is always locked. You walk east into the nave between a small sea of church benches; above you are the timber beams and badly-painted walls we have already met; far left and right, the transepts. Approaching you from both sides, the aisles are lined with stone pillars.

Look right. The south aisle houses an old vestry, since partitioned into a unisex toilet and miniaturised vestry for Falkirk to hoard his teabags and biscuit tins. Further along is the pipe organ, do you see the heavy curtain by it, the burgundy one? Good. Now, turn around and look up.

What you see is a balcony, directly above the narthex. Its decorated stone balustrade is appealing, is it not? As dated as the church itself. If you want to sneak a peek, go and draw the burgundy curtain. A narrow, helical staircase spirals upwards, its metal railing and steps painted black. It winds, round and round like the skeleton of an upturned python. Ugly, isn't it? Climb it.

You find yourself on a small landing. Face west and keep walking, it is not far.

Turn right. You're there, you can now wave down at me from the balcony, or Haunted Balcony, as Little Rona dubbed it. If there ever was a ghost up there I only saw it once and too briefly, barely more than an outline. You see, I thought it was my mother. It certainly resembled her photograph, but my aunts kept so few after she died and I knew her face from nowhere else.

I have introduced you to an integral element in this story: the gallery.

The gallery was shady, charming in its way. The stair was marked 'Private', for boring reasons, I assumed, because, unless they were hiding a bomb up there, sensible reasons are pathetic to a ghost-hunting seven-year-old. I, who otherwise knew every yard of the church, was magnetised to this unexplored zone, leaving me ravenous. I *had* to see it. You see, I was adventurous but shy, and unknown territory made me wary, so I would stand by the narthex, staring longingly upward, hungrier with curiosity every day, awaiting a feminine spectre that never reappeared, drawn nearer and nearer.

I remember my aunts nagging Falkirk to fill that disused space with their local choir group, perhaps the only occasion when I sighed along with him. A pair of busybodies they were, with their choirs, church meetings and charity events, and their clique stank of perfume, worse than the overbearing altar flowers.

During one such church meeting, I gave in and stole away under the burgundy curtain. *More*, I thought, placing my small hand on the railing. *Come on, just one more step.* I placed my small hand on the black railing, daring myself, excited and nervous with a child's instinct that I was not supposed to be there, it was naughty. *I could get in trouble. They might shout.*

I was over halfway there, growing confident, feeling triumphant already …

'Rona! Where are you? C'mon, Button, we've got the bakery and market before dinner.' Cue the clogging of Aunt Alison's Sunday heels in my direction.

I ground my teeth with frustration. 'We'? They always said that, '*We're* going there', '*We're* doing this', '*We're* having that', as if I was ever given any say in the matter. I hated their endless shopping excursions worst of all. Hell, I hated *them*, especially for the interruption. I took one last miserable look at my unreachable destination and descended, furious with myself. If I'd had more guts and climbed faster ... Dammit!

Next Sunday evening I tried again.

November 1998.

Due to bust pipes at the community centre, my aunts begged a reluctant Falkirk to grant them the church space for a charity meeting after the evening service, ten or eleven fellow church-goers in attendance. Falkirk hovered over the proceedings, pacing and pacing the chancel, constantly checking his watch, colour rising. I saw him, his jowls were getting redder than clown rouge. By eight o'clock he declared they had ten minutes left, no more.

I was an equally reluctant witness. Earning my pivate time meant first playing puppet to my aunts' scripted instructions in front of their friends: Mrs Mc-Something and Mrs Et Cetera saying oh what a lovely dress I had (I never picked the damn thing) and oh what a big girl I was becoming. After my dutiful 'How are you, Mrs Wotsit?' and 'Thank you, Mrs Thingy,' I was freed and skipped off to my usual haunts.

Aunt Alison called after me, 'Be sure you don't knock Minister Falkirk's nice lilies over!' I wanted to shove them down her perfumed throat.

From behind a pillar in the south aisle, I made sure the coast was clear and padded towards the burgundy curtain. The leviathan pipe organ gleamed its savage smile, my inanimate spy. I moved precariously, fearing the instrument would snitch on me in a storm of trumpeting keys, ducked behind the curtain, and released my breath.

The python's black skeleton hadn't run away since last week. There it waited, daring me again.

Step, step, step ... I paused. *Can't see where it goes.* I

couldn't gauge my distance. Without daylight, the stair simply disappeared into greyness, the way Mrs Aldridge taught us to draw shadow with the edge of our pencils in school. Its tenebrous landing might not even be there, it might just climb on and on forever. Where had my confidence gone? Tonight, this once adventurous platform was the shaky plank of a pirate ship. The railing was clammier, I felt misplaced and all I could do was cling to the logic that if I made it so far last Sunday, I could tonight, and more. *Probably boring up there anyway*, I reassured myself, and went. Step, step, step, step, step … I paused, this didn't feel right, but I was losing time.

I was not even halfway. Step, step –

'Oi! YOU!'

He leapt out at me from the top: an oily, grimy, pug-nosed face of stubble. What happened next came too fast, I wouldn't clearly recall who did what until hours later when I sat, hunched on my bed, still shaking, trying not to cry in case my aunts saw fit to tell me off again. I still hear his nasty voice to this day.

'Oi, little bitch! Whaddafuck you think you're doing? You can't come up here. Get out of it! Get!'

Heavy trainers thumping, he lunged and proceeded to wrench a healthy clump of hair, roots and all, from my tender young scalp.

I tumbled.

Stinging fire shot through my palms as I landed at the bottom of the stairs, twisting an ankle, a flush burning my forehead scarlet, my first experience of true panic, it was surreal.

The pug-nosed sentry was coming down, so rabid I thought he meant to beat me lifeless. He appeared middle-aged, wiry in a tatty shirt and combat trousers, sickly bags hung beneath his eyes and a repulsive line of fluid dribbled from his nostril, but his most sinister feature was an uncontrollable twitchiness as if ill, too innocent was I to recognise a drug addict when I saw one.

I couldn't get up.

Can't move, something has me pinned flat, the killing weight of a massive log – no, the leathered sole of a giant, holding my neck down. Must be a giant, for no person is this strong!

Prostrate on the floor, the use of my neck disabled, my entire view consisted solely of the helical stair and pug-nosed man, tipped ninety degrees. He had stopped shouting, pale and mute.

'Feeling skittish, Daniels?'

A man's voice. Not the booming I expected of giants, and not Falkirk.

I watched the pug-nosed sentry. My forgotten hair glided down from his fist. This 'Daniels' had magically transformed from barking farmyard pig into a jittering guinea pig, stunned by this out-of-view Goliath, in fact he was now twitching so badly I thought he might trip and fall on me.

Of course, my aunts and their clones had heard the uproar. Anxious footsteps and various utterances of 'My goodness!' were travelling down the nave.

'Here they come,' said the unseen giant above me. 'Or did you plan on howling any louder before *she* does?'

Without a word Daniels bolted up the stairs, and a magician somewhere must have waved their magic wand, for the weight lifted and I could move again.

Nobody there. No giant. No Goliath. I was stupefied.

I tottered from the curtain into a crowd of Sunday winter dresses encircling me, Falkirk amongst them, and it was he who incriminated me. 'She ... she must have tried wandering to the gallery,' he said, glancing upward, eerily tranquil. 'It's private, love. No access.' He said no more.

As to my pulled hair and damaged ankle, an abused kid knows no better with an army of adult fingers waggling at them as if they agreed with my punishment. Off I was trotted, due a day's scolding from my aunts, 'Did you go bothering the man?' and 'Well that's what happens when you're a bad girl!' and

'Big girls don't cry!'

On our way out, the shiny jaws of the pipe organ winked over its wicked grin, guarding the burgundy curtain, an oily bully somewhere beyond. So that was the ghostly trick of the gallery, another bully. I felt I had lost all right to even glance at the balcony, to think such a nice thing had a 'Daniels' living in it! *Is that how it works?* I thought. *Why are the nicest things given to horrible people? Or is something beautiful a lie in itself that only likes cruelty for company?*

I was dragged out, limping and shaken.

20th December 1998.

The cosiness of St Patrick's made it a favourite for Bronmeg Primary School's Junior Christmas Choir Recital, not that I joined the choir by choice; my dipped toe was an inconvenience of my pushy aunt's contriving. Closer to the event, our choir rehearsed there three times a week after school.

A child's year is a lifetime, and when the winter sun sets early you feel a pang of liberation to be outdoors past your bedtime. But this rebellion limited me to the church, where the presence of gormless classmates violated my private bond with the place. Children can be cruel, girls crueller, and matriarch Naomi Brennan was a ticking time bomb waiting to disembowel me, the school runt. She hated me in class, she hated me in the playground and she hated me here, joining the choir merely lit the fuse; spitting on my sheet music, stealing from my school bag, putting gum in my hair, getting everyone to laugh at me.

That night the taunts came to a humiliating head. With tears. During the interval I sneaked off, hid in a shady corner of the north transept and snivelled, as formal a resignation from the choir as I cared to give, bullied in and forthwith bullied out.

In the transept, my small size was well concealed by the chunky memorial tablet of a certain Lord William Menzies, a

Renaissance patron of St Patrick's interred in the wall beyond. By this memorial and coat of arms stood a large oak cupboard, older than Queen Victoria, younger than the church, embedded in the outline of a doorway in the wall, fitting like a glove. Its double doors were always bolted and it never occurred to me to wonder why the keyhole sometimes emitted a draught, like breath. Banishing myself there, wiping my nose on my sleeve and feeling sorry for myself, this deserter would be lying to you if she denied a furtive pride in making an unearthly new acquaintance that evening. The draught spoke to me.

Three nights later, after having painstakingly gone out of my way to avoid any future collisions with the odious Daniels, to my utter bewilderment *he* approached *me*.

The choir recital, attended by parents, locals and teachers, commenced in the late afternoon, the eve of Naomi's reckoning. I had no more premonition than anyone else.

The church was packed. Candles tinted the holly, nativity scene and Christmas tree with appetising splendour while the ruddy cheeks of proud parents lined the front pews. Aunt Alison did her best to rattle my conscience for quitting the cute vocal mania; water off a duck's back when this safe distance from the choir was, for me, a reprieve. I had spared myself the torture for a change, no matter what Alison said.

The recital ended, applause ensued. Parents and children lingered, buttoned their coats, shook hands with Falkirk, with other parents and with teachers and exchanged mince pies. My aunts joined in the polite anarchy.

I stayed in the pew. I had been a reader from a young age and I was attempting to wade through *A Christmas Carol*, a toilsome mission for my tender years. I remember the page I was at, too, easily distracted by the gritty elegance of John Leech's Dickensian illustrations. It should have been comical:

'... the dying flame leaped up, as though it cried "I know

him! Marley's Ghost!" '

Here was the illustration, inky and moody, the flame transformed into a momentary beacon complete with funny little facial wail, illuminating the spectre of Jacob in chains, horrible, lanky, bloodless and wide-eyed – just like the figure standing over you, Rona?

I gave such a start that my book fell.

Daniels stood there like a zombie, gaunt and unhealthy, glaring at me with irises like pebbles, his unblinking whites so wide you would think the eyelids were snipped off. A deadened beat of silence stamped between us and the recital attendees, footsteps, candles and voices became a dense hum like water in my ears. Finally, Daniels spoke, tonelessly, without any reaction to my reaction.

'I was told to give you this.'

He gave it.

Chore completed, he crossed the nave, as unnoticed as any ghost should be. As he withdrew behind the curtain, sounds of the living returned; families jingled car keys and pulled rambling classmates apart while my aunts talked to too many people as usual. The pews were vacant but for me.

On my lap sat a new addition. A soft toy. A monkey. Made in China for all I knew, you could find thousands similar in any cheap toy shop across the British Isles. Its arms and legs were hacked off, coarse fluffy stuffing hung out in tufts. *Have you heard of the Three Wise Monkeys? Wise or unwise?* I hid it under my coat.

As we walked home, my reasonably sensitive Aunt Pam tried to cheer me up. 'Thought of all you want from Santa, Button?' she asked.

'Are there books on the Four Wise Monkeys, Auntie?'

'Another book!' exclaimed Aunt Alison, a veteran *Eastenders* fan who only liked her Dickens with ketchup. 'Well, you can't be getting that!'

'No, dear,' Aunt Pam agreed. 'There are only three wise monkeys.'

'There's four,' I mumbled.

None of it made any sense until word spread through school about the news headlines a fortnight later.

10th January, 1999. Happy New Year.

Was I a good girl? Did I not always do as I was told? I did what my aunts told me. I did what the closet ghosts told me.

Classroom mutters surrounded the absence of my school enemies until the dawning awareness brewed over me like a rain cloud, chasing me from school, all the way home, all the way to bed. Nightmares clustered in my sleep: I was in the corner of the transept, sliding towards the cupboard, I tried stopping myself but the ground was a belligerent downward slope, wouldn't let me stop, sliding into the keyhole, kicking fruitlessly. *Tap-tap. Feeling skittish?*

I woke in the safety of my bedroom.

Giants.

This Sunday morning my aunts were shaking their heads, gasping over their boiled eggs and pristine teacups as they passed each other the newspaper while the radio reported news of murdered innocents.

During church service that day I made my aunts angry. Despite threats of a smack and no dessert after Sunday roast, I refused to be dragged anywhere near the north aisle, the transept was too easy to see. A globule of guilty sickness had grown in the pit of my stomach and now squirmed there like a fat worm, getting bigger. *The news headlines. Rumours in the playground. I've done something bad. Noise on wood.* My fertile imagination saw the antique cupboard fly open and swallow me.

I buried myself under my coat, huddling up on the pew.

'What's wrong, Button?' Aunt Pam was shaking me.

'What's all this silliness now?' interjected her boisterous

sister, approaching with her hero Falkirk in tow.

'She's scared of the cupboard,' Pam answered, uncurling me.

'Can't do anything with this niece today!' Alison brayed. 'Imagine! A clever girl like that scared of a poor old wardrobe. And get your feet off the benches, Rona, you know better!'

'Oh?' Falkirk said coolly. 'The cupboard in the corner? Why is that?'

'She woke us up crying last night,' said Pam, trying to put my coat on. 'Said she had a bad dream.'

'Did you?' he asked me.

I was too put on the spot to respond. Falkirk expressed no interest in children and habitually refrained from interacting with me, why should I learn how to talk to him now? In any case he smiled, treating me to a rare view of his yellow teeth, the only thing worse than his glower.

'Oh, I can nip those bad dreams in the bud,' he sang. 'We can solve that!'

He vanished beyond the burgundy curtain. I heard voices. A minute later he returned, striding towards the item of furniture itself. A key clicked in that big keyhole, the doors opened. There. Falkirk proudly presented a rectangular space: wooden base and sides, the basic dimensions of any cupboard, stupendously uninteresting, fabulously tamed – and completely featureless. Emptier than Mother Hubbard's, not a brush, not a shovel, a cheerless bit of carpentry.

'See?' he happily declared. 'Better? No spooky nightmares. Just a cupboard!' For emphasis, he innocently *tapped*! the wooden base.

I ran from the building, a loose coat sleeve dangling inside out.

~

New school term. My classmates constantly harangued Rob for any leaked news of Naomi, Jason and Stephanie, while the teachers were sworn to zip-lipped discretion, as if children are incapable of concocting their own nasty conclusions.

The snow was reduced to slush, meaning dirty puddles and wet socks. I spent lunchtime in the school library and fished out an encyclopaedia.

The Three Wise Monkeys:

A proverb of Japanese folklore dating from the 17th century which teaches the means of living well by ignoring wicked thoughts or deeds, signified by three symbolic monkeys in specific postures. The monkey *Mizaru* covers its eyes for 'See No Evil', *Kikazaru* covers its ears for 'Hear No Evil', with *Iwazaru* covering its mouth to symbolise 'Speak No Evil'. Lesser known is a fourth monkey, *Shizaru*, possibly originating from ancient Chinese texts, often depicted as folding its limbs or covering itself between the legs, to symbolise 'Do No Evil'.

Is being Number Four what you want?

After school, I went straight home to my room and sought out my gift from the closet ghosts. Its synthetic insides were spilling out from the four hacked limbs, leaving small mounds of sandy particulates in my mahogany drawer like artificial snow, a repugnant texture offensive to the touch. I got rid of it at the bottom of our kitchen bin under as many food tins, junk mail envelopes, ready meal packages, used teabags, biscuit wrappers and hollow milk cartons as I could cram on top.

I made no connection between monkeys and giants, it was years before I forgot to avoid the north transept, and Shizaru did no evil by forever holding her peace. They would have dismembered my body.

Chapter Two

Seventeen summers later I found I was destined to be home-less. Aunt Alison had passed away at Marie Curie hospice; her sister Pam would soon follow.

I am bastard born. My mother died when I was too young to remember. My father? I doubt he was even aware of my con-ception; no memoirs, photos or accounts of him were offered in my aunts' house, nor does he matter when I stopped caring long ago. Adopted by my two aunts, sisters of a departed grand-mother, we lived in middle-class suburbs a short distance from St Patrick's in the large town of Bronmeg, Warwickshire. To be fair to my deceased aunts, they were determined to raise a well-to-do young lady because our house stood a hair's breadth from council homes with an undesirable reputation for crime, drug-dealing, muggings, gangs, you name it.

Solitude came as no burden to me, it was the *want* of solitude that usually fuelled my problems, not that I was an unpleasant girl, and though not without friends, they were few in number, coming and going with the tide. My greatest weakness was my sensitivity: just as I automatically absorbed atmospheres, if I sensed danger or reproach, I shrank into inconspicuous ether. My high school guidance tutors sent notes (without my knowl-edge at the time) to Aunts Pam and Alison, recommending they 'push' me to be more outgoing and socially active, 'Being cruel to be kind' as the smug old motto goes, my oh my what wisdom. I didn't understand what their problem was when any idiot knows nothing makes you lonelier than a crowd.

You may conjecture that the generation gap in my family relations was key to my vulnerability? I would disagree. Meek, natural-born shyness emits a vapour to predatory classmates; they circle you, from a distance at first, sniff-sniff, getting closer – eventually one takes a nip. Then a bite. Before you know it you're the centre of attention, and *my* school included kids from the crime-ridden council estate near our house. You can imagine. I learned to keep my head low, learned to walk a pace quicker past swarms of lingering youths outside fish and chip shops, learned the best routes to avoid dodgy streets and the safest times to wait at bus stops, even when it put me out of my way.

Mind, I was not above re-merging from those teenage years with a subtle dusting of grit, namely smoking and an adequate lexicon of therapeutic profanity. Miraculously I managed to keep my smelly addiction a secret for years, until that evening before Aunt Alison's funeral when her tired, weakening, seventy-six-year-old sister stopped me on my way to bed and said, 'Um, I'm out of cigarettes. Mind if I have one of *yours*?' A stunned pause. 'How long have you been smoking?' she added with a copious dollop of sarcasm. Not the first time I had underestimated long-term smoker, retired dancer, and, I suspect, former rebel, Pam. I had to love her for it.

I hit nineteen and went to university, stuck on ideas for a career path and hoping for direction, and considering my love of books and collections, I half-heartedly started a BA in Archiving. I didn't finish the course. I may as well tell you that halfway through my degree I attempted suicide.

My tuition money had dried up anyway and the future was bleak. Bleak because I also ran out of gas. Something was already dying in me. Who or what to blame for this? A rocky childhood? My aunts? Depression? The planet? A child may want to be a million things as they grow and progress, but not everyone progresses inside, and as sure as society dictates how to process the fresh, unspoiled slate of a child's mind, we are not clones; some bulbs need to sprout and blossom on their own, not be carved by invasive input from all angles then forced onto a conveyor belt with the rest. Try that and you could smother them, kill them even, asking me to press buttons I didn't have … Christ, just let my mind *breathe*! But no, the older I grew the thinner it spread me until the world shrank into a thimble, ambition drained and my slate was grey, something was lost.

As for tuition fees, when I discovered I was at university on borrowed time, I searched for ideas, alternatives, any ambition at all, and found none. There were too many dreams of what I wanted to be, so many that they overwhelmed, overlapped, conflicted, fell through, cancelled out and murdered one another. I had chosen the archiving course because it was available and intellectually doable. Not financially doable. Well, sigh, I made plans to return home.

On the eve of dropping out I was invited to a classmate's birthday party with vodka, cider, the works. The voice of alcohol is a nasty daemon to have on your shoulder. Not in my right mind, I passed out on my dorm bed with rum and two full packets of paracetamol in my belly. Woken later by nausea, I wound up on a hospital ward for two days and three nights.

I went home with a single suitcase, collapsed veins from their umpteen blood tests, and told Aunt Pam nothing – her clock was already ticking with colorectal cancer.

The chores came down to me as she grew frailer, her tumour steadily winning. You could have folded those two foul wrinkles drooping from her neck into tortillas. Speaking of necks, mine grew stiff with nodding at her solicitor's reminders that our house was rented, the bank account dwindling, and my current situation wouldn't keep my head above water after Pam expired.

We got through three more years, I was often melancholy and, notwithstanding the obvious, unsure why. I did errands for Aunt Pam and her friends, I mowed lawns, pet-sitting, house-sitting, I passed my driver's test, I temped in office jobs, turned the leaves on my calendar, and – like my emaciated love life – hailed constellations at night and forgot their names by morning. I collected Aunt Pam's prescriptions, fed pigeons, ate chocolate for breakfast, vacuumed, plucked my eyebrows, brushed my hair and took long walks.

I did odds and ends. I smoked cigarettes. I did nothing. It's awful to feel the need for something without knowing what it is.

And I visited my church. Avoiding services, St Patrick's became my reading room. Falkirk looked ill lately, and though rumours abounded of a heart condition, his dilated pupils, baggy eyes and twitching now reminded me rather too much of Daniels, St Patrick's verger and handyman as it turned out, who never seemed far. Falkirk addressed him as 'Ian, wash this!' or 'Ian, fix that!' Daniels also had what you might call dodgy-looking 'friends', thugs more like, occasionally passing in and out of the church gallery between sermons, leaving a whiff of cannabis behind. So, Rona dutifully reports this violation to Minister Falkirk, who emerges from his vestry, lit cigarette between his yellow teeth (indoors!), saying oh it's no problem, all is hunky dory. Shut up, Rona.

Daniels and I ignored one another despite a grinding temptation to return the favour and wrench *his* hair out. Besides, adult sense teaches us that certain memories are an overwrought child's imagination. Because there are no giants.

I scattered Aunt Pam's ashes over Bronmeg's River Bridge, and have now brought you to the summer of my twenty-fifth year.

~

Twenty-four-hour summer days are hogged by greedy light and hungry heat, reducing the cooling breathers of night to a cameo role. On the twenty-eighth of July, midday, the church was floodlit with golden sun, bathing the nave and I in stained glass rainbows. This day, this unforgettable day, set to demolish anything my twenty-five years had prepared me for.

'Rona? What are you doing in here? No services at this hour.'

Falkirk snapped me out of a dour stupor in the front pew, bent over a copy of Thackeray's *Vanity Fair* I wasn't reading.

'Sorry? Reverend Falkirk, I'm often here. Sorry, I was … was reading.'

'Why?'

I flinched at his derision. 'It's not a problem, I hope? I mean, you know I'm usually here alone.'

Falkirk stood over me, beetroot, flexing his fingers and glancing around restlessly. I took his irritability with a grain of salt; his being a reserved, self-contained man, our lifelong acquaintance was so far impersonal.

'Are you ill, Minister? Is there anything I can do?'

'Hmm?' He bounced as if seeing me for the first time.

'Reverend.'

'It's a –' he coughed into his fist, 'a grand day. Why are you not outdoors?'

'I needed to think. I'm in trouble.' With so few people to speak to, the landlord's henpecking phone calls and my funds virtually zero, for what it was worth I let it spill. 'My lease, it's finished, the landlord's selling the house. I don't want to wind up homeless or in a hostel. I'm freaked.'

Falkirk, nodding impatiently, didn't seem to hear me. So much for reaching out.

36

'Have you seen my cleaner,' he asked, 'Ian, at all?'

'Er, sorry, no.'

'Well, he washes the floor soon, so no visitors till next service, I'm afraid!' He was leaving me. 'Use the aisle exit. The front's locked.'

With that Falkirk opened the small south aisle door and vanished into his vestry before I had the chance to pack up. Hurt and rushed, I was nearly outside before realising I had almost forgotten my Thackeray novel, and doubled back –

What's that smell?

– to squeeze it into my handbag.

Picture me doing so; take a snapshot with your mind: my elbow raised, open bag hanging at an angle, motionless. This is how you would see me. It is no photo. Something has stopped me.

The smell.

A deep breath.

That's smoke.

Smoke, serious smoke, comes from no cigarette. I raised my nose and scanned the chancel, inhaling repeatedly. It was getting stronger. I walked at a dreamlike pace, my bag still hanging open, taking in long, deep breaths. To the south it thinned, so not from outside. West? No. I searched eastwards, treading in and out of colour and shadow between the stained glass reflections and pillars of the north aisle. The smell was thickening. Moving through this empty church drenched in summer sun, I was hauntingly loud, for the building had an uncanny intelligence – it answered you, pitching echoes at its convenience. Today, it was rearing at me.

Something's burning.

And here we are, the north transept, unchanged in seventeen years. I turned in a circle, concentrating. Without warning the smokiness condensed so rapidly that I spluttered.

There it is. It couldn't be, and it was – smoke leaking through the huge keyhole in the cupboard's double doors. The cupboard with nothing inside. Whisperer's doors. Monkeys. Memories of a kid's imagination.

There was no alternative explanation. Fire.

'Falkirk!' I shouted. 'Come quickly! There's a fire in the crypt!'

No answer.

Smoke was bleeding through all the chinks in the cupboard now, not just the keyhole. *A piece of furniture. See, Rona, just a silly old cupboard.* I must have been a cowardly sight, tarrying like a fool outside the locked doors, watching smoky poison seep into my beloved building, unsure what to do, coughing, frantically fumbling for my phone to call the fire brigade. Dear God, Reader, the doors flew open.

He either leapt or was thrown through. Filthy smoke billowed, ecstatic in its release as he landed face down at my feet.

He was half-eaten. His hair had singed away to smouldering roots. Third degree burns coursed up his body. His shirt and trousers were charred to crusted edges, some fabric melting into his flesh. His flesh, what there was of it, puddles and pits, he was covered in deep oval bites, whole chunks of subcutaneous tissue missing from his waist, his thighs, his arms, burned charcoal at the rims and pork-pink at the centre. A pool of blood and saliva gargled from his mouth, his leg quivered. Ian Daniels was still alive.

I froze in a soundless scream, rooted to the spot.

He's still alive.

There was something. A single distraction, the only thing that could distract me, in the tunnel of dense pitch straight ahead. A pair of eyes stared out at me from the darkness. Something, taller than I, marked me with two small lenses floating in the smoky murk. It was all I saw, two iridescent discs of grey-blue, like the lion, the wolf, leopard or hyena retinas in your night vision cameras. I had no protection, no perimeters, no safety fence; the animal sees you, you have to stare straight back.

The eyes moved. In a flash Daniels was sucked back in by the legs. He screamed. The doors slammed.

My hands shot to my mouth. For an instant I could only stand there, paralysed, tasting the leftover vapour of meat in the air. I shuffled and, with a cry, fled. I would not make it to the exit.

It was Falkirk who caught me.

He sprang from the aisle and seized me violently around the waist, throwing my handbag and scattering its contents all over the floor. He was pasty with perspiration, panicked and delirious, laughing and shrieking insanely like a madman.

'No, no, it's all right! It's all right, everything's all right, we are in the house of the Lord, in his hands pray with me!' Falkirk called wildly to the ceiling, raving and hyperventilating, hoisting his wriggling captive towards the vestry. 'All is okay is okay is okay! Pray with me, child! We are okay, everything's okay, in the midst of life we are in death in the midst of life in death, *pray* with me! Haha, blessed Lord deliver us unto thee!'

'*Let me go!*' I screamed, wrestling. 'Let me out! *Get me out of here!*'

Falkirk's sleeve was rolled up to the elbow. A full syringe jiggled loosely over his forearm, the impression of a needle tugging his saggy crook.

'All is safe, yes, yes!' he raved, jamming his salty fingers down my throat to choke my cries. 'The child is safe! You interrupted my medication! Interrupted me! Here!'

Falkirk kicked the vestry door open and hauled us in. Pulling the syringe vial from his arm, he proceeded to assault mine with it.

'N-no, don't!' I yelled. 'Stop!'

The tranquilliser worked fast.

Drowsy. Shapes and shades swimming.

I came to, slumped in an uncomfortable chair at the coffee table in Falkirk's tiny vestry; a compact box of sink, kettle and shelves housing his disgraceful mess of tattered bibles and outdated ledgers. An overhead bulb hummed. The single window was a classic Gothic slit, scarcely adequate for a kitten to squeeze through.

As for our minister, he was sitting opposite, lighting a cigarette and twice dropping it.

I wanted confirmation that I was waking from a freakish dream. Falkirk destroyed this for me. Beady with sweat, he bowed over a trail of something too similar to talcum powder on the table. One wet snort and it fired up his nostril. He noticed me, wheezed, and waved the now empty syringe vial before throwing it into a bin.

'Just a trifle midazolam,' he said, his joints convulsing in a horrible dance. 'I find it alleviates the burden of endurance, ha. You're safe, you'll be safe here.'

I wanted to run and couldn't; the tranquiliser had left me dizzier than the worst hangover.

'You're insane,' I croaked.

Falkirk chuckled. 'Hehe! Yes, yes,' he said, taking a bottle of single malt from the shelf. 'It requires being insane. Requires it!'

I gripped the edges of my seat. 'Please don't hurt me.'

The man collapsed with laughter into his chair. 'Ahahaha-hahaha! I? Haha! Do I look like I can? Does it look like *I* have to?' He poured whisky into a plastic cup.

That cackling of his! I didn't know this man, did not like this side of the dark horse one bit.

'Let me out,' I pleaded, carefully, searching for whatever steady tone might strike reason with this maniac. 'I have to get out of here. You can't keep me here. I'm scared to death.'

'Welcome to the club. *Salut!*' He downed the single malt.

A series of pictures was unravelling: smoke, meat, animals overlapping with memories, nightmares, wind through keyholes, and a kid who knew no better, talking to cupboards. I thought out loud: 'The closet ghosts.'

'Ha, closet ghosts,' Falkirk slurred, draining his cup. 'They'll like that.'

I dug my nails into my scalp, recollection flooding me. 'The fire!'

'Will be out, I should think,' he added, pouring more whisky. 'They're a treasure trove of tricks.'

I tried to stand, wobbling. 'Daniels …' (*He screamed. Slam!*)

'Fool of a man!' Falkirk raged, lifting his cup. 'Stupid drugged fool of a man! Starting fires! What did he expect? Common-minded ingrate!'

'What's in there? We have to get out!' I edged clumsily to the door. 'Will they come here?'

'No, child,' he said condescendingly, drooling over the bottle neck. 'Not by day.'

'I saw him. Daniels.' I tottered, needing to empty my stomach but more than anything needing to escape, useless as my legs were. The zip of my jacket made a crude rattling noise, I must have been shaking all over.

Falkirk frowned as if offended. 'Why do you call him that?'

'What? I don't know!'

'Ian lived anonymously. How do you know his surname?'

'He …' I drifted. 'Cos giants don't exist.'

'Talk sense!' he shouted, slamming down his cup.

'*Sense?*' It was all I could take. I dashed for the door and yanked the handle, locked of course.

Falkirk leapt up and pinned me there. 'I know not of giants,' he growled, 'but *They* exist!'

I couldn't fight him, the aftereffects of the midazolam rendered my arms flimsy tentacles and my fingers were still numb. Nor could I dial for help; my phone was lying out there in the aisle somewhere along with my handbag.

'Who are they?' I cried.

'I said how did you know his full name?'

'They called him that!'

Falkirk recoiled, releasing me. 'When?'

'When I was a kid.'

Fresh perspiration dripped to his collar. 'You saw them?'

'No.'

'Don't lie to me!'

'*No!* They whispered through the doors. I was just a kid!'

'They *what*?'

He moved away, sauntering as if hopelessly lost. 'You're too lucky to be alive. I can't believe you're still alive. *Youuuu*,' his tone rose, damning me with a deranged glare, 'sneaking around my church! Poking in corners! Why did you always sneak?'

He advanced. I thought he would hit me.

'Leave me alone!' I shouted. 'Don't touch me!'

Instead he dropped into his seat, rubbing his temples. 'How is she still alive? Why? *Why?*'

Falkirk's floundering emboldened me. 'Who did that?' I demanded.

He hunched over his knees, in no hurry to answer, his eyes watery jelly, struggling to find the words. 'You saw Ian's whippings out there,' he said. 'That's what they are.'

'Animals?'

'If you truly believe your Darwin books, we're the animals. Their fodder. Our fluids are their nourishment. They feed like immortal fleas. Beasts. They live here, this place is theirs, you can't fight them. Daniels, he … Hahahaha! Fool wouldn't listen! Do not judge me, Rona.'

I saw what I saw beyond that cupboard, what Falkirk believed, and what I could never believe. After seeing a burned man die, if I submitted to Falkirk's mind I would lose mine.

'I want none of your madness,' I said. 'You're high. It's nonsense!'

'What do you think you saw? Deny it all you want. What do you think did that?'

'An animal.'

'What could do that to a man, Rona Dean?' He laughed evilly, standing. 'Do you want to find out? Shall I put you in there and show you? Yes! Why not?' He came at me, waving keys. 'I'll take you down there, shall I!'

I broke away and ran across the room, preparing for a counterattack. No need. Falkirk sat again, out of breath.

'Don't you understand?' he panted. 'Lucifer's leeches. Hunters! And you know you saw no animal, or you'd ask *what*, not *who*, did it. Do you deny its eyes were level with yours, tall as a man?'

'No,' I denied, convincing myself. 'It was an animal!'

'Your closet people,' he continued, 'used to *be* people.'

'You let them stay here?'

'Are you an idiot? *They* let *me* stay here. Imagine the consequences if I thought I had a choice!' Falkirk shook his head despairingly.

I observed him. For years I had trusted my rationality, earned and prized my secularism over my aunts' theism. Here sat a man, an insignificant minister, keeping me here against my will. Which do I trust more, my reasoning, my eyes, or this drug addict?

'I won't listen,' I decided. 'You can't expect me to believe this.'

'Doesn't matter,' he said, drinking. 'You will.'

'I'm not safe in here. Get me out!'

'You are safe. I told you. The sun.'

Another dizzy wave and I reeled again. *Daniels' flesh, scooped out in chunks! I'm going to see this day for the rest of my life.*

The haze cleared. 'Daniels,' I said. 'He started the fire?'

Falkirk cradled his cup like the Holy Grail. 'I'm a shoe-string drug addict, young lady. Daniels was plain scum. His job here took its toll, but depraved scabs like him were suitable.'

'For what?'

'Just a routine watchdog. A ghoul. Their errand boy.' He poured another whisky, gulped it, and pointed upwards. 'Where did you think he slept and snorted his dope?'

The gallery. Yes, that I could perceive. A kid comes snooping by a criminal's hideaway, he chases her downstairs.

'Falkirk.' I rocked, steadying myself. 'Christ, what they did to him.'

'Foolish man,' he repeated, tipsy. 'Idiot man!'

What Falkirk did next, raised the hairs at the nape of my neck. Meeting my gaze, he gave me the most sordid possible simper you could imagine. A minute ago I would have said Falkirk was in shock too. Nope. Wrong. The man is twisted!

'Take heart,' he condescended. 'The abominations spared you. You'll be safe in your bed!' He broke off, thinking to himself. 'Bed …'

'Open this door. Please!'

He answered, deep in thought. 'You plead as if I'd grant your wish.'

'I won't talk. I'm not stupid! Please. I've *got* to get out. Falkirk?'

His self-absorbed trance was unbearable. 'What did you say,' he said, 'about losing your house?' Too calm, far too calm.

'Do you hear me? Falkirk!'

Falkirk swirled the drink around in his cup, mesmerised by it. 'You're going to be homeless and jobless. That's what you indicated, wasn't it?'

I was to be driven mad! *How dangerous is he?* I browsed the vestry for defensive weapons. Pencils, a kettle, a blunt bread knife on the counter.

Suddenly Falkirk turned to me, as civilised as a lawyer with a wealthy client. 'Rona, I think I've sussed why they didn't kill you. In my experience, this is on condition of us coming to an arrangement. Huh, subtle message on their part. You must trust me. I know them of old.'

Pausing to check me, he then delivered the most fateful line of all.

'As of today, this church has a job vacancy.'

I did not hear that, Minister. Will not hear you.

I went as grey as my voice. 'I don't know what you're talking about.'

'You're hired.'

This was not up for comprehension. Neither of us spoke for a minute.

'You sit there and talk like that,' I seethed. 'How can you sit there? How can you sit there and … and … How can you think I'd ever come back here?'

'Collect yourself,' he said, rising. 'Let's have some water. Water. We need it.'

He poured two cups and made me sit.

'I repeat,' he continued, 'your life was spared on condition. You'll have a place to sleep. You'll be paid for cleaning duties, by me, out of my pocket, same as Ian was.'

'You've lost your mind.'

'No, you're not using yours. Drink your water. Now listen, listen too carefully! I cannot vouch for your safety if you refuse. Do you think you can run away? You're broke, you're helpless. Worst of all, you're a witness! They'll rip you to a hundred thousand pieces, then rip *me* to a hundred thousand pieces for letting you go. You could try running. Try. They'll even grant you a head start for sport. I'll share this with you: it is my belief they see through walls, into dreams, echolocate for miles just by breathing!' He added whisky to his water. 'It's a simple job. They leave messages on the altar. We must protect ourselves, don't you see?'

I lay my head on the table, tired of begging, tired of seeking a way out, my all-important disbelief flitting into hiatus. 'That's obscene! I can't, I couldn't hold myself, I can't bear it in here ... please, I beg you, Falkirk, don't do this to me, dissuade them, say I'm gone. You can't possibly think I'd do this!'

'Don't you think they'd see through a lie like that water in your cup? Consider what you saw, what they are. God save us, child, they're loose out there by night. Every night! You and I are the only safe people in the world! Yesterday you were fair game. Today? Can't you see you've no choice?'

'I'll do anything else! Anything you want, only please don't make me. I'm not strong, I can't, I want to go home, Christ, I just want to go home!'

'You virtually have no home,' he said jubilantly. 'Describe what they did to our late Daniels. Tell me.'

'Stop it.'

'Describe it!' He banged his fist on the table, spilling water.

'Burned.'

'Mutilated. I saw it too. You witnessed option one, I'm proposing option two. Refuse and your body will never be found. I can offer you my prayers, not a grave, no wreaths, no headstone.'

Fuck your prayers, Falkirk.

'Why not you?' I protested. 'Why can't you do it? You're the minister. Your house is outside.'

'Because I *am* the minister!' he blasted defensively. 'I'm the harmless front cover. I have a position! I'm too conspicuous. You wouldn't be. Think!'

Slimy coward, drowning in your drugs while others face the flames. I wanted him to have a heart attack, I hoped the rumours of his ill health were true; not a day since infancy had I done anything to offend him, let alone ruin his life.

I goggled at him. 'You put me in this position, you're telling me I have to be a servant for monsters …' I hugged myself. 'I thought I knew this church.'

Falkirk slurped his whisky. 'You should have left when I told you to. Now you can't. More water?'

Chapter Three

I had so much to wade through in our old house; my aunts' home, my home, the landlord's property, purely because he held the paperwork. I went through their possessions, prized, forgotten and miscellany, so many things, Pam's smell on the duvet, blankets and chairs, and I laughed fondly at her foul perfume still clinging stubbornly to the wallpaper. There were photo albums, volumes of them, black-and-white, photos from when they were girls, younger than me. Shelves of crockery, framed paintings, furniture and clothes, clothes, clothes – all destined for the flea market.

It was over, twenty-plus years.

'Yes thanks, Aunt, I'd love a cuppa,' I said to the scrubbed mortuary of a kitchen. 'Don't ask where I'm going. Please.'

That was the straw that broke me awhile. I dropped the huge boxes I was lumbering about and took my usual space on the couch for the last time, a couch by rights the landlord's. *But how can that be? This is the couch where I grew up watching cartoons and Sesame Street every day. I sat right here when Aunt Pam timidly explained what menstruation is. Where I crawled through years of tedious homework. Where I watched the World Trade Centre fall into pyroclastic tsunamis of rubble.*

I didn't realise I was welling up until I sniffed. From infant to teenager to woman, a miniature lifetime here, gone. It was hard. It was very hard. *What the hell's going to happen to me?* I swore there and then I didn't care what it took, whatever else happened I would not end up like Daniels.

I spaced the move over five days. Falkirk permitted me to sleep at my house until I finished packing, provided I report to the church every day where he already had me started as a domestic and tea lady. He told me this much: on the evening following Daniels' death, an urgent meeting was called by what he pompously referred to as 'aforementioned parties', where the recent change in circumstances was discussed. Trying to imagine Falkirk in civil discourse with – what? Animals? Devils? – was indigestible; all I could picture was Daniels' cooked body and the shapeless presence of whatever beast had finally found me.

Disembodied whispers, tappings on wood and memories of the choir crept into bed with me in my increasingly bare room. As nightmares broke up my sleep, I sometimes thought they leaked from my brain like smoke through a keyhole and were now at liberty, wandering about the house.

Not by day, Falkirk had said.

I kept indoors at night, bar once. Exasperated by broken sleep, on the eve of moving out I scampered to an off-licence to buy wine. The streets were perfectly empty, noiseless apart from my footfalls – and that other pair of footsteps, the ones that stopped when I stopped, that walked when I walked.

'Falkirk?' I called, knowing he was nowhere near.

Silence. Humid summer evening silence.

I'm being watched.

That was why I refused to part the curtains; it's why I felt this home was not mine anymore. The worst occasion was a night when I woke from another dream of Daniels gargling on bloody phlegm, grabbing my ankle and pulling me into the smoky plughole with him. I sat up in bed and saw my window open an inch, voile curtains sighing in a light breeze, the bedroom looked as if it had woken up before me. I moved to switch on the lamp.

Somewhere downstairs a door closed.

My circulation stopped. My blood crystallised. Do not ask how long I lay there, rigid. A long, long time. Oh yes, dear, I was being watched! They made no big secret of it either, just enough to keep me leashed and terrified.

Moving day arrived.

Is it not somehow violating to see a 'For Sale' sign on the lawn of the home you've known all your life? Today hardly seemed right for saying goodbye, it was bright and sunny; the leaves were juicy green and daily life plodded on in my neighbourly street with blasphemous tranquillity. Aunt Pam's rose bushes were in full bloom. Who was going to look after them now? Would the new buyers be gardeners? Would they demolish her hard-earned rock garden and turn it into a garage? I locked the door and put the keys through the letterbox, stooping to peer through, glued to the doorstep. There lay our kitchen at the far end of the hallway, its green felt message board dotted with vacant multicoloured pins, no more bills, no hastily scribbled phone numbers, shopping lists or postcards ever again. The kitchen bin where I'd chucked the dismembered monkey stood hollow. The counters were too squeaky-clean. The ten-year-old toaster looked brand new. The mopped floor was spotless and unfriendly. Junk mail had arrived today, I'd left it on the mat where I now heard my key land.

I couldn't go, not yet, this place suddenly felt more my home than it ever had in my whole life. How many times had I skipped through the gate to this doorstep in my school uniform, wielding the key now lost to me, how many, never imagining this era of my life could end?

I said goodbye, then repeated it. Repeated it, repeated it.

Go, Rona.
I turned and walked away. I would not run.

~

St Patrick's Church, Clayburn Avenue. I transported my belongings in six cardboard boxes to the small gallery, already ridiculously cramped with discarded church ephemera and Daniels' single mattress. A dismal sight.

I set down the last box, arms aching, then set about making it as homely as pathetic circumstances could allow. Bed cover, duvet, quilt. *It's dusty and filthy up here.* Behold, Rona's mysterious gallery: magnet that drew a seven-year-old, threw her downstairs, and forsooth sucked her back up kicking and screaming. Pam and Alison were dead. Daniels was dead. The house was sold. I lived here.

~

I wished Falkirk wouldn't go. He was a coke-snorting coward, yes, that we have established, but in that capacity, I – fresh young watchdog with no criminal record and no uncouth addictions beyond nicotine – could hardly blame him. Years in his grim position had slotted him into that niche; in other words, get someone else to do it: '*I have a position! I am vulnerable.*' So I've heard, Falkirk, though for your choice of adjectives I should make you eat your crucifix.

The summer day was mercifully long, though this proved a mixed blessing. The hours I brooded away in the gallery, mounted only to burn out in a landslide of anxieties. How the glamourous weather, happy passers-by and radiant sunbeams mocked me! Safe in the sun, Falkirk says, that same sinking sun punctuated by the hour hand of my alarm clock, by which I sat, cross-legged as my anxiety grew with the lengthening shadows. I was to sleep here, alone, with them, Falkirk was going to leave me here. I rehearsed how I might ask him to stay for as long as possible, just for my first night. Daylight keeps them away, he'd said, at night they're 'loose'.

Incidentally Falkirk was unusually gentlemanly today, all sweetness, apologies and patronising speeches. He tediously overstressed how my new occupation was simple and invaluable, that Daniels lasted nearly twenty years here, and that only his suicidal behaviour was his downfall. No hard facts, no specifics. 'Them.' How many were 'Them'? *What* were those 'aforementioned parties' that disengage fist-sized scoops from your anatomy at will?

Practically rocking in the gallery, on my fusty mattress bed with a relentlessly ticking alarm clock, I searched for any past traces of bravery in my life that I could bring to the oncoming trial. Flight being a death warrant, I formulated a lame plan to be inconspicuous, to keep my distance, to stay up here, to basically hide! My sole talent if ever I had one.

Please don't go yet, Minister, not on my first night, please, just stay until I know I'll be all right? – my planned request. I harboured no affection for the man, but he would be my last glimpse of the world before these front portal double doors were locked.

And so they were. He locked them. Closing time.

I had never seen the church so dimly lit. A paltry glow peeped from my bedside lamp up in the gallery, while a burning altar candle cast jumping shadows about the chancel, oddly devouring more light than it gave, jerking restlessly on its wick as if feeling my heartbeat.

Falkirk shut up his vestry and hurried to the altar, busying himself with papers, sermon readings and bills, any excuse to ignore me as he crammed them into his bag. I dallied behind him at the chancel, more than one obvious question on my lips, my courage waning at his show of nervous haste. How the hell could I ask him to stay now? He would leave before I got a word out.

I began shyly. 'Is, the …'

Falkirk spun around, impatience stamped on his profile. I pleaded, 'Is it really unavoidable to stay here every night?' Idiotic question of course, if far better for being a thousand combined.

'Yes,' he said abruptly, stuffing his bag. 'It's necessary in case of any, er … requirements, messages, um … You'll see.' He stroked his stubble. 'There shouldn't be any problems, I think. They've been informed, er … It's fine, they know how things go. You may not even see them. In fact, most of the time, you won't.'

'Falkirk?'

'What!' he snapped. I knew his earlier show of cheap sweetness couldn't last.

It dribbled out. 'You're leaving me behind with … Falkirk, I still don't know what I'm dealing with.'

The minister slapped his bag shut with a whack; he may as well have slapped *me*.

'Oh yes you do,' he replied, meeting my gaze for the first time in hours. 'Even *if* Lord Byron, Stoker and Polidori knew bloody nothing.' The man was practically running for the south aisle door, sparing me a final (and is that a resentful?) look. 'I'll say this for your sake,' he added with a half-turn: 'They're for-midably older than whatever storytellers named them. Do not address the undead by such tacky modern labels. They don't like it. The truth is, Rona, I'm not sure *what* they are.'

He made a dingy silhouette in the outline of the opening doorway, its steely hinges cutting straight to my eardrums like glass. My parting words weren't much more than a futile mur-mur.

'Please don't go.'

Falkirk swung his bag over his shoulder, we sounded miles

apart:

'I'll have a copy of the aisle keys for you tomorrow, good-night, andmayGodbewithyo–'

He left me. Boom. Clink. I'm locked in.

I looked about me.

~

In my memory, I am standing on the chancel step. The minister has just left. A single lick of fire flutters beside me, casting a bright ring on the altar tablecloth. I hear nothing but my own breath and heartbeat reverberating from chest to fingertips. The flame has grown in height ('I know him, Marley's Ghost!'), bouncing voraciously in its brass holder where weeping wax collects in a melted bowl around the wick, I watch this tiny well fill up with clear liquid until my eyes water. The obstinate candle is more master here than I, my breath sends it dancing, otherwise everything is completely quiet and completely still, I could sink my teeth into this solid air. The aisles left and right are threatening, I know for a fact there are a dozen hiding places in the arcades. The ceiling, successions of diagonal beams crossing like great stripes, meeting in the centre of an arched roof, from the gallery to directly over my head. Though I feel the familiar presence of my church, tonight its beams, pillars and ceiling, ten times higher by candlelight, are disapproving strangers.

That is how I remember it. The image is imprinted on my mind and bones and veins. Ask me any time about St Patrick's Church, and that memory always, always, takes the lead, the opening seconds of my first night there alone.

What time is it? After 8:30 p.m. Late enough.

I lifted the candle-holder and hot wax trickled onto my finger. Wincing, I held it steady and started for the coiled python stair. It was necessary to be slower than I liked; the candlelight would illuminate a pew or a step then plunge it into darkness, tripping was a hazard. The silence encased me like porcelain, ready to scream treason if disturbed by the slightest touch; in terror of breaking it I tread softly as possible, flinching as grit scraped too loudly under my feet. Petty sounds you ignore by day, amplified by night. The thought of disappearing into the long black tongue of the north aisle did not appeal, however, shadows are deceptive and the wall emerged closer than expected. Had I rushed I would have collided with it.

I paused, unsure why, looking out from the pillars into stillness. The candle only revealed a row of pew benches; beyond that, there could be anything. I sniffed the air, no sound, and carried on.

Taking great care brushing by the burgundy curtain, I reached the twisting metal steps, still bearing the sign in big red letters: 'Private'. I tore it off.

The narrow steps which once permitted a child's shoes were now not so accommodating and I was obliged to use the railing. It was as gelid as I knew it would be. *This is the spot where Daniels pulled my hair and I fell. Another man, not a giant, an unnaturally strong man, stepped on me. Daniels was afraid of him. Feeling skittish?*

Once sure my bedside lamp would guide me from the landing, I blew the candle out. Its silky smoke, almost luminous, raced vengefully upwards as if to call out, 'Here! She's up here!' I waved it away, I needed to be invisible, needed to use every wit in my being to be silent as a mouse. Risking the remotest chance of being seen ('Rona, I'm not sure *what* they are') was categorically unthinkable when forced to wait defenceless without any foreknowledge of what to expect or when! Fear wrapped me in elastic bands from head to foot.

Get up there, hide, and stay there.

My bedside lamp cast a lemon oval over my unassuming patchwork quilt, pillows, books and ashtray, a poor scene in this foreboding cave. It was a little bit of *me*, the only homeliness I could preserve here. I dived onto the mattress and pulled the quilt around me. Outside the lemon oval stood my cardboard boxes in piles of two, along with the church's disused chairs and more forgotten piles of I don't know what, covered in thick dust and feathery fronds of old cobwebs connecting them to the low ceiling. I would have to get used to that. At least my ashtray was a welcome sight, smoking indoors being a compensatory indulgence Falkirk permitted me.

I waited.

Two hours and half-a-dozen cigarettes later it was dark outside, and paramount invisibility necessitates switching off your lamp. It took all my courage to do so.

Waiting.

I sat with my knees under my chin, sore arms wrapped around my legs. The boxes and junk surrounded me like a mini fort, sketching an illusion of security. *Maybe I am safely out of sight, and didn't Falkirk say I'm unlikely to see them anyway?* In spite of myself I began to settle.

Waiting. Breathing. Waiting.

A noise!

True fright is an iron dart striking your solar plexus. I seized myself and listened, my insides knotted wires. The noise had been very faint, a shuffle, and not from up here. Did I really hear a noise? It's an old church, after all. Mice? Peeling paint?

Waiting combined with fear will drain you; something has to give. The balusters of the gallery balcony were a couple of metres away, narrowly spaced and stout enough to conceal me if I spied through. Sleep being out of the question, it was now or never.

Slightly bewildered at my boldness, I was compelled to lie belly down on the floor, straining my upper weight on my elbows, nose between the balusters, the lower half of my body on the bed. It was gruellingly uncomfortable. I wondered how long I would be able to stay like this, but I could see much more from here. Street lights stole their way through a few glass panes, outlining the chancel and nave in achromatic lines, transforming my church into a Victorian ink drawing.

My mind floated with the passing minutes. I considered how flat and two-dimensional the place looked, recalling my last glimpse of Falkirk, marking his hurriedness with a kind of sick nostalgia as he packed away his books of frayed covers, ledgers, everyday papers, everyday things! Normality. Right now, it was something I wanted back, these trifling glimpses of a now-alien world where all is predictable, stable and secure, where I don't feel like a grub on the end of a fishing line. I was being set adrift. Absurdly this nostalgia reminded me of how I felt just before an accursed week-long sports field trip in Year Two of high school, waiting with my peers at the train station: I didn't want to go, was willing the platform to glue my feet where I stood, trapped in a butterfly net with abrasive teachers, high-pitched classmates and the odour of rubber soles. Other waiting passengers lining the platform were symbols of freedom, adults not subject to this entrapment in the name of policy, an entire spectrum of lifestyles with different destinations, free from compulsory academic enlistment. It was an escape I would have traded my left arm for. When the train departed, I'd plastered myself obsessively to the window, passing everything I so dearly linked with home. Talking to Falkirk's shoulder blades earlier, I'd felt that train speed up again, pulling me further and further away from a life I had undervalued, passing familiar fences, buildings, rear gardens and people and his papers and books and bags zooming by faster and faster, me desperately wanting to reach through the train window and grab them to pull mys–

Click.

Did you hear that, Rona?

Cli-klick.

Rona! Get down!

A metallic scratching broke through the wilderness and swept it away. It came from a distinct corner in the north transept. I lay flat.

The cupboard opened.

I'm only seven years old. I've done something bad. Wise or unwise? Frosty wind made moan, have you heard of the Three Wise Monkeys?

Three people walked out.

Two men. One woman. The first was of medium height, wearing a loose business-like jacket, open and casual. His shoes had a gentleman's shine and were surprisingly soundless on the floor. The woman I discerned by her frame, long wavy hair and frilled ankle-length skirt, almost bohemian. The third locked the cupboard. He was the tallest, burly and bulky, his head largely devoid of hair.

Their finer features were indistinguishable in the dark.

The first man wandered to the chancel. His slow walk reminded me of that lazy swagger you see in cocky young salesmen, taking his time, fists in his trouser pockets, brushing aside the corners of his jacket in two triangular flaps. He sauntered about thus, absently eyeing the scenery like a disinterested house buyer. Now and then he scratched his head under a thick crop of sandy-brown hair, fidgeting, loitering at the altar, kicking some leftover petals around with the toe of his shoe, playing with bits of candle wax on the altar cloth and flicking them away.

The woman reached inside a small handbag, took out what appeared to be a notepad and exchanged some words with the bulky man, too quietly for me to hear. She uncapped a pen and scribbled.

The swaggering first man took a handful of something from his pocket, raised his arm high, poised theatrically, opened his palm and let it empty onto the altar. Whatever it was it scattered in dozens of tiny fragments.

It was confusing. I couldn't make it out. *This* is what I'd been waiting for? I hadn't expected a million bats to fly from the transept, but neither could I process these three emerging from the cupboard of my nightmares, the portal to 'far away' where wise monkeys live with ghosts and mutilate children. They could be any three people you saw every day! Yet in all this I failed to question why they used no candle, no light source at all, how they moved through the dark seamlessly as I glazed over them, the burly man, the woman –

My heart stopped in a ball of dead ice. The first man, his pivot …

He *sees* me!

I ducked behind the balcony so fast I nearly split my chin.

Found. Seen. Caught. I cowered into a ball and covered my face, determined not to move for however long it took. It was all I could do. What the hell else could I do?

From the chancel came a muffled voice or a soft laugh, then deathly quiet. And this was worse, the most dreadful quiet! I sat there waiting for God knows what, buckled in the balcony with my head between my knees, every single muscle in my body clenched, tight, *tight…*

'Yoo-hoo?'

It was a punishing night already. Ages spent waiting, fearing for my life, homesick and exhausting every precaution. I had blown it, too, for now they were calling me directly, calling the girl who had sworn to be invisible.

His call bounced off the stone columns, inviting, sarcastic and unsurprised, making it all the more commanding. For a second I even felt foolish; such summons merited acknowledgement. Either way I was in no position to ignore them.

Slowly, slowly, I came into view.

There they stood. The first man was now facing me full-on; the woman seemed more interested in her notepad, and here

I was, submissive in my birdcage, admitting defeat. The man inclined sideways and waved mockingly, 'Hello,' then gestured towards me with a supercilious nod. 'Hmm, see? There she is!' Amazingly, they then continued to ignore me as if nothing had happened, and that's when lemon light flooded the space behind me.

I wheeled around with an inadvertent shriek.

Outlined against my lamp, the bulky man, pressing the switch. At my gasp, he rose to his full height, glanced around, and made a seat of my stacked boxes where he now perched wordlessly, contemplating me.

In the spotlight and cornered, I cursed my premature curiosity: step on a crack, sneak a peek and you blast all precautions out of the water. It had put them twenty steps ahead of me, for now look, one of them is up here! Taking charge of my lamp!

Pressing my spine against the balcony, defences forfeited, I resorted to the white flag. 'I'm sorry, I didn't mean, for disturbing, I mean, I was put here by Falkirk, I ...' I sounded like a housemaid that had broken the family china, unsure of how best to address them. 'I was only here by instruction –'

He cut me off. 'Uh-huh, fine,' he muttered impartially, with as human a voice as any.

He would pass for a man in his forties, and, judging by his build, very strong. His scant hair was fuzz, his head round with thin, severe lips and brown eyes, which I thought glinted momentarily. In future, I would learn he seldom spoke, and that when he did his voice was deep, low and monotonous, though I'm sure that larynx could resonate like a trumpet if he wanted it to. Adding to his Eeyorish demeanour, he had a rather offbeat mobility, moving with a detached heaviness in all he did.

But none of the above, none of it, is what really struck me.

Unlike downstairs, the bedside lamp generously exposed his features. Now, how do I describe this to you?

When Aunt Alison died a few years earlier in the Marie Curie hospice, I took the phone call giving us the news. I thought it would take forever to traverse those chlorine-bleached corridors with underlying whiffs of defecation behind closed doors, Aunt Pam resting her weight on me, tediously hobbling along that never-ending damn corridor and sobbing into a hankie while passing nurses marked us. I despised the display it made to be seen this way. I was supposed to be feeling gushy and charitable, mourning her sister, my Aunt Alison, when in truth I found I felt precious little; what does that even mean? They laid her washed and dressed in a sort of customary mourning room, her parting snippet of luxury before the morgue. Reader, have you ever seen a dead body?

When you have known someone many years, you take for granted their animation, asleep or awake; a slight plumpness, the living cells pulsing beneath. As I looked down at my Aunt Alison, subconsciously waiting for her chest to rise and fall … this was not my Aunt Alison. The best description I can give you is *a badly done wax effigy*. Her forehead was ivory, I had never seen it that colour before, not even on her sickest days, likewise her cheeks, eerily free of wrinkles where rigor mortis was setting in, making her three times thinner. Her head was propped up on a pillow for appearance's sake; it did not have the desired effect: her blood, out of a job, had pooled and settled in a lagoon, blooming in a thick red band around her neck. Though I am not spiritual, I can understand why people believe in souls; there was no feel of *her* in that room. It was a carcass. It taps your deepest primal nerve. She was cardboard, artificial. I repeat – a badly done wax effigy.

Now, please, if you will, imagine this shell opening its eyes and moving about. Have you seen the acerbic mimicry of European marionettes, lifelike expressions contoured with ravenous life*less*ness? This, I tell you, is what switched on my bedside lamp.

Meanwhile – *What?!* Mumbling voices. Footsteps on the

python stair.

No time to prepare myself. The woman loitered at the far end of the balcony, settling her gaze upon me. The first man strolled confidently ahead of her into the gallery as if quite used to it, hitched up his belt, swiped a bit of dust from the junk fort, blew it off his fingers and turned to the trembling heap on the floor that was me.

'In person. Rona, isn't it?' He held out his hand.

Meet Serge.

He has just taken your palm in his, trapping an icy pocket of air in between them. He has asked you your name and you're not sure if you heard him or not. His gimlet stare is disarmingly penetrating; a pair of arrows are behind his pupils ready to fire and gouge yours inwards. Your new acquaintance stands before you, broad-shouldered, relaxed, and remember for future reference his classic postures: arms akimbo, folded or in his pockets. I would seldom see exceptions. Despite the surprisingly human teeth, his friendly smile belongs to a tiger. He knows you're scared. You'll do as he says, he's in charge.

Though as I write I now know him better than I have ever known anyone, I could never have guessed what age he tried passing for and his voice was no help either. The fact is that while I guessed the apparent ages of the other two, this one was impossible. Impossible because he did not look remotely real.

This spectre that called itself Serge, this thing touching my hand and speaking to me, was what no unwary observer could ascertain as being anything other than a mummified corpse. His deeply sunken eye sockets were encircled by purple-navy rings wide as his eyebrows. Skin taut over shrivelled cheeks as if pickled, clinging to bone, made him so unbearably thin his overbite bulged behind wizened lips, accentuating the cadaver. Deltas of thin blue and red veins stood out on his jaw and forehead. His pallor was not sick milk like the large man's, more ochre-grey and flaking like parchment. You believed if you so much as touched him he would disintegrate into powder like my cigarette ash. Where the other two were haggard, Serge was desiccated. It was painful to see. That and the blatant defiance of nature in this pseudo-human mimicry made him diabolic. Such a thing should not be moving and speaking! It wreaked havoc with my whole basis of rationality, stamped it to a pulp and rewired it from scratch.

But fragile as he seemed – just to give you an idea of his physical strength – his brief handshake instantly pulled me to my feet like gravity working in the wrong direction. His mere presence, intimidating and imperial, ruthlessly dwarfed the bigger bulky man. Every minute detail of how Serge carried himself had a subtle air of command, and though confident without vanity, a snide sliver trickled through his sweet tone.

His stare was the most striking of all; no apologies for re-turning to this point because it is extremely difficult to describe our interaction without stressing Serge's wide-set eyes. They were the sharpest of the three, grey-blue with large whites and a vulpine sparkle under the brow of an eagle. They held you with invisible hooks, hinting many more questions than just your name, retaining everything you said without even listen-ing. Serge never looks *at* you; he looks *into* you.

There. Now you've met him.

He gestured to the big man. 'That's Hector,' who nodded, 'and this is Edith.'

No sooner had he spoken then the tall woman whom I would always know as Edith came striding towards me. She seemed older, I assumed late fifties. The elegant clack of her heels under the bohemian skirt, her mauve coat and sway of reddish-grey hair, shone its own sense of authority.

'Hello, Rona.' She took my hand.

The voice was silvery, though I detected wear and tear grating in her throat and couldn't quite place the accent; English, like Serge, with slants of French and Dutch. Though gaunt and dishevelled, I saw she masked it well with bright lipstick, rouge and excessive layers of foundation. Her hazel eyes were not piercing like Serge's, merely watchful, her guarded tone and expression giving nothing away. And there was something ageless in her stately walk, as trained and disciplined as her stance.

Satisfied with the introductions, Serge swung his hands into his pockets. 'So what are you doing hiding up here?' He asked this as you would an infant.

How could I answer? Deer in headlights, I tried to concentrate. In the background Edith passed a small silver case of foundation to Hector.

'This is where Falkirk put me,' I said, my mouth dry as the Sahara.

While I spluttered the above, longing for the best and expecting the worst, Serge picked up my cigarette packet from the bed. 'Yes, yes, yes,' he said, feigning woundedness, 'but weren't you coming down to see us?' He passed me a cigarette and lit it with a knowing smirk.

Hector stood, powdering his complexion to shades of buff. Serge took his place on my boxes and boyishly dangled his legs over the side. 'So, remind us please, Rona, what exactly is Falkirk's little setup here? What's the plan?'

Despite Serge's amiable tone he was devilishly hard to read. I may as well have been scrutinised by a reluctant job interviewer. Plus his query knocked the wind out of me. '*They've been informed. We had a meeting.*' Sure. Thanks a bunch, Falkirk!

'I thought you knew,' I stammered. 'I mean, he told me.'

Serge gleamed. 'What, trusting a man of God? Got you there, didn't he!'

I summarised for him my being homeless and jobless, which he interrupted before I slid into another nervous ramble. 'But what about his villa over there?' he asked. 'Is Fickle Falks so touchy on letting out rooms to the homeless? God's work, amens and whatnot. Your cigarette's getting lonely.'

It had burned to a droopy worm of ash halfway to the filter. I dutifully inhaled. 'He's very guarded about that,' I babbled, unsure of what I was saying. 'He says he's vulnerable.'

Edith snorted.

Serge guffawed and slapped his knee, smiling from the others to me. 'Hehehe, what-ho for pious candour! *Acta deos numquam mortalia fallunt* and so on, wouldn't you say?'

'Serge?' Edith threw him the silver foundation case. He toyed with it absently where he sat, observing me thoughtfully.

One more uncomfortable pause under those probing eyes would lose the battle for my self-control; another second and I'd implode! I drivelled, for gap-filler if nothing else.

'Falkirk left me instructions. I won't be trouble.'

Serge waved it away. 'No, er, actually it's as well you're here. A favour for us, if you wouldn't mind.'

He hopped off the boxes and rejoined me at the balcony.

'See that gunk I dropped on the altar? Do not clean it up. Your predecessor allowed a gang of dealers to use Menzies' crypt for their drugs storehouse, not that I recall giving permission. Our altar decoration is their vandalism, we don't partake. Leave it. It's your minister's mess.'

'Yes.' I complied, servile come hell or high water. 'I will.'

'Ta. Oh, and by-the-by, *never* take "instructions" from anyone else in our name.' He topped this off with a wink. 'Cheerio.'

They were going. On his way out, Serge nudged Hector, who accordingly zigzagged to me, rumbled something along the lines of 'Good evening', and followed.

Their footsteps grew distant. The south aisle exit opened and closed. I wished for stillness, received it, triple-checked my hearing and wished again.

(*What ails our recurring doorkeeper tonight?*)

Acta deos numquam mortalia fallunt. It means 'Mortal actions never deceive the gods'...

I crumpled to the floor. Seconds passed, progressing into minutes. A cloud of disturbed dust rose and twirled in the heat of my lamp. My cigarette packet lay open next to my lighter on the patchwork quilt. Shadows hung, dead cobwebs fluttered.

Oh my God.

I didn't know it then, but the only reason I survived that night was because I conquered my reluctance to touch their hands. It was harder to do than watching Daniels die. First test, passed.

Chapter Four

B-beep, B-beep, B-beep, B-beep

Consciousness dawning through closed lids, the world a sheet of cloudy pink blood vessels.

B-beep, B-beep

I felt for the alarm clock: 7:30 a.m. A full three hours sleep after a night huddled on the mattress debating whether or not to switch off the lamp.

Rona the Church Cleaner had the daily duty of rising at this hour to prepare St Patrick's for its congregation, and when less frequently the building also played host to young couples riding nauseating rainbows of happiness in factory-processed veils and extortionate floral buttonholes. I believe you call them weddings.

The congregation's elderly crowd were retired pensioners who had quite forgotten me since I renounced my churchgoing in adolescence, hence the unlikelihood of their late friends' niece being recognised – 'All grown up! Have you not found yourself a nice young man yet?' This was a mercy and a necessity that cannot be overstated. Falkirk would have agreed.

My role entailed the never-ending job of keeping appearances tip-top, this meant ordering from florists, sweeping, brushing, polishing, wiping and tidying, the extent of my training being a dated shopping list for polishing supplies, bleach and disinfectants, courtesy of the minister. I gave it a permanent home in my pocket. Though not quite a full-time job, I set my alarm early because, groggy as I was, I feared sleep. I feared dreams.

Chilly water from the rickety tap in St Patrick's toilet filled my cupped palms, and, *splash*, onto my face. Again, *splash*, and again, again, a hundred times to be sure I was awake and not in some warped purgatory: I had just seen, on the altar, solid proof of the past twelve hours.

Sprinkled gloriously in the chancel were the contents of what appeared to be a huge ashtray. The tablecloth was littered, stained taupe with stubs, butt ends, filters, cigarettes and joints like a hive of dead bees, some fallen to the floor, reeking of cannabis and tar. That was not all.

Commanding the summit of the pile, folded in half like a landscape greetings card, perched a spotless piece of paper.

Please find here cause for our disappointment.
You may save yourself the trouble of offering names.
Yours in fondest confidence,

E.

Written underneath in a different hand:

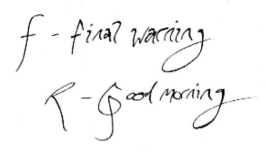

f - final warning

f - good morning

Do the drug dealers have Falkirk so wrapped around their little finger that he grants them access to the Menzies crypt beyond that threshold? Such foolhardiness is suicidal!

Falkirk arrived and I prepared to explain their message, standing prim and ready with their note in my hands. He saw me and stopped. I bade him good morning – he eyed me as if I were mad. Fine. Courtesy dispensed, I delivered their message.

Falkirk negligently scrunched it into his fist. 'Clear this mess up!' he said. 'Fresh altar cloth.' And off he strutted to the vestry.

'But Falkirk,' I gaped, 'th-they told me no. They said to leave it.'

'And spray the place! Doors open in ten minutes.'

End of discussion.

Never take instructions from anyone else in our name. What a way to start. Their very first request, disobeyed thanks to a snorting minister.

'You're welcome, *Falks.*'

An Indian summer was upon us. Much of the day I spent sweeping up and down, a longer job than you would expect with the benches, nave, vestry, chancel, narthex and transepts to cover. My biceps hurt, strands of hair stuck to my greasy forehead, and when I opened both portal doors to air this greenhouse there was no wind outside, leaving the church a stifling cocoon. In this tropical micro-climate, I washed vases and changed nosegays, acquiring a substantial powdering of yellow pollen in the process. Slouching with lethargy and lack of sleep, I found myself brooding over the flimsy stalk of a dying rose, its sad head drooping, its petals falling to the touch, a suffocated victim of human adoration, loved to death. Never to this day have I understood why people pick flowers only to watch them slowly die, it's ludicrous.

I kept out of the way when services were on, feeling a delightful pang of liberation with my intervals of crafty cigarettes as the congregation tripped in. There they went: captive children skipping by in their Sunday best; a pair of identical twin boys in identical attire; a tiny girl in her impressionable frock, a haunting copy of me seventeen years ago. I looked away.

While my old adversary the pipe organ played inside, the price I paid for these cigarette breaks was exposure to a scorching sun. You can protect yourself against cold weather, but persistent heat with no breeze? I thought I would frazzle. An unreasonable part of my brain almost convinced me that last night was an illusion; the poignant normality of daytime, bright skies and warm-blooded people everywhere certainly made this a worthy argument, the contrast was too dizzying.

Meanwhile the Devil's advocate, my wrist-watch, begged to differ, and as evening approached, normality conspired to be the big, wicked illusion. Night was inevitable, I had nowhere else to go, and as the hours ran away from me, so did my spirit. I retired to the gallery, wanting sleep for a weapon, wanting to wake up to the sound of Aunt Pam's radio and her coffee bean grinder.

The mattress was rough but the quilt silky. My joints, worked and sore, sank into its sea of foam. The gallery ceiling, a few beams, streaks of shadow, grew dimmer ... dimmer.

I slept through the night. I heard nothing and saw nothing.

The next day it rained. Being less busy than the day before, I grew self-conscious of slacking off and made a mental note to stretch out cleaning duties between the days, lest Falkirk saw fit to cut my hours, hence my already measly wage.

I was thankful for the cooling rain and for my sleep, I wished every night could be like last night, horribly aware that an excessive dose of sleep paves the way for a shorter one. The front portal was closed and locked, Falkirk went home without a goodbye. Lights out.

… Dammit I couldn't doze off! I flinched at the slightest sound, from the rustle of the quilt to a creak in the mattress. Some streets away, a fire engine roared.

Speckled flesh burned aubergine, red cavernous chunks.

Shut up.

He must have died in such pain.

Shut up, shut up!

Overcooked human meat. My God, the doors flew wide open.

After much tossing and turning, that plane bridging wakefulness and sleep crept in, that place where dreams unfurl, random doors open in your brain and foggy voices overlap, fizzing out, some even calling your name, jerking you awake. Voices. Whose voices? No, it's my aunts making a clatter, brewing their midnight Ovaltine.

I snapped awake to the sound of footsteps.

Shoes were crossing the chancel. I shrank under my quilt until the noise died away for what felt like ten minutes, though it was probably only two. The bedside clock said 8:50 p.m. I would not sleep for hours.

The coiled stair is behind the curtain. I'm running to it, trying to. It's only a stride away. I push and push with all my might and can only move centimetres. I push and push. The stair is shiny, appears to be sweating. The tepid railing slides through my hand. I try the steps, running, running, moving nowhere; my foot slurps through the stair like butter. I'm trying so hard.

It's too hot. I see Falkirk through the railing, scorning me.

He has no eyes. His eyes are gone, fixing me with two bleeding holes. He knows exactly where I am.

'Look what you did!' he shouts. 'Because you didn't brush the aisle. Sweep properly. Pray with me!'

Strict Aunt Alison is laughing at me from somewhere, cackling like a witch. 'Oh-ho! That's funny, Rona, that's funny, ahahaha!'

Help me, steps, please*!*

It's right behind me, the thing I'm running from. The longer I'm stuck here the closer it gets. It's coming, a tarry cloud big as a giant. Don't look back, it's coming! The stair is 'Private', won't let me climb, running out of time –

My eyes opened.

2:30 a.m. I stirred, listening out.

My uncompromising bladder stirred with me. I had sworn to myself never to move a yard from the gallery by night, but at less than a minute to the toilet and back I'd be very fast. I listened again, stalling, fighting the need to urinate and squeezing my legs together, not that my bladder was fooled for a second. Nature always wins; when I could stand it no longer I slipped from the quilt.

Unlit solitude will transform anywhere. St Patrick's slept like a charcoal tomb, I had to feel my way without a candle, tiptoeing in socks because the church kept only one battery-powered torch, miles away under the vestry sink. Naturally we were out of batteries. In my briskness, making it to the toilet felt too easy, even the flush was muffled. Thus relieved, some confidence restored, I swung back out into the aisle.

The chancel was lit up.

A gasoline lamp, the kind I knew only from antique shops, sat on the altar. Less passionate than a naked candle, it cast a homely glow, three-dimensional and neat, on the tablecloth and walls, awaiting me. One of the cupboard doors hung open. My insides lapsed.

Before I could sneak away, a man strolled from the cupboard, kicked it shut with his heel and took a seat on the chancel step without acknowledging me, unscrewing a green glass bottle of dark fluid in his hand. His thick hair was a familiar sandy-brown, almost fair, and his double-breasted jacket hung open, also adding a familiar style to his walk. Circumstances aside, visibly you should find no cause for alarm, were it not for his disquieting presence, a passive shrewdness spiced with casual listlessness.

'Hello,' he said eventually.

The nose. Same wide-set eyes. Same hair. The swagger. The voice.

– How long did I stand there embarrassing myself, questioning my eyesight? I couldn't help it; the more I gawked the more it hit me. It was remarkable. It was absolutely remarkable!

He was alive. Where there had been flaking ash, bloomed a vanilla skin. No desiccation or ugly veins crept across the jaw. He could pass for thirty to forty, but if you judged him handsome it was an unconventional handsomeness; his inverted triangular profile, eagle's brow and straight Greek nose gave his whole persona an angular feel. I laugh to recollect how baffled I was, but to see actual muscle in his face, take it from me it really was … quite incredible.

Of course, he saw my childish ogling.

'Hmm, yes,' he said, swigging from the bottle, 'we're all a little better tonight. Still recovering from the fire, and summers are lean times. We'll improve as winter comes, the nights are longer.' He secured the bottle cap. 'How's the Rona tonight?'

'I – I'm well, thank you.'

'Come over and sit with me a minute.'

Unwise to refrain. I obeyed. Whatever happened, stiff, dry-mouthed and white with fear as I was, I would sooner stay composed than go out in hysterics.

Serge picked up a random hymn book.

'We appreciated your manners the other night,' he said drily, flipping through the pages without interest. 'Not exactly Renoir material, are we?'

I held my tongue.

'How do you get on with Falkirk?' he asked, flipping away.

'I've known him all my life,' I said, 'only in passing.'

Serge skimmed the pages like a deck of cards, creating a small wind in my hair. 'Like hymns much?'

'Not really.'

'Or Menzies' bonafide house guests?'

'The drug dealers? I don't know any of them.'

He snorted, not meeting my eyes. 'No, of course not. What is it you *do* like, Rona Dean?'

A vague question. I tried to guess what answer he was browsing for. 'Um, books,' I said, flustered, feeling sheepish. 'Stained glass. The smell of the old stone.'

This caught his attention. The hymn book flapped shut.

'How are your dreams?' he queried after a moment.

I held my breath, sensing his subtext.

And as if to confirm this, he probed further. 'Do you still smell it?'

'Smell?'

(*Daniels' pig nose, human pork. He screamed.* Slam!)

'The *stone*,' Serge answered, playing me with impressive timing. My shoulders fell, relaxing the tiniest bit.

Sniggering in his victory, Serge now swivelled and faced me directly. His tone grew serious. 'The circumstances by which you came to our attention are an unceremonious jolt in plan for us. Do you understand this?'

'Yes.'

'Do you know why you're here?'

'Yes.'

'Do you know who we are?'

I nodded.

'Do you know what we are?'

'I think so.'

'You *think*.'

'Falkirk said –'

'A man of God *said*! Enlighten me.' He grinned venomously. 'I'm curious. He never calls, he never writes. With what epitome of damnation does he baptize us this year?'

My heart quickened, for all I knew I could utter the wrong answer on pain of death. Lucifer's leeches, according to Falkirk.

'I can't remember,' I lied. 'He sai–'

'That comprehensive, was he?'

'He said this place belongs to you –'

'That was sweet of him.'

'– and that –'

'All right, all right. To be continued.' He stood with the bottle. 'Leave the lamp. And please never lie to me again, don't waste your time, eh.'

He didn't wait for an answer. 'We'll talk.' he said. 'Later.'

With a nonchalant wave, he left the church by the south aisle, St Patrick's unused fire extinguisher hanging neatly by the door.

Fast forward to the next evening when my mobile phone rang ten minutes after midnight. The caller: St Patrick's vestry.

I answered. The phone went dead.

As I crept to the balcony, I saw someone lighting the gas lamp on the altar, someone huge. Hector. Whether I made any sound within normal hearing range or not, *he* heard it, and beckoned me down.

Once I reached the chancel, Hector was gone and from the cupboard flowed Edith in a sweeping breeze, trailing her frilled purple skirt, carrying a large shapeless bundle in a sealed cloth bag.

'This here,' she said, setting it on the altar, 'you'll forgive us our fastidiousness. I understand Falkirk gave you launderette details. If there is anything in need of mending, ignore it, unless you're a dab hand with a needle.'

Her face had a natural tinge tonight without the aid of foundation, and I'd swear her cheeks were fuller. While I stood there trying to remember the last time I'd ever picked up a needle and thread, a voice projected from the front pews.

'Hehe, one thing at a time, Eddie.'

Was Serge there before? He had appeared from thin air!

'Can we agree on tomorrow for all this?' Edith asked me, prodding the bundle.

I blinked from Serge to her. 'Yes, yes of course.'

Then to add to my bemusement, Hector re-emerged carrying a second bag of the same and married it with the other bundle on the altar table. Serge sniggered, reading my uncertainty. 'You won't be washerwoman every day,' he said.

'Is there anything else?' I asked, knotting my fingers behind my back to stop a nervous fidget.

'Yep,' Serge announced, swigging from another green bottle.

As if on regimented cue, Edith and Hector immediately left the altar and joined Serge in the pews, sitting a row behind him.

'Be seated, please,' he told me. 'I think we need a chat.'

I had to be ready for utterly anything and this militant invitation did not console. Clinging on to the fact that nobody had hurt me so far, hiding my clenched fists, I joined them in the benches, though, having no excuse not to sit in the front with Serge, I gauged a cautionary space of two feet from him.

'Maybe you should light a cigarette first,' he suggested rather caustically. As I did so, Hector reached over the bench and handed me a miniature bottle of Sauvignon Blanc. 'That's for now if you want it.'

Serge began.

'We would like you to tell us exactly what happened in here on the twenty-eighth of July, this year of our Lord and so forth.'

They all waited.

My God. Put squarely on the spot. What sort of version could they possibly want when they already knew the answer? *Is this another trap, being made to spell out the worst horror of my life under the keen scrutiny of its very instigators, a sitting duck in their firing line?*

'I was here,' I said, 'reading. There was only Falkirk and myself.'

'I gather this would be somewhere around midday.'

'Yes. I smelled smoke and traced it to there.' I pointed to the cupboard. 'I called to Falkirk. He wouldn't answer me.'

I bit my lip.

'I saw ... I mean ...' I rubbed my nose, agitated. *Please don't do this to me!* 'Quick, it was very quick.'

Serge gestured at the wine. I opened it, hoping this account would be enough for them, and drank, stalling. Alas, their deliberately drawn-out silence was not encouraging.

'Rona,' Serge finally said, 'we can sit here all night if we have to. The sooner we've settled this the sooner you can flee to your third- or fourth-hand mattress.'

I puffed on my cigarette, bitterly conceding I was too obvious for them. *Don't think, just talk. It's the only way out.* Shutting them out of view, I bent forward, not far off the way you instinctively curl to protect your vital organs when threatened.

I spilled it. 'Bitten, burnt, dying. As you know.' Shaking, I gulped the wine impulsively; it was easier to talk without facing them. 'Then Falkirk tranquillised me and shut me up. Is that enough for you?' I said, cracking with an unexpected spark of defensiveness, 'Will that suffice?'

Not a blink amongst them. They sat unperturbed. I may as well have been making small talk.

Serge went on pecking. 'So the reason you haven't contacted the authorities yet, is …?'

He sounded accusatory. Rona didn't tell the cops, ooh what a bad girl! This wasn't an interview, it was a gauntlet.

'Common sense,' I replied. *And you were in my fucking house.*

'Oh.' He slouched. 'But then you're not so very "common", are you?'

Another edgy beat passed. This time it was quiet Hector who spoke up. 'Did you know him?'

'Barely,' I replied.

That was when an object, round and hard, was tossed over from the second row and landed on my lap. Dry, grey and smooth as polished clay, two symmetrical hollows goggled up at me over a single row of teeth pressing a semicircle of small crescents into my palm. The world clouded.

The cupboard slammed, carbonised tissue scraping a trail of charcoal to the door, the world standing still, me, every muscle locked. This was how I sat now, entranced by those concave orbits, barely a mark left on the thing. Its lower jawbone was missing.

'Daniels had a typical history,' Serge elaborated. 'Prison, drugs, theft. He had your job for nineteen years.'

Whaddafuck you think you're doin'? You can't come up here!

This hollow, inanimate object on my lap had once shouted at me and pulled my hair out. Seeing his molars now resting in my hand, I tried to imagine Daniels shouting again with that absent jaw. I couldn't.

Serge continued. 'Falks walks around high as a kite most of the time, going through expendable bad boys to do the dirty work when he hasn't the stomach. Try knocking on his door at night, he never answers it, heh.' He chuckled, relieving me of the skull. 'Then one day, Mister Daniels fills this hovel,' he tapped the cranium, it made a dull tinny noise, 'with, oh, whatever narcotics you like, and takes it upon himself to pay us a flammable visit. Perhaps we'd made him uncomfortable. I blame your funny face, Hector!'

Edith sounded sceptical. 'I'd have been more interested to see Falkirk's face.'

Serge rested his elbow on the pew, knuckles under his chin, studying me. 'How long do you see this new setup going on? Tell me the truth.'

I had to tell him I didn't know.

'How are you feeling, Rona?' Edith quizzed, narrowing her eyes.

I opened my mouth to say something. Air fell out. Another beat passed.

Then another.

'Rona!' Serge shouted.

I jumped as if smacked.

'Do you know what hematophagy is? It's the correct term for whatever Falkirk called us which you were too modest to tell me last night. We're not serial killers; our sanity's fine, thank you. Nor do we appreciate the subjective term "monster"; have you ever heard of the undead building nuclear weapons? What you're looking at are three parasites that exist to kill people – are you telling me you can look us in the eye and handle that?'

And there it was. He had hit the very quick of my predicament where I hadn't the guts to. I sat with, by all accounts, a 'monster' sponging the scales from my eyes – Handle it? *Think, Rona! He isn't fucking about.* He knew me, he remembered, did that grant me immunity? Three children were mauled to death. And I, my innocence was taken, they poured the blood of three children into the hands of an unsuspecting seven-year-old, I was dirty already from a deal with the Devil. But I'd told no one. Nor planned to. What did that make me, monstrosity or victim? He was waiting, I had to say something.

'I've no choice,' I said. 'Falkirk said you'd find me.'

'Falkirk, Falkirk, Falkirk. Falkirk says this, and this, and this! Will you stop saying that, please?'

'Very well – I don't know where else I'd go. I'm befouled. You saw to that when I was a child.'

'Starting as you meant to go on, eh?'

That sparked an angry flame in me.

'I didn't start it,' I said.

Serge rested lazily on his knuckles again. 'That's the bit of a politician's answer, isn't it?' he sighed.

Another pause, cunningly timed to unsettle me. He went on.

'Isn't it, er, somewhat more the reality that what you haven't seen yet, can't hurt you yet?' He lightly touched my forehead with the tip of his finger: 'In here?' He repeated the action over my heart: 'Et cetera?'

Worse yet, he was correct; Daniels' death was the tip of an iceberg. Serge patiently awaited a response, patiently watched me struggle, patiently spinning Daniels' skull on his index finger by the eye socket.

'I'm under no illusions,' I said.

'Illusions?' he probed, taunting me with a phoney frown. 'What sort of illusions?'

I was stuck, really stuck, helplessly glancing towards the gas lamp as if for help. It must be seldom used, I thought, sitting on the altar, the antique brass obscured by a solid layer of grime and fluffy dust cooking in its heat, surrounding it with a luminous aura, the only light in the church, asking no questions, inviting me in, what a nice place to lose yourself.

At a loss, I allowed a single word, a name, to wisp by my lips.

'Shizaru.' Do no evil. There was no more to say.

A sobering moment later, Serge straightened in his seat. 'Well done,' he said quietly. They all stood.

Next thing I knew, Edith was bolting the cupboard and Hector was at the aisle door. They were going out. It seemed hours had passed, and yet there was a distinct difference in the density of the air, as if a weight had dropped and settled.

I motioned to the lamp. 'Serge? The –'

'Keep it.'

I was left alone again. It was the first time I called him by his name.

The gas lamp's tiny brass handle was just wide enough for two fingers; its seductive pear shape glowed by me in the gallery where I lay smoking, the taste of wine still in my mouth. They had mentally slapped me about whilst also reaching in and untying a knot. I felt unusually calm. Their faces drifted through my mind in turn, from Serge's interrogating orbits to Edith's high cheekbones, a hundred questions unravelling.

What the hell has happened to my church? Serge spinning Daniels' skull by the eye socket, Falkirk with his drooling jowls in this whole setup, and why *did* you never tell anyone about the monkey or Daniels? You're sinking into this, yes, because you were powerless not to, but don't you want to climb out? What is it about them, Rona? They move, walk, speak and stare differently, always taking their time yet so quick and unnaturally sharp, as if there were ten extra eyes behind the pairs already in their heads, and their inflexions, their mannerisms – they stand out, dimensions away even when sitting right next to you, like tangible holograms. If I am a bad person, whom do I confide in? They have me; what do *I* have?

I stubbed out my cigarette and turned down the lamp, forgetting my electric one.

Chapter Five

The launderette was a dismal shack in the middle of Bank Street, four blocks away, on a main road of rush hour traffic, fumes and littered pavements where overflowing public bins drew half the wasps in the county. Grime nearly painted out the faded yellow lettering of Bank's Launderette & Dry Cleaners, leaving its windows opaque, and when I blew my nose upon entering this shack, my hankie filled with unmentionable pollution from outside.

My mood was not eased by the weight of the bags. I took care to be there early in the morning as, even on a weekday, customers lined up fast and seats were limited. I opened the load, unsure what to expect.

The clothes were nothing extravagant, mainly shirts, trousers, skirts, blouses, and tops. The stench didn't emerge until halfway through. The usual with dirty washing is a stale, dank odour; I waited for that smell to worsen, and was met with another.

A comparison springs to mind here. Aunt Pam's deterioration became apparent after I quit university. She was unable to keep house, the sink was overrun with unwashed dishes, her carpets rotten with mildew and every hard surface wanted a polish. Upon opening the fridge door, forgotten chicken fillets, green lamb's liver and rotting vegetables hit me with waves of putrid decay. Shortly before Pam died I was her full-time Home Help.

This smell could not fool me.

I should have inspected the garments sooner. A third were blotched with brownish-maroon like spilled coffee or gravy, spreading out from sepia nuclei in circles; they swiftly vanished into the washing machine. Next, four women's tops, untouched for so long they stuck together by dried, scabby fluid. The deeper I sifted through the load, closer to the main source, the unmentionable core, the worse it stank. I held my breath and gulped hard, determined to keep my morning tea down.

Found it. A man's shirt, pale green, folded lengthways, partially burned, several buttons missing, jingling change, an old bus ticket in the chest pocket. It felt terribly wrong, hard as cardboard, not like fabric at all. With immense revulsion I unfolded it, slowly peeling one crispy sleeve from the other in a long, screaming, torturous *tear* as if separating two strips of gaffer tape stuck together. The shirt was opening up.

Worse than I imagined. I gagged. It was cemented together by a lake of solids and aged blood, caked on, riddled with lumps of solidified clots and hundreds of pebbly specks dried black, hard and sharp like flecks of bone. I was looking at human gristle.

I dropped it, forcing back another lurch. *Meet their eyes and tell them you can handle this, Rona?* How was I supposed to wash this? I could barely touch it!

On this thought I happened to catch my reflection in the concave window of the washing machine door, its curved glass bending and distorting the line of my brow into something like a wrinkled goblin's: *Shallow girl*, said the voiceless face. *How inconsiderate of the dead to dirty poor watchdog's fingers. But you've always been a good lass, doing as you're told, even by them.* Especially *by them.*

Feeling diseased and stained, I brushed my palms together, desperate to scrub them. I was literally washing people away, destroying fingerprints of their last screams forever.

I waited in the chancel with the lamp, laundry and its despicable garment that evening, pacing, debating the idea of leaving a note to explain the ruined shirt instead of seeing and telling them outright, because it was early yet, and after a day without food my reviving stomach eventually persuaded me out to the nearest shop. But upon returning via the south aisle door (I rarely used the front portal anymore), I froze on the threshold: one of the cupboard doors was ajar, and did I hear the faintest piano music a second ago? I moved inchmeal, closing the exit without checking over my shoulder.

'Aha!' Serge barged in behind me and we met face to face.

I leapt, stifling a scream. Paying no heed to my fright, he locked the aisle exit himself and walked me to the laundry, a large leather case under his arm.

'Excellent,' he said. 'Any problems?'

I dug for the shirt of gristle. 'This,' I said. 'It wouldn't wash out.'

(*Silly girl. Why else do you think the clever beast asked?*)

Serge had already whipped the shirt from me and was holding it aloft for inspection. 'Ha!' he laughed. 'Hector's a messy clod.' And to my great relief he ungraciously tossed it over his shoulder without a care. This relief would be very short-lived.

He picked up one of the clothes bags. 'Assist. The passage gets narrow and it saves two trips. You'll want the lamp.'

He could not mean what I thought he meant. Surely he couldn't!

To my horror, he did. He wanted me to pass through that cupboard with him. It had digested me in dreams, monkeys and ghosts lived in there, they tapped your name, they breathed through keyholes, they dismembered children and their toys in the portal to 'far away', a whisper so friendly 'depending on the friends'; it's how my church had seduced, used and tricked me, it was impassable – and he wanted me to *go* in there?

I stood mortified, hugging a laundry bundle, the lamp wedged on my fingers, a seven-year-old adult standing where I watched Daniels die on a day of sunlight and smoke, reliving the weight of his skull on my lap.

The cupboard opened into a dusky throat of uncertain depth and inside, not far off, stood the woodwork's ultimate deception, a detachable base, propped up, now facing sideways against a long wall of sandstone brick, a scent of damp earth wafting from within. My bowels jellified, *He really expects me to do this.*

'I don't think I can,' I said, hypnotised by the sight ahead.

'You were a bolder brat than that,' he remarked.

I shook my head like a ninny, knowing I would lose, knowing disobedience was suicide.

'Really, sorry, I can't.'

The hard way it is then – said Serge's expression as he came to me, unfazed, moved behind, and unceremoniously drove his knees into the back of my legs. Forward! Pointless as it was I instinctively gripped the oak casing around the doorway, gasping, resisting him, and all I gained for my efforts was his chest between my shoulders and his voice in my ear:

'Poor show for a watchdog, Monkey. Choose or we decide.'

That reminder got me moving, I walked into far away. Dear oh dear, what a child will believe.

I raised the lamp.

Unlock any average cupboard and as a rule you are not supposed to see what I saw. Come with me, go a few feet straight, past the detached base.

The close corridor is about twelve feet long. Halfway down on your left is an opening; take a peek while Serge locks us in.

Meet Lord Menzies' crypt, minister and magistrate in his marble sarcophagus. Not much else to see in there? You'd be a teensy bit mistaken. Spot the far corner behind Menzies? Yes, very out of place, that carrier bag, and a discarded syringe on the floor confirms it. Seems Daniels' guests enjoy this sepulchre for more than just wacky baccy, and no fair guessing as to how Minister Falkirk procured his precious nose powder, the carrier bag's bulging with it.

Taking no interest in the sepulchre, Scrge walked straight past it and turned right, so let us now leave Lord Menzies in peace, and proceed with caution! – the next diversion is too easy to miss without nocturnal vision.

Serge stopped at a high gate of wrought iron, blended into invisibility with bars so close together you could hardly poke your pinkie through, I would have overlooked it without Serge's guidance. 'Watch this carefully,' he said, wielding a crooked key. Where you expected a handle or lock, was a square metal plate; Serge twisted this nifty device in sharp jerks until an internal latch clicked, lifting the plate to reveal a hidden keyhole. Using his key, the gate pulled with a squeal, swinging and locking automatically when shut. Now you can't get out.

My breath fogged up the lamp glass. The instant drop in temperature and the lack of direction or air circulation in here tricked your brain into feeling crushed, even following Serge by lamplight I still bumped into walls more than once, relying on the scratching of our shoes on the floor for sensory backup. And it was just as well, because if he hadn't stopped suddenly I would have fallen to my death: beyond the gate was a short landing, cutting off dramatically like a continental shelf. The severe drop plummeted into a near-vertical stairwell, straight down, a trench descending to what seemed infinity, for it devoured my lamplight in gulps. Each stone step was deeply sunken in the middle with overuse, which made carrying the clothes bundle awkward and we had to descend sideways, in single file, the gas lamp jiggling dangerously on my knuckles.

Again, there came music, only this was no piano, indeed I couldn't have been more surprised to recognise a 1920s recording of *Send Back My Honeyman* by The Virginians. There was something unearthly in that eager foxtrot, the way it sang to us in this underground nosedive devoid of visual cue; were we nearing the music or was it coming for us? The melodic ghost of another age hungrily vying for attention from an unknown source sent shivers down my spine.

All too soon the song finished, the jazz ghosts faded.

Now all I could hear were my boot heels in sync with my breathing. Being harried into this pit had stretched my courage to its absolute finest strands, and so it was by a most unforgiving twist of fate that what happened next, did.

Out of the darkness, two bright eyes flying toward us –
'*No!*'

My shock was unstoppable. I dropped my bag with a cry as the retinas melded into Hector's face, unfortunately by then it was too late.

And, *pop*. Every ounce of my fear, teetering on the edge since the day a half-eaten man died in front of me, crystallised in that exact moment and exploded, levelling me. No matter how tough you fancy yourself, you cannot predict your reactions, and I for one could suppress it no longer, the upheaval to my life had been too rapid. I lost it. I broke down.

I covered my face. '*No!* Sorry-I'm sorry-I'm sorry …'
Dear God the doors flew open animal eyes he's still alive slam*!*

'SorryI'msorryI'msorryI'msorryI'msorry*I'm sorry*!'

I'm sorry. Heaven knows how many times I said it. It was inevitable really, released like a spring by the worst trigger Hector could have inadvertently pulled. I sat on the step with my face in my hands and let it sob out, humiliating myself and powerless to stop; if they were going to kill me for it, let them kill me.

I was vaguely aware of Serge passing him both laundry bags, saying, 'That shirt had to go,' and Hector withdrawing downstairs. At length, Serge's steady voice came to me.

'Rona? Rona, it's all right. It's just because you had the lamp on. Come on, you've seen the same thing with cats.' He passed me something from his pocket, a wet wipe. Wonders will never cease.

'I'm sorry, all right!' I burst, not myself. 'I'm in that gallery every day scared it's my last. I'm scared to sleep, I'm scared not to sleep, please don't fuck around if you've nothing better to do. Shit, *shit*, I'm sorry!'

'But why would we kill you, Rona?' he said, mildness itself. 'There's plenty to go round. Wipe your face. Breathe.' He waited another minute before taking my elbow. 'Good. Now, stand.'

As he carefully raised me I saw lamp sitting undamaged on the step, having been miraculously caught by Serge when I dropped it, still I was not ready to get up, let alone imagine going any further. I needed more time to recover, and there is a kind of sensitive tranquillity that blankets you after a breakdown, a sort of weightless suspension zone you are loath to be taken from.

'Right, we're going downstai– Yes, you are, Rona!' he said as I resisted. 'You can walk, and we need you this evening. I didn't bring you to sulk on the steps all night.'

I hated him for making me.

After what seemed like an age, the stair ended in another passage with an opening to the left.

'Here we are,' said Serge.

I followed him across patches of dry earth and uneven paving into a small vaulted chamber. In the centre stood a high wooden table with two high stools, near it a very old French sofa, threadbare with faded dye, though I made out embroidered landscapes, symbolic peacocks and eighteenth-century lovers under pear trees. I envisaged this item being once upon a time luxuriated by the posteriors of eminent aristocrats in a shimmering drawing room of aromas fair and foul; wines, hand fans, perfumes and unwashed sweat glands seeping into the material. Here it sat tonight, tired, dragged into an unfamiliar century, sagging and begging to be put out of its misery. On this sofa sprawled Edith, ankles crossed, reading a hardback volume in Chinese print. She regarded me with minimal interest.

Opposite the sofa was a Georgian desk bearing the source of that eerie jazz music: a battery-powered record player.

'That lamp's running low,' Edith criticised. 'Purchase gasoline. You're the one who'll need it. What was all that drama upstairs?'

'Technicalities,' Serge answered, resetting the record player.

'I got a fright,' I said, resentful of being downplayed. 'Hector startled me.'

Oblivious to my speaking out of turn, Serge adjusted a pocket watch. 'He may be early again, Eddie,' he told her.

He?

Serge opened the dated leather case, tatty at the seams, fastened by a single brass clip. A surgeon's case, blocky, the sort I'd always imagined nineteenth-century physicians carrying around hospitals for wounded soldiers, healing the sick and infirm with giant butcher knives, chloroform and leeches. No such thing here. Its contents were shiny and modern; Serge unveiled a bizarre combination of very thin plastic tubing, a small plastic box and more wet wipes.

'Normally,' Serge explained, unloading the instruments, 'I do this myself, but the gentleman you're about to meet is too fragile to manage evenings much longer. So, Rona, this is something you're going to have to learn.'

He and Edith exchanged a few sentences in a foreign lingo, and whatever was said, it sent her from the chamber, up the long flight of stairs to the church while the record player sang out some crackling tunes from Glenn Miller.

Serge motioned me to the table. 'Have a seat. Ever donated blood?'

I replied in the negative.

'Effectively that's what this man does. We treat him well enough for his services. He's in his twilight years and loaded with haemochromatosis – too much iron in his system. Without us he would die.' Serge uncoiled and displayed the tube. 'The fancy name for this procedure is a phlebotomy, what you otherwise know as bloodletting.'

He passed this highly disagreeable tube to me.

'I'm not asking you to sit a calculus exam!' he said at my hesitation. 'It's simpler than it looks.'

My attention shifted to the leather case. It reminded me of a trip to the Royal College of Surgeons Museum in London during my teenage years.

'Robust, isn't it?' said Serge, fiddling with the brass clip. 'It fell into my hands in 1819 from a medical student in Edinburgh. Conrad Docherty. Young man, quite useful. Look.' He reached in and retrieved what at first resembled a broken piece of pottery. 'Souvenir that escaped the graveyard. There's where Conrad sawed along the temporal groove. And that section's her parietal bone. See, there's the suture where it joined the occipital.'

Alert as I was, I couldn't resist feeling along the cranium's winding suture lines; they looked like a bird's-eye view of rivers meandering through the countryside. A woman's, he'd said. What in her lifetime would she have thought of the cap of her skull being handled by us strangers two centuries later?

'Conrad narrowly escaped the noose for bodysnatching,' Serge added. 'Pah, every student dipped in it.'

'What happened to him? I asked. 'The student.'

Serge shrugged. 'He graduated.'

Edith reappeared in the doorway with a second lamp, lighting the way for someone on the stairwell.

Serge stood. 'Here he is.'

Edith departed as a sluggish pair of feet approached, and into the vault shuffled the very last thing I expected to see. A hunched little old man. His flushed face was red as sunburn and he clutched a plastic shopping bag close to his navel like a pathetic shield as if it were his last line of defence, his puppy eyes filled with vague uncertainty. I immediately felt for him.

Serge strode forward to shake his hand, brimming with droll gentlemanliness. 'Good evening, Derek. How are you?'

The man, Derek, lifted his weary gaze to the God-like boss and gave a phenomenally genuine smile, creasing his lineaments in a dozen new wrinkles. 'Fine, fine, yes, thank you, Serge, yes.'

'Come on in. Watch your feet.'

Derek regarded me with a measure of uncertainty.

'This is Rona,' Serge explained. 'She hasn't been here long. She'll be looking after you later.'

I greeted him, hoping for a trusted ally. I needed one. 'Hello, Derek.'

Serge was adjusting the record player again. 'How are you feeling, Derek? Be honest now.'

'Yes,' Derek stuttered, sitting on the French sofa, 'I – I'm taking my greens, doctor, heh!'

'Rona,' said Serge, 'would you take him that water and move those chairs over too.' It was not a question. I did as I was told.

'I, heh, I brought my sugar fix,' Derek added, taking a packet of biscuits from his shopping bag.

'Good, good.' Serge took the medical tools and two empty green bottles to the sofa, then passed me the packet of wet wipes and opened the plastic box. 'Wipe his arm, Rona – just here.'

I moved stiffly, wiping Derek's blue vein, more than positive I would never have the competence for this bloodletting task. His elbow crook was already dotted in a cluster of green bruises from God knows how many previous trips; the poor man's illness had turned him into a pincushion. My own arm tingled with the memory of Falkirk tranquillising me.

'Watch how the needle attaches,' Serge demonstrated. 'Discard afterwards, we'll leave you details for getting new kit. I'll do this now. Next time I want to see you do it yourself. Make fists for me, Derek.'

In short, the objective of all this was filling bottles, a full two pints worth, with Derek's surplus blood. Serge chatted to him on and off; they discussed news, politics, their mutual taste in music, but despite Serge's genteel manner it was a blatant front, screamingly so, the way he used him.

Watching Derek, too, he was a conundrum; either a supreme actor who saw through Serge's patronising, or all the more pitiful. Derek reclined, sipping some water. And this was how we three sat, Glenn Miller playing in blissful ignorance from the vinyl disc. I wanted to smash that record player off the wall.

Suddenly Derek spoke to me, catching me off guard. 'Do you like Duke Ellington? He was the best in my day, you know.'

Who? Serge saved me the embarrassment. 'I have the records somewhere, Derek. I'll dig them out next time. Okay,' he removed the bloodletting utensils, 'that's you.'

Benny Carter took over from Glenn Miller.

Derek offered no thanks when I helped him with his coat, taking more interest in Serge, who was – ah! – counting out a thick wad of paper money. 'No hospitals, as per usual,' Serge ordered, paying him. 'You know how to get in touch. You have Rona's number now. Call *her*, remember!'

Derek hastily pocketed the cash. 'I'm not well, Serge. Getting too hard to go out at night.'

'We know, we know,' he consoled, half-heartedly patting Derek's sleeve. 'Rona will take care of you in the afternoons.'

Derek rambled on. 'I get – get too tired, you see?' He might as well have grabbed Serge's collar. 'It's too much. No, too exhausting at night!'

Serge mechanically repeated the performance. 'One more night, then the evenings are yours. Let Rona book your taxi next time. That's what she's here for.'

What I'm here for. Edith returned to escort Derek out and Serge disappeared for a while, leaving me in the chamber with the gas lamp and Benny Carter. I lit a cigarette. They wanted me to do daytime bloodletting down here? But where else – the blessed daylight of a public church? Or how about the Menzies sepulchre, exposing Derek's sweet anxiety to thugs shooting up with spliffs?

I exhaled a cloud of smoke. I had no way out of this job.

Serge re-entered in his outdoor coat. 'Derek's a tidy crumb for the pigeons,' he said, switching off the record. 'Two pints is a joke. We humour him while it's mutually beneficial. If everyone were a haemochromatosis sufferer they'd be erecting churches to *us*.'

'You trust him?' I asked.

'He trusts us. That's work enough.'

'How? How do you earn his trust?'

'By being Me.' He gave a moment for that to sink in. 'Mind your lamp.'

We were climbing the steep stairwell out, Serge marching in front.

'Go on,' he said out of the blue.

'What?'

'Ask away.'

Serge had no need for psychic ability, not with his perception.

'That man,' I said. 'Derek.'

'Um-hmm?'

'Why humour him like that if his donation is a joke? You'd rather scare than kill him?'

'Watch yourself, he's a lot braver than you. The hospital has his details, as do certain authorities. He won't risk spending his remaining days in prison.'

Prison. I lagged, which is why Serge turned to me, his eyes catching my lamplight. Two animal retinas flickered. They were grey-blue.

I stopped walking.

Two iridescent discs I'd seen before. My senses instantly refilled with smoke. I didn't scream this time, did not drop the lamp. *You.*

It's you. Daniels dying, but for a single distraction, the only thing that could distract me …

Serge halted. He faced me. Took a step. Two steps. Three. He was an inch away.

'Take a good look.'

Everything slowed down.

'It's called *tapetum lucidum*. The light from your lamp went into *heeere* …'

He lifted my index finger and rotated it over his eye, his tone a soft, cruel, Arctic freeze.

'… *behiiind* the retina …'

An alarming smile drew his lips over his teeth, an inhuman smile. *He's sneering at me!*

'… reflecting it out …'

He redirected my finger to my cornea.

'… to you.'

My hand was dropped.

'And that's why we don't …' He flicked the lamp with his fingernail.

94

Tap
'… need …'
Tap
'… this.'

The next five seconds in there with him, with his scowl, were awful. Oh, but the speed with which the chameleon switched from bestial to vibrant!

'That's enough for now,' he said, marching resumed.

I felt malevolently kicked. Why would he do that? Why play nice when I cried, then press the nerve deeper with a red-hot poker?

'Serge? Do you hate everyone who isn't you?'

He twirled about on his heel, pert as springtime. 'Did you rehearse that enchanting iota of profundity in a mirror? On-ward trot!'

We reached the nave, where Hector and Edith were waiting. Serge wandered, ostensibly on a planet of his own, scanning every brick, column and pane of glass.

'Winter comes early this year,' he said. 'You'll be seeing a lot more of us.' From his inner pocket he took two keys bound together with a ragged piece of string: one small with a single oblate loop; the other large, rusty and shaped like a miniature hammer. He held up the small key, 'For the transept,' and the large key, 'For the gate.'

He dangled the keys over my nose. I took them. Tonight I had been tantalised and reluctantly engrossed; my breakdown on the stairs earlier had broken more ice than my spirit; a lay-er was blown away, knowledge intuitively exchanged as those keys changed hands. I crossed my first bridge at that point.

They proceeded to the aisle exit, stepping over the gored shirt lying on the floor. I couldn't believe I had forgotten it.

'The shirt?' I called.

In passing, Edith slapped a sticky post-it on my wrist. 'On the altar with this,' she said. 'Goodnight.'

'Compliments of the house,' said Serge on his way out.

I didn't bother folding up the shirt. Falkirk would find it lying on the altar with its note in the morning.

I walked up to bed, refusing to look back at the crossed bridge collapsing in flames behind me.

"To Falkirk With Love",
Ian Daniels

Chapter Six

So went my introductory nights with the Three Wise Monkeys.

Plot the tale of a child conversing with whispery monsters. Picture anything you like: tendrils, horns, pointed ears, dragons' eyes, scaly goblins, gnashing canines, bat wings, talons; God knows the clueless child would agree with you. Would you have envisaged our three mutual friends, well-dressed if not ostentatious or tawdry, who spoke an endless array of languages fluently, who even demonstrated passable manners to push my buttons? Having survived my introductions, they proceeded to play me, and very well.

In the weeks that followed, unwinding routine put me into an uncertain state of solidarity. Autumn arrived. I was known as Cleaner/Verger to the congregation and Watchdog to other parties, whose revenant physiognomy notably improved with the shortening days. Our summer is their winter.

Shall I give you an idea of what their post-its said? I'll start with the most common chore: travel arrangements. Usually by taxi; private cars are too traceable. Whether travelling together or separately, week by week Serge, Edith and Hector's destinations spanned as random a spectrum as the irregular hours they kept. Though I never asked questions, they hinted that since police inspectors seek out patterns like dogs dig for bones, predictability is taboo. Their geographical knowledge was encyclopaedic: they knew every alley, street, park, lane, footpath, bridge, garden, river, canal, square, hill, market, attraction, terrace, avenue, thoroughfare, road, highway, passage and estate – not only in all boroughs, but in the neighbouring counties too.

I accumulated quite a collection of cab company business cards and countless false names. Where modern technology gives freedoms, it castrates others: calls are traceable too, hence taxis were never directed to or from the church. On my easiest nights they either walked or took trains; a more typical evening required two return trip taxi bookings to wherever; others demanded multiple unplanned stops, goodness knows why.

The truth is their existence was an unenviable state of perpetual hiding. No matter how erratic or pedantic, their habits were invaluable safety nets, because as far as the world is concerned, they do not exist. They are anonymity itself, prepared with fake identification for all crises, which, given their veteran ingenuity, were exceedingly rare.

For a start, Clayburn Avenue – a street of Georgian apartments for middle-class pensioners – was one of the dullest streets in town. Also, closely surrounding St Patrick's south and east towered a twenty-foot wall of Victorian brick. If three shady individuals happened to emerge under cover of night by this façade, you'd need better than X-ray vision to outsmart them. If *I* barely saw or heard them, you would have no chance in hell. How could you when by all accounts they do not exist, understand?

Next in my duties: launderette several times a month. Notwithstanding my initiation with that outrageous shirt, I needn't exhaust the details here, suffice it to say the unpalatable particulars neither improved nor worsened.

This, believe it or not, is how they settled me in – taxis and laundry. The easy part.

No one can walk a tightrope forever. And sure as human eyes will adjust to the dark, shapes take form; cracks that were always there widen until you cannot imagine how you missed them before. You loosen. You adjust. You see things you may not want to.

Their collective character began to peep through.

It started with the phone calls in the middle of the night. I was under the impression, by their assurance, that their single mobile phone was for emergencies only. First lie.

For example, after midnight, *ring-ring*: 'Change of plan; new booking, please.' Command duly obeyed, I would nod off again, then, *ring-ring*: 'Diverted routes, we've changed our minds, book us here, book us there.' Why can't you call them yourselves, I ask. No can do, they say, phone numbers are recorded. It got ridiculous, four to eight calls a night, tossing my sleeping patterns around like dice until I overslept in the mornings, subject to unpleasant greetings from jolly Falkirk, no less. What could I do when they knew I had to let them have their malicious fun? Would you have argued with them?

After a fortnight of this and a fourth call at 3 a.m., exasperated, I planted myself in the nave with my phone, book and gas lamp, foolishly thinking the thirsty flame would prevent my nodding off. In short, I – so far unaware of how it feels to watch your soul chip away – lost and sleep won. This was the night my real job started.

The jolt of a tectonic arm shook me.

'Rona!'

Serge and Hector towered, visible definitions of no-nonsense moods, their complexions filled out, ruddy and fleshy, their orbs bloodshot. Such an alien contrast, to be so liverish and inscrutably healthy at once.

Something inaudible groaned in the background.

'Rona,' Serge repeated, 'you're wasting the gasoline!'

Edith was unlocking the cupboard. Tired and woozy,

I thought I was seeing double: her whole configuration was askew, she had three arms, an extra leg; an unnatural shape, carrying something. Someone.

Four went in that night. Sometimes five, sometimes six. Three always emerged twelve hours later. Don't ask me why they sometimes brought their spoils home and sometimes not. Dear Reader, the most frightening thing is that you get used to it. No, no, don't argue with me, there's no point. You do.

It was a technical job, a practical job. The mop and I became lonely friends and I worked fast. Do you honestly think I took my time erasing the sight of it in the nave or on the altar, the tablecloth or door handles, a smudge on the pillars, a smear on the floor? You can't simply take a saturated cloth to it either, because too much water dilutes the mess and then, well done, you've spread it into a puddle. Don't waste time. Hell, don't waste cloths!

You look at those stains. You think. Thinking is bad. Or think if you want, go on … Uh-huh, see?

Blood. Did you hear them tonight? How many did they bring? Alive or dead on arrival? Did they suffer? You can't tell when a swift bite to the carotid causes unconsciousness. Arterial spray? Not necessarily. Once I chanced a glimpse through the balcony: in Hector strides, disproportionately light on his feet for such a heavy male; as with Edith he is all multiple limbs like an Indian god, four arms, legs and two heads, somebody's neck in his suction cup of a mouth. And that night they spilled not a drop! On purpose, of course; I doubt a single stain in that church was accidental, they were far too sophisticated to leave a mess without artful subtlety. *Bring her closer,* that was their idea, *bring her closer.*

It emerged that Serge had a genius for tidiness, whereas haughty Edith, ignorant phoenix too used to having her arse wiped, made quite the point of taking the proverbial and creating extra work for me. (I could see why Serge nicknamed her 'Eddie', a style-cramping nudge she had to live with.) One night I overheard her say after leaving a mess, 'She's a church cleaner – make her "clean"!' I always wonder if Serge had something to say about that, because the next morning an interesting post-it appeared on the altar, reading: 'Apologies. E.'

Edith was subdued for a few nights. Only don't let that soften you towards them just yet; don't let them thaw then refreeze you as they did me when for all I knew it was most likely a scripted ruse. The minutest variation in your reactions could make the greatest difference to their judgement, hence they ran hot and cold, stand-up-sit-down, folding you into origami until you see-sawed on eggshells, precisely where they wanted you.

But indeed, as Falkirk said, half the time you never knew they were there. Up on that mattress I learned to clock their routine roughly by sound. (Hear No Evil: that's one down.) A third of the time, you heard it, but not once did I hear a scream. They never scream. What you get are grunts, moans, groans, maybe a whimper, otherwise the dying are always mute. Men or women? Both. Fifty-fifty. Whenever the coast was clear I had to scour the grounds with a fine-tooth comb, erasing traces of everything from human hair to fallen bus tickets, sweet wrappers, receipts, fingernails and lemonade puddles from dead bladders. I wish I could tell you those victims were undeserving criminals or ne'er-do-wells. Sorry. Judging by the countless possessions I destroyed, their palate was indiscriminate, and possessions tell you a lot, even the wallpaper on mobile phones, or (worst of all) sudden texts popping up from kith and kin; friends, colleagues, husbands, wives, partners, parents, children. I would raise a hammer to smash a phone and bingo, here beeps a 'New text' alert, frightening the life out of me:

'Dad? Outta milk. Ur late!'

First time that happened I cried.

Wham, my hammer comes down. Daddy becomes scales and a split SIM card. You had to get rid of phones before anything else, no exceptions whatsoever! After that you destroyed remaining detritus at leisure, via plain old-fashioned refuse disposal or our good minister's garden incinerator. Not a single policeman knocked on St Patrick's door, at least not initially, that episode is for later.

Falkirk kept to himself. It dawned on me just how unapproachable that morose man really was. His parading alone shouted royalty next to little me, the invisible go-between, the expendable asset. This is what slowly sank in as I grew accustomed to my hovel of a gallery.

No captive in my unsung niche could ever take the outside world seriously again, and with that comes an isolation morphing you into your own subspecies. As the weeks passed, I found myself diminishing into the building's foundations. My movements obeyed its daily rhythms, my body joined every shadow, rising and shrinking with the hours, here, in the only place that made sense. Conscience became the best and worst word in the universe, feeding off me until I had no stomach to feed myself; I lost weight, I swore not to end my days as a Daniels replay, and if I heard more than I cared for in the middle of the night I buried my head under the pillow, wilfully suffocating myself. It was this deal with the Devil or my life. I chose. It was no fun and, so help me, I chose.

Did their eyes glow like in the movies? Never, and exposure to street lights cancelled out their modest *tapetum lucidum* anyway. Did they have the enlarged canines everyone talks about? Not that I saw. Such was my ignorance, for I only knew what I'd seen. Early days, dear, early days.

Nevertheless, the privileged safety and infinite danger of my position were intoxicatingly paradoxical. You have to be careful with that sensation, it starts things. Rash things. Mistakes.

I am sure you understand by now there was not much pride in this job, figuratively patted on the head like a good watchdoggy, have a biscuit, because their sardonic pokes were self-explanatory: what good are you to them if you lose your fear? I promised myself I'd never forget that.

Damn you, Rona, you promised ...

Oh, and incidentally, those weeks also included my second meeting with Derek.

Chapter Seven

I rolled over to my faulty alarm clock to see how late I over-slept this time. Christ forbid Falkirk should make the coffee himself! You could set your watch by his disapproving scowls. What can I say, Minister? An atheist is a lost soul, are they not, can I take that damning label as licence to sleep in, please?

I reached for the clock, yawning. What I saw startled me with a whip crack, and it wasn't the hour.

They were up here last night. The clock ticked away cheer-fully, blindfolded by something taped to its face: a creased business card, printed in bold capitals.

COLE'S MEDICAL SUPPLIES
306 Sanders Avenue, Bronmeg

Written in red pen over the print, a large letter 'S' com-manded the centre. Medical supplies, for Derek? He was due here tonight, same time and place, nevertheless with this card I had a new errand on the other side of town.

It cost me two bus trips to reach Sanders Avenue, a cheap district of greasy spoon cafes and second-hand stores at the east end of town. The exterior of Cole's Medical Supplies was tackier than its business card and the door jangled on a tin bell as I went in.

What a mess of a place. Boxes, bandages, bedpans, used wheelchairs, stethoscopes, pushers and the obligatory first aid kits stacked beyond capacity. I half-expected to see artificial limbs hanging from the ceiling like a doll's butcher shop. Dwarfed under all this paraphernalia was the shallow booth of a counter and a man whom I presumed to be Cole seated behind it. Unshaven, late thirties, lanky black hair and tattooed biceps, reading from the sports section of a newspaper. Music and football results blared from a portable radio on the till.

As the bell announced me he glanced up, taken aback at being disturbed in his reading by the audacity of intrusive customers, probably ready to kick me out if I requested any items not in stock. Apprehension speeded me; this pasty man had an air of the highly strung, and I quickly noted the bags under his eyes. Just like Falkirk's.

'Hello,' I said, handing him the initialled business card. 'I'm to show you this.'

Confused, Cole gave me a very thorough and, I thought, rather inappropriate looking over.

'Where's Ian?' he demanded.

This guy seemed no friendlier than the Daniels I remembered, they would have loved each other. Oh well, so much for modesty.

'Dead,' I replied without pity.

Cole shuddered, muttered 'Fuck' under his breath, and eyed me again doubtfully, reinforcing my repulsion towards him.

'Just … Just a minute,' he said, vanishing into a storeroom of sorts. 'Wait there!'

A minute later he returned with a large paper bag sealed at the top with lethal-looking tape. Derek's bloodletting gear. Taking it, I burned with curiosity. If he knew Ian, precisely what else did he know?

Cole resumed his position with the newspaper. The scene was closing too fast for me to compute; this place was disagreeable, Cole more so, but I couldn't leave it like this.

'What?' Cole barked. 'You can go now! No charge, you should know that.'

'You knew Daniels? Ian?'

'Maybe.'

'Do you know *them*?'

'Nope,' he replied, nose reburied in his sports column.

'So how –?'

'And I don't need to!' he snapped. 'I get enough of my own, sister.'

'Oh,' I said, decidedly fed up with his company anyway. 'Right then, cheers.'

I turned to go.

'You and me,' he called, gesturing symbolically. 'Same watchdogs.'

What was he expecting in return, some sort of tribal salute? 'You said you didn't know them,' I replied icily.

'No, slow bitch, the fucking *job*.' He paused deliberately, radio voices filling the gap. 'We don't talk about it,' he added, a feral light in his eye. 'We never talk about it. We never see them.'

If he means what I think he means … Christ, how many of Them are there?

'This is the part where you piss off, by the way!' he said. 'See you whenever. If ever.' With an ugly smile, he flipped to the football headlines and bit off a stick of gum.

I left that cesspit and went to find a taxi rank. *Now it's my turn to piss off? You're the one pissed off, mate. Pissed off cos you're shit fucking scared. So am I.* I searched the sky. Brighter today. Sunlight. Daytime. Borrowed time.

From across the street a sign for a hardware store jumped out at me. I went to buy gasoline, a spare torch and batteries. Twenty minutes later I was sitting on a comfortable taxi seat laden with two bags, whizzing by pedestrians, people, normality, shopping, lunch breaks, buggy brigades, headphones, citizens, short lives, mortal lives, livestock grazing in the sun. I pinched myself. You and me, he'd said. Same watchdogs.

The livestock passed me in a queasy blur with or without the taxi, slipping away, and would continue to blur, week by week, until the whole world fell into superficial background noise.

The church was a tip in the aftermath of a wedding that day. Unfashionably late, I made a mad dash from taxi to gallery, rushing by stragglers in tuxedos to change my shoes and stow the medical bag, hoping to buckle down before bumping into punctual Falkirk. My growing antipathy towards weddings peaked whilst battling die-hard wasps browsing the vases; bridal processions love to leave doors open.

Another smell reached me as I scooped up weepy mother-of-the-bride hankies from the front row. I inhaled like a dumb sniffer dog, seeking out the source, and found it. *Not there. Please not from there.*

It was. It was smoke, too, but not that kind of smoke, seeping from a certain transept I was supposed to be guarding like a Doberman. A human laugh came from inside, definitely human. Oh no.

Whether or not they knew of Daniels' death, Falkirk had allowed them in all the same. That idiot let them in! So Falkirk has his own key now. Thanks for telling me, Serge! Daniels' buddies sounded exactly as I remembered them – inebriated, high and aggressive.

I wanted to vanish. They could appear at any moment. Trouble is, it was my job to kick them out.

Another laugh came from inside as the pungent smell of cannabis oozed out. Falkirk's carelessness baffled me. Any earlier and the wedding stragglers might have thought *me* the pothead, sweeping his floor, though I cared even less for what prudish spectators might think of my broom in their mouths. Our good minister was demonstrably absent.

'You hypocritical tool, Falks,' I growled. Falky, Falks, their nicknames for him were getting catchy.

The voices were getting louder. I decided to get out of their way, to escape outside, scoop up confetti and hope they would leave soon. Yes, a plan.

Not so fast, Rona. From the cupboard poured a fresh cloud of smoke as four intruders tumbled out, beer bottles in hand, the oldest-looking a thickset, egg-faced ogre with puddles of perspiration spreading from his armpits. At his side was a black-haired ratty man. While the third, and shortest, male appeared to be an attractive young boy, thin with curly shoulder-length hair, dosed up and being physically supported by a stocky female with dreadlocks. With the exception of the boy, who could hardly stand, they were all obnoxiously loud, their lingo punctuated by expletives. The older man was cruelly shining a pocket torch across the senseless boy's swimming pupils and laughing, a horrible laugh, like smashed plates clattering off the pillars. Requesting my torch back or speaking to them would be madness.

I wormed my way to the south exit, attempting invisibility. Some watchdog you are, Rona.

'Hey!' they yelled.

Too late. Thugs are seemingly magnetised to anybody walking alone, especially a female.

'Oi, cheeky bitch, I'm talking to you!' hollered the ogre. His attentions were echoed by the troop, excited at the prospect of a new scab to pick; they could smell my fear.

I was escaping, pretending to be deaf. I was going to make it.

An explosion of brown glass hit the aisle inches away, spraying me with malt. A giant Rorschach stain of liquid and bottle fragments discoloured the wall to buff. The bastards had thrown a beer bottle at me.

I raced for Falkirk's house, hearing more breakages and jeering from the churchyard, it being their customary tradition to smash bottles on gravestones. Later that afternoon I would be scrubbing graffiti from the eighteenth-century epitaph of a certain:

HERE LYES **UNDER MY COCK** KATHERINE STRATHEARN.

A few minutes later Falkirk joined me in the nave, pointing and barking this way and that, shifting from heel to heel. His bleary eyes and ill pallor were getting prominent these days.

'Keep the front open to get the smell out,' he grumbled, 'and get this glass cleared up, for goodness sake! What have you done with the air freshener? Open the south door as well!'

I glared at him. I had nearly acquired a broken bottle in place of a head; beer was splattered down my side, my clothes reeked of it. The nerve! Falkirk with his twitching hands and double standards. Fuck this.

'Just hang on a minute!' I argued. 'Where were you? Anyone could have walked in. The smell is everywhere.'

'They never stay long,' he said. 'You'd rather they use your gallery like they did with Ian? Stop interfering. We both have to see to our own, don't we? Hurry and wipe down that wall before someone *does* come in!'

Oh, Falkirk. Did you really think your gruffness could intimidate me now?

I stood perfectly still. 'You do it, then!' I said fearlessly.

Falkirk's face was disbelieving.

'You clear the mess out here,' I said. 'I have to clear the mess in there.'

I fed fresh batteries into the spare torch, passing Falkirk as I dished out Serge's keys.

'How did you get those?' he exclaimed.

'They were given to me,' I said, a little too proudly, as I

entered the cupboard and locked it, shutting him out.

The torch sprang into life, vigorous and ready. I winced in the sudden light. *Bam* came the stench of cannabis and urine. Religion itself fails to enchant me, but that such tiny, imbecilic minds should dump their crap all over this humble place, made me sick. Fresh graffiti covered the sepulchre and Menzies' sarcophagus; no doubt the grisly thugs had tried opening it, unsuccessfully. There were butt ends, beer cans, syringes and, lest we forget, their grotty carrier bag in the corner. I refused to go near it.

It was horrid, uncomfortable, mucky work, grovelling with the torch, shuffling yard by yard to see what I was doing. A few spiders and mice scuttled off my brush and shovel, investigating its charming pile of accumulating treasure. I had to take great care with my hands, especially where I found discarded needles, not to mention an old condom, solid as pavement gum with congealed semen.

A good thirty-something minutes later, I bagged the refuse and got up, passing the locked iron gate. The barred mesh was invincible, but you might easily have squashed through all the stubs and joints you liked, condoms included. I directed the torch, hoping against hope the thugs had spared it. No such luck, Rona.

Sure enough, the filthy pigs had battered the gate for all they were worth, and failing that, their Plan B was to put the impenetrable in its place by chucking more litter. I sighed.

I have met clever minds who debunk gut instinct as a myth, and others who swear by it. As I poised with the key and twisted the trick lock, I cringed with an insoluble certainty that if I moved beyond this point, they, down there, would know.

You're mad, Rona, don't go in there!

The key had trouble finding its place in the lock. I felt it catch, thought it had jammed, took a chance and turned it anyway. Victory. The rusted hinges screamed as it pulled open. I grimaced and slowed, tugging gently. This only made it louder. I held my breath. A valiant swing and … Done! I stepped onto the landing.

How far away is Far Away? Hello? Like it or not, they were somewhere down there.

Nor does it rain, it pours: five steps down, more stubs, more work to do.

The gate's swinging shut!

I got no further. I lost my nerve.

Seven o'clock. Bye-bye, sunshine. Street lamps hummed.

'He said you'd be hanging about, waiting to be asked,' said Hector, stepping from the cupboard. 'We've been awake an hour.'

I was followed in, through the gate, downstairs. I owned up earnestly, ready with excuses. 'The druggies were here again today. I swept away what rubbish I could.'

'Don't bother explaining what we know.'

'Oh.'

'Everyone leaves traces everywhere.'

We found Serge sitting at the table in the bloodletting vault. 'Already?' he said, taking Cole's medical bag from me. 'You should have left it on your way here this afternoon.'

'I scooped away their rubbish in the crypt,' I repeated. 'I was outnumbered. They threw a bottle at me.'

'Tut-tut,' he patronised, sifting through the medical kit. 'What to do?'

His lack of interest floored me; I thought he would at least be outraged at Falkirk if not me.

After the necessary preparation with fresh needles and tubing, Serge bade me sit and rolled up his sleeve. 'Here,' he said, presenting his bare arm, 'practice on me. There's the vein.'

'Excuse me, why can't Hector or Edith do this for Derek?'

'Because this early in the evening,' he said, picking up a

needle, 'freebies require a hand of restraint.'

They were hungry. In the cage with tigers, I took the needle. 'Tell me what to do.'

He talked me through it, criticising and appraising. 'Diagonally … No! You'll need to be tougher than that, Rona, stop wimping out … Yes, better. Nearly there.'

His jacket off, me touching skin normally hidden under stylish sleeves, the pale underside of his forearm was a contrasting landscape of body hair and rocky muscle. It was a new familiarity, being this close to him, especially someone I supposedly feared, and is that him nuzzling my hair? No, he hadn't moved, but whenever I returned my concentration to the needle, there was an overwhelming sensation of his breath. I could not interpret what I was feeling; if I was uneasy or not. In this freezing vault, a current of surreptitious warmth swelled in my abdomen. I worried he was reading my mind, feeling his eyes sink into the top of my head, watching me touch him. I pushed away an uninvited awareness of how his skin would feel under my tongue.

Serge removed the needle. 'Do it again,' he said cynically. 'Get the angle right. If you can stab me you can stab anything.'

Two needles later seemed to do it. Derek arrived shortly after, armed with his packet of biscuits, pink wafers tonight, the same hunched shuffle and stammer, same gallant greetings from Serge before he left me alone with Derek, me the nurse, he the patient.

We were both at a loss for conversation. It was tense. *I* was tense! Connecting syringe to tube was the simple part; in my nervousness I gripped the needle too tightly and Derek had to help me find the correct vein, which I wiped repeatedly, procrastinating while Duke Ellington melodiously assured us *It Don't Mean A Thing*.

I withdrew, despairing, wiping my brow. While I apologised for my incompetence, Derek was obliviously tapping his foot and bobbing his head to the Duke's swing. He caught my eye and, instead of berating me, twinkled!

'Nineteen thirty-one, that was,' he said, nodding at the song. 'Know what we'd tell the new military nurses, girls younger than you, dear, who swayed at the sight of blood? "First dame who stitches me up gets silk stockings down her knickers and a free dance!" '

He laughed so jovially that I joined him; it was the ice-breaking green light. I tried the needle again. Success.

'I feel quite the square,' I said, 'not knowing Duke Ellington.' The flow stalled. 'Please keep making fists, Derek.'

'You and the Duke?' he said. 'Too young, silly. Heh!'

'I know, damn my eyes.'

The others were gone, we had privacy, and I so many questions, God how I had them, but to badger an old man cornered by leeches? Then again, ooh I say, where was that nervous stutter he performed so convincingly around Serge? His speech was as fluent as the jazz sax playing in the background. Interesting.

'How long have you been doing this, Derek?'

'Over two decades, dear.'

'For Serge?'

'Oh, yes.'

'You must know him well.'

'Since 1944. That doesn't mean well.'

Not what I expected. 'Really?'

'I don't ask him much, dear. Heh, funny world. Very big and very small. Funny world.'

Since World War Two! Derek could be the treasure trove of answers I craved. I felt shy requesting a tutorial on his coping mechanisms, but it could save my life.

'What's he like, Derek? Really like? All of them. Because I don't know! I'm lost!'

'Oh, my dear,' he said sadly, 'are you doing all they tell

you?'

'Of course! Sweet shit, I have to! Sorry.'

'You're in a good position, you know. Think how many meteorites from space might hit us whenever we walk out our door – they discriminate no more than a hungry hunter. You and I practically have licence to deflect meteors. Why're you here, anyway? What happened to the horrid one? Serge wouldn't let him do this. You must be a good girl.'

'Daniels? He died.'

'I see,' he said, chillingly unsurprised.

'He did something crazy.'

Derek laughed. 'Hehe, what more to expect from a Daniels?'

'He set fire to the underground somewhere.'

I said this with ease, not anticipating Derek's reaction. He changed completely. His jaw plunged to his belly. 'What in the name –? What in the naaame ...?'

'I saw what they did to him.'

Derek wasn't listening. 'I don't understand,' he said to himself. 'Even for a mad dog!'

'Daniels was an addict,' I insisted. 'Sick in the head.'

'No, no, that still doesn't make sense!' Derek reeled, nearly spilling the blood bottle.

'Please, Derek, please hold your arm still. Thank you. You see, Falkirk said Daniels went mad.'

'Falkirk? Hmm.' He sounded doubtful. 'Never liked the man.'

We sat on that note for a minute. I wanted to beg for help of some kind, any kind, if only I could find the best way to ask. 'How do you feel about being party to all this? How did you cope for so long?'

'How could I not?' he said casually.

'Well, I know you're ill.'

'Hehehe, yes, he said you were new.'

I recalled Serge's mention of prison. 'How did he convince you to do this?' I asked, assuming it was blackmail.

Derek frowned, genuinely astonished, you would think I had asked what country we were in. 'He showed me,' he said.

'Showed you?'

Another change came over him, and this one I really did not like. He shifted himself upright with renewed concern, but not for himself. 'He … Has he not shown you yet?'

'I saw Daniels, if that's what you mean.'

'Oh. Oh.' He trailed off. Whatever he wanted to say, it was smothering him.

I tried to help. 'Shown me, you say?' It could mean anything.

'He hasn't.' Derek was talking to himself again. It frightened me, the way he searched the air aimlessly, wagging his head as if my words were torturous spikes, agitated, upsetting the needle and tubing.

'Oh, careful! Please be steady, Derek.'

He steadied unhappily.

'I only meant,' I continued, 'how you met them. You don't have to say.'

'My dear, I know this church inside out, lopsided and upside down. Draughty old gallery, isn't it? Stock up on your woollens.'

Former watchdog.

'You're kidding!'

Derek patted my hand. 'I remember it like yesterday. I remember having no choice. I was in and out of the army, then in the Home Guard, helping folks to the bomb shelters in air raids. I was a churchgoer at that age. A sultry wet night. Their wardrobe wasn't locked. Thought I'd struck gold. "Think of all the people we'll shelter. The thanks I'll get!" Whack, the door closes behind me. Dunno who did it. Frightened out of my wits I was. Cos I heard him coming. Plodding. From below. From here, coming for me. He was whistling. Whistling that tune playing a few minutes ago. It's a bad thing, to be afeared. You know that, of course. Oh, it's a bad moment!'

The bottle was about to overflow. I switched to a second bottle, spilling drips on the floor. 'You survived, though,' I said.

'Who knows how Serge judges.' Derek shrugged. 'His perception … It's not of this earth.'

I attacked the subject, guns blazing. 'How did you cope? How bad does it get? I can't help being scared, Derek, please help me. I swore I wouldn't end up like Daniels!'

'My goodness! Forgive me, dear, but you're working for *them*. Best left for you to find out. Pardon me, I can't reveal too much. He'll read it in your face if I do.'

My spirits fell. 'What I mean is you lasted this long, and retired. It'd give me hope if you explained how.'

'They promised me something, dear. I couldn't accept. I left.'

'Accept what?'

He continued his story, evading my question.

'I went AWOL, peripatetic. Bounced from Paris to Madrid to Athens. I thought they'd forgotten me.'

'They came after you?'

'I didn't know for decades. Yes. They were always there. Serge, I'll tell you, he's a respected singularity. He – is feared. Retired, like me. But he is known. If he's after you, you're good as found. They edge closer. They tease. I jumped city to city, thinking I'd lost them. They like to *play*. You'd best learn that, by the way, their games! My advice? Go along with it. You won't win. Treat them better than you're treated if you want a hope in hell. They breathe with the winds. I think they hear and see ultrasound, infra-sound, every wavelength, who knows what else. I'll never fathom them. I've tried. I was a haunted man, but I learned to live with them at my tail.'

'I don't understand. They didn't punish you? Harm you?'

'I don't like to think,' he said. 'Insurance, that's what I was. I think Serge smelt it in my genes, this blood iron illness dragging me.'

'And here you are.'

'Yes! Hehehe, here I am. As are you, my dear.' He was tiring. 'I think I'll take a biscuit now.'

'I'd free you from this if I could, Derek,' I said, handing him the wafers.

'No.' He chuckled grimly, chewing. 'I'm an old man. But Serge, he ...'

Derek briefly lost himself, nodding incessantly; it kindled a new spark of curiosity I would live with for a very long time.

'Do you know his true age?' I asked, truly thinking he might.

'I, the ...' he faltered and, with that anti-climax, giggled. 'I'm a handsome teenager!'

There was a peculiar aura of serenity about Derek, and in spite of his torment I think I began to understand him: he was glad of his mortality.

'Do you think it a bad thing?' I asked. 'Their age, that endlessness?'

He stammered again. 'I, I ...'

'They asked me,' I coughed nervously, 'if I could handle that they kill.'

'Do you like cats?' I swear that's what he said next.

'I hate 'em,' he continued. 'Never mind, heh! Do you think if mice wrote storybooks, cats would be the goodies? While folks adore cats, then make films about nasty Martians destroying us! I know how you feel. There's no easy answer.'

Derek sank into the sofa with extraordinary coolness.

'Perhaps when he shows you, you'll comprehend what life really is.'

Shows me. That pretentious new phrase was already annoying me.

'Do they still frighten you?' I asked.

Derek considered me before answering.

'If there is a greater danger than knowing them,' he said without blinking, 'aren't we, am not I, damned enough without being worse?'

Two pints drained. At Derek's insistence, I accepted several biscuits and offered to see him safely to his taxi outside the church portal, where I shook his hand as we said goodnight. I watched, breathing tasty night air as the taxi lights blinked and disappeared around a corner.

The street was empty, I could be standing backstage in the one-dimensional scenery of a deserted theatre: lights out; a painted public park across the road; a few collapsible plywood buildings; the high wall a cyclorama curving around St Patrick's, and, hugging its side, an orchestra pit – the graveyard.

Not as well-kept as it should be, overgrown and abused by certain thugs with their glass bottles and canisters, this graveyard, though meagre, was dominated by its own personal lord and master, a yew tree. Sacred creatures. I have heard tell of these masters lasting over five thousand years and still retaining their vibrancy, as alive as you are, evergreen, never especially tall but broad, wide and grand. Its extensive crown, many metres across, overhung a permanently bare patch of earth where light was a rare visitor and vegetation unwelcome. There stood my beauty, undaunted and lionhearted, as lifelong an acquaintance as St Patrick's. The trunk was peeling in vertical seams of new versus dead wood, and aged gashes cut through the centre, an open body dissected so slowly by time it survived the process; you might have fitted a whole person in there, and I have childhood memories of splinters under my nails, cracked bark in my sleeves and green needles in my hair to testify to it. For many a church in Britain you will find a yew tree older than its accompanying buildings, and with good reason: their spiritual influence long preceded Christianity, survived its incumbency, and will succeed it. It is not for me to say precisely how long a yew may live. Mine grows there yet.

There was no wind, no sound except the oddly comforting hum of distant traffic. Orange streetlamps shimmered in rainwater puddles, and as the last house light flicked off, I had Clayburn Avenue entirely to myself, and I was in no hurry. There on the pavement, I inhaled evening. Night time has a smell, and in autumn it is the best smell in the world, an earthen savour of gold, auburn and musk made to blend with smoky dusk, breathing fresh life into me every time. It always revived my only happy memory of primary school, of heading to the gymnasium at six o'clock in full costume for the Halloween party. The delight with which I skipped down the road in my witch's outfit, my aunts barking at me to slow down, kicking up mound after mound of dead leaves so high the crackling flakes landed on the rim of my pointy witch hat, me tingling head to toe with excitement at the bittersweet gift of a few hours out of three-hundred and sixty-five days to be permissibly wild and otherworldly. Nothing is more fragile than happiness, or freedom for that matter.

The evening was mild, and they were out there somewhere. *I smell a rat in you, Rona*, spoke a demon in my ear. It was true, I did harbour an evil wire of curiosity, for if I honestly preferred ignorance, why secretly mull over their whereabouts? Why more than once had it crossed my mind to skim through the newspapers for any articles on missing persons? Dangerous ground, that, you could drive yourself insane. Printed photographs of their faces ready for me to cut out with scissors, turning them sideways, upside-down and full circle to snip around the images. I could cut and paste a whole scrapbook if I wanted! That character from the previous week, captive in Edith's arms, groaning and breathing, boy or girl, deserving or not, they were a lost cause. It would either break or numb me, so which was worse? Balancing in the middle like this, the see-saw was not going to hold, how was I possibly going to last long as Derek simply by clinging to his meteorite-proof philosophy? See no evil. Hear none. Speak none. Do none?

It was after ten o'clock, Derek's health prohibited me from smoking around him and it was three hours since my last cigarette. Rolling my tobacco, scanning the scene, I turned and beheld St Patrick's brown outline, the spire, its trefoil windows, my fortress, claustrophobic and uninviting, looming above its inmate. There was nothing in there for me right now, I couldn't face going inside yet.

I wandered the small graveyard. Most of its summer weeds were withering, the grass soft but for a few twigs and dead bracken crackling under my shoes. Before familiar shapes owned up to me I nearly lost my balance; so many once-vertical headstones now lay flat on the ground, some literally broken in two, eaten by lichen and disappearing into the soil, their weathered angels' faces and forgotten names facing the sky. I must have felt more respect for the dead than for the living, imagining how grieved these souls would be if they knew their sole reminders to the world lay almost as buried as their bones. Put more plainly, the graveyard was a mess, half-full of toppled dominoes of the dead.

In any case I had fewer scruples about stepping on said dominoes than risking injury by edging around their tricky outlines at this hour. As a child, I used to hop from grave to grave like stepping stones in a pond, a leap here and a jump there, eighteen hops in total, all the way to the yew tree without touching the ground. Tonight (why not?) I relived this childhood ritual in a minute of ageless abandonment, cigarette pinched between my lips, my short break from a melancholy church where I was denied sleep anyway. My phone was in my pocket, and no calls yet. Good!

Hopscotch – on I went. Step on a crack, fall and break your back, hop-skip-jump. Landed! Hello, yew. I lounged about there, finishing my roll-up.

Through dense foliage the tree's spiralling needles rocked up and down in a modest breeze, the upright headstones immovable shapes behind it; arched graves, square graves, rectangular graves, small, large, nothing you hadn't seen before. Then a shudder ran through me: one of those outlines, round and uneven, did not belong. I stooped and saw that the outline didn't change relative to the backdrop either, it was the only unfamiliar feature so far.

A streetlamp wavered momentarily and again the shape was wrong, too high up. It had moved. More importantly, it was no part of the churchyard behind the tree – it was right in front of me.

'Evening,' it greeted.

The voice and thick crop of hair were unmistakable.

I jolted to my feet, holding my ground by sheer willpower. Met with a stereotypical nightmare of churchyards, sitting in a tree, watching me for how long? But I knew him, and so long as Derek promised I could deflect meteors …

'Good evening, Serge.'

He bounced down from the branch and approached me, hands in his pockets, as informal as you please.

'Are you any the wiser yet?' he asked.

'Excuse me?'

Serge smiled playfully to himself, pretending to take in the surroundings with his idle swagger, his signature presentation. 'Your idolisation of the decrepit,' he replied.

'Derek?' I said. 'He told me about the army and Home Guard.'

'Do you like him?' he enquired, propped roguishly against the yew trunk.

I straightened, feeling defensive. 'Yes. I do, actually.'

'He's a product of his era, madam.'

'Oh?' I raised a sceptical eyebrow.

'Derek's killed *plenty* of people. Women, too. He's a war criminal, perchance he neglected to mention that? I wouldn't fit a halo over his bald patch yet.'

That shut me up a moment. I re-gathered my disillusioned thoughts. 'Does that make me a product of *my* era?' I sulked.

'Most people are. Children. You, of course, are not People. That doesn't make you anything special, just you.'

'Just me.' I sighed, trying to hide how easily that got a rise out of me. 'I wonder what that is.'

'Guess.'

'I don't know. Scared?'

'That's redundant.'

'Curious, then. You don't know the questions I need to ask.'

'I disagree. This, for instance.' Serge gave the ground a couple of stamps. 'Do you know where you're standing?'

'I pass on trick questions.'

'Thought not. You're a few dozen feet above the vault where you drew blood.' He indicated from church to graveyard. 'For over three hundred yards across, four dozen yards down is the original monastic settlement.'

My eyes widened, drawing a rough schematic in my head while Serge pointed left and right: 'South and north-west,' he elaborated. 'A thousand and twenty-something A.D. if memory serves.'

'The vaults below? But that goes all the way to under Delfour Road, over there!'

'Give yourself a gold star,' he said sarcastically. 'The staircase you climbed passes under there ...' he walked me across the graveyard like an ordnance surveyor, 'through this section, then towards Delfour Road and Rennet Street. Just.'

'It sounds like a labyrinth,' I said.

'You grow fanciful, Rona. Check yourself. And shout Geronimo.'

'Pardo–' Geronimo. I tripped over another flat headstone,

landing on my side. 'Ow!'

'Check yourself or prepare to fall,' he said, ambling over.

I cursed and sat on the grave, digging out my tobacco. Serge found himself a tall monolith opposite me, rested against it and folded his arms, musing over the graves while I rolled my filter. He went quiet for a minute, gazing ahead, in thought.

'Did you never wonder,' he said mistily, 'why some church-yards have so many fallen headstones, and some don't?'

I followed his gaze, not really caring. 'They're labelled un-stable by the council?'

Serge pursed his lips with a light smirk.

'Once upon a time ... in various places ... decay walked the streets at night. Rats swarmed in and out of homes like ants, in and out of bodies before their flesh was cold. People lay yellow and dying in their beds, flies tickling their foreheads and dried vomit on their pillow. The very rooms dripped with sweat. The stench of sickness swam through villages like smoke. On win-try nights it *was* smoke, vapours from whoever coughed their last cup of blood or lanced their last boil that day.'

His sly storyteller's voice was intensifying per sentence.

'Scavengers followed stench like ravens follow wolves. Where once-green fields fed sheep, human bones jutted through mounds of earth, covered in rooks by day and dogs by night, digging,' he mimicked the clawing of a hound, '... *digging*. Roads were deserted, no horse carts trundled to market days and travellers were taken at dusk, families picked off, one by one. Windows broke; by morning the masters walked in to flapping wings and black feathers everywhere, crows startled from a new corpse polka-dotted red by their beaks. Everyone blamed the Almighty punishing them, trying everything to ban evil spirits. Garlic above locks,' he was bending forward, very slowly, closer and closer to me, 'crosses on doors, bonfires. Send your beloveds to the grave with rocks and logs in their mouths. Even mirrors were smashed in case the departed souls *crept* inside.'

On the word 'crept', Serge scuttled his fingers up my hand like a spider. I winced, he sniggered.

'The sick and the dying are so often buried alive, for no one wants plague from thy neighbour. What would *you* do? Buried at the drop of a hat or burned if they were lucky. Oh, but if their family made a mistake!'

The whites of his eyes glared, a piteous furrow darkening his brow as he bent closer to me. Drama or not, what had started as an entertainment was rapidly becoming too harrowing to watch: his macabre theatricality, though deliberately exaggerated, hinted the faintest smudge of sincerity in there somewhere.

His voice dropped to a ghastly husk.

'They scratched at the door, trying to scream. So weak. *So* weak, Rona. Screaming inside, screaming outside, fingernails chipping off, their hands stiffened to *claws* and faces shrinking till they imploded from desiccation. Even the starved guard dogs were too scared to attack. Wailing for help with no breath, their skin cracked and split open from exertion, then their withered limbs buckled, locked and snapped off when they tried to stagger. Couldn't see, their eyeballs rolled back in their heads to pulps of pink veins. No energy, they'd spent it all trying to get home again, chewing away their own arms and lips until their mouths were gone, it was the only strength they found, *surviving* themselves to death.

'The parish fell into panic. Graves were exhumed, caskets unearthed. Their hair had grown, gnawed insects were stuck in their teeth, grinding clack-clack with their jawbones, lip-lessly calling for help. Then they were decapitated. And if not burned ...' Serge raised his arm, presenting the flat stone dominoes about us, and mimicked the cry of a crazed peasant. 'Cover the grave mounds with stone! Block them! Hurry, don't let the dead climb out!'

We froze in position. Count to ten, Rona: one, two, three …
Almost. He had *almost* had me.

'You prick,' I said wryly.

Serge threw his head back and laughed. Touché. I fetched
myself up from the ground. 'Yes, that's one fall I won't give
you,' I said, brushing down my jeans.

Do you think I sounded convincingly sporting? I think so.
His performance masked as a gag had deeply unnerved me and
I wanted to get in out of the dark. I needed to. Fast. I had never
seen anyone or anything's pupils dilate so fully: his grey-blue
irises were completely gone.

Our enigmatic raconteur blithely promenaded inside while I
bolted the aisle door.

'Where are the others?' I asked.

'Revelling. We're not joined at the hip, you know. I was
waiting for you out there. Some news. Our beloved Falkirk is
ill.'

'I fail to see how that's news.'

'Hospital-ill. He finally brought some heart palpitations on
himself, bless him.'

'How serious?'

'Serious enough to keep him a few days.'

I reddened. Falkirk would be replaced, so what about me?
I was a squatter there, hell my general situation was a test of
endurance at best; for it to be blown out of the water was more
than my strained mind could wrestle with.

'But, the thugs, they were here today,' I stammered. 'They
might be back, and what's to happen in the meantime?'

'Less noise, woman,' he said, moseying without a care in
the world. 'In pickles like this the parish sends a substitute for
sermons and what-have-you.'

Substitute? Heaven's sake, a baby knows that!

'Sorry, Serge, but if you'll pardon me, fuck the sermons.

Only Falkirk knows I sleep here. What's to happen? It can't go on as normal.'

'You tell me. You're a big girl. St Catherine's Hospital, by the way. And stop pacing, you'll make me dizzy.'

I paced regardless, on the verge of panic. 'Whatever temp they pull out of a hat will find out I squat. On top of that I'm unofficially employed, paid cash in hand.'

'Awww.'

My guard folded. 'Right. Fine. Meanwhile you don't know how long he'll be gone – if I'm found out, who'll deal with Derek, the chores, the nightshifts, your damn *taxis*?!'

Oops. Temper, Rona.

Next thing I knew a modern set of pin tumbler house keys was flying at me. I caught them just before they busted my nose.

'His villa twenty metres away doesn't belong to the parish,' said Serge. 'Thank me later.'

A trio of keys affixed to a key ring; one for his car, two for the villa.

'Are we happy?' he asked as you would a spoiled brat. 'Indeed, said temps don't expect gallery gremlins and tend to arrive sharpish in the morning. That means tomorrow. Haven't you some moving to do? Goodnight.'

He left me in the nave.

I moved. Quilt, pillow, ashtray, alarm clock and the few clothes I could carry. I set the mattress inconspicuously up against the gallery wall and coated the balcony in air freshener.

Falkirk's villa was a stuffy airless tip with food in the fridge past its sell-by date and four bedrooms with fusty spare mattresses left behind from some previous family decades ago. It was past two in the morning when I pulled the quilt over my head and gave St Patrick's the finger before nodding off.

Chapter Eight

I overslept, a worrying habit. Waking in Falkirk's villa, I forgot where I was until I stretched. Nine o'clock in the morning, damn, another wedding to prepare the church for, and with a substitute minister plopped into the mix it was set to be a hectic day.

The temporary minister, Berwyn Howell if I remember correctly, was a bubbly, dimpled, ebullient tub of a man, if somewhat lighter in the intelligence department. He read sermons too slowly, wandered the church to kill time and was in serious need of retirement, but where Falkirk was bumptious and dogmatic, Howell was a softly-spoken song of belief that all was right with the world and everything in it. When I introduced myself and explained my role as cleaner and verger, this easy soul greeted me happily, glad for the extra bit of guidance from an insider, this breath of fresh air who would never in a million years suspect a subterranean dominion infecting the entire building.

I did plan on visiting Falkirk in hospital, but this was not to be the day; I had the wedding fallout to sweep up, exasperated by two whole boxes worth of confetti dumped outside the front portal. I got to work as the last few wedding guests sauntered by at their leisure, stepping over my brush and shovel, thoughtlessly kicking extra confetti into the gutter before driving off with cursory glances, repeatedly catching my warped reflection in their car windows.

Sweeping is a nice mindless job, the brain has wiggle room to wander where it likes, to graveyards, old aunts' houses, tunnels, cupboards, and with enough of those reflective car windows driving by, why not stray into a maze of magic mirrors while you're at it? Where's Rona? Is that her? Or is *that* her? Which is it? Ah, there's Rona, sweeping away, one of her anyway, she and her broom, partners in crime.

Enter Sunshine Rona: today she clears pretty confetti and bouquet petals thrown by happy relatives, bridesmaids and cute flower girls.

Last night?

Enter Disfigured Rona: she and this exact same brush were woken at 4 a.m. Ring-ring. *Good morning, Rona, we're home-sweet-home, how do you like Falkirk's palace? The nave requires your attention, cheerio.* Three pairs of muddy shoeprints, trails of dirt, blonde human hair complete with follicles caught on a brass nail in the cupboard door handle. And droplets, hardening to jellified rubies, droplets on the doors, on a pew bench cushion, droplets in the chancel, bleach them before they seep! My tools are sweeping up confetti; less than twelve hours ago they swept gore and mud. Which mirror has your soul '*crept*' into, Rona; how did his scuttling spider fingers feel? *They like to play*, Derek says, *you'd best learn that, their games!*

I was interrupted.

– Interrupted in my reverie by the unwelcome sound of voices coming from across the street, voices I recognised, too close for comfort. My grip tightened on the brush. Yesterday's thugs sat on the park wall of Fergus Green opposite, smoking joints and babbling their usual colourful lingo. Shit, it didn't look like any accidental rendezvous either, they were lingering and, I think, waiting for me. Three this time. The egg-faced man, the big stocky woman, the young boy they practically carried out yesterday, and they were not going anywhere. Hang on, a boy? I squinted.

By gum, it was a girl! A classic tomboy. I blushed at my mistake, if a tad too late, because unfortunately this tomboy, sharp little thing, caught me staring. I hurried in my sweeping task, dreading a cacophonous sequel to yesterday's 'Oi, cheeky bitch!' any second. When nothing happened and the confetti was gone, I chanced a quick look before going inside; big mistake, the man was lumbering across the road towards me.

'Hey!' he called.

Within seconds he had closed the distance between us and invaded my personal space, shepherding me against the portal jambs. Checking to see the coast was clear, he used a hushed tone. 'Hey, go and open that tomb for us, would ya?'

'No, I can't do that,' I said feebly. This was no meteorite I could deflect in broad daylight.

'C'mon, give us the key! We'll only be a minute.'

By his intonation they assumed the crypt their territory. Interestingly that made me angry, cockroaches mocking the tigers. *And it's a crypt, not a 'tomb', imbecile!*

'I don't have the key,' I said, edging for the front portal. Lying was the easiest part of my job.

Meanwhile, across the street, the stocky woman was smoking a joint, bored with the proceedings. The tomboy however, had slumped forward and, incredibly, was smiling at me. Seeing she had recaptured my attention, she opened her mouth and slowly rolled her tongue along her upper lip in a way that could only be described as flirtatious. Discombobulated, I tried wrapping it up with this ogre, whom I subconsciously dubbed Egg Face.

'Falkirk's in hospital,' I said. 'He has the key. I'll tell him you were here but there's nothing else I can do.'

'For fuck sake! Can't you get it from his house? Just go

find it!'

Egg Face's fuse was lit and he was not going to take no for an answer – thank you so much, Minister Howell, for your heaven-sent timing!

'Hello!' Howell bubbled, happening upon us in his harmless buffoonery, rubbing his chubby palms together. 'Everything all right?'

This knocked Egg Face unawares. He drew away, outnumbered, and stormed off, cussing with the others.

'Anything to worry about?' asked Howell, keeping his opinions to himself.

'No,' I replied, playing it safe. 'The street gets some characters, it's okay.'

The ironic predicament of 'playing it safe' heavy on my mind, I lit a cigarette and retraced my path along the churchyard's stepping stones. Daylight made it quite impossible to believe that right there was the flat headstone where I sat with Serge standing over me, against that monolith, telling stories with a grim grain of truth, impaling me with two swelling ink blots for pupils in cloudy whites. (*'Screaming inside, screaming outside, fingernails chipping off ...'*) I tread wet grass, bracken and stone, mentally tracing out my imagined schematic of some elaborate underground labyrinth stretching from here to Delfour Road and Rennet Close, where under twenty-first-century cars roaring their fumes and radio music, slept the church's oldest residents, buried in its mazy skeleton.

I knew Howell's fortuitous timing was only a temporary reprieve. No thanks to Falkirk I was on borrowed time; Egg Face may well return tomorrow or the day after with his bottle-wielding army and no Falkirk to negotiate with, leaving who? Me? I think not. I had the mettle for three inhuman revenants and none for a single Egg Face.

I took a deep, long draw on my cigarette. I was going to have to speak with them. Them.

I managed to persuade Howell to let me lock up at night and assured him I certainly needed no lift home. Come early evening I patrolled the nave, jingling my keys, mulling over how to explain my latest dilemma.

At this premature stage in my relationship with the trio, Edith and Hector were openly tight-lipped. Serge did all the talking. Hector was an odd specimen with his inanimate gaze and daunting size, though under that monotone bearishness I sensed a milder creature than his commander. As for lofty Edith, she was clever enough to keep me guessing, but if as intelligent as Serge, she still hadn't half his intuition. I tried putting my finger on exactly what made them tick. If you are tempted to label Hector the big dummy and she a debonair grimalkin, bear in mind I had so far seen only what they were capable of: I hadn't seen *them*, not really. What had I seen? *Tapetum lucidum.* Dilating pupils. Desiccated flesh. Not much.

Has he not shown you yet?

I caught my breath on that thought, booked their taxis and decided to potter on the balcony until they emerged. I had my lamp and a book or two. It was the safest option. The last thing I could have anticipated was a visitor waiting in the gallery for me.

I pulled down the mattress in case I dozed off, grabbed a warm jumper and slouched over the balustrade, preparing for however long a wait.

'*Pssssst!*'

'Fuck!' I shot around as my heart hit the ceiling.

A delicate boyish frame, tucked between the boxes like a gnome, picked itself up out of the shadows, griping. 'Jezuz titty-fuck it's crap up here!'

The skinny urchin coughed and straightened, betraying a whiff of cannabis. Wiry umber hair fell almost to her shoulders in two uneven crops; she wore a torn denim waistcoat and heavy leather boots. I recognised her immediately.

'Shit!' I gasped. 'You can't be in here! You have to go! How the hell did you get in?'

The androgynous face with its bright eyes bounded towards me in a childish hop-skip. 'Oi, yeah, luv, I've been hanging around. Where's the key?'

Despite the company this lip-licking tomboy kept, I instinctively surmised she was a different side of the coin from Egg Face. She was not remotely sweet, bashful, mature or decent, nor could I detect any real aggression in her. This girl I am introducing you to – I may as well say now for your benefit – was a very singular character indeed!

'How did you get in?' I snapped.

She kneeled on the mattress, making herself quite at home for an intruder.

'How the fuck d'ya think?' she chirped. 'I've been up here! I tried the cupboard. Let us in or Gaz'll thump me.'

She said *Gaz* as if I should know him.

'Jesus,' I groaned, recovering. 'I told you I don't have it! Who else is with you? Are they outside?'

'Nah, just me,' she said, settling into a cross-legged position. Digging out filter papers, she talked through a plastic pocket of weed in her teeth. 'Gaz wants that stuff soon. He's raging. Got orders to fill.'

'Orders?'

'Duh! The shit through the wall, babes. Got any roaches?'

I threw a cigarette to distract her. 'Please don't smoke joints in here or I'm screwed.'

'Spare me,' she moaned, lighting the cigarette and exhaling a cloud of smoke. 'You went to Bronmeg High.'

'How did you know that?'

'Saw you before my suspension in year four. Never same class though.'

'Oh. I don't remember.'

'You were the loner, no boyfriends.'

I coloured. I did not appreciate reminders of being the school runt, thanks. What was I supposed to say to that? Apologise or something?

'I just liked my space,' I said, averting my eyes.

'Do you shag girls?'

'*What?*'

Now *there* was a question I didn't see coming; not even the high school bullies threw that one at me!

The tomboy leant back and relaxed against the wall, smoking away. 'Girls,' she replied. 'Should probably make it Plan B.'

Was she making fun or not? With this crazy character, I really couldn't tell. She spoke as if she had known me for decades, no respect for discretion, tact or conventionality whatsoever.

'I don't, thanks,' I said, sounding haughtier than I intended.

'Why not?' She asked this as if it were nothing.

I was not used to being queried so frankly, especially by this peculiarity from Thugland I only met a couple of minutes ago. 'I'm straight,' I said. 'Period.'

She exhaled a smoky 'O', stuck her tongue through it and refastened a bootlace. 'Up-fucking-tight is what you are. Bet I could sort you out.'

I gaped, an involuntary snigger escaping me. Was she nuts? She spoke with such impish sincerity!

'You're the most direct person I ever met.'

'Roll me one of those, will ya,' she said, passing me a half-finished joint.

'I don't do weed.'

'Why?'

'Tried it at uni, never took to it.'

'Uni? And that's why you now sleep in a fucking church?'

'I'm homeless.'

'How?'

'You ask a lot of stuff,' I said, forgetting to check my watch.

'You're high, aren't you?'

Either that or she has ADH-bloody-D, I thought. She was a bizarre mish-mash of hyper-alertness and idleness, her eyes either darting here and there or chilling out, and though a couple of years younger than me, I had to admit her offish chirpiness suggested a lot more spirit than I possessed. Yet I discerned a tragic streak juxtaposing her sparkly bounciness, the self-harm scars on her forearms for one thing, not to mention yellowing bruises on her wrists.

'No,' she replied. 'No real high, thanks to you. Gaz is gonna be on your arse soon if you don't watch out.'

My resentment for Falkirk intensified, he who put me in harm's way, safe and cosy tonight in a hospital bed.

'You're with them?' I asked. 'That gang?'

'Why not? Fuck-all else.'

'I don't understand you people.'

'I don't understand you fucking halo-heads. So if you're not after a shag, why were you ripping my clothes off out there with your face?'

'I thought you were a boy.'

I instantly regretted shooting my mouth off, thinking I was in for a punching. Instead she laughed hysterically.

'Hahahaha! Was I hot?' she asked, drawing on the cigarette. When I refused to answer, she teased, moving in close. '*Was* I?'

'How should I know?'

'Ah, fuck off.' She slumped against the wall. 'But yeah, how would you?'

I was very uncomfortable with *how* comfortable she was getting. 'Aren't you going soon?' I said impatiently.

'The fuck's your problem?'

I remembered to check the time.

'*Shit!*' I bolted up. 'It's late! You need to go! If the minister comes I'll lose my job!' Another easy lie.

'I thought you were homeless.'

'I am! I didn't say unemployed.' I went to the balcony, making agitated fists. In under ten minutes that cupboard would open – the consequences of being caught entertaining forbidden company did not bear thinking about.

Infuriatingly she remained cross-legged on my mattress, puffing smoke. 'Minister had no problem letting us in here.'

'Not now, things have changed! Come on!' I moved to shove her. 'You have to go!'

'Flash me and I will,' she joked.

I couldn't believe this, she wasn't moving.

'You'll get me in serious trouble! The other minister's coming. He'll call the police the second he sees you, I swear!'

Magically, this seemed to convince her. 'Fuck sake!' She stamped out her cigarette and stomped to the aisle. 'Get the key from him, would ya, or Gaz'll raid his house.'

I just wanted her out. Now!

'I hate what you do,' I raged, panicked and heated, pushing her to the aisle exit. 'I hate what you take, and I hate drugs!'

At this she angrily grabbed my collar and yanked me towards her. 'Bitch! Don't be a fucking nun *all* your life! Go finger yourself.'

The tomboy stumbled outside, raised her middle finger and wiggled it in that suggestive manner. 'See ya, sexy.'

I shut and locked the door, feeling like I'd just been hit by a freight truck.

A close shave. They would smell her for sure. Great, now I had two things to confess to my overlords. I needed some water; I was sick of fearing blame for others' mistakes, sick of worrying about thugs and definitely sick of waiting every night, my mind playing every possible outcome in loops.

As I ran the tap in the vestry, something caught my eye. A flat ivory square on the coffee table, ominous and unmissable against the polished mahogany and biscuit crumbs. I scowled at it. I despised it for being there. I drank and refilled the glass.

Howell had left his newspaper.

The Bronmeg Post, coincidentally lying where Falkirk had told me, 'You and I are the only safe people in the world.'

A single flip through would take seconds. From my safe distance at the sink, I knew if I spurned that newspaper its presence would only swell, radiating like a vengeful searchlight from the vestry to the balcony, its ivory pages glowing neon. I could easily toss it in the bucket, but that would mean touching it, and that would mean feeling discarnate screams eating my fingers through the dusky texture, begging me to honour them by reading in shame or suffer their muddy blood to seep through the pages.

Do it this once, Rona, get it out of your system. One skim, that's all, honour the dead with one skim, no more, it's not my fault!

Defeated, I pulled the chair aside.

Heartened to find nothing remotely significant on the front page, I modestly flipped through. Airbrushed celebrities in size zero attire reminded everyone that healthy girls are ugly; politicians posed with phoney promises; multinational contracts were signed for tax-dodging corporations; another 'Miracle Baby' survived premature birth.

As I gratefully skimmed through safely uninteresting stories, a horrible thorn in my gut warned I was not off the hook; it was in there somewhere, a buried spike waiting to cut me. I reached the final pages: car sales, TV guides, Howell's unfinished crossword in blue biro … It was almost too merciful.

With lighter spirits, I flipped the featherweight leaves backwards, relaxing. Headlines, bold print, small print, large print, 'Funding under threat …', '£OFFERS£', '… announced future of …', 'Manager takes legal …', 'Remains thought to …', 'Jury still out over …', 'Award for school team …', 'MP challenges accusations of …'

Remains thought to

Yes, I saw it. Yes, I passed it. The thin pages quivered in my fingers.

I could close this paper right now, chuck it in the bin and have done with it, I don't have to look, is it my fault I'm here? Go upstairs and have another cigarette!

I closed my eyes, and turned to the place.

Remains thought to be missing Farrow couple

Under the headline, two monochromatic photographs: a brunette woman in a striped pullover, lipstick, dangly earrings; a balding man, small moustache, posing on a pub stool. Both middle-aged, both healthy, both normal, completely unwary. Paper ghosts.

> Police believe they have uncovered the remains of Mr Richard Farrow, aged 44, and Mrs Jacqueline Farrow, aged 39, mother and father of two, at a building site in Kerry Park following a six-week police search. The bodies were found in an advanced state of decomposition. Detective Inspector Lowrie confirms, 'Though cause of death has not yet been established, these deaths are now being treated as suspicious. We are conducting DNA tests on the remains and welcome the assistance of any possible eyewitnesses who may have seen them on the night they disappeared.'

> Mr and Mrs Farrow were last seen on 10th September at 10:30 p.m. this year leaving the Crannon pub on Smithson Terrace in Bronmeg, Warwickshire. Mourning friends described the deceased as 'a delightful couple always game for a laugh.'

I remember sitting there, hunched over the page, gazing through the newsprint I'd just finished reading.

Always game for a laugh. Dad? Outta milk. Ur late!

Denial upstaged my premeditated guilt. News articles like

this were no landmark; you heard them on the radio and TV I don't know how many times, was I supposed to beat myself up over every missing person on Earth from now on?

But Kerry Park was local. I knew that building site, my taxi had passed it on the way from Cole's shop. I sipped my water, blank as a sheet, deciding to call it a night and retire this paper to the bin as the next page fell. There it was. The word I did not want to see.

'Missing'

I set my head in my hands and rubbed my eyes. Okay … okay …

Appeal For Missing Students

Police are appealing for information following the sudden disappearance of Michelle Burnham, 18, Christopher Epton, 19, and Austrian exchange students Kassandra Berg and Jonus Koertig, both aged 18. The four youths were last seen together at the Students' Union of Bronmeg's Maple Park College around 8 p.m. on Tuesday 30th September. Their friends and family confirm it is very out of character for them not to get in touch and strongly urge anyone with information to …

Under the newsprint, four individual photographs of blithe young faces. The tap water curdled to slime in my stomach. Here they were, another sample of Rona's treachery to her race. There would be more.

Funny, though, the way the regular news articles affected me too, how glimpsing beyond the fence whacked me with hot air. My entire consciousness circulated this church; my every nerve was dictated by the minutest change in light, super-highly attuned to the most indiscernible noise in this big stone cage. The newspaper was a compelling window reminding me how quickly I had forgotten there was a world outside, and, what's more, from my remote island this bleak realisation made me neither happy nor sad.

The church and I, one of us was bound to change, and St Patrick's hadn't budged. Dirt and death beneath, me relegated to some unknown slot in between. Ever since fish crawled from the sea there would always be something crouching at night.

These students were dead, I knew it.

Enough. I pushed the paper aside and refilled my glass, gulping it twice.

Edith came in.

Knock-knock-knock. Without waiting for an answer, she sailed in confidently.

'Ah, Rona. Will you come with me, please?'

How unusual to see her fully illuminated in electric light. Her hip-length hair was tied up in large pins, leaving a few wavy curls loose to frame her jawline. Under the insensitive vestry bulb her contours shone razor sharp, betraying the heaviness and imperfect texture of her thick foundation. To behold her, dressed so respectably, then to think of those news articles … It was ridiculous! Not just Edith, the three of them. How do you picture a murderer, Reader – an ugly drooling man hiding in shrubs with a butcher's knife, perhaps? The impossibility even made me slightly glad to see her.

She marched regally ahead. I trotted to keep up.

'They came here today,' I said. 'The drug dealers. One sneaked in. I got rid of her.'

'Uh-huh,' she said. 'We heard.'

Heard. Oh dear.

'They won't get the key,' I stressed.

Edith opened the cupboard. 'Save it for Serge. Did you know they also left this on the floor?' She passed me the older battery-powered torch; the thieving tomboy must have left it there earlier. 'Now follow me, and don't lag.'

I switched off the church lights behind us.

'There are a few places I need to show you,' Edith continued down the stairwell, kicking aside a tiny mouse nearly impaled by her heel. 'We have instructions from Serge to expand your duties, especially now.'

'May I ask what?'

'You've been given some idea of the other vaults, I believe. You're to have access to several as of this night, with our guidance.'

'I see.' I hoped she would elaborate further, but she remained tight-lipped as I followed her to the bottom, past the bloodletting vault, past Duke Ellington and Glenn Miller. She kept going. Where? In vain I tried calculating our depth in metres or feet, bracing myself for any dangerous unseen steps or some Greek-style labyrinth suddenly unfolding before me, complete with Minotaur at the centre. I wished Edith would slow down in case I lost her, never bargaining for what I was about to see next.

Edith halted so abruptly I bumped into her.

Straight ahead: a wall. Dead end. Uninteresting stone. It led nowhere.

'Back up.'

She reached for a chunky metal latch attached to a three-by-three-foot square of criss-crossing iron bars, built into the floor. Very impressive iron, durable enough to resist the teeth of rust; whereas the jagged latch was a sorry sight, worn to a ghastly faecal brown, misuse it at the cost of ripping your hands. The trapdoor was a personality unto itself, a credit to its bygone era.

Edith gave it a pull. All the way up it went, obediently submitting until the latch rested on the dead-end wall.

'Now,' she said. 'Observe first.'

I shone my torch into the square cavity.

It swallowed too much of the beam, limiting detail to a set of stone steps no wider than the trapdoor, descending to the right

with an unprotected drop on one side. This threadlike staircase
was more ancient and heavily used than the other, laced with
feathery cobwebs stirring in the light beam.

'This here,' she emphasised, 'is the entrance you will use.
I'm going to take you in a couple of directions. You'll only be
seeing so much tonight. Understood?'

I nodded in earnest.

'Follow closely,' she said. We disappeared under the floor.

Lead the way, Reader, you are torchlight, that makes you
my eyes.

A short twelve steps down eliminate any fancies of entering a great chasm or pit. Forgetting to duck, you hit your head
on a ceiling only five feet high in places. You find it hard to
breathe in here too; I'm afraid you'll have to learn to live with
coughing up catarrh in this underground ice-box. The air tastes
chalky because your movements have disturbed a surface layer
of stone powder, its grains flying in your lit breath like midges.

The base of the steps is a T-junction of three separate routes,
each about four feet wide. Look up at the trapdoor: the steps
coming towards you hug a wall to your left, to the right is the
short drop; fall from it and you're level with us at the head of
a long, long passage disappearing eastwards into nothingness,
greedily devouring the reach of my torch.

Staying where you are, face west and you'll see the same
passage continues to a high archway with no door. Touch it
and your fingers come away gravelly with crumbling sandstone, the lost work of a Celtic floral design carved in a labour
of love centuries ago, yet everywhere the stonework appears
blackened, as if burned.

A quarter turn north reveals a much shorter passage ending
in a bolted wooden door riddled with woodworm. Edith leads
us in this direction, not to the end; there is an opening on your
right into a domed vault.

'For the time being you'll be working in here,' she indicated. 'I shall explain.'

Initially all I registered was a shambles, a jumble of paper mounds everywhere, too befuddling. Adjusting my torch, I illuminated the room.

It was absolutely packed, floor to ceiling, with books.

Stacks and stacks of them, piled highest in the corners, grading in height like a metropolis towards the centre of the vault. Hardbacks and paperbacks of infinite size and thickness from tiny to gigantic, towers tall and thin, stocky and short, falling over each other or scattered, many books so old the covers were sponges. What little I saw of the floor was a scrap paper carpet; you couldn't put your foot anywhere without suffering another stack to collapse.

Skirting the vault were sets of ragged cabinets with glass-covered shelves containing yet more books, painted and sculpted with wooden cherubs, rams' heads, human figurines, diamonds and stars. Not only were they smashed and cracked, their sides were toasted, several beyond repair.

'This is the library,' Edith said. 'What's left of it.'

I understood her. Sadly, most of the books were done for. If you have ever seen an office fire you will know the flames send papers into self-sustaining whirlwinds, and here's what remained, a patchwork carpet of brown, brittle paper slates. The blackened sandstone now made sense. Daniels.

'The damage continues, unfortunately,' Edith said. 'Daniels was uninformed as to our whereabouts, so he ignited as many rooms as he found.'

'I am sorry,' I said automatically. Another lie, Rona? Not sure.

'Well, that can't be helped now,' she said. '*This* can. The idea is, Rona … We've been here quite a long time. As you see, we collect a substantial amount.' She picked up a carbonised book, its spine and most pages burned away. 'This, for instance,' she threw it over her shoulder, 'is now muck. You understand? We

can't be here all the time and must take advantage of the longer nights while we can. There's plenty more besides here, but
Serge says this is where you're to start.'

I recalled enough from my university days to know that
many of these books were valuable, an archivist's dream come
true. It was a travesty, an absolute travesty.

'Did you know about my archiving degree?' I asked, suspicious.

'Nope. Nor could I say I care. Come.'

She ushered me back out into the north corridor. I stalled
there a moment, drawn to the worm-eaten door at the end.
What puzzled me was its absurdly modern padlock.

'Not that way,' Edith said, leading me to the high Celtic
archway. 'You may as well see this while you're here.'

Memories. Curse them. I miss my vaults.

When I walked under the archway onto solid stone, what I
heard, I never expected. Not merely an echo, but a *travelling*
echo, the first since leaving the nave. A gentle, organic resonance communicating with some hard surface high above me.
I looked down at my feet to see a paved floor, cracked here and
there but uniform. I let the torch overtake me.

The floor went on, and on … and on. The torchlight caught
an arch, then a pillar, rising and curving into another arch. I
followed them, they duplicated, again and again for about sixty
feet. It was an arcade, like St Patrick's. My torchlight climbed
with the last pillar, ten feet, twelve, higher … higher. The top
corner curved into a semi-circular dome forming a wall at the
far end. My torch climbed higher yet. This was no claustrophobic, shallow, stuffy chamber. The detail opened up to me
beautifully, and, a stone at a time, unveiled the cause of the
ethereal echoes.

Diagonal and transverse ribs snaked out from each pillar
to join a crystalline network of multiple boss centres and in-
fillings like mighty stone cobwebs. The vaulted ceiling was a

transfixing specimen of Gothic architecture, supported by these multiple arcs, some ribs with fallen stones like missing teeth. Suddenly I realised why my body had relaxed without hitting my head or straining my spine – no stooping required here. I was standing perfectly straight under a ceiling over thirty feet high. Its majesty fell over me.

The pillared arcades were symmetrical, running the length of the room on both sides and, judging by the fathomless shadows in between, sheltered more vaults beyond. How many I was not ready to imagine. I turned in a hypnotised circle. Compared with the rest of this underground, I had walked into a Great Hall. My favourite smell, that noble unspoiled stonework, was free to circulate in this airy chamber and fill my rejoicing senses like springtime. I was in the heart, the very subterranean soul, of my church. And yet there was something unaccountably oppressive about this enrapturing Hall; the very atmosphere could skin you, it wrapped twine around my gut.

This was only the outline of the Hall itself. The echoes might have been louder if not for the contents.

Everywhere I looked there was furniture, packed in every available square foot of space under the arcades and, like the library, creeping outwards, invading the floor. A sharp sting pierced my vision as the torch reflected off a mirrored display cabinet inlaid with boxwood and decorated with painted flora, accompanying a team of others lined with brass and wooden columns. From the walls to a metre away – cupboards, oak presses, portmanteaux, tables, units, a six-foot triple candlestick holder of tired old silver. Wooden beaks of eagle armrests screaming at me from Elizabethan box pews. Beech frame sofas of padded leather, once wine red, now ripped and pink. Yawning drawers of grand bureaux, overflowing with papers, pamphlets and letters handwritten in quill pen and tied in lace. On my left slumbered a grand piano, furry with dust and dotted with spurious fingerprints.

Part One

The scents of musty aged fabric and wood were exhilarating; hardly a single era seemed to be missing from this exhaustive collection of multiple ages surrounding me, albeit falling apart with overuse and disrepair. Nor could my eye run over the same detail twice; everything boasted something new in neoclassical or art nouveau, Celtic, Georgian, Victorian, medieval, Eastern or Baroque design, contrasting generations ruthlessly dumped together. Overwhelming, too much to take in! It was like standing in the middle of the world's most disorganised antiques warehouse.

Except for the centre of the Hall. There items were purposefully set and devoid of dust, a sign of recent use.

Don't move. Stand still. You should be able to hear it by now.

Tick tick tick

Their grandfather clock, the Hall's most faithful servant, stood guard over a long dining table covered in Renaissance cloth, surrounded by three chairs, each unique: one gilded in ebony and ivory, supported on marble legs of talons and lion paws; the other a Gothic choir stall, armrests moulded with animal heads, the crest rail with a fleur-de-lis.

The third chair I mistook for being the plainest, with its low base and rounded crest. Close up, it mesmerised. Below the seat its four legs were heavily panelled together like a box, and decorating it top to bottom without symmetry or repetition, meticulously sculpted figures, geometric forms, lozenges, foliage, birds and beasts covered every square centimetre.

'Byzantine,' Edith commented, noticing my interest. 'As you can see,' she idly gestured about us, 'more losses.'

I did see. Of all the above, I am sorry to say the only beauties to escape the fire were the central table, its chairs, the clock, piano, and precious few others. Priceless works of carpenters and master craftsmen that had survived centuries – scorched, crisped, charred, fragmented, wood burned white.

'This kindling must be swept up and disposed of,' she said. 'Soon. I dare say much of it should have gone decades ago.'

'The fire, how did you contain it?'

'You tell me.'

Seeing I couldn't, she dipped behind a pillar and retrieved a large bright red cylinder. A fire extinguisher. Grossly out of place as it was, I felt like an idiot.

'Six in total,' she elaborated. 'We're not antediluvian to excess! It isn't the first time these vaults have faced vigilante conflagration.'

She mindlessly chucked the empty cylinder away, hitting a toasted desk and sending an impressive fountain of splinters into the air, at which I would have jumped had I not been distracted by brisk footsteps clapping under the archway behind me.

'Good evening!' Serge called as he paraded into the Hall, followed by Hector.

He proudly meandered, smooth as a river, through the obstacle course of destruction and twisted around, splaying out his arms and smiling with a bitter tinge of mock enthusiasm.

'I see you've discovered our *boudoir*, more or less! Has Edith given you the spiel?'

'Yes.' I nodded politely. 'I'm amazed. It's dizzying.'

'Why not?' he goaded. 'You didn't think we only entertained ourselves with a record player, did you?'

I flushed, struck by the sight of them standing here in their modern clothes amidst relics that had no place in this century. And yet despite the aesthetic contrast, unlike me they made no clash whatsoever, but blended in perfectly, the paradox only serving to further accentuate their authenticity.

'The losses,' I said, searching for the right words, 'they're extraordinary.'

'Lot of rubbish!' In that same moment he suddenly *kicked* over the remains of a bench with unjustified violence like an unhinged youth, shattering what was left of it forever and giving my heart an electric shock.

I think even Edith and Hector felt the sting. There was something very off in that antisocial little micro-burst, there was no need for it.

Anyhow, the mercurial creature then stood arms akimbo, quite collected, and looked from me to Edith. 'The, er, library?'

Edith was unresponsive. Cue me.

'When do you want me to start?' I asked.

'Whenever.'

'Evenings, I presume?'

'No,' he breezed, hands in his pockets. 'Not necessarily.'

'You mean I can come down whenever I want?'

Edith spoke up. 'When you want. *Where* we want.'

'Not tonight,' Serge said. 'On that note, Rona, I'll see you out. You're hungry.'

He escorted me to the trapdoor.

'I think I am peckish,' I said. 'I hadn't realised.'

'You're giddy,' he replied, 'and your colour's changed.'

Serge saw me all the way to the nave.

'Proceed,' he said.

'Sorry?'

'Your vivacious vixen.'

Rona, you headcase! Vaults, books, Grand Hall, even the ticking grandfather clock had re-jigged me enough to forget the tomboy.

'She sneaked in,' I started, catching up with myself. 'I don't think she's dangerous. I sent her away. Her friends though, they're threatening to raid Falkirk's house.'

'If it happens again just let them in,' he said, stunning me.

'But I thought you despised their mess. More than anything I worry they'll break through the gate.'

He tutted sarcastically. 'Ah, yes, you tidied that up for us the other day, didn't you? That sepulchre's nothing to me in any case.'

Serge's finality was inarguable. I shut up.

He took a seat in the pews. 'You never tell us much of yourself, Rona.'

I stopped in my tracks, hardly knowing what to say. Where did *this* come from? The only presupposition I dared allow myself was their indifference to me, and now here's Serge, slumped and sedate in that pew. *And he wants me to talk? Fuck you.*

Rona, dear, if you knew how well Serge heard this, heard every tiny electrical signal from one side of your brain to the other!

'It's not a trick question, you little wench!' he teased, motioning me nearer.

I struck a reticent pose and sauntered over. 'You have but to ask.'

'Why did you enjoy our transept corner so much?'

'I enjoyed many corners in here, Serge. Usually hiding from my aunts.'

'Your aunts.'

'They will fuss over a child. They moved here from Krellingsgait to adopt me after my mother died.'

Serge fiddled with a piece of loose thread on the pew bench, thinking to himself. The torch beam spread wider up here than below ground, replacing my trepidation with a kind of possessiveness. *I live in this church. Is it not my territory too?*

'Rona "Dean",' he finally said. 'Of the Krellingsgait lineage "Dene"?'

I shrugged.

'Love child or bastard?' he poked. 'Which do you prefer?'

'I don't care. My aunts wanted a God-fearing piglet. They said it was unnatural not to have a mother and father.'

'Don't say *unnatural*. I never want to hear that word from

148

you. There's no such thing. By rights the term's an abomination, but ...' He tittered. 'No, just more anthropomorphic claptrap.'

In this repose, I used the opportunity to watch him properly, taking in the trillion-and-one tiny characteristics that made up his presence, struggling to segregate them. His every gesture was naturally choreographed without effort; his swerving inflexions refined every cadence into delicate pulses with a style I had never seen anywhere before. I could taste his words.

'And where are those fussy aunts now?' he asked.

'Gone. They were much older.'

'And why is your phone not buzzing with friends and suitors?'

This time *I* tutted.

Taking that line of enquiry as settled, Serge reclined, glanced around, and gestured at the stained glass windows. 'Have you a favourite?'

Rather a sudden change of subject. I browsed about aimlessly. *Come on, Rona, you know these windows!* Then it came; in fact, it was easy.

I walked closer to him, following the north aisle. 'There.'

I pointed to a two-light divided window. On one side was a female figure, on the other a small dragon by a horse, crescent moon and horizon. Inscriptions of yellows and pinks adorned them, but that was not the true fire; what I loved were the Prussian blues and indigos enclosing the image in delicious chaos. In sunlight, it bedazzled. How people passed it by was a mystery to me.

'The shades are so beautiful,' I said, sitting on the pew in front of his. 'I could look at it for hours. Actually, I did.' I smiled. 'You see, I never really took to religion. I daydreamed while Falkirk preached on.'

I could never have told you what Serge was thinking. He glanced at the window. 'That's St Hannah,' he observed. 'The artist was Spanish.'

He considered me, cogwheels turning.

'Why did you leave your degree?'

Did Falkirk tell him that? Did Falkirk even know about my degree? Search me. Either way I wished Serge hadn't asked. It shamed me to remember.

'Money,' I half-heartedly replied. 'Tuition fees.'

Nope, he wasn't satisfied. It was the only thing I could read in his face. I took a breath. Try again.

'I suppose ... I suppose when you want to be everything, you wind up being nothing. I don't know how else to answer you, Serge.'

'No, you don't know how,' he condescended. 'Only *what*.'

'You don't have all night.'

'If you don't tell it, I will.'

'So why bother asking me?'

'Because it belongs to you. And secrets age the heart. Especially when locked away. Until you lose the key. Then one day you forget why you're searching for it, so you search even harder, for nothing.' He followed up this profound speech with, 'That and you might as well have the honour of entertaining me while your pain's young and fresh!'

'Huh!' I weighed his expression; it was frivolous. 'Very well,' I said. 'I'll be a sport.'

I told him. It didn't take long. Of course, he behaved like Serge. Of course, he sat deadpan throughout.

'Anything else?' I sneered when finished.

Serge yawned. I'm telling you he yawned! And shook his head.

Neither of us spoke for a while. This should have felt unnerving. Strange that it did not. The seats were accommodating and the torch a solemn comfort, no need to spoil it, no need to speak. It was an easy silence.

That's why I broke it. 'Do you have any favourites? The

150

windows?'

'Oh …' Mildly surprised, Serge thought briefly, and then relaxed his elbows over my bench. 'Four back on your right.'

I aimed the torch past him.

'The Angel Wrestles Jacob,' he said without looking. 'It's unusual. The angel's face, wings, body and gown, they're all stained deep red.'

I knew the window.

'Your age,' he said. 'Remind me.'

'I'll be twenty-five in a few weeks.'

'I see.'

Serge rose, my cue that we were saying goodnight. He grinned – not unfriendly; menacing. Two weeks ago it would have terrified me. 'You'll still be too scared to come down to-morrow, won't you?'

'I have your permission.'

'The trapdoor's not as heavy as it looks.' He went.

I called after him. 'I'll update Falkirk in hospital tomorrow.'

'I give not a shit what Falkirk thinks.'

I returned to Falkirk's villa, my mind feeding off the subtly electrifying image of Serge's walk, his vocal timbre a zeph-yr blowing through him. Absently digging for the keys on the doorstep, I tried visualising Serge in the modern world and failed. I found nowhere to place him because he wasn't even a caricature of anything, no culture or era I knew anyway, for such countenance cannot be taught. It raised questions as to age and origin I had no place asking. I often thought I wasted my breath talking to Serge, that if I kept my mouth shut he would still hear what I said and more; there was no end to how he studied me. Is there any personality anywhere in the world throughout time that he hasn't met?

By now my stomach was complaining. I went searching in Falkirk's freezer. I had forgotten all about the newspaper.

Chapter Nine

This was the same damn hospital where I visited Aunt Pam in her final days of cancer.

Many people are nauseated by hospitals. I don't know what bothers them. The smell? The patients? The noise? Hospitals never upset me. I find them rather stimulating, there's always something happening.

St Catherine's was a vast expanse of nineteenth-century architecture recently upgraded with gaudy modern blocks slapped onto the exterior, ruining its symmetry with the best of intentions, I'm sure. It still looked like architectural vandalism to me. Rising high above it pointed the Victorian clock tower of the original building, its cockerel crest obsessed with due north.

When I'd visited Aunt Pam I was given clear directions; today I had none amidst the multiple new entrances for Inpatients, Outpatients, A&E, Staff Only, Students Only, Surgeons Only, Child Support Only, Radiology Only, Counselling Only. You would think a hospital so pretentiously boasting its outstanding upgrades might spare you the burden of getting lost. I felt very conspicuous, sticking out like a sore thumb to passing nurses in blue scrubs, traipsing around the hospital's seven buildings only to wind up where I started: the grotty rear door of a kitchen. Aha, the side they don't want you to see, covered in filth and grease you could never wash off your hands. By the door were two giant steel bins where buzzing flies combed mountains of used soda cans, bottles, napkins and mouldy canteen leftovers. *Where the hell am I?*

In front of me a large concrete hut for electrical mains said, 'Danger of Death. Keep Out', pummelling a black stick figure with a miniature lightning bolt. From behind this a car engine started, guiding me to a massive parking area; at last, some form of civilisation, there should be decent signs nearby. I gingerly made my way along the pavement past square windows of one-way glass offering unflattering reflections of my windswept hair.

I was under no impression Falkirk would be thrilled to see me. I could easily talk about bubbly Howell to pass the time, and if his view on the drug dealers was anything like Serge's, I did not imagine this visit taking long. I wanted to strangle the old fool with a stethoscope for leaving me open to Gaz's threats and beer bottles, especially after having known me since infancy. It hurt. More than anything I wished Serge would just tell him off. I would have to be mature with Falkirk. I would be affable. How do you wipe away twenty-plus years of treating someone politely even when you don't want to?

This pavement wasn't leading me anywhere.

'Fuck it.'

I found a public bench and lit a cigarette.

Smoking on hospital grounds with the occasional ambulance driving by, not very politically correct, is it? In no mood for Good Samaritans with disapproving looks, I subconsciously hid the cigarette and tried to get my bearings: large car park, a few members of the buggy brigade (please don't tell me I've strayed to the maternity ward) and a big fat shiny pair of automated doors actually going somewhere, thank God.

I zipped my coat. The weather was changing. A breeze I

would have welcomed a month ago found me today and decided to gnaw. Soon the rains would accompany it.

A bout of laughter sounded from the car park. Father and mother were ushering a noisy infant boy into their vehicle. The child clasped a toy windmill, jumping up and down in whiny tears for the sake of some vital cause only he knew. The mother laughed. The father laughed. I was disenchanted. That family knew nothing.

I smoked on the solitary bench, my island in their inflated, polluted sea.

According to the receptionist, I had two corridors to hike then a third turn left, straight along the next corridor and on through a pair of automatic doors where the cardiac ward was second turn after a few more lefts here and rights there. She finished her all-knowing speech with, 'Follow the arrowed signs.'

In awe of her impatient assumption that I should remember her directions upon one hearing, I set off. It wasn't until the third corridor that clear signs sprang up like rabbits from a magician's hat. The rank of chlorine and closed wards made every section indistinguishable from the next, five or six replicas in all directions; nurses pedalled patients by me like traffic, navigating maps branded into their psyches. I would have to worry about finding my way out later.

At length, a large pair of double doors ended my search, guarded by a written notice ordering me to disinfect my hands before entering – lest, heaven forbid, I'd wiped my palm on their kitchen door, no doubt! I went in with sticky disinfectant snaking between my fingers, absently wiping my hands on my coat. The cardiac ward was brighter than the others, two sets of four hospital beds flanking a path to the nurses' bay. I enquired there, giving his name.

As the nurse directed me to Falkirk's bed a twinge of unease decelerated me; he was not expecting me, and I myself did not know what to expect. Much as I maligned him, he was a man who felt unsafe, spiralling into his own private hell of narcotics with vipers on all sides. This I empathised with unconditionally. Time with the true guardians of St Patrick's had twisted him into a dour-faced shell, preaching the word of God through a mannequin. Did he resent me for being fresh with age, a light still at my core where his had died? I'll bet he either prayed or pissed on his Bible every night.

I reached his bedside sooner than I was prepared.

His complexion was a queasy straw yellow. A cannula jutted from his arm and hidden pads under his hospital gown sent his vital signs to a screen. I went unnoticed as he leafed sluggishly through a magazine, submerged in a pillow.

'Hello,' I announced, as meekly as I could.

This kicked Falkirk into reality. He noted me with some astonishment.

'Hi,' I repeated. 'I hope this is an okay time.'

He goggled around the ward as if to ask, 'Is she supposed to be here?' Other visitors congregated at beds, carrying chocolates and grapes. Grapes, the quintessential hospital token. I had brought nothing. I felt a bit naked at my thoughtlessness, even for Falkirk.

Adjusting to this unpardonable change of scene, he shrugged uncertainly. Curtains around hospital beds cannot be drawn unless the doctor pays a royal visit; every patient is on display for anyone to see. I remembered the lack of privacy too well. I found a chair and sat down awkwardly.

'I won't keep you long. Just wanted to see how things were going.'

'What do you mean?' he grumped.

Not the best way to start. This was definitely an unwelcome visit; perhaps my presence had thrown a javelin at him. I shifted in my seat. 'I mean, er, how are you feeling? I heard it's a heart problem.'

'Hmm,' he mumbled, paying more attention to the blanket covering his legs.

I tried to sound charitable. 'What did the doctor say? Is it serious?'

'Were you sent?' He sounded disturbingly grim, miles away.

'No,' I stammered, pinched by the shady accusation. 'I'm here of my own accord.' When he made no reply I gathered my thoughts and carried on. 'The substitute is Berwyn Howell. He's okay.'

'Hmm.'

Another grunt. My words were bouncing off his eardrums like tennis balls.

'Howell doesn't seem nosy. He won't be a risk.'

'Hmm.'

This was not going far. In this bright ward with scrubs, grapes, chocolates and people, mentioning thugs and monsters seemed outrageous. I could stick with chatting about his health and Howell and wrap up this conversation in five minutes before he noticed I had no shitty grapes.

'Don't you want to hear about the church?' I asked. 'Any updates?'

'You've come here with something to tell me,' he said, darkening enough to unsettle me.

No chickening out now. 'Not very much,' I said. 'I had some trouble yesterday.'

'From what?'

'Your friends. They –'

'*Friends?*' An ugly grimace distorted his features, turning my stomach. Whomever we associated with, I wanted no part of his haunted brain, and to be in its firing line smacked of unclean vapours. I hated sitting this close to him.

'Your friends from the street,' I said.

The pique in his eye worsened. 'As opposed to yours?'

Wary of time and place, I leaned in and whispered, 'The

dealers, Minister. The gang.'

He held my gaze, leafing through the magazine, mocking me. I wished I hadn't come, but if he insisted on behaving this way I may as well get it over with – if I didn't tear up his sodding magazine first.

I reiterated the ordeal from the previous day, of Egg Face and their threat to raid his house.

Falkirk redirected his trance to the ceiling. 'What's it to you?'

The skin tightened around my bones.

'To me? To me it's being threatened by a band of thugs, is what. It's being target practice for glass bottles. It's not knowing where's safe to sleep.'

Whatever was on that ceiling, it fascinated Falkirk, he was lost in it.

'Did you hear me?' I pressed. 'I don't need more reasons to fear for my safety.'

Falkirk burst out laughing, shut his eyes and fucking laughed. Fair dos, actually. Safety? Really, Rona, how jejune can you get? He lay there with his foul laugh drooling gunk down the creases of his mouth. I let him chuckle it off.

'He – and I don't mean Howell – gave me your house keys.' I threw this in with virulent timing.

Falkirk snapped out of his trance. 'Why?'

'Inconspicuousness,' I shrugged. 'Can't have Howell learning where I sleep. Plus if one thug already sneaked in, so can others.'

Falkirk wrinkled his nose. 'How obliging of him. I hope you said thank you. It's your job to chase out thugs and eat glass bottles. Do you think *They'll* put up with that incompetence much longer?'

'Please.' I couldn't look at him, he made me sick. 'Please don't talk to me like that.'

He swivelled to his beloved ceiling. 'You foolish girl.'

Foolish? Foolish!

'Falkirk,' I rasped, restraining a shout, 'I've only done everything I was told, by you as well as them.'

He held his inertia.

'Well, I don't suppose it matters in any case,' I said, reclining, testing him. 'He said to let them in next time.'

'He's playing with you.'

'What?'

'He said no more people in.'

'I know, Falkirk, I saw his message to you, but that's old news.'

'No! He told me.'

'How d'you mean? When? I don't get it.'

'No, you wouldn't! He took away my key for the cupboard.'

What? *Final warning*, according to Serge, then Serge changes his mind ... and now ...? Dammit, Falkirk, what are you saying?

We were interrupted. 'Hellooo there!'

In pedalled a rosy nurse, wheeling a tray with a square monitor and a long thick cuff of black padding. I recognised it at once. They're horrible things.

'Am just gonna take your blood pressure, okay?' The nurse was Scottish, a bumpy, cheery female. 'Weather's getting gloomy now, isn't it!' she chirruped. Having no appetite for small talk, a puny smile was the best I managed.

A beep sounded and I watched the cuff tighten around his bicep. Memory pulsated through my body: only one other person in the world knew of my suicide attempt; three nights on a saline drip in a hospital bed, hooked up with tubes on either side like Frankenstein's bride, blood tests until my veins collapsed and urine samples in patient toilets without locks. And those damn blood pressure readings, the bands of that torture device tightening until I thought my fingertips would split open and spurt, lying there convinced the machine had malfunctioned or that they had forgotten about me and it would go on and on tightening until I screamed.

'All done, cheers!' the nurse sang, bundling up the cuff and wheeling away.

The sound of chatty families and friends flitted around us while Falkirk deliberately ignored me. I would not visit him again, but I refused to wimp out.

'He told me you were here,' I said. 'How did he know?'

'Don't interfere.'

'Interfere? Whose idea was all this? Remind me.'

'Don't let them get inside your head,' he said. 'We must all answer to God, damned or not.'

I sat gobsmacked for a minute while Falkirk floated in his oasis. So unfair to be roped into this by a man who takes no responsibility when imps like Daniels start fires and dump syringes where the wild things are! Plus I resented the insinuation that this coerced collusion ranked me with the damned. I resented that. Strongly.

'I don't think I'm damned, Falkirk.'

'Isaiah,' he droned, preaching. ' "We are all infected and impure with sin. When we display our righteous deeds, they are nothing but filthy rags." '

Speak for your 'damned' self, I mouthed noiselessly. There was not much else to say, except maybe a minor bit of news.

'Do you know when they're discharging you?'

'Few days,' he drivelled. 'Then a spa.'

Spas now! Yes, stay tucked away, Falks, as if they can't find you there. This evil thought caught me off guard.

'Okay. Er, when you get out, just so you know, I'll be –' I hesitated. Some nameless hunch warned me against telling him. I dismissed it. 'I'll be in between the vaults and church by day.'

Wow! I suddenly had his undivided attention.

'The vaults?' he said.

'Yes. They took me there last night.'

'What for?'

'The fire caused a lot of damage. They want to clear the rubbish, simple as.'

'What rubbish?'

'Why, the fire.'

'What about it?' he snapped.

'I'm telling you,' I emphasised, bamboozled, 'it caused damage. They have so many things down there, if you'd seen it …'

His revulsion made a dramatic comeback. 'You didn't earn that! No one's allowed in there! What do they want *you* for?'

'You're not listening to me! I'm explaining. They have incredible things, burned, for clearing, that's all! What's wrong?'

Good grief. Falkirk was trembling convulsively.

'Not even Ian was allowed down there,' he said to himself.

'I have his keys,' I said. 'I don't know why you're surprised. Isn't that what you put me there for?' The rash pride in my tone startled me; I conquered my reluctance to touch his arm. 'It's okay. I think I'm okay. I'm dealing my cards right.'

'What right have you to think that?' he hissed.

'All I'm saying is they could treat me worse. Yesterday Serge –'

'*Hggghhh.*'

'Yesterday *he* talked to me. I think it helped. Please don't look at me like that!'

Falkirk was eyeballing me as if interrogating a criminal. 'What are you saying, girl?'

This made no sense. He was asking me different versions of the same question over and over again and his vicious glare did not help.

'All I'm saying,' I attempted, 'is I haven't been treated any worse than can be expected.'

Falkirk was really shaking now, sitting up, eyes wide and

rabid. I couldn't twig what on earth had triggered him so; I had but two images to count on: thugs throwing bottles and Serge resting his elbows over a pew, talking about stained glass windows.

'I know it's crazy,' I said. 'It confuses me, too, but if they put me in a position of trust, the – Falkirk! Wha–?'

He had grabbed me.

At my use of the word 'trust', Falkirk popped like a champagne bottle. His knuckles clamped painfully over my bones, tormenting every nerve in my forearm as he used all his strength to pull himself up from the bed. I was so startled I could only gape; he looked desperate, so desperate! A sweat broke out over his brow, his face and bulging eyes full of deranged terror. In this momentary switch he had gone mad, I was honestly scared. Pulling me closer, spittle shot through coarse morning breath as his lips curled over two rows of gnashing teeth in a deep guttural growl.

'You … have … no … *IDEEEA* … how *brutal* he is!'

I tried wrestling him off but he held fast to my jumper, jerking me sharply. 'Stop it, Falkirk!'

A visiting family had fallen silent, semi-masticated grapes and chocolates in their mouths. We had an audience.

'No idea!' he yelped. 'None! None!'

He released me and crashed onto the bed, dripping delirium, laughing and snarling. 'Look at you! Didn't even bring me something from Menzies' crypt, nothing to keep me going, you, you stupid, stupid whore!'

He coiled up, raised a sweaty fist and punched his forehead several times. I stood speechless, holding my injured arm, unsure what the hell to do while Falkirk writhed before me, burning in his own fire. He is guilty, I thought. He may be damned, but he is also an addict, an addict in the talons of serious withdrawal.

The now not-so-cheery nurses took over, their practised

simpers more or less telling me to clear off before my unsavoury presence locked down the entire ward as a quarantine zone. I required no assistance, I wanted to run. I didn't bother saying goodbye.

I left the hospital feeling both angry and at fault. Having no talent for confrontations, by self-deprecating default I always worried, rightly or not, that I was accountable. And yes I lit another cigarette.

Chapter Ten

On the bus home from St Catherine's Hospital.

Home. Not much else to call it. Falkirk's stuffy villa was certainly no home. Its lungs infected yours with fuggy old carpets and damp. The cave-like interior shrank stubbornly from daylight under stunted ceilings, jammed windows and custard curtains from the 1970s. From the outside, the villa might have been beautiful with all the charming aspects of a late Edwardian dwelling. Inside it carried his muggy scent, plant pots with dead plants, yellowed wallpaper, basted kitchen towels and foamy toilet plugs blocked with his pubic hair. It would be pointless to tidy. Who knew what I might find if I lifted a rug? No, it was not Home, haunted by his own discontented heart.

Falkirk's methods of persuasion did anything but convince me. 'Brutal'? Well, Minister, if they punish thugs who burn them and their treasures to cinders, *you* would think that. You know they have you by the balls, Falky, so let your King James Bible paint all incarnations of Hell you like, but not on me!

I put his tantrum down to withdrawal paranoia and thought no more of it. I would gladly have kept Howell instead, an unrealistic option.

I lifted my sleeve. Yep, nice juicy plum bruises on the rise where he had tried pulling my arm off, spitting desperation and

damning me for not bringing his grapes, aka narcotics. Bring il-
legal drugs into a hospital? *Search for brutal in a mirror, Falks,
and pick on someone your own size!* His mania loomed more
tangibly in my shaken-up mind than Daniels' chomped body;
home was the church, home was the gallery, that's all I knew.

I pressed the bell for my stop.

I fleetingly mentioned the hospital visit to chatty Minister
Howell; cue his wholehearted prayers for a quick recovery and
would I please pass on my best wishes! Unable to picture the
two men in the same room, I went about my duties, polishing
and brewing coffees. The day was over too soon, and by early
evening I ran out of things to do – above ground, that is.

The vaults. I had extra duties now, and whenever I wanted,
too, according to Serge with his omnipotent grin, challenging
my nerve to go there alone. *'Will you walk into my parlour?'
said the spider to the fly.* The sun sank low behind Clayburn
Avenue before the church closed. I procrastinated as long as
possible, waiting for Howell to go home, and besides, you can't
go diving through wardrobes in plain sight like *The Chronicles
of Narnia.*

Meanwhile another problem developed. My unpaid payday
was yesterday; I now had thirty-four pence to my name and
harboured no desire to revisit St Catherine's on the subject. I
was broke and unfed, and the vestry's stale biscuits made for a
poor dinner. Falkirk's decomposing fridge contents would have
killed me. *What now? Do I borrow from my benefactors or
starve?*

The onset of short winter days always sneaks up on you.
In my fruitless search for food in Falkirk's kitchen, I missed
Howell locking up the church and driving away.

I was at the sink, scraping jellied grease from a pan.
The library, Rona.

Tick-tock, washing dishes, drying dishes, running out

of excuses, running out of reasons …

You have their permission.

Not yet, not yet, pots, library later. (Alone.) Yes, yes, that's a good plan, wash up, then go.

Procrastination, cowardliness. I was proving my sagacious boss right.

Rona, you're out of pots to wash.

Not yet. Not yet!

I moved to scrub the counter by the kitchen window, a window with curtains I had forgotten to draw.

It glared through the glass at me.

Large and rectangular, taped to the window on the outside, its frail edges fluttering. Not a note. The print was an ink drawing, aged and faded on sooty paper.

Dominating the image, a fat band of two parallel lines ran through what resembled an ant farm, illustrated with the finest nib. Top right of the image, faint quill strokes named both town and county, quaintly ending in '*shyre*'. A cross indicated north.

Unfastening the window, I delicately peeled off the page and examined it. How intricate. The ant farm was, in fact, a cluster of squares within squares making up a hundred teensy houses and rooftops in scattered rows, enclosed by a town wall from which scrawny roads branched out like tree roots. On closer inspection I found a market square, a twin-turreted building suggesting an armed gatehouse and further roads cutting through surrounding farmland. Though oversized, the domineering thick band was self-explanatory – Bronmeg River, dashed by bridges and tributaries lined with endearingly dainty tree symbols. Its style suggested Middle Ages, otherwise I recognised nothing from the present day. No street alignments matched and even the bridges were alien.

The map's alluring detail held me like a magnet as I examined it again and again. Unfortunately, it had been very recently vandalised with large slanting quill strokes, scribbled on by far the most lonesome spot:

Here, a solitary spire in a field where Clayburn Avenue had centuries to be born. The sender needed no introduction. They were awake.

Répondez s'il vous plaît? Fly to spider.

Trapdoor not so heavy, eh? My, they will have their fun. Serge made a chump out of me; I heaved and pulled, metal groaning in my fists, using my weight to hold up the corners or it would fall and clamour. After several pauses and yanks, the iron square resentfully balanced, too far to crash. The black mouth lay open.

The torch felt slippery, sliding in my palm as I held it too firmly, four knuckles peaked like the Swiss Alps.

Inside, the ceiling felt lower still. With no Edith to rush me, I took in the surroundings. Here's the T-junction, there's the bolted door and modern padlock, the archway to the Great Hall, and that other passage, the endless eastward tunnel where my torch refused to reach the end.

I heard something.

It was distant, a very faint muffled rumble, starting and stopping. I walked in its direction, a few steps east.

… Vrrrm-rumble …

A mischievous sense of liberty briefly overtook my fear, filling me with a reckless hunger to explore. The vaults were open to me without threatening to chew me up and spray me out; the torch batteries were recharged, its beam wide and obliging. *I think I know what that noise is.*

What, traffic? I may be in a catacomb but I know my own

century, thank you very much, and that, *is traffic!* If my coordinates were roughly correct, the distant roar was coming from Delfour Road. It had to be! The irony of being within hearing distance of internal combustion engines was hard to swallow in this parallel universe. I stifled a careless laugh, swiftly covering my mouth. *Shhhht!*

I realised what I'd done. Edith had told me, 'When you want, where we want,' and this disobedient watchdog had just wandered off-limits by over twenty feet.

Too far!

I caught my breath as icy goose pimples spread across my arms. Controlling an urge to race, I returned to the T-junction as quickly as I could, the library eclipsing in my light as I ducked to enter. Serge's grey-blue retinas flashed up from where he perched on the floor.

He sat there quite leisurely, on a stack of books amidst paper towers, face down in an open volume on his knees.

'Isn't it amazing,' he said, leafing through, 'the forgotten things you find when clearing out?'

Haphazardly recovering from my fright, I stepped through the mess. 'Thank you for the map. Would you like it back?'

'Hmm? No, no. What did you think? 1147 A.D. Most of the bridges are gone now and the river was wider. Did you see the well?'

'No.'

'You will,' he said, reading.

I assessed the paper tumult. 'Should I start at the edges and work my way in?'

'Speaking of which,' he said, setting the book down, 'pass me those scrolls over there, the smaller ones.'

He pointed to a corner with over forty parchments loose and bound, squashed together, some untouched by the fire and some toasted. The nearest literally fell apart in my hands.

'Shit, sorry.'

Serge held out his arm expectantly. 'Just bring them all.'

I searched him for any tell-tale signs of the brutality Falkirk seemed so sure of. Useless. In this library exploration, his attitude seemed demonstrably civil tonight, enthusiastic even. I had shared secrets with Serge; our previous talk in the nave stroked my core with a clement feather, I was starting to let go.

Stooping, I gathered as many as I could carry, scrolls within scrolls, huge and tiny, many loosely rolled in pairs and falling out of each other as I wobbled. Serge stood and relieved me of a dozen. At his side was a stack of seven massive books, he added more to the makeshift stool and patted the top, inviting me to sit. Taking the rest from me, he ignored several scrolls and perused others, unrolling them, examining them from all angles, cocking his head, disregarding one after another. Maps and charts, every single one. I wanted a closer look, wishing he would explain them to me, especially one enormous map he unrolled to about four feet, riddled with annotations and labels in Old English around an island so clumsily delineated it resembled the cross-section of a brain. I nabbed Serge before he discarded it.

'Where's that?' I asked.

'Don't you know home sweet home when you see it?' he said. 'The unshakable wisdom of 1335.'

'Britain?' I exclaimed, reaching for it. Rivers of obscene width cut through pale green land, dividing it into blotchy chunks and fat curves. 'London is halfway to Bristol,' I said, indicating the cartographer's hilarious geography, 'and Canterbury is where Brighton should be.'

'The idea,' said Serge, preoccupied in his search, 'was to define lands by river routes, that's why they're painted so thickly. − Ah!'

Finding the needle in the haystack, he held out a smaller map for me.

'Look, Rona, here we are by the sixteen-fifties. See, Bronmeg's town wall is almost gone. When Cromwell's Ironsides were raiding and arresting priests, the church above wasn't rebuilt yet.' He tapped a spot on the paper. 'There is no hint of St Patrick's here.'

Bronmeg's streets had multiplied, spilling over the original boundary; our specific location revealed nothing but a broader road, some farms and a tree. The yew.

'And the original spire on the twelfth-century map?' I asked. 'The one stuck to the window?'

Serge eyed me, the corner of his mouth curling into a sly gloat. 'You're in its bowels.'

Serge and the others left me for some time, with basic instructions to round up the library's survivors and ditch anything unsalvageable, a batch of modern refuse bags at the ready.

The library collection was as fathomless as Mary Poppins' handbag, making it pernickety work separating charred shreds and blackened bindings from the 'possible' rubbish, especially things still loosely bound or containing undamaged artwork, too tricky to tell. The archivist in me couldn't bring herself to throw them *all* away; I had half a mind to keep a secret stash of unclaimed souvenirs.

The vaults were always Siberian. My teeth chattered, twice I hit my head, and acrid dust nibbled my wrists to furious itching. On an empty belly, I eventually slowed and made a spot on the floor for some rest. Good God, my watch said 2:40 a.m. I had been on my hands and knees for over six hours and barely made a dent in this conflagrated paper lagoon. In fact, the mess looked messier.

I languished in this snug city of books, an archivist's dream within a nightmare. The floor was unforgiving on my backside, but it was such a mercy to let my muscles relax. I hadn't realised how tired I was. As my neck lolled, the domed arc ceiling returned my gaze, stones dyed warm apricot in the torchlight. From somewhere through a mist I heard the grandfather clock … *Tick … Tick*

'You're on flexi-time, not night shifts. Go to bed.'

I woke from a doze to see Serge, disconcertingly tall in the stunted doorway.

'Sorry,' I said, rising. 'I didn't mean to doze off.'

'Polite apologies are boring,' he replied. 'Edit them out.'

Uh-oh, he was in a mood; unwise timing to mention my overdue wages from Falkirk. But I had to unless they wanted me to starve. What a soul-destroying moment that was, watching Serge listen with the officious scepticism I predicted, hearing me stagger my browbeaten way from start to bitter end of the degrading request.

'Why didn't you ask Falkirk?' he interrogated.

'Truly, Serge, he was in no state …'

I stopped talking – Serge had caught sight of the ripe bruises on my forearm.

Smirking to himself, he burrowed into his jacket. 'Treat this place like a hotel, don't you? How much are his bread crusts?'

'Forty pounds a week.'

If you think this a tyrannical wage, Serge's expression might have agreed with you. 'I know,' I added. 'For food and fags. My free room and board is his reasoning.'

'*Christian* reasoning,' he muttered sarcastically, counting out some paper money in his hand. 'The virtue of poverty.'

He gave me almost two hundred pounds to last until whenever Falkirk paid me, which remained to be seen and could take weeks. Do not suppose Serge had any interest in spoiling me.

Exiting the library, whether by fatigue, tiredness or both, I made the mindless blunder of giving myself away.

'I could have sworn I heard traffic,' I said, pointing east.

Serge, perceptive monster, slowly swaggered towards me. I bit my tongue too late.

'Did you now?' he smoothed, cool as a cucumber, letting

the uneasy pause swing. 'I should think you would. Drilling, too.'

'Drilling?'

'Um-hmm. Pipes. Roadworks. That sort of fun.'

'Is there any risk?'

'Of their drills staking us through the heart?'

'You know what I mean.'

'Below Delfour Road. A road is a road. There will be *road-works*.'

To my amazement he took my elbow and led me eastward, over thirty feet down the off-limits passageway. He gestured upward, gentlemanly, informative, and holding me by a very short leash.

'A dozen feet up, water supply pipes coming from that direction, right along here, following a hundred feet, dividing a dozen more times. Electric cables cut straight across. And don't forget your good friend the sewers. I ought to know those streets, madam. I designed them.'

There was something unutterably wrong and ten-dimensional about this long passage, it did not fit in with the world above or below. Its hallucinatory depth warped the east wing into a hideous surrealism, expanding, contracting and plunging. It screwed with your brain like putty, inviting you to walk on, never reaching the end of its vanishing point teetering on an event horizon.

And that was all I managed to absorb before Serge's authoritative leash reversed us. I thanked him for the money and he thanked me for my help. At ease, Rona, you needn't have feared! You appreciated his mini tour, he was accommodating instead of angry and you escaped any chastisement, let off Scot free as a bluebird, how forgiving of him, insert smiley face. I slept soundly.

Bluebird Rona. Gullible. Young. Stupid. I'm glad she's gone.

Chapter Eleven

In my life, I have not always started as I meant to go on, continued after starting or damn well started at all. Nevertheless, the library was started.

Every day after church closing time, I made my way underground and went to the library direct – no mischievous wandering, no unauthorised exploring – for weeks. Weeks, it took! A bit excessive for a mediocre-sized vault, you might think? I would say don't get me started, alas an avalanche of pages, prints, mezzotints, handwriting and illustrations, beautiful, drab, exhilarating, funny and ugly, from Ancient Greek to the mid-1900s, sails through my mind as I write. I will never forget it, they numbered in the thousands.

After dividing, subdividing then re-subdividing, categories into subcategories, etc., etc., between so-named Worthless, Unsure and Keep piles, many items getting mixed up and confused, it soon became apparent this job was going to be far from simple. I was dealing with a multi-dimensional spectrum of damage. The easiest to bag was the burnt snow of scraps and shreds for the Worthless pile, which became a straightforward hoovering operation; next were incomplete volumes and books partially reduced to charcoal with, miraculously, sections still in pristine condition, and pages (I personally believed) worth preserving including chapters, drawings and scriptures missing their bindings, freely scattered all over the place. To add to the confusion, many rogue extracts were wedged inside surrogate volumes where they had no business being. How they got there was anybody's guess, though I gained the impression they were habitually shoved in wherever without consideration. These orphaned pieces earned a separate pile; matching them up and locating their parents could take a lifetime.

I became so tenacious in my cataloguing that a paper fort accumulated around me like a game of cowboys and Indians, including a small build-up of damaged souvenirs that, if unwanted, I may ask to keep. For a thankfully fleeting, outrageous moment I considered classifying everything librarian-style; I would not have gotten very far when so few items were in English, in fact name any other language and I'm sure it was there. I waded through Latin texts from 800 to 1400 A.D., gold-painted monastic inscriptions framed in green, and purple floral patterns enclosing hand-painted figures of huntsmen and rabbits. I sifted through monks' paintings of embossed throne rooms, figures in robes and furs, noblemen in tunics, hose and pointed shoes, medieval women in wimples at hand looms, the symbolic Wheel of Life with serfs rising in status from peasants to kings, indolent donkeys harassing a friar and bipedal boars jousting the Knights Templar. Not a single speck of these pages was untouched by exquisite embellishments; the majesty was so tireless I could exhaust my eyes to tears on their infinite Celtic fractals and still never fully complete my visual journey through the artistry.

Sound romantic enough for you? It wasn't. I learned the hard, hawking and coughing way to religiously keep a bottle of water and tissues by me, initially pulling my collar up over my nose, later never entering the library without tying a cloth around my face like a highwayman: throughout the vaults, irregular patches of yellow and turquoise fungus caked the underground mortar. Before you knew it, you were breathing it in, and in the library more than half its books were illegible with dry rot and grainy dust; your hands and wrists itched furiously with it, it was horrible. I would literally inhale this stench for hours; fluids, hankies and gloves proved essential. Essential! God help you if you were asthmatic.

The worst smell came from a Turkish book untouched by the fire. Its musty pages were in a horrendous state where purple, black and brown mould had started from the edges and worked its way in, burying the lost text, its curved corners softened to wool and its sorry leather cover about as hard as foam. This may once have been a great work, a priceless artefact of history or the lifetime achievement of some hopeful scholar, now age made it a spectacular relic to view – repulsive and unreadable to handle. In another volume to have escaped the fire, the pages were perfectly dry and pearly white, an Arabic text, neatly written in red and black ink. This I banished to the Unsure pile: the entire book was a block of Swiss cheese. Unless someone had attacked it a million times with a hole punch, the devoured carcass in my hands was hopelessly perforated with burrows, possibly bookworm or the larvae of spider beetles, a bane of archivists; the poor thing lay in tatters.

The topic of mould and bugs brings me on to the lesser-known diminutive residents of the underground.

Rodents will gnaw anything. Meaty leather book bindings? No problem. I was never a girl to be frightened by mice, and they lost their fear of me, running over my feet like greased lightning, fast devils, on their own stringent schedules like clockwork, who was I to interfere? One evening, while the Three Wise Monkeys were out, I rested the torch on a stool of books to whip out another hankie for regurgitating yet another glob of catarrh (I shouldn't complain, having been a smoker then). Suddenly the torchlight wavered, a shape crossing it. My eyes automatically shot to the doorway. Nobody there. The light wavered again.

On the wall opposite the doorway, in the torch's orange spotlight, rose the terrorising shadow puppet of a great dragon. A dragon washing behind its ears.

The mouse sat on its hind legs in the warmth of the miniature sun, cleaning itself on the book tower, a four-legged king of the castle. Though I kept still, I'd flinched enough for it to stop and contemplate me, an animal I could flatten at will, but I came here often and, seeing I was no threat, the mouse resumed his or her self-scrubbing.

'Are you getting used to me?' I asked it.

The mouse paused, sniffed, and squatted to groom its belly of chalky-brown fur.

'Bold, aren't you? You do know it's dangerous here? Falkirk sets mouse traps all over the church. He won't even let pigeons on the spire outside, he had spikes nailed into the ledges, in rows, it looks like a carnivorous stone cactus.'

I don't remember much of what else I said, except that I meditated on this fuzzy tenant for the longest time.

'I'm getting used to Them,' I said at length, whether to myself, the mouse or both, I don't know. 'That isn't right, is it? *Am* I getting used to them?'

The mouse brushed its nose, twitched its whiskers and set to work trimming its claws.

'Fuzz ball, everywhere is dangerous. Promise me you'll never get used to *me*.'

No answer from the mouse; bathing accomplished, he or she scampered off.

I generally found it impossible to work my way through the library without hungrily browsing more of its contents than was perhaps necessary, and during my third week, I made a discovery that knocked me sideways. A scroll, the oldest yet, unrolled to over five feet long, *so* painfully fragile that if I lifted it by both ends and held it taut the midsection would fall away, leaving its brittle edges between my fingers. The material was of papyrus, a grid of vertical strips and stem fibres where they were mashed and adhered together, now incomplete with holes and accretions. Papyrus very rarely endures in this country; just by unrolling it I'd inflicted fresh cracks and tears through the fading heads of eagles, jackals and several vertical rows of Egyptian hieroglyphics.

Barely able to contain myself, with nail-biting care I cleared a space, set it on the floor and squatted over it. The scene was a funerary text, a figure lying on a table carved with a lion's head and legs; over him stood the figure of Anubis, embalmer and guardian of graves.

'There should be another piece of that lying around some-where,' Edith said, announcing her presence in the doorway.

'Edith,' I said, shifting on my haunches, 'you need to store this between taped glass sheets. Now. And keep it dry as possible. I can't believe it's survived here this long.'

'Hmm, yes, that thing isn't going to last,' she said emotionlessly, kneeling beside me.

She delicately lifted an end. I immediately grimaced, naturally fearing it would crumble under anyone else's touch. With trained patience, her bony fingers hovered over and snaked down a line of hieroglyphs, reading, her long, unpinned hair falling over her shoulder. The effortless concentration in her hard face and serene eyes gave her the statuesque countenance of a Madonna, I marvelled at her in that instant.

Then, with frigid abruptness, she rose, claiming the price-less relic in her fist. 'We should throw this out. Serge wouldn't like it.'

'Throw it out?' I gaped. 'How can you? Why? It's irreplaceable!'

Edith fired me a flinty warning look, shutting me up.

'There are some things,' she said evenly, 'he would rather not be reminded of.'

Without another word, she gracelessly gathered up the papyrus and went. I sat there, gutted for the loss and for the censure, unable to ask for a story I may never learn; they have too many.

I saw little of Serge during those weeks. In fact, I saw little of any of them. I grew accustomed to going down alone, keeping a stock of batteries for the torch and replacing them probably more often than needed. Nobody objected to me smoking, though I forbade myself from smoking in the library, from which Hector periodically lumbered, in and out, removing my bags of paper rubbish without comment. None of them asked any questions, which often left me uneasy in case I had unwittingly made a serious mistake or thrown out something I shouldn't have; it caused the Unsure pile to grow until it became ridiculous and ruthlessness set in.

I still house a few souvenirs from that library, including the crumpled heap of magazines I found bulging from a cabinet drawer. This cost me two hours' truancy, sitting on a makeshift bench of hardbacks, poring over an authentic series of Penny Dreadfuls, ten pages per edition of Spring-Heeled Jack, Wagner the *Wehr*-Wolf, Sweeney Todd and the over-romanticised Dick Turpin. Sold, I lost all track of time, unwillingly drawn in, repulsed yet unable to ignore the crude Victorian drawings of villains' faces twisted into vulgar screams of rage, eyes bulging, on tatty paper in a bad state of decay. So much in this library cried out for professional conservation.

It was on this perch that Serge and Hector happened to find me. I sprang to attention, caught in the act.

Serge sighed. 'Take them if you want,' he said dismissively. 'Is that refuse bag ready to go?'

'Yes.'

'Show her, Heck.'

Hector strode in and ducked for the bag like a colossal hunchback, dwarfing the library to a doll's house and gesturing in a deep voice straight out of Jack and the Beanstalk, 'This way.'

Serge didn't come with us.

I followed Hector into the Great Hall. Burned and unburned tables, clocks, cabinets, chairs and sofas swept by as we cut straight through them, past the central table and grand chairs, under an archway and into a tiny vault at the far-left end. This area was new to me and I spun in disorientation before Hector came into focus, facing a wall, or what should have been a wall.

'This is where you'll dispose of the losses,' he said.

A large section of masonry had either collapsed or been knocked down long ago. At my feet lay a heap of chunky bricks; in the wall itself, a massive gash gaped from the ceiling to my calves, large enough the fit the two of us, as if some mighty monster had squeezed its head through and chomped a gnashing bite. Jagged masonry lining the cavity made it savage, too easy to imagine that if I bent over the edge, the bricks would crash shut like huge molars and chop me in two. Within the gash, my torch shone off the interior of an enormous vertical stone cylinder, its geometric precision an eerily charming contrast next to the ragged hole. I heard a dripping.

Hector then said what I knew he would.

'This is the water well.'

I stepped up for a better view, balancing my grip on the edges, my foot on a fallen brick of debatable stability. Twisting my waist to a funny angle, I directed my torch upward to see a choked throat, nothing above but a blockage of slimy bricks, caved in long ago. The truth is I was afraid to look down: because I smelt it. Worse than the laundry shirt of gristle. Worse than Daniels' cooked meat. If I inhaled I knew I would vomit.

Hector's robotic voice hummed on.

'Dug for the monks in 1130,' he said. His breath smelled of rank haemoglobin, its metallic flavour mingling with the sickly-sweet stomach acid rising to my mouth. 'You're roughly a hundred feet from the bottom. Above are yards and yards of rubble, pipes, buildings. This is where we intercepted it, about halfway down. It's useful.'

With that declaration, he hurled the refuse bag into the chasm. A second passed.

Pffud

I looked in.

A hundred feet? The bottom seemed a lot closer, filled with rubbish, not water. The torch beam was wide but not bright enough to interpret a great deal. Well, to be fair, Rona, there lie your bin liners. Bits of scrap wood. A couple of books. A shoe. Oh God –

I bounced out of the gash, pricked by reality. *The smell. A shoe ...* I didn't want Hector to see my colour draining, but it took some heavy-duty self-restraint to hide my nausea without running. This smothering box vault, the smell and that noxious drip-drip-dripping fooled me into thinking the walls were moving in like tar bogs.

'So now you know where to find it,' Hector said, showing me out. 'Have you seen the other rooms yet?' Unusually chatty, for him.

'No,' I replied.

A minute longer and what else would I have seen in that well? They expected me to go there regularly, dispose of the 'losses', just another part of my job. Don't think about it, Rona, do – not – think! Desperate for distraction, I focussed on the nearest thing to me, the first thing I saw, the Byzantine throne, trying to picture Edith in it, then Serge, then Hector. Who sits there? ('Remains thought to' ... Don't think.) Come on, Rona, guess; whom might (A shoe, missing students, photos in the newspaper) this chair fit? (A trainer, that shoe was a man's trainer – Stop it! Stop thinking, Rona!) Whose throne?

My watch said eleven o'clock. I wanted my bed, my stomach was curling inwards and I needed fresh air, but for appearance's sake I normally never finished my night shifts until they went out, and when Hector vanished through the trapdoor I reckoned he was the last to leave. *Go, hurry, leave me so I can smash my head off the walls. Why the hell did I open that fucking newspaper?* On my way out, I dashed into the library to fetch my bottled water.

Serge was standing alone by a book cabinet, absorbed in a small hardback. He acknowledged me without moving, reading aloud.

' "I am the self-consumer of my woes. They rise and vanish in oblivious host ... Untroubling and untroubled where I lie, The grass below, above the vaulted sky." Heard of the poet John Clare?'

'He wrote that in the 1840s,' I answered. 'In Northampton Asylum.'

Serge closed the book with a cosy, agreeable thump.

'What's wrong?' he asked without needing to look at me, casually replacing the volume.

'What do you mean?'

'What did I say about lying to me, Rona?'

The blood rushed to my face. You'll lose, Rona. Save it, he probably knows the answer already.

'The well spooked me.'

'And the army of skeletons inside, I suppose?' he said, smiling subtly.

'I saw nothing like that.'

'Rona's Universe certainly did, bless your mortal heart and come with me.' He walked past, nudging my elbow. 'C'mon!'

Here we are in the Hall again, Serge striding in front of me like a general.

'Three hundred and nineteen feet down, eight-and-a-half feet wide, almost a millennium old and she's scared of it!'

'I'd politely apologise if you hadn't told me not to.'

'Ha! A snippet of the real Rona. We like it when you do

that.'

Mid-trot, I was again distracted by their three chairs, neglecting my footing and smacking directly into Serge. I nearly fell over. He touched the gilded ivory chair.

'Egyptian. Edith's. A bit extravagant for her. She never even met a Nubian. But,' he shrugged, 'finders keepers.'

Finders keepers? An appallingly clichéd scenario popped into my fancy. I saw Edith spectacularly devastating the sacred entrance of some Pharaoh's priceless tomb, luxuriating like Cleopatra in its riches and keeping them for herself. I could see it, oh yes, I could quite easily visualise her!

Serge marched me towards an arcade. 'How much have I told you of the vaults so far?' he demanded. 'Humour me.'

'Erm, the original monastery, eleven-hundreds, under Delfour Road and Rennet Close, um …'

'And what do churches keep in their vaults? Turn off your torch.'

'But, how can I?'

I hoped against hope he was joking. It was unimaginable. Not here. You're kidding, not here!

'Like *this*,' he said.

Before I knew what was happening he snatched my sole source of light. Click.

Blackout.

My brain signalled instant visual memory of Serge's face floating in mid-air, spectral as a photo negative, his hair and retinas glowing silver – fading.

Now I was completely blind. I fumbled at the air, petrified of hitting obstacles, gasping as Serge's palm closed around my wrist. His touch was like rind, my pulse drummed against it, both of us knowing one squeeze, a single squeeze, and he could pinch my hand off. He led me faster than I preferred, a low obstruction hitting my toe, a stone step perhaps, then the texture of the ground was changing, getting coarser, walking,

walking ... Don't trip!

His voice came, too near and too far at once.

'I don't like repeating myself. What – do – crypts of the latest celebrity god – keep?'

'Bodies,' I blurted.

'My. How dramatic.' He dropped my wrist, leaving me there.

Shit, where is he? My breathing sounded unusually loud in wherever he had taken us, somewhere with a low ceiling and stale air richer in stone powder than oxygen. My feet shuffled on some potholed surface and a piece of straw crunched under my heel. How many seconds passed? Seven? Ten?

What do churches keep?

'Graves,' I said, in a voice I didn't know.

'*BOO!*' – A torchlit human skull shouted in my face.

I yelped, stumbling backwards. 'Serge, dammit!'

Serge appeared behind the skull he was holding. However ancient, however wise, I swear Serge's smile, his real smile, belongs to a small boy. 'Haha! Here,' he said, tossing the skull at me. 'Educate yourself!'

The fleshless head grinned up in my hands, its smile widening, teeth parting as a hairy spider scuttered from its mouth –. On impulse I hurled it past Serge. *Smash! Clatter!* It landed in a hidden cranny somewhere behind him.

'Stupid Rona!' I growled. 'Just a spider.'

Serge's countenance glazed over to verglas. I always hated it when he switched like that; how do you deal a card against quicksilver? He took a step closer, offering my torch, dead-faced. 'Why don't you go find him and apologise, then?'

The beam glared in my face, diminishing his outline to greyness. I took it. The pitted floor was a lonely lunar landscape, unaccustomed to receiving company, our shoes leaving incongruous prints in the chalky regolith like astronauts. Pointing my torch, the chamber passively relented to exposure.

On opposing sides were four rows of three rectangular niches dug lengthwise like shelves, floor to ceiling.

'Meet the resident monks,' said Serge.

Each niche contained a skeleton. The interments fitted snugly, naked with mossy fungus growing out of their cranium sutures. Others were incomplete, missing a femur, humerus or most of their rib cages. Inches from me, a monk's toothless jaw, gawping, or was he laughing at me? More worryingly, I made out a distorted heap in the far corner, hip deep: hundreds of hollow orbits ogled sideways, at each other, at the niches, at Serge and me, at the ceiling, thousands of teeth beared, calling, singing and laughing at nothing in particular, all human, and nobody to hear them.

I gawked blankly, unsure what I should be feeling. There were so many, too many.

'Why did you bring me in here?' I asked.

'Bones, Rona.' His voice was sombre, almost tender. 'Just bones. It's all just bones down here.'

Numbed by the old well and jaded by his tricks, I hesitated on the way out. 'Serge. Do you like it here?'

This question caught him out somehow, he did not answer straight away.

'The price of any world being yours,' he said after some thought, 'is there's nothing left to gain. This place is part of me. Not purely me. It is full of me. That doesn't mean *all* of me.' Without any notable change in his expression, Serge could morph from winter, to summer, to adamantine. 'Remember about Derek tomorrow,' he then added, switching again!

'Any word from Falkirk?' Serge enquired, holding the trapdoor for me.

'Still sulking in his spa in Warwick,' I replied, climbing through. 'Probably sleeping through AA meetings. I don't care. He freaked me out, Serge.'

He shut the trapdoor and presented the way out.

'After you. Go on, big girl, it won't be the first time I've followed you in the dark.'

Serge and his games. Mindful of being trusted ('trust', Falkirk's nemesis word), I accepted the challenge, walking the same route where they must have dragged Daniels to his death. *Did they flay his skull before or after his heart stopped beating? Am I afraid?* I felt Serge's shape behind me, his broad chest, his frame, his leather soles gaining the space between us. *He's enjoying this.* An unexpected flutter circulated me, a tingling. It wasn't fear. Hours later in the gallery I was to wake up with my hand between my legs, and I would not have him know this, not under any circumstances!

I had never left the church with Serge before. Outside of the aisle door you stepped onto a grassy nook, confronted with the high façade a few feet away which ran the length of the church's south wall, curving around the chancel to a dead end, hence I always turned right, walking to the pavement and then right again, past the front entrance and graveyard to reach Falkirk's villa on the north side. Serge did not do this. His mood switching to distant mode, without requesting a taxi or any chores from me, he murmured goodnight and walked off in the wrong direction: left.

That façade was unassailable without a pole vault or a ladder, certainly high enough to shelter the grassy nook from streetlights. Away into this he dissolved, I lost all sight and sound of him. A tremor in my nerves warned that I was prying, poking my nose in where it had no place. *Go away, Rona, move on; you're spying, mind your own beeswax.* But that tasty seed of covetous curiosity had taken root, and lately it was germinating; every night its scent grew stronger and my fear weaker. Where the hell did he go?

I heard a rustle. Grass. It got faster. Faster, faster-faster-faster –!

Running. He was running on the grass.

I couldn't see a blasted thing, entirely reliant on my ears while the wind distracted me, branches shedding crispy leaves in micro-storms around my ankles.

He ran, fast as a rabbit.

What happened next proved only too well how little I really knew of the beings I worked for. Even after this many weeks I was none the wiser as to immortality, fangs, superpowers or which of your favourite monster myths were true or false, I promise. Your mind sees what it wants to.

But I *had* seen things, not illusions! Why shouldn't I fully believe what I saw now?

In a fraction of a second, the moving sliver gained momentum, jumped and disappeared over the twenty-foot façade of solid brick. Up and over. I rewound this snapshot too many times, overanalysing until it became a useless merry-go-round in my head, muddying the recollection. It was gone. He was gone.

'Serge …'

The wind blew papery leaves in my hair, they whispered with me.

Chapter Twelve

Derek rained a neat puddle into the nave, shaking his umbrella.

'Oh, the showers, yes, getting wintry now. Heh!'

His arthritic hips and spine held him in a rigid hunch which must have been painful. It was a miserable day. An overcast sky undermined the stained glass and dimmed the unheated building, creating a dismal atmosphere for both of us.

Derek was an hour early. I hadn't seen him come in; he could have been waiting there up to thirty minutes while I mopped between the pews. I identified him from eight rows away by his halo of vulnerability, sitting patiently in his raincoat, staring at the chancel, through it, past it.

Howell ate his sandwiches in the vestry and the church was deserted for now; getting in and out of the cupboard should be safe. I called out to the war criminal sitting second row from the altar. My heart fell at the slowness with which he turned around. He was a tough fugitive, but I saw precious little happiness in him, nor, if I'm honest, much remembrance of any.

Derek was not very talkative today. I offered him the torch when we passed the iron gate, but he refused.

'Sure you're okay on the steps, Derek? They're so narrow.'

I caught myself talking in whispers. At this stage (though I had my suspicions), precisely where the underground residents slept was an open-ended question, a forbidden question.

Whereas Derek answered, loud as you like, 'Oh, yes, dear, don't fuss. I, heh, I've had worse!'

He shuffled very slowly, descending sideways like me. Edith, Serge and Hector could hop up and down here like crickets. I generally maligned this stair, its treacherous condition, the steep drop should I fall, the duration. I counted them once. Eighty-seven. With Derek in tow this could take an age.

I scoured for more small talk.

'How are you feeling these days?'

'Oh, I, er, I'm not very well,' he stuttered. 'I have a spot of influenza, and I-I get very tired, dear, you know.'

Influenza? And he came out in this weather? The flu, at his age! I wanted to speak with Serge, beg him to spare the man.

The record player and gas lamps awaited us, along with the surgeon's case virtually commanding the room.

'Derek,' I said, lighting the lamps to bring some futile cheer to the place, 'does your doctor know? Your blood condition?'

Derek unscrewed a flask smelling of delicious hot chocolate and opened a packet of custard creams. Good man.

'Oh, no!' he exclaimed. 'No doctors, dear. We can't have that! Have some hot chocolate while you work?'

I fiddled about to get the record player going. 'No, Derek, you drink it. No rush. Have your biscuits. I wish you weren't outdoors with the flu; don't turn me into a mother hen.' I felt so patronising. 'Any requests? There's, um, Cab Calloway, your Duke Ellington, Earl Hines, Harry James …'

'Harry, dear.'

I set on the record, sat and wiped his weary battered vein, thinking myself a heartless bitch.

'It's getting too hard for you to come here, Derek.'

'I must, dear.'

'Was it Serge who ordered you to keep your condition a

secret?'

'You know he did, dear.'

Ouch! A pang of ridicule in his tone there?

Derek's eyes were closing. He wanted sleep, and still his fist faithfully opened and closed to keep up the blood flow, loyally feeding the leeches that had chased him all over Europe.

Then he spoke, not a stutter within earshot, smooth as a young man.

'Forging names and composting bodies is a lot trickier these days, don't you find?'

My recoil was the exact response he wanted to that question within a question. He nodded chillingly.

Women, too. He's killed women, too.

For a second my sympathy for him evaporated. What a sheep I was, to think Derek incapable of planting a seed of fear. You should have seen the twinkle in his cunning eyes.

'I suppose you want to know about me,' he said. 'Well? Why the butterflies, dear? I wasn't a double agent for nothing. Leaders hop landmines with spies for shoes. Benevolent leaders fail because they don't backstab. Evil leaders do, that's why they win. But hot-headed stars burn out too soon. The leaders who endure – they know to tread somewhere in between. Sound familiar?'

'Us?'

'Serge. Pick a side if you must, but never forget whose side you were on first: yours. Our world is saturated in corruption, whereas their world, I …' Derek weakened, paling. 'I think I'll settle for the boring, corrupt human world, dear. If you please, I hope that summarises. I'm too old for the past. Too bad I still have the marbles.' He tapped his patchy scalp.

I straightened the plastic tubing; the infuriating thing coiled if left loose. His blood snaked through, stalling, leaving clear gaps then resuming, racing from him with fresh lustre in a crimson worm. My stomach knotted to think of the red liquorice shoelaces we used to eat in the school playground.

He dozed afterwards, the infection heavy on his lungs, I heard them whistling each time his diaphragm contracted. I sat at the table, contemplating him. Double agent, war criminal, spies, the undead, a piece of work you are, sir. What about children, have you killed children, too? Maybe.

Derek out of action, I was unable to tear my gaze from the vault entrance. With no other way out, the room was open and naked. My imagination couldn't help filling its vacant doorway with inhuman forms come to visit us, their faces bloated with rage like the Penny Dreadfuls, froth drooling to their waistcoats, piercing me with their beady pupils.

When I'm with those three I forget the nightmares. When I'm not?

The most vivid of recent dreams had me wandering my aunts' old house, perilously feeling for light switches in bare hallways, lace curtains blowing from open windows and no front doors to escape through. I have no control there. There is a creaking, a dragging, a stifled laugh, a door closing somewhere. Sooner or later I enter a room and two animal retinas without a body are hovering, mid-air, waiting for me, and when I run I know they're chasing me, two lasers burning into my scalp, gaining. People say you can't see colours in dreams, I beg to differ, because those retinas were not blue-grey, hazel or brown like my overlords'. They were green.

The record spun to its end. I changed it to Cab Calloway and mulled over my patient, their donor. He is bonier. He is kind. He's a killer. He is dying. Oh, Derek. I let him sleep on.

An hour passed. Howell would surely notice my absence soon.

'Sorry, Derek.' I shook him gently.

Derek nagged me for letting him sleep. He even tried to give me the rest of his custard creams.

I cared not a fig if my constant locking and re-locking of the gate seemed pedantic, it was an occupational requirement, though I did secretly ask myself what I was more concerned about, being their good girl or, was it possible, remotely possible, I felt protective? While Derek waited, I locked it on autopilot: metal latch down, key in, twist it, and (a trick to this) jiggle the key as if jammed, then twist in reverse. Serge's contraption, of which he had many, apparently.

'Don't come here again until you're healed, Derek,' I said, not that I wagered money on his longevity, not a pound coin. Nor was Derek listening, anyway, fixed on the locked cupboard door.

I suppose I knew what was wrong instantly. There was no need to ask, but oh God I didn't want to know! He could only be pointing like that for one reason.

'I think you have a guest, dear.'

I heard their voices too. Shit. Shit, shit, shit! The door rattled – a pause – then *furiously!* Through wood snarled the familiar voice of an angry man losing control, overlapping with a girl's voice further away.

Wet panic fizzled in my abdomen. Their shouting would draw Howell, and Howell possessed no key. He would call the police! Scenarios like this demanded quick thinking. Derek and I couldn't hide in here all damn day.

The door rattled again. Then, *bam!* That pig was trying to bust in. Not that he ever could; Serge's mechanical prowess went beyond trick locks.

'How concerned should I be, dear?' Derek asked.

If it happens again just let them in. Serge's advice.

Falkirk's advice? *He's playing with you.*

Bam! The cupboard shook.

Derek nodded. 'I've seen this problem plenty a time. The longer you wait, dear, the direr.'

I clasped the key in my fist like a gun. 'Stay by me, Derek.

190

It's okay.'

I braced myself, used the key, fast, and thrust the door open with more strength than I knew I had.

You cannot blame me for anticipating every aggression and hostility under the sun from the intruders. What I hadn't taken into account, however, was their assumption that the sepulchre was empty, that the very last thing they expected to see was myself and a frail old senior citizen materialize from an exploding door like something out of the Twilight Zone. Two utterly flabbergasted thugs jumped back with genuine fright, none other than Egg Face and Tomboy.

Without wasting a second I pulled Derek with brute force, dashing; I could not escape fast enough. They gawped at us on the way.

I shouted to them, 'Don't take long!'

Outside the front portal Derek shoved me off.

'Silly, silly. There, now!'

'Sorry for dragging you,' I said. 'It's Falkirk's unsavoury compatriots. They snort Devil's dandruff in the Menzies crypt.'

Derek shrugged and coughed. 'All sorts of the usual, nothing worth bothering. Though if I still had my Luger pistol it'd be yours, forgive me. Now, dear, I'll call you if I can't get outdoors next time.'

'Take care, Derek. I mean it.'

He lifted his hand in farewell and crossed the street, heading to Fergus Green. I felt compelled to watch him go.

I should have called him a taxi. Christ, you thoughtless bitch, you always do it for Them. He's on his last legs. Why didn't you call him a goddamn taxi?

I lit a cigarette to wait the thugs out. I never saw Derek again.

Rain spitting. I idled in the grassy nook between the church and high wall, partially hiding from the street, in battle with the raindrops dampening my cigarette. Ten minutes since the thugs went in, Egg Face presumably being 'Gaz' the drug dealer; the state of his nostrils alone suggested he sniffed more than he sold.

Gaz, short for Gary. Huh! The first guy I'd ever dated was a Gary. Nice enough bloke, even an interested bloke. Congratulations, Loser; when you were eighteen, somebody was actually interested in you! Now as I skulked outside St Patrick's with my tobacco, part-time cleaner and accomplice to supernatural murder, the very concept of dating and relationships was a mystery to me. Me, a dud battery in her mid-twenties. *Fuck it*, I thought, *maybe that's why I smoke too much.*

'What, in theee *fuck* was that?' Tomboy exclaimed, stomping around the corner to find me. She came outside alone, dressed in thick striped tights and jeans ripped off at the thighs, carrying a sizeable backpack over her jacket.

'What the fuck was what?' I retorted, ready to fib all I wanted.

'What was granddad doing in there with our stash? What the hell were you up to?'

Tomboy was a bag of nerves. I read fear in her, but not of Derek and I leaping from cupboards.

'Never mind,' I said. 'Your piece of shit supply is untouched.'

'Try telling that to Gaz. He's paranoid as fuck, going apeshit in there! I had to pack the rest of his supply out. He's pulling the plug.'

'Not my problem,' I said, pretending to be tough whilst backing further away from the front entrance.

Tomboy followed me, not taking the hint. 'Thanks a fuckin' lot, cos he'll make it *my* problem.'

Unfortunately, I believed her. Tomboy's previous bruises were today upstaged by a new violet shiner on her jaw. This Gaz was a nasty piece of work.

'Is he your boyfriend?' I asked, nodding at the bruise. 'Charming.'

'No, he's Annie's bloke. I live with them. What were you two doing in there?'

By "Annie", I assumed she meant the stocky girl with the unfriendly face. Annie and Gaz, match made in heaven.

'He's just an old man,' I said, 'helping me bin the mess you leave! You think you can go in there whenever you like? What if someone saw you? What if they called the police?'

The tomboy slumped against the church with me. 'Keep your knickers on. Why would a bendy fossil help you in there?'

Technically it was a fair question.

'He just did, okay? He's decent.'

'Fuck off,' she winked. 'I saw his condoms.'

'Hey, shut up, that's sick.'

Ah, but she was giggling. 'Sooo, this is it, yeah? You passed me up for Rumpleforeskin in there?'

In spite of myself it took effort not to snigger. The tomboy was infectious. 'Cut it out,' I said.

She was laughing now. 'Did he bend you over the coffin?'

'Ugh!'

She stepped sideways, studying the building. 'Could I crash here, by the way?'

That she asked me at all, as if I'd say yes, was crazy. I nearly bit her nose off. Then I compared her carefree sparkle with the bruises. *Poor kid*, I thought. *Who could beat up that?* Even so, I did not know her. What if I suggested a spare room in Falkirk's house and her whole posse showed up?

'No way,' I replied. 'How long is he going to be? I think the minister's inside.'

Tomboy shook her head, lighting a joint. 'Nah, he went out. We saw him. Gaz's having a meltdown in there, so I'm out here ogling your tits.'

This sprite simply couldn't keep a single thought to herself.

Though endearing, I predicted it cost her.

'There's nothing interesting about my tits,' I said.

'Really? Show me.'

'Sod off!'

'Okay!'

I could not believe what she did next. Up went her top, in front of me, the street and the House of God himself, bra-less. An elderly couple nearby were in danger of finding themselves a hostage audience. It lasted a fraction of a second, long enough for my cigarette to drop into a puddle along with my jaw. By now she was exhausting me.

Then it happened.

Gaz would not have seen me. If the tomboy hadn't given me away, if he hadn't seen her talking to me, none of it would have happened. But he did see her, meaning he found me too. His face was scarlet with rage, making him ten times broader as he charged directly at us, huffing and puffing straight past her, straight up to me.

To remember is to see it in slow motion: his two fat arms, big filthy hands, a huge *push*!

Smack! My head hit the church wall.

With one blow, he shoved me out of pedestrian view behind a buttress in the grassy nook. The world swam in spots, a razor sheet of hot electricity blazing through my skull. My legs forgot how to work and I heaved with nausea. I vaguely recall the tomboy tripping around to us, paling, the forgotten joint dangling between her fingers.

He kicked me.

That gorilla-strength kick … My throat made a distinct *uhh* noise, then no more; all wind abandoned me and burst forth to the skies. A shockwave rippled from his club-like knee embedded in my gut; the pounding would leave bruises for weeks. Gaz plastered me to the church, holding me fast so that the brickwork chiselled mercilessly at my spine.

Another horror filled my vision. A polished switchblade reflected the murky clouds, moved under my chin, and aimed, pressing. *Tsssssss!* He cut me. A trickle of something wet and warm ran down my neck into my blouse, joining the spitting raindrops.

'What's happened to my stuff, you CUNT?'

I was beyond sense; all I registered was pain, too dazed for fear. Gaz must have repeated the question, for he shook me and shouted again. As my double vision coalesced, his face amalgamated into every penny dreadful villain I had ever read.

I fought to find my voice. 'Wh– I –.' Too soon. I had no air to speak.

'There's a kilo of my stuff missing. Where the fuck *is* it?'

'I – I don't –'

Gaz shook me again, bouncing my head off brick until the stinging drew tears.

'I don't know,' I said. 'Don't know about it. I don't know what you mean.'

He kicked me again, same place in the gut.

My breath, just restored, fell from me with such force that I fell with it. Blistering flame burned my scalp as he pulled me up by the hair, wielding his knife from my neck, to my bust, to my waist, down … down. That savage slice of metal was positioned at my groin, exerting pressure on the zip of my jeans.

Gaz's eyes shone wildness.

'You a virgin?' he said. 'Are ya?'

The blade pressed into my zip, pushing further; any harder and –

'What, ya shy?' he snarled. 'I can find out. Your mummy tell you what a virgin is, luv? I'll find out!'

Heavy beads of sweat trickled from a pulsing vein on his forehead and dripped onto my collar bone, diluting the line of blood running under my blouse.

From a million miles away I heard Tomboy say, 'Gaz, she doesn't do –'

A swish of his left arm! Gaz lashed out in a great arc as if parting half the Red Sea, his fist landing square on her temple, knocking her sideways. She doubled over, holding her head soundlessly, too used to the blows.

'Did you even search her, you stupid bitch?' he bellowed.

His thick hands tore into my pockets. Everything was turned out. Suddenly my clothes, my body, were not rightfully my property; my lighter, spare change, tobacco and filter papers went flying, all destined for the damp grass and puddles. I would never get a dry cigarette out of them now. He missed the tiny pocket in my jeans where my keys, Serge's keys, were kept. God almighty, if he'd found the keys!

Meanwhile, Tomboy gingerly righted herself, cupping her fresh wound, a new shiner on its merry way.

'I did search her,' she lied. 'She's a halo-head, got fuck-all.'

'You were in our fucking vault!' he barked, chip sauce and lager breath. 'Who was the old fuck?'

My choices were to either speak, risk a third kick or rape via switchblade, if that telling bulge in his trousers didn't beat him to it.

'He wanted to smoke,' I whimpered.

'Fuck off!' His blade hacked off a button above my fly.

'That's all!' I croaked. 'He wanted a cigarette indoors out of the rain.'

Whether he believed me or not it was too late for more excuses. Gaz stopped shaking me, a hopeful sign.

'Where's Falkirk?' he hissed.

'Warwick.'

Dear me, did I just say my lying made me hopeful? What a fool. I was rewarded with another shaking and a third suffocating kick, powerful enough to make me vomit in my mouth.

'You expect me to believe that piss!' he shouted. 'Do I look stupid? You deaf?'

The biological fact that it is impossible to speak with the wind kneed out of you was lost on Gaz. His blade cut a hole in my denims. 'Answer me or your period comes early! Do. I. Look. Stupid?'

Oh, to give this pig the unthinkable satisfaction of answering him! That he could reduce me to this! But what would *you* do? The knife tip pushed in, touching the surface of my pudendum.

Pride withered. My lids squeezed shut. I moaned a pathetic 'No.'

'Louder.'

'No!'

Though the buttress concealed us, from the pavement yards away came the buzz of chatting locals, a pack of blissfully unaware people. Welcome to the afternoon church service, my devout congregation. This grassy nook was losing its privacy.

Tomboy saw them. Bright and alert, she anxiously rocked from side to side, rubbing and flexing her fingers.

'Gaz,' she said, 'not smart. There's people. She's seen your face. Lost your temper too soon again.'

I think the presence of people convinced him; in fact, they may have saved my life, for Gaz stopped, conflicted and panting. His knee unpinned me. In other words, he happened to notice what he was doing: he had a live one, potential eyewitnesses included. Could he believe a church bitch, if only half-heartedly?

He was trembling with frustration.

'Good girl,' he eventually said. 'Tell ya what. Guess what, I'll let this one go, ya lucky bitch. Ain't I a sport?' He smiled like a hound. 'Be good and tell us where the wrinkly old cunt lives, yeah? The one you came out with, where'd he go? Cos this knife wants to fuck you!'

I had absolutely no clue where Derek lived, thank God for

small favours. I admired Derek and valued his confidence, but be honest, you yourself don't know how you would behave with a knife at your groin.

'Delfour Road,' I gasped, it was all I could think of. 'Don't know which house.'

'And he's got our stuff?'

Gaz's knife held its position, Reader, make no mistake! I shook my head miserably, bracing myself for more bruises or worse.

'You be smart and tell Falkirk for us, yeah? I'll only warn you this once. If I find you're fucking with me, I'll break in your cunt like a real Virgin Mary! But don't you worry about that, dawlin', yeah? We'll take back every gram he fucked off with, straight from his holy arse. You pray for that. You fucking pray for it!'

The knife vanished. Gaz retreated, changing his tone like a character actor. 'Aww! Brave bitch, ain't she, Alice?'

Alice. She stood across the grass from us like a pole in a desert, the congregation growing in number not far behind her. The Christians sounded so loud and cheerful today. Were they always like this?

Gaz joined the magic mushroom he called Alice. 'So you just fucking pass that on, luv!' he finished, directing a dirty fingernail at me.

Alice dithered on the spot, stiff as a statue. I think she tried to approach me, saying something; whatever it was I missed it because Gaz's grimy paw slammed on her slender nape, violently shifting and marching her off. *That hurt her*, I thought.

Alone at last. My body was waiting for them to leave, and now it slid, slid, slid down to the grass. Every muscle sighed. Baked air from my caved gut steamed past my lips. I did not want to be found, wanted to be left in peace. A shielding cloak of greyness stole over me, my body ached and jarred, oh but I didn't have to move! I rested my cheek on the cool church stone, damp blades of grass licking my cuticles, staring in a sort of netherworld through the uninteresting buttress, pretty bricks lined together with cement, glistening like enamel in the rain. I learned their every imperfection, pebble, chink and curve that afternoon. Raindrops fell on my upper lip; they tasted rusty.

The bleeding had lessened. I touched a trailing line of blood, dried and peeling, from the shallow cut on my neck. Two maroon blotches stained my blouse. The dated mirror in the church toilet was a framed oval dangling above the sink, lit by a slim mullioned window. I had been crying without realising. The pipe organ and congregation chorused their worship from the nave, worlds away; I'd hobbled past them inconspicuously to get here, every movement sending rods of pain through my pelvis. I held up my palm in front of me, it hung there, quivering of its own accord. It took three tries to get a decent grip on the tap. The water here never heated up.

I doused my neck and chest. I wanted to bleach my clothes where I still felt the pressure of his knee, I wanted his breath out of my hair, I needed a shower, needed to sponge every minute of the last hour off me. A hot lump on my scalp warmed the raindrops in my hair; I tested it with the lightest touch. *Ow!* It would require sleeping on my belly, likewise inflamed lobster red. There was no returning to work today. I would wrap up in bed, phone Howell and plead sickness.

The sermon wasn't over yet. I exited the church with what crippled speed I could, scared of venturing outside again, but I had to. As I unlocked the door to Falkirk's house, the sound of singing churchgoers glided past my ears.

'Happy birthday, Rona,' I said.

Chapter Thirteen

I knew I was not alone as soon as I woke up. Through the open doorway I saw that the downstairs light was on, illuminating the upper landing in a dusky peach.

I'm sure I closed that door.

Sitting up brought fresh waves of pain and set my bruises pulsing. I lay there until they passed, listening. Noiseless interludes were broken by creaking floorboards, the weight of someone walking. Falkirk must be home.

Keen anger resurfaced. I wanted to show him the handiwork his bosom buddy had made of my neck today. *It sure as hell wasn't me who nicked a kilo of their drugs, Falky. Want to see the bruises too? No, I don't care how bad a mood you're in! I've already been battered today. I'd do another round if it meant taking you with me!*

Feeling around for my clothes, I saw the time: 9:30 p.m. Five hours sleep in total. Hold on, they'll be awake and their taxis aren't booked yet. Damn! Or, wait …

I stayed absolutely still, locked on the peach dimness.

Falkirk?

Whoever it was, they had seen me semi-comatose in this guest room and left the door open. Would Falkirk drop a hint like that? Had he walked to the bed? Breathed over me? My slumber was so deep I hadn't even dreamt.

I slipped into my jeans and tread softly to the landing. The movement grew louder; a clang of cutlery, a mechanical hum rattling from the kitchen. Good, the kitchen was furthest from the front door; I could sneak past Falkirk and grab my shoes without being noticed. I needed to apologise to Serge and the others for sleeping late and – Oh! What's that?

The heavenly vapour rushed to my nose on the way down. Inside my kicked abdomen a shrunken stomach bumped awake with fireworks, surfing me towards the smell of garlic, cinnamon and coriander orbiting a buttery nucleus of tender meat, rising, circulating the house and pouring down my throat. I tasted its succulent juice in mighty gulps, scent drawing me on a cloud downstairs, past caring for precaution. Damned or not, Chef Falkirk, I could think of worse ways to be woken up.

The kitchen was deserted. In a frying pan sizzled thick slices of the beef I'd purchased earlier that week, lightly browning at the edges around a pink centre. My mouth filled with saliva, biting the sweet fragrance.

'Aaaand here she is,' he said, outlined in the hallway behind me.

Where did all this come from? For me, still groggy, it was too much of a jumble-bag to process; if cooking food signified their anger at my lateness tonight, I was still upstairs asleep and this scene was a dream, far easier to believe!

'Hello,' I managed, rubbing my eyes. 'I know it's late. I didn't mean to sleep so long. I was ill.'

'Um-hmm,' said Serge drearily, sauntering into the lounge. 'Yes, yes, we know. Edith! Check her.' His tone was not a request. You might open and close elevators with that voice.

Edith's wavy hair brushed my elbow as she swept into the kitchen, her bony fingers touching my scalp where a lump tingled, making me hiss. I remember a cold prickle running up my sides as her piercing pupils expanded and contracted like camera shutters, seeming to peer straight through me. Convinced in her examination, she told Serge, 'No concussion.'

I felt a nip of intolerance. I would have happily told them about my attacker if they extended me the courtesy of asking, preferably *not* via impersonal taps and pokes. The attack was my experience, it had happened to *me*; I didn't care to be speculated over like a lab rat, not today.

'Excuse me,' I said. 'Can you please tell me how you know this? I am here, you know. You *can* ask. I'd prefer that.'

'Sing your opera if you must,' Serge dismissed. 'Later!'

I motioned precariously at the hob and a bottle of Cabernet which had also mysteriously appeared, bewildered.

'Is this for me?'

'No, it's for Her Majesty Queen Elizabeth the Second, fool.'

'Don't tell me you knew it was my birthday, too.'

'I suppose we do now.'

I was too muddled to pursue explanations, and it would be a long time yet before I fully comprehended the inherent danger behind any offbeat acts of generosity from those three. They ate nothing.

I dined in the lounge, poorly lit under Falkirk's cheap lamps blotched with foul-smelling coffee stains and greasy fingerprints, one lamp illuminating the couch, the other a TV opposite. Their substandard condition plunged the centre of the room into full shadow and the remainder in sepia, creating a mixed atmosphere of undecided comfort. Then again perhaps the alien smell of good food helped. In the absence of adequate dining space, Falkirk's coffee table, ruined by countless cigarette burns and ring marks, was so low it defied logic and craning forward to eat over the plate did no joy for my kicked abdomen whatsoever. Nonetheless I ate, faster than I should have! The meat replenished my energy and swept away fatigue. Afterwards, I automatically searched for my lighter before remembering it was in a puddle outside along with my poor tobacco. As I inspected Falkirk's ashtray for butt ends, a small rectangular missile, unopened, packaged in plastic, skittered across the coffee table and hit my plate. They had thought of everything tonight.

Serge was wandering restlessly up and down from lounge to hallway, refusing to stand still, looking bored and restless, not much of a digestion pill when it made me equally restless with a cherry of mortal anxiety on top. There was absolutely no clocking his moods. By stark contrast, Edith, completely relaxed, reclined in a leather armchair and crossed her ankles on a footstool.

'May I tell you?' I asked, desperate to share the pain of my afternoon with someone.

'Sing away,' Serge malingered, 'though I can't see how it's any concern of ours.' He was perusing Falkirk's bookshelf, picking out volumes, glancing at the covers, flicking through and tossing them over his shoulder.

My spirits sank back into my bruised gut. *I may as well be static from the radio to them.* I half-heartedly explained the events of the day, keeping it short.

'All I can do now is tell Falkirk,' I finished. 'As if that'll help. I'm sure he's the culprit.'

'Well,' Edith said, 'you needn't worry about the library tonight.'

'You're done in there anyway,' Serge added, perusing another book destined for the dingy carpet.

'Really?' I asked.

'Yes. You've wasted enough time. There's more important work. Don't look so trodden upon! Come down and pick your paper souvenirs and that'll be all for tonight.'

I ordered myself not to be disheartened by their benumbing lack of concern; proof, unfortunately, that I was.

As we left, Serge said, 'Eddie, bring the rest of her Cabernet.'

Rona Dean could never have predicted the evening of her twenty-fifth birthday. It begins with me following Serge and Edith under the trapdoor, my torch illuminating his thick hair and navy-blue business jacket over his casual trousers, Serge's unchanging style of informal formality.

I foresaw nothing more eventful this evening than taking my pick of library ephemera, which had since accumulated from a handful into a small hill. No way would they allow me to keep the lot, surely.

'So, this is it.' I blushed. If only they had given me time to filter it and avoid this embarrassment!

A mass of lightly toasted medieval illustrations, Edwardian posters advertising circuses in London and Bath, the Penny Dreadfuls, Victorian newspapers, a season ticket to the Great Exhibition at London's Crystal Palace in 1851, and one incredible London flyer dated 1645 with a drawing of a beak-nosed old lady in a scarf under the headline:

Eighteene Witches, a Lift of the names
of thofe executed and their Confeffions.
Emila Parron, Frederick Lewif, Helen Scarp...

I had poured over that witch-finder flyer a number of times with bittersweet fascination, imagining 'their confessions' under God knows what torture: thumbscrews, the boot, the rack, lack of sleep; everyone is breakable sooner or later.

'You'll find a bag for that in the Hall,' Serge answered, almost yawning. 'Come grab one.'

Of all their underground requirements, illumination is not one of them, so judging by the pre-lit candles and gas lamps in the Hall, they had been expecting me all evening. We found Hector slouched over the grand piano, drinking from their green bottles.

'Well?' Serge called.

'Almost done,' Hector replied.

The piano's coat of dust was almost gone, an attractive spruce wood peeping from underneath; you could see the signs of polish. The lid was up at its maximum height, bass and treble strings exposed. Hector inclined over the soundboard with what appeared to be a tuning fork, a mute felt hanging from his pocket.

Serge positioned himself over the keys while Hector poised with the tuner. The peals! The piano strings were glorious, bounding off the vaulted ceiling and quickening my blood to exhilaration. Sleepy air stirred in the turbulence. With a maestro's concentration, Serge's fingers rippled out scales like interference patterns across water, pattering the keyboard up and down. Then he would stop, pressing a number of keys at once, padding from high to low octaves, instructing Hector.

'Middle C … G … A-sharp. And, er, all of those.' Serge swiped his finger up a dozen keys, ending his assessment with a smart *prrrrrrit!*

My fingertips tingled.

In my aunts' house, a cheap, run-down piano used to occupy the gloomy recess of our lounge. Never had my aunts made the effort to hire a tuner, never. Being a passed-down burden from a distant relative, it was not technically mine, but from the ages of five to ten I spent years of hours at that tired instrument, so chronically out of tune that I formed my own idea of what keys lay where, all in the wrong places, of course. In this pathetic set-up, I did my best to drum out melodies learned by ear, and, with no one to help me, eventually managed crude renditions of some nursery rhymes and basic songs. We were an odd but, I think, appropriate match, sitting together alone, existing out of tune with the world. My aunts would scold, 'Why don't you go outside and play with the other kids? Look! They're all having fun in the park!' Children my age, hogging the swings, compet-

ing on see-saws, boys kicking girls off the climbing frames –
and I hardly knew their names, no love lost for me. Then one
day I came home from school. It was gone. My splintered old
friend with the broken voice, passed off helpless, they had sold
him without so much as warning me. Pam and Alison stood in
the kitchen, cooking fish fingers and baked beans, explaining
light-heartedly like sensible, mature adults, 'Oh, of course it
had to go, taking up space over there. And selling that piano
brought in good money, little miss! It bought your lovely new
school uniform for next term. That'll be nice, won't it? Oh, that
reminds me, Mrs Greer's coming to measure you tomorrow.
Mind you stand still while she pins you. Oh, now, now, you're
not going to cry like a *baby*, are you? Big girls don't do that!
Look at her, Pam, blubbing over a silly old piano!' I got a row
if I ever cried in that house. I knew I would then. My heart
sank into my shoes; I bit my lip hard, but the waterworks were
coming, squeezing out, and the fish fingers were nearly ready.
I went to my room, buried my face in the sheets and wept so
they wouldn't hear, wept until my pillow soaked through. A
piece of my heart had been taken away, not even a goodbye for
my tuneless companion, the only thing as out of place as I was.

Now, there, in the vaults, my feet wandered to their piano
ahead of my brain.

'It's a Bösendorfer,' said Serge. 'Not the grandest but, who
knows, we *may* be waking her up. Try that C again, Hector.
Yes, and – no, no, wait for it! F-sharp.' He worked the keys
again. 'All right, getting somewhere. Have a drink, Rona.'

Edith placed the Cabernet on the table. 'I'm afraid we don't
habitually indulge in silverware,' she said, 'but I found this lying around.'

She placed a pewter goblet by the bottle, a shallow cup atop
a tall neck and base, shaped rather like the chancel's candlestick holders. Wine, a grand table, music … *My birthday*, I
thought, filling the goblet. Between you and me I'd have settled

for drinking straight from the bottle.

Serge the tenacious perfectionist took the tuner from Hector and made his own adjustments, now and then sprinkling a few phrases that promised something beautiful only to terminate in meaningless scales. 'Did you know we have a birthday girl in our midst, Heck?' he said, his face full of a musician's concentration.

'Rona,' said Edith, 'look behind you. See that large wardrobe with the inlaid frieze?'

I searched with untrained eyes. When it came to antique furniture I was an imbecile. The astute woman directed me. 'Warm. Warmer. Colder. Much colder. No, next to it, the barrel columns. If you open the bottom shaft you'll find a plethora of bags.'

Wedging my way between an oak dresser and a pillar, I reached a wardrobe panelled with a brass handle etched in curling grooves. From its shelves, a million other things besides bags fell out: scarves, shawls and gloves, moth-eaten and tattered. I took the largest bag I could find, an enormous saddle satchel with heavy leather straps over double casing, goodness knows what age. Putting the calfskin to my nose, I bet the sweat of horse loins still lived in there somewhere.

Edith lounged in her grand Egyptian chair; she could certainly pass for an exotic queen. Serge left the piano and joined her. *Now* I saw who sat where …

I knew it! Serge blended into it effortlessly, the joined legs making a cushioned slide as he moved it, and though he seated himself as casually as any man, together they might open a crack in the earth's core with a single thunderous syllable. The throne was harsh and beautiful. Like its occupant. Need I say which chair he took?

Edith dealt a deck of cards on the tablecloth. Don't ask me what card game they absently played. They sat at this for a time while Hector worked with his tuning fork. I sipped my wine, feeling self-conscious and desirous of an alternative to their tatty sofa covered in rodent droppings.

I discreetly edged to a Dutch armchair by the arcade. 'Is it all right if I ta–'

Snap!

Like a pistol shot. The crack of Serge's knuckles ricocheted off every stone in the Hall. It burst my eardrums. It split the air. I froze, along with my pulse, over the armchair.

Serge had simultaneously snapped his fingers and was pointing at me. My heart still stops when I remember that moment: he sat upright, as frozen as I was, one long, great, terrible finger directed at me like a jousting lance. His eyes shone daggers. All heat fell from my pores.

A beat passed. Edith continued (if somewhat slower) handling the card deck. Serge remained solid as granite, pointing like a damning, unblinking seraph. His only movement was a slow, *slooow* shake of the head – an imperial, invulnerable, *No*.

'Not in here,' he said gravely. 'Not with us.'

Cringing, I straightened, not knowing what had hit me.

Serge lowered his arm and slouched over the cards. 'Yes, that's something Edith and I never got used to.'

The sounds of piano-tuning resumed over my pounding chest. Edith, unfazed by the whole thing, shuffled the deck in satisfying thumps off the thick tablecloth.

'You'll have to make do with a bench or stool, I'm afraid,' she told me, smiling at Serge. 'He will insist, won't he? Personal chairs are rather recent. Late 1500s.'

'Hmmm,' he droned morosely, laying down a card, 'that's still a little soon for me.'

Hector passed into the sea of furniture and re-emerged with a rustic square trunk lined with iron hardware on both sides. Setting it by me without a word, he returned to the piano. My 'chair', I presumed. Honestly, if I needed any stronger hint of status! I thanked Hector and sat with my goblet, sniffing a crumb of empathy in his mute assistance.

The trunk was sturdy and took my weight. Serge smiled at my sorry wee throne, shuffling the deck.

'I'd gamble sand is still embedded in there,' he said, 'straight off the Mercia clipper ship in the 1780s. You're not entitled to chairs unless you're of noble birth. Didn't you know that?'

A pregnant pause as they taunted me with raised brows … then fell into laughter.

'Just a custom of ours,' Edith rejoined. 'Most customs die with time. Not so with us.'

Backtrack a few centuries and you get a day in the stocks for dressing above your station. Even sitting down? I swallowed more wine. Hell, I finished the goblet, swallowing their elitism with it. Custom or not, the gunshot of his reprimand rang in my head.

'So, no one contacts you on your birthday,' Serge remarked, deck-dealing with Edith. 'No acquaintances whatsoever. I find that hard to believe.'

'You've asked me that before,' I moped. 'Again, the answer is no. I don't even use social media these days.'

At my mention of the internet, Serge sighed over his cards. 'Interesting. There was a time when diaries were private and expression had to be earned. Now *every* voice is a whore. Too many voices.'

Perhaps it was the wine speeding my tongue or some trace of adrenaline letting my thoughts slip out, or maybe I just wanted to snatch a chance at regaining their favour, either way Serge had touched on a topic that interested me. I threw in my tuppence worth.

'What might count becomes lost in their noise,' I said. 'Overuse kills purity. Originalities become banalities. Soon everyone is bored.'

I caught myself with a gulp, having shot my mouth off. I needn't have worried.

'If they learn no other expression,' Serge added, head down, dealing another deck with Edith, 'they'll spin round and round in that cyber ants' death spiral until their brains dry up, then blame everyone but themselves for becoming empty static. There's sheeple for you, Edith.'

'It's always been the same, Serge,' Edith replied, blasé. 'They've always been this way. They proudly ride the tide of their fads, high on it for a time, leaving behind forgotten hiding places for us.'

'*Do* they?' Serge challenged, forgetting the cards a moment and eyeballing her. 'Privacy is a critically endangered species, madam. My amateur contraptions may be lost under the seabed but I warned you a hundred times, Eddie, once the cat's out of the bag industrialisation is exponential. Caution, milady! By all means hold out your goody bag for detritus but don't think they can't track you with it.'

Unwilling to provoke a debate, Edith occupied herself with card re-shuffling while Serge slid the wine bottle across the table for me. I refilled my goblet, relieved at not having to ask.

'May I smoke in here?'

They nodded indifferently.

I had to silently agree with Serge. While Big Brother kept constant watch outside, there was little to envy in such a vulnerable underground minority, only a fool could perceive otherwise. And yet, people continued to go missing around the world every day, never to be found …

I contemplated them. Historically speaking, my present company was the product of unshakably different worlds. The mayflies in your back garden live for a day, then die, while we go on for decades. People, are their mayflies. I could not imagine the spirit it must take to be dragged through exponential technological change in a blink of human history, it would break my heart in their shoes. The very soul of their mental and physical survival was the ability to adapt; that takes more psychological strength than brawn. No wonder Serge required invincible sagacity, no wonder they nurtured inhuman sensitivity, by experience alone they must see humanity's storms coming like satellites spot typhoons. Animals, all of us – mayflies, cockroaches and tigers, people are Nature's playthings, zipping by like the seconds on that grandfather clock. Time is lonely and the world is beautiful; most never live long enough to fully comprehend that.

The grandfather clock chimed. It chimed eleven times, a snipped porcelain *ting*. I wandered around their table to where it stood resolute like the shell of a king. The body was of walnut, decorated about the face with helical columns embellished with glass under Corinthian hoods. The clock face itself was hand-painted, numbering phases of the sun and moon. Standing this close, the steady beat of its pendulum penetrated, ever so gently, under my skin. I longed to mischievously open the door and peek inside, nor would I have dared.

I must have stood transfixed in this pose for some time, because Serge appeared at my side.

'Work of Charles Embaldt,' he said, 'carpenter, Lord Menzies' valet and former watchdog. I'm rather fond of this.' He stroked the polish. 'Custom made for us in 1698. Grandfather clocks were originally crafted by coffin-makers. Hence the name of its casing: the "sarcophagus".'

He paused … then flung the case door open. I flinched. Serge laughed.

There hung its heart, long, dull and metallic, swinging left-right, left-right. It seemed the instrument sucked up all time into its sarcophagus, leaving us suspended in a paradox with the pendulum's heartbeat.

I blinked – a full five minutes we had passed in this snug suspension.

'Serge,' I almost whispered. 'The man who hurt me today.'

'No,' he said quietly, reading my mind. 'More coward than

211

killer, Rona. Or you'd be dead.'

He drew out a set of keys and jangled them at Edith.

'Another vault,' he chimed at the others. 'Why not!'

He and Edith led me from the Hall, past the library to the worm-eaten door. The padlock swung on its metal chain above the original, larger keyhole beneath, a plump beetle crawled from it. Using his smallest key, the hinges busted in excruciating thunderclaps as the stubborn door cranked open bit by bit.

The interior of a box-room was revealed. I navigated with my torch and found nothing save one object.

'Hello, Sam,' Serge announced.

Facing us some feet away, fat, formidable, jet-black, proud and terrible: a gargantuan safe. The hulking cube of Edwardian metal greeted us with a great brass eye, encircled by the manufacturer, *Samson White & Co. of West London*, in orange paint.

'This is the Treasury,' said Edith. In we went.

Serge unlocked the safe, which yielded noiselessly and smooth as silk. 'Treasury' conjures up images of mountainous paper money or bars of gold; I felt a twinge of disappointment to see only various shelves, deep and shallow, containing not gold or bound bills, but boxes and chests.

Contents thus exposed, Serge promptly left us. Clearly only he had the authority to use Sam's key.

Edith took boxes from the cabinetry and laid them on the floor. 'As you've gathered,' she said, 'we drag leftovers in our wake whether we like it or not. At any moment in time it is impossible to know what will be priceless in future. But not always impossible.'

She demonstrated, opening a box, then another, and another.

I never believed my eyelids had the power to open so far. My jaw dropped to my throat. I soon had to steady myself against the immovable Sam.

Glittering up at me: diamonds, gold, silver, rubies, pearls, amethysts, garnets, sapphires, tanzanite, emeralds, topaz, platinum, blue zircon, turquoise, tourmaline, amber, peridot and jewelled crucifixes. Single, double, triple and quadruple chains crowned with more jewels and divided into necklaces, earrings, bracelets, anklets and rings. Brooches and pendants of art nouveau chiselled the sweat of rainbows into insects, butterflies, spiders, birds, flora, dragonflies and laurels of more than the eye could untangle in styles of art deco, Greek, Roman, Japanese, Arabian, Saxon, Viking, Celtic, Renaissance and hundreds of Georgian shell cameos.

'It's your birthday,' she said plainly. 'Pick one.'

Speaking was initially out of the question. How could I possibly choose from all this?

Edith slouched against the safe. 'Mind not to take all night.'

'I'm overwhelmed, Edith. Thank you. How far back do they go?'

'Far enough and more,' she answered. 'I wouldn't expect them all to be in one piece. Choose carefully, if I know anything of it I'll tell you.'

The bangles on her wrists, the rings on her fingers. In an underground of mould and soot, Edith knew opulence yet!

She was correct about their condition. Some chains were broken and many bore the naked wounds of missing gems, several chipped lockets hung permanently open, pocket watches were smashed, and a set of diamond-studded quartz teeth had eight molars missing.

I had no excuse for being remotely picky; their collections were unmatched, each item priceless and too good for me. I so rarely had the means or occasion to wear jewellery, there truly *was* the danger I could be there all night; I may never get the chance again! Wary of the ticking minutes, I grew hastier, overturning ruby clusters, emerald brooches and tangled Lavaliere necklaces of sapphire and coral.

Music echoed from the hall, the piano was in tune. Edith folded her arms, tilted her head and meditated on the distant melody.

'What is right for you,' she said, 'often finds you first.'

That is when something small, round and phosphorescent winked at me from the bottom of the box. I lifted it, unwinding a skinny chain of fine silver, so delicate I thought it might dissolve in my palm if I held it too long. Holding it up to the light, a spherical piece of magic dangled like a raindrop inside a hollow loop of silver: a dragon's egg of opal.

Opal. A mineral of fire and sky. It instantly bewitched me with diffractions of luminescent purple, lilac, electric blue, green, blots of red-orange flame and aquamarine floating in an indigo mist like interstellar nebulae, galaxies in my very hand. If the wine made me tipsy, swimming in this micro-cosmos rendered me quite drunk. How can anyone not fall in love with opal? It penetrates the senses. It pushes every single button. I wear it as I write.

'I think you've made your choice,' Edith observed. She knelt and studiously brought the pendant closer. 'Hmm. Venetian. No earlier than sixteen-eighties, I think.'

'Opal,' I said dreamily.

'You do right to trust your instincts. Where I come from, opal is a talisman. It embodies the strength of every gem hidden in its spectrum.'

She closed each box with a clap and returned them to Sam.

I raised the chain over my neck. 'May I?'

'It's yours,' she said, shutting Sam's cast iron door.

The opal sphere rested light and cool against my breastbone. Hector appeared in the doorway, holding my saddle satchel.

In the library, I loaded the satchel full to bursting, fearing damage to the paper keepsakes. 'Is there anything else I can do tonight?' I asked, hoisting the leather strap over my shoulder. 'Taxis?'

'You haven't finished your wine,' said Edith. 'Drink and

214

humour us.'

Humour them indeed! But the alcohol was speedier than my slackened wits. Edith strode into the Hall and gestured at my neck. 'Serge? Pendant. Venetian. I gamble 1680?'

Serge rose from the piano stool and came to me. Without a shred of discretion, he raised the opal from my chest.

'No, you're wrong,' he told Edith, examining it. 'Sixteen-thirties.' Rather arrogantly, his finger then digressed upward, from the pendant to my knife wound.

'Blade sharp,' he muttered to himself. 'Metal shabby.'

There I was, standing on display like a dummy in a clothes shop, surrendering my personal space. Serge, no fool, snickered at my pique.

'Oh, dear!' he said. 'Haha. Someone dance with the birthday child for your-pick-of-a-god's sake!'

I glimpsed Hector testing a wind instrument, a recorder or perhaps a flute, I didn't find out which, because no sooner did the music resonate then Edith pulled me into the centre of the Hall as Serge started on the piano. My satchel slipped off.

Edith stepped from side to side, bobbing up and down, pulling me with her; goodness knows where my feet were supposed to be moving.

'Forgive me,' I said urgently. 'I can't dance.'

'You already are,' she said.

'Stop complaining,' said Serge. 'Use your ears.'

Edith led me in an unusual sort of waltz. 'Of course, this is cheating,' she said. 'The correct steps – are this.'

She took position at my side, lifted my hand in the air and paraded me to the rhythm: two steps forward, two sideways, right, left, and again, counting with me. Then, as the tempo wove and mounted, without warning she wheeled me in a circle. Serge made Hector take over while he kicked burned obstructions out of our way to make a rudimentary sort of dance floor, placing the wine goblet in my free hand just before Edith

215

spun me again. When his piano resumed, the melody wound its way into my mind, a light tune with the mellowness of autumn fruit. I hear it to this day.

'What dance is this?' I asked her.

'Galician,' Edith explained. '*Mandad'ei Comigo* by Martin Codax. It means My Love is Coming Home. A popular cantiga in its day.'

She sang as she led me. Edith has a rich and piercing voice, a high-toned complement for the piece, reaching crescendo two or three times. Just as I was getting used to the dance steps, the tempo played faster and faster, Edith pulling me centrifugally like a puppet on lengthy strings. An unsure laugh escaped me. Under the compelling melody I was held hostage and swept up, whisked about the room as if weightless, breathing red wine.

Ceiling, cupboards, pillars, bureaux, chests, table, clock, lamps, cabinets, sofas, piano, chairs, Serge and Hector swirled, swirled, swirled and danced with me. I was whisked and whisked.

'Edith sang in the courts,' Serge commented. 'She's had many a heel dance under her larynx.'

I believed him; their incantation is of a style none save their kind remember. Neither would you: the *joglar* Martin Codax died in the 1200s.

I have some general recollection of reaching Falkirk's villa that night, the world in colour and my head waltzing. The tune plays on.

~

Let this be a lesson to you if you empathise with the Rona who pooh-poohed Falkirk at every opportunity: predilection will walk you off a cliff before it occurs to you to mind your feet. Whilst I was too busy sniffing the daisies, brewing storm clouds above had gathered into two colossal eyes. Soon they would see me.

Chapter Fourteen

Falkirk reclaimed his pocket-sized empire later that week. Howell wasted not a minute in sharing the happy news, beaming his affable smile and clapping his hands. He had received the phone call from his superiors: Falkirk was much refreshed from his luxurious spa break, no doubt keen to get home by this evening, and today was Howell's last. We exchanged our mutual thanks and farewells.

And so, back to the gallery and grubby mattress it was. I had precious little of mine to clear from Falkirk's house, I made the bed, washed his dishes and took my clothes. Passing through Falkirk's lounge, out of the corner of my eye I saw seven or eight books strewn across the carpet. I laughed to remember Serge graciously tossing them over his shoulder.

Learning how to behave around Serge was an ongoing process of decoding. His humour could set you at ease one moment, you would assume you knew which way the ball was rolling – then, like the butterfly effect, a shadow falls across the sun. He disturbed the temperature of every room he entered. He was a walking thermostat, you could go away feeling elated, mystified or cloaked in thorns, him weeding out your precautions every step of the way. This cat's radar defied physics. Fortunately for me I (thought I) had tweaked those strings: I had called him 'a prick', I had reflected his sarcasm, partaken more than once in his sardonic duel of wits and gotten away with it; I fancied myself as in tune with his patterns as any hapless soul could be. So, quite impressed by my painstakingly acquired armour, I, self-proclaimed confidante, played the careful trooper, sniggering at his vandalism of Falkirk's lounge. I even felt a spoilsport for replacing the books on the shelf.

Rona Dean. Barely months their watchdog and already the expert, eh? Of course she would have denied this accusation, then absently fantasised regaling the secrets of her profession to a lecture theatre next time she swept St Patrick's floor. Anything to feel safer, lest ye judge too harshly.

I was not immensely sorry to leave the religious drug addict's villa, but for my concerns about certain thugs. I had had my dose of warnings, very soon so would Falkirk. The knife wound from Gaz was healing too fast, I'd wanted Falkirk to see it at its worst, fresh and bleeding to blame him with.

His violent fit at the hospital made the idea of seeing him again unthinkable, nevertheless, he was on his merry way back! *He may put money in my pocket, but what authority has that insufferable man, considering?* For insufferable was exactly how I saw him. His latest stunt with pinching the drugs had cost me up front in pain and injury, I felt determined to shove him into their limelight, *he* could deal with Prince Gaz for a change. *Let him bear his own burdens, and as to his health, may the Devil take the hindmost.*

With that bedtime thought I retired to the gallery.

The three were out on their prowls and their nocturnal game of piss-taking phone calls had ceased. I was being given more respect; in thimblefuls perhaps, but respect. With my library mission accomplished, their in–out patterns and occasional hellos had recommenced, nice simple routine.

It was getting harder and harder to ignore my mental battle of fear versus awe, most days I couldn't tell the difference.

Their knack for invisibility, for instance. There was too fine a line between fearing their mysteries and revelling in their confidence. Their stealth challenged logic; I would see them in my peripheral vision yet not see them; they would switch between spaces, disappearing and reappearing simultaneously. As for their sense of smell, underestimate that at your peril. But it was more than simply sight, sound, touch and scent: the four combined was like nuclear fusion, elevating their sensory range to an alternative dimension above the rest. I imagined they could *feel* people, the minutest change in wavelengths from however far away, the electrical charges in your body, infrasound through pavements, dozens of eyes on the back of their heads. Your world is far smaller; if your average cat or dog outwits your senses, what were my three masters capable of?

I switched off my lamp.

What time is it? How long have I tossed and turned? An hour already! Why am I not asleep?

We've all been there, the body is spent yet the brain jogs. Behind droopy lids my mind was restless, meaningless gibberish churned inside; the vestry radio, the rumble of launderette washing machines, the clip-clop of pensioners' shoes echoing down the nave, the beeping of traffic, the roadworks drilling on Delfour Road, a wolf whistle from civil servants in orange helmets and luminous yellow jackets. ... The roadworks.

My eyes opened.

The roadworks. The drilling. Going on for how long now? A month? Longer. Why were they drilling? What for? And Serge, so complacent on the subject. Archaeologists find underground tunnels all the time –. Oh now don't panic, Rona! Serge told you not to worry.

I changed position in bed and pressed my eyes shut.

That hole in the road had become too familiar a sight, pipes thin and fat, splayed like arteries in an autopsy, electrical cables running alongside them like rubbery tendons. The men needed ladders to climb in – ladders, Rona! And was the site looking bigger when I passed it today? It was. My God it's directly above their vaults. Serge is not worried so I shouldn't be worried, he has the authority, but …

I rolled over on the mattress. The image of naked pipes gaped behind my lids, crying for help like a wound, and wounds need healing, before the infection deepens, digging deeper, deeper. Cities always change, buildings change, sewers change, pipes change, sooner or later they … *Argh!*

I sat up.

It had started. The seed of paranoia was planted and spreading across my mind like a virus. Until I found out precisely why they were drilling, what for and how far, I would never be rid of it. Was it not my job to know, my job being the sole reason I was still alive? During the day they were helpless!

I swore there and then to keep a close watch on the roadworks. *I was wrong*, I thought, *mortally wrong to overlook this. If it's the worst news they'll shred me for not forewarning them sooner.* During the library cleanout, the sound of traffic had been a rare, distant hum, but a hum getting louder. *Oh God, oh shit, this is a real problem.* From that point on my anxiety was unquenchable; I could not afford to fall out of favour with them now, not after plucking their delicate wires as you would disarm a bomb!

Tomorrow, I resolved, tomorrow for my sanity I will investigate, soon as they switch on their machinery. Heaven's sake, they needn't discover the underground by direct contact; there are other ways of finding out, aren't there? Radio waves or geodetic signals, whatever it is; Christ, I'll be damned if they try that shit. The very thought of a dozen men in orange hats traipsing through *their* vaults, *their* possessions.

Now, you, on the other hand, Reader, might herald the elimination of a monster's lair as the world's best news and encour-

221

age me to feel the same. How run-of-the-mill. Congratulations. Though I didn't classify myself as a monster just then, I was already changing. You should know that by now, better than I did.

I ground my teeth. When you have a bee in your bonnet it's hard to be objective.

Tomorrow. Tomorrow …

I tried to sleep.

~

The next day began as no antidote. For starters, Falkirk was up with the lark and in church before I got dressed, an hour and a half before morning service. You couldn't mistake his start–stop strut.

I peeked over the balcony. Must say, for a yellow-toothed cocaine addict who nearly dislocated my arm the other week, he looked tip-top. Naturally I received no apologies for his behaviour in hospital, nor much of a hello for that matter.

I dressed and switched on the kettle in the vestry. No more biscuits, Falky, sorry. Invoice Howell. I watched Falkirk, waiting for him to be stationary. Our minister was never in the habit of relaxing. He strutted past me, doing a lot of evasive nonsense. He came in, dropped his bag, picked it up, carried it this way, carried it that way, on the counter, off the counter, took bibles and papers from his bag, opened it, closed it, and went off to do something else – buggered if I knew what – proud as a peacock. He asked me to pour the tea (he was nearer the kettle than I, by the way) and made to resume his strutting crusade. This morning charade in the name of Strut seemed phoney as hell; he was prepared for a confrontation. Unbelievable. *You really are unbelievable, Falkirk. Fine, want to play?*

'I was attacked last week, Falkirk.' My answer to his tea request.

He pirouetted. 'What was that?'

Oh, his innocent brow rising!

'You heard me,' I said.

He recoiled as if I had gone for his balls: is this the five-year-old who skipped up and down the nave just to hear her boots echo off the ceiling? Falkirk could easily have stolen from the crypt before Serge took his keys away, it added up, he was the thief. But for the briefest second I questioned my judgement.

'What on earth do you mean?' he said defensively. 'Attack? What attack?'

'Your friend. Gaz? I'm sure he'd be hurt if you didn't remember him.'

'Well, I can't predict how they're supposed to behave. They're nothing to do with me.'

What? Oh! I flushed.

He took a timid step backwards. 'I mean,' whined the holy martyr, 'you know they're not my sort of people. You surely know to steer clear of them.'

A classic. Accused blames the accuser for accusing the accused to screw with my mind, hoping I drop the subject while he opens his Get Well cards from the congregation.

'Stay clear of them?' I replied. 'Do you think I went up asking for *this*?'

Cue the big reveal. I showed him my midriff: but the bruises were nearly faded. I touched my neck: the cut was no worse than a scab. Failed by my own evidence.

Smug satisfaction dawned in Falkirk's eyes. 'Humph. I thought you were told to "let them in". You certainly seemed sure of yourself!'

Molten fury rose in me. Wait, is that him walking away?

'You pompous …'

'*What?*' he retorted, brimming with replenished confidence. 'Who do you think you're speaking to? I've dealt with Gaz for years and never put myself in careless danger. So if you disobeyed a certain someone's instructions …'

'I let them in. That's why it happened, damn you.' I was doing my best not to yell.

'Ha!' he cheered. 'So you blame me. How rich! I warn you Serge screws with your mind and you blame me. At least I know better than to anger a gang; anyone with common sense would.'

'Don't you dare talk to me about common sense, Falkirk. It happens you're the one who pissed Gaz off.'

'I'm sure I don't know what you're ta–'

'Heart palpitations my arse! I'll more easily believe you overdosed.'

'Keep your voice down!'

'The drugs you stole. The bastard gave *me* the kicking.'

Now it was Falkirk raising his voice. 'I'll never dignify that accusation with an answer! How dare you!'

'How dare I?'

'Well,' he raised his arms in a most antagonising make-my-day shrug, 'what else is there to say? Either you've been neglectful or thugs have simply behaved like thugs. And I'll thank you not to point vulgar assumptions in my direction again!'

I could have cried from frustration. The biggest problem was that I had nothing to prove Falkirk really stole from Gaz. Pride kept vigil on both sides.

'I'll fucking thank *you* to appreciate Gaz could've killed me!'

'As is demonstrably clear, he did not. If you think such inebriated people are more than cowardly smoke and mirrors, then you grew up watching too much television.'

My mouth fell open. *What am I, five? Am I actually hearing this? Look, there he goes, prancing out, his nose twice as high.*

I marched after him.

'In which case, Falkirk, you can test that when you speak to Gaz, which will be very soon, and, I quote, he'll "get back his stuff straight from your holy arse". Unquote.'

Part One

It was time for my cigarette break, an unscheduled one. Theatrical exits aside, it was not impossible I could be wrong, plus it disturbed me that Falkirk's prognosis echoed Serge's; Gaz, 'More coward than killer'. Calling the police was no option either. Protect the vaults, protect myself.

Speaking of which, drilling started from over a block away. I made my way to Delfour Road.

Not my favourite street. Whatever optimist built this dowdy idea of retail hubbub did so with the M40 in mind, connected to Delfour by and A-road: a commuter's route, the commercial connection, the taxpaying trail of innocent primates severed from their beds at the call of corporate puppet masters. Make your mark, clock in, get in line! Twenty years ago, much of Delfour Road did not exist; where my five-year-old self once knelt to blow dandelion puffballs and pick brambles in autumn, my twenty-five-year old self now pressed pedestrian lights to wait for the green man. The traffic was busy this time in the morning, both lanes were full, heading for the M40.

There is an ethereal liberation in being an outsider. I had no part in their daily routine, no family to support, no house, no bills, and not really any friends to write home about. I was a fly on the wall, a pigeon in the street, I might as well have been a hologram. Granted, the government may have my details, my disused bank account, my National Insurance Number, but where was I in its big machine now? I was flitting on air with my tobacco, time to kill, and one or two wolf-whistlers' brains to pick.

The state of the roadworks was worse than I thought. Not only did they extend closer to the churchyard, seven or eight civil servants completely disappeared into a caldera deep as … What was it Serge had said? How far above the vaults? The obstructive traffic cones were a nuisance, I would have to stand on top of the office buildings for a decent risk assessment.

I lingered awhile, finishing my cigarette. The workers jeered and barked orders at one another, stooping, lifting, carrying and climbing, calling to whoever was with whom, rowdy and cacophonous. A wave of reluctance swept over me. Their rough complexions and gruff voices were not my idea of inviting. I mentally scripted what would hopefully be brief but effective detective work, wearing my best Miss Friendly-Pretty-Curious-Citizen mask, lest any of them should get the wrong idea and follow up the encounter by chasing me with their phone number.

I smoked my cigarette to the filter, procrastinating, taking out more filter papers to roll another. *No, Rona, get your shit together.* I so seldom communicated with the outside world now, not that I missed it much. I walked shyly, indecisively, to the nearest hard hat. He was fairly young, younger than I, perched on the top rungs of a ladder. I did not want to have to shout over that deafening drill, it seemed to stop and start with a mind of its own.

'Hiya.' I waved.

'A'right, luv?'

'Hi, what's –?' The drill started up. No choice but to shout. 'What's the drilling for?'

'Replacing pipes, luv.'

'It's quite deep. How far is it going?'

Another man in hard hat and overalls butted in, older, with the manner of a foreman. 'G'morning. Can we help ya?'

Immediately I was discouraged. This foreman did not seem best pleased to see his younger workers distracted. Not an unkind man, if very much the law-abiding Jo Average; you could practically see the holes for puppet strings through his palms.

I repeated the question for him.

The foreman nodded in no uncertain terms.

'That's right, luv, installing more pipes and water drains ready for the new warehouse.'

Come again? A new building?

'*Ware*house?' I blurted, Miss Pretty-Friendly-Whatever-Face, poof, gone.

'The Mezdon Retail Storage Warehouse, lav. Council say there's a lot of potential space down there.' He was pointing directly into the hole.

The accursed drill chose that moment to resume digging, drilling down, down where there was *a lot of potential space*, into the last protective barrier between this world and Theirs. Mine, too.

I inwardly reeled. 'A lot of potential space' underground. A lot of vaults underground. The terrible, unflinching confidence in that foreman's voice, his voice of normality in the gloriously illuminated and spectacularly blind twenty-first century; the voice of humanity that went for pints with mates, had council meetings and reality TV, sold you phones for filming tragedies instead dialling emergency services, then served its over-populated self with storage warehouses for tax-dodging giants like Mezdon. The humanity that ripped up brambles and puffballs has just stumbled upon extra 'space' – no – a lot of 'potential space'! Humanity's greatest legacy – 'Wherever you are, Potential Space, if we find you, you're ours. *Nothing* will be left alone. Because we're Humanity! We are the Omega. We write things on paper and deem them higher than the laws of Nature and Physics put together. Know why? Because they're *our* laws! Three cheers! We have Mezdon, drills and councils, Mother Nature, what do you think you're gonna do about that? Nothing. Buy yourself a telly, eat chips and shut up.'

My gut rose up into my throat. *Tell me this is not happening. Potential space?* Sparks flew into my vision. How much did he know? How much did the damn *council* know? Maybe there was still time. I had to grab this chance.

'Potential space?' I asked, trying (bloody hard, actually) to steady my voice. 'What kind of space? How do they mean?

Where?'

Two other workmen pushed past me carrying more pipe casing. That did it for the foreman's patience. I was in their way.

'Sorry, luv,' he said, practically shoving me aside. 'Need to ask you to move. Look, if you've got questions, you're better talking to the council. Like I said, we take instructions from them. On ya go, we need to get on here!'

The young guy on the ladder was giving me a puzzled look. I couldn't blame him, I was ready for a swoon. No wolf whistles for Rona that day.

The council was my next lead. I groaned. Try telephoning any town council about anything, never mind roadworks, well-meant endeavours rewarding you with forty-minute waits in a queue of hapless citizens put on hold, chaperoned by the world's finest selection of elevator music that had no business being written let alone heard, cursing you with an earworm for the day. Should you have the good fortune to be answered (akin to winning the lottery jackpot), it seemed a matter of policy to pass you on to the village idiot. This could literally, no exaggeration, take all day.

'Well, which department is it you *need*, madam?' said a terse female voice on the other end of the phone.

'Planning and Development, please. I have an enquiry.'

'And what sort of enquiry, madam?' she asked in her politest what-the-hell-do-you-want voice. There were offices for Building Warrant Applications, Reviewing Warrant Applications, Conservation Applications, Regeneration Applications, Local Planning Guidelines, Enforcement Guidelines, Public Access Strategies, Permissions for Public Development, and General Complaints. Paper paper paper paper paper paper.

I answered her question, reiterating the foreman's addendum on the Mezdon warehouse.

'One moment, please.'

On hold. Ladies and gentlemen, more elevator music, cunningly designed to frustrate the hapless caller into hanging up. My cynicism was cut short by a prompt response.

'Hello?' A husky male voice spoke into my ear, I heard his moustache rustling through the receiver. 'This is Drake Windridge. Can I help you?'

I had temped in enough offices to recognise a council official when I heard one. I pictured a beefy man with permanent creases on his nose, blustering under a collar and unimaginative tie.

'Hello,' I said. 'I'm sorry to bother you. I was looking for anyone who could tell me about the roadworks going on at Delfour Ro–'

'Uh-huh.'

Ah, an interrupter. Oh goody, seen my share of those, too.

'I'm told Mezdon are building a new warehouse ther–'

'Uh-huh, uh-huh.'

Christ.

'– and the roadworks already go fairly deep, re-laying pipes and –'

'Uh-hmm?'

Is the guy even listening? An uncomfortable cough came from the other end.

'Well – ahem! – yes, I can confirm that Mezdon put forth a bid. If all goes well, construction is due to be completed and opened this time next year. You'll find the details on their website.'

A dismissive tone if ever I heard one.

'It's okay. I don't need that,' I said. 'It's the location itself I'm interested in.'

'There are no other planning bids at this time.'

All at once his tone darkened.

'Are you calling from the Local History Society, by any

chance? Because if so, I should think the National Trust made it perfectly clear, madam!'

Blimey. To hell with it, I hadn't the energy for another confrontation this morning.

'Excuse me?' I said. 'No, not at all. I don't even know them.'

He sounded unconvinced; I wouldn't want to be his secretary on a bad day.

'That may be the case, madam, but I've had to deal with a great many phone calls from the National Trust this month. As Regional Planning Divisions Operator, I find myself having to repeat here that I work for the best interests and priorities of Bronmeg Council. I hope this is coherent.'

'Why is the National Trust interested?'

'The site is historic, Miss, er …?'

'Cartright.' Giving false names was second nature to me by now.

'Within the next two months the deadline for their investigation expires. At the moment, their progress hangs in the balance. I am quite certain, Miss Cartright, the Mezdon bid will pull through.'

A historic site. So they know that much. I'd heard enough of this Windbag or Windridge anyway, whatever his name was.

'All right,' I said. 'Thank you for your time.'

'Yes. Good morning.' Bang goes his phone. Creep didn't even have the courtesy to let me cut him off first.

I wish I could tell you my day got better than discovering the National Trust switchboard used no elevator music. From them I learned that the archaeologist in charge was a man named Dudley Flotterstone, that he worked part time between the Trust and the university and, whaddaya know, just happened to have arrived at the Trust's office.

'Good morning,' I said, crossing my fingers. 'Is this Mister Flotterstone?'

'Speaking,' replied a clear and vibrant voice.

'Hello, I'm a resident of Delfour Road where I understand you're the expert with some interest in the building site there. I just spoke with a Planning Permission Officer at the council.'

'Haha, how nice for *you*!'

I decided I liked this guy; he felt as warmly about the council as I did.

'Hehe. Yes. They said I may speak with you about historical interest in the site.'

'What is it you'd like to know?'

'I was there today and the workers are digging very deep.' *Digging very deep.* I was sick of saying this line; my innards filled with sand at the thought. 'I suppose I'd hate to think a Mezdon warehouse would spoil any historic site.'

'I would hope not,' he replied. 'Rest assured the National Trust has dibs in this case, at least until Mezdon wields its corporate scythe! Haha. To answer your question, yes, we have reason to believe there are possibly remnants of settlements dating from 800 A.D. to the eleven-hundreds. Two to three hundred square yards of the area was religious in nature, according to some references of the period.'

A twinge of pride nipped me. *I could have told you the same word for word, and more, pal.*

'What are you planning?' I asked.

'That really depends. Soon as the GPR gets in it'll speed things up.'

Alarm bells went off in my poor head, which was set to ache for the rest of the day. 'Excuse me. GPR?'

'Oh, beg your pardon, Ground Penetrating Radar.'

Radar.

The alarm siren flared neon red. Radar, a ticking time bomb. The vaults would show up like jumbo brain tumours. From some murky dimension Flotterstone went on talking.

'… technique used in geophysics …'

The phone was slipping through my palm.

'… is ideal for this work and the penetrating waves relay a strong signal …'

My knees were going on strike. High tech remote sensing. Ground penetration. I had heard of this technique. It had been waiting, with me in denial, to be said out loud and here it brayed into broad daylight, hitting my dread right in the jugular. I hadn't wanted to believe it; it would end everything.

'… radio waves reflect variations in signal from any subsurface structures for us to build a picture. A lot of limestone on the site helps …'

I envisaged Flotterstone's enthusiastic smile, his educated eagerness.

'Which means,' he continued, 'the deeper they plan on digging, the better. That way the signal relays further when we get there, up to sixteen metres subsurface maybe.'

I was looking for somewhere to sit down, the cigarette I had lit lay smouldering and forgotten in a pavement crack.

Drills, radar. A warren of secret passages lighting up on Flotterstone's computer screen, next an avalanche of daylight filling the orbital cavities of a hundred sleeping skulls. *Why did I wait so long to find this out?*

A parched croak came from my larynx and somehow formed itself into words. 'And when is this being done?'

'Oh, the GPR in a few weeks, funding permitting. The roadworks are dithering with pipes for our leeway.'

'And, um,' I swallowed, 'what do you expect to find?'

'Rather speculative, we hope maybe some burial sites. You've probably heard of that great breakthrough with the crypts found under Coventry Cathedral, for instance, and there could be more. It's exciting but we have to await the GPR. For now, the best news is until that's out of the way, hot shots like Mezdon will have to tread their water, ha!'

So enthusiastic. He has to be so enthusiastic, doesn't he?

'Hello?' he says. 'Hello?'

I barely heard him, I was away somewhere else. The monstrous vaults, even Serge, suddenly looked so fragile. You're a nice man, Flotterstone, but I'll have you know I saw what they did to the last man who tried flushing them out, I saw the fist-sized chunks they removed from his love handles, his leg, quivering, I saw it.

'Hello there?' says nice Mister Historian.

My hearing returned with the reverberating *slam* of their smoking cupboard door.

'Hi, yes.' I was out of words. 'Thanks for your help.'

'Nice talking to –'

Tap. *End call.*

I sat on a public bench in Fergus Green.

Welcome to the crossroads. This was the hour I split into two separate Ronas. I very seriously debated not telling them. Not Falkirk, not Serge, not anybody. It was my hard-earned chance to liberate my conscience. Investigations concluded, I processed my findings, envisaged the outcome, and lost myself in it ...

A thunderous crash as bricks, pipes, cement and concrete collapse into their underground, reducing it to a naked trail. Darkness is raped by diagonal rays of daylight, solitude evaporates. Hills of jawbones scream up at the twenty-first century, some in protest, others crying bravo. Cobwebs melt in the solar radiation. Down comes more masonry, thick machetes of sun slashing further and further towards the Great Hall, towards me, *crash*-slash, *crash*-slash, *crash* ... Pow! Gone blind. Can't see. Serge? Edith? Hector? The next crash buries me, time, history, their treasures, their stories, them, forever. Exposed.

A week ago I would not have believed it possible. They were so mighty, so permanent. They had come this far. They had danced with me.

I don't have to tell them. I can go on with routine, have them trust me and they won't know. Silence is easy.

As easy as your sensuous silences with Serge, Rona?

I will not tell them.

I smoked cigarette after cigarette, promising this over and over. A week, I thought; that's all I need, a week of watching them trust me, it'll be so easy, *should* be so easy.

But I was torn.

Or could I drop them a hint? Yes, okay, that's fair, mention it in passing ... Then what? Wake up, Rona! Hint a syllable and Serge will see through you like tracing paper. Well done, the best way to invoke their wrath – withholding vital information!

Leaving them to their fate was the moral thing to do, the right thing, the human thing to do, and make good my escape while they were distracted.

Sure, Rona. How does Paris sound? Or Madrid? Or Athens? Derek liked it there, oh, wait a sec ... Uh-huh! Damned if you do or you don't, sinner.

This moral platform was not feeling quite so steady. The secret would not be so easy to keep, it was slipping away from me already, it was going to bleed, I could feel it. Which option, which sin, was greater?

I have grossly underestimated their hold on me.

No option satisfied me, nothing worked. I shivered in the October breeze, the opal pendant warm against my breast plates, demons and angels arguing on each shoulder. Their debate raged.

They're in danger. If they came this far for nothing then so have I, me, so-called 'deflector of meteors' locked into their world. Fancy reacquainting yourself with the outside world of human mayflies, Rona? *Could* you, now?

I was offended, that's what I was, offended for Them. They were death defined. They were also matchless. Plus, there was another issue at stake: being homeless and jobless; where to go?

Part One

I found myself helplessly watching my moral compass make a devious, unforgivable U-turn, slowly, carving my conscience with the ruthless logic of Mummy Nature.

After all, did ancient civilisations, say, the Native Americans, show contempt for the buffalo they killed, their staple diet? No! They respected them, respected all animals they hunted. My subterranean beasts respect me because I have a job to do, it isn't in their interest to hurt me, they said so, even gave me a birthday gift, look! And now they're at risk because human mayflies want a piece of the pie?

I stamped my foot, ignoring glances from gawky dog-walkers, unaware I had already made up my mind.

I stormed past Falkirk, not giving a shit whether he scowled at me or sang *Ave Maria.*

I spent the rest of the afternoon with the weight of potential catastrophe looming over me. Falkirk, thugs, drugs, were gone from my mind. I smoked myself silly in the churchyard, crouching on fallen headstones. The hours dragged. At cleaning, mopping and dusting I slouched, unable to concentrate. The roadworks drove me mad, even indoors I thought I heard it drilling into my ear with the proboscis of a giant hornet.

Where the Rona of hours previous had taken a vow of silence, a very strange, unforeseen desperation possessed me, blurring the moral crossroads to an intolerable itch until it didn't matter whether I told them or not – I just wanted rid of it! If there was no solution for the danger they were in, what difference did it make? The longer I waited, the sooner I needed to tell them. The urge to get it off my chest built into a fevered frenzy, for anxiety slows time, I longed for night to come and thought the day would last forever just to punish me.

I remember it was the 24th of October, sunset due at six. I became a slave to my wrist-watch and must have checked it a thousand times that afternoon, minutes apart. Patience is like an elastic band: stretch it out thinner and thinner and –! The sun lowered in the sky, shadows lengthened, and the more minutes dragged, the more irritable I became.

I was no stranger to the vaults now, and during my library shifts Serge or Hector had emerged as early as 5.30pm, encouragingly soon. I rocked with relief at this realisation, feeling part of the weight lift already. The hour hit four-thirty, with any luck I didn't have to wait much longer.

The shake of a lamb's tail and I was checking the time again. I considered and reconsidered, dithered. The lamb shook its tail once more, twice, thrice, I checked the time, considered, reconsidered … considered. *I'm not unwelcome down there, I know the underground, they know me.* I reconsidered. *No, I'll wait.* I went looking for something to do, smoked again, checked the time again.

I could have waited for them.

Eventually I dropped my brush and shovel, pacing furiously. I wanted *rid* of this burden, the proboscis of a man-made hornet, an itch demanding to be scratched, the cork on a bubbling bottle, the drill in my head, boring in, drilling, itching, *itching*!

I shudder to remember my audacity. The shame. That I had the nerve to worry, the inexcusably reckless nerve to underestimate more than just their hold on me. I could have sat in the nave with my hands on my lap like a good watchdoggy. I could have booked their taxis as per instruction on that morning's post-it note.

You really could have waited for them, Rona.

One of my earliest memories is of a vinyl record of nursery rhymes. Its cover is the first thing I see: sharp-featured kings, queens and animals with spiky hair and narrow slits for eyes, painted by some avant-garde illustrator. These figures gave me the creeps. And of all the typical mundane ballads every child learns, there was one track I never warmed to and never will. Why? To a four-year-old, some misinterpretations conjure up butterflies and bluebells; others spawn trolls under a bridge with tiny glowing eyes, bodies of coarse mangy hair and clawed hooves.

Oranges and lemons, say the bells of Saint Clemens.

Recorded by a children's choir of high-pitched harmonic catcalls, whenever the tune played I braced myself. I don't know why, but for me the off-kilter melody disguised a sinister countdown, a hungry ticking masked by innocent voices – for who could understand better than a child that those were really the bloodthirsty squeals of baby demons? Sharpening their incisors under angelic pouts, daring me to stand nearer the record player (*What's the time, Mister Wolf?*) for as long as I had the guts. Their game was this: wait until the final verse, and if I fled the room just in time, ran as fast as my small legs could fly before the last line was sung, I was alive. Trip or leave a foot in the door? Sorry, you're dead, they got you. In the end, I couldn't listen to the record anymore; the troll had set up home under the bridge and was waiting to sing. I hear it yet, writing this page with one hand, tapping my forehead with the other; it's in there.

Here comes a candle to light you to bed. Here comes –
Run, baby Rona. Run, run!

Everyone experiences these one-in-a-million coincidences when you think of something and then it happens, usually nothing earth-shattering. Unimportant factoids. Like Derek's words resurfacing as I passed the bloodletting vault on this day in October at 5:10 p.m. '*Because he showed me.*'

Ah yes, I remembered that conversation now. '*Has he not shown you yet?*' I hadn't thought of it in weeks. Were I more sensitive, I would have felt his words following me to the trapdoor, desperately fluttering at my nape with feather-light fingernails. Derek had trembled.

I could not reach the trapdoor bolt.

What? Come on, you've done this often enough!

My back wouldn't work. Another two inches and my fingertips would be brushing the bolt. Why couldn't I move? I was bent over like a photo of someone in mid-fall, my muscles and bones had turned on me, and though the urgency of Delfour Road prevailed, it was obscuring a separate, submerged awareness.

D-a-n-g-e-r

My own DNA knew it before I did, switched the controls and locked my joints so now all I could move were my fingers, wriggling mid-air like a speared bug. My body understood more than my mind.

Come on!

I gave up and stood upright to give my spine a rest. Almost at once I felt safer, I even retreated five steps, six, seven. The trapdoor grew smaller, lonelier … I turned to leave.

What, call yourself a watchdog? Big girls don't cry! They'll laugh at you! They know you, for Pete's sake! It's okay!

Every individual is two in one: who they are versus who they want to be, forever arguing until you can't tell who's who. Anyway, if They were nowhere to be found, I had a note prepared, summarising the urgency, ready to leave on their Hall table. All well in hand, you see!

Too late anyway, I've left my scent, they'll know I was here. If I chicken out now it may destabilise their trust in me. Not good.

When I lifted the bolt, it screeched so piercingly that I grimaced and my ears rang. Had it always done that? I delayed the trapdoor midway, waiting for the screech to dissipate, then gave a swift, almighty *pull*.

Clunk. It opened, a young scab ripped from the wound. It bled black.

Part One

~

At 5:50 p.m. on the 24th of October 2014 on Clayburn Avenue, a young woman named Rona Eleanor Dean staggered out of a wall in the north transept of St Patrick's Church, crying and screaming in livid terror. A beard of blood coated her chin and neck in a wide crimson band, soaking through her shirt in streaks. Salty tears cut through it in pink canals, stinging her mauled face. The glass of her torch was cracked, its light busted. She slammed the door of an apparent cupboard behind her, leaving a red palm print, and careered into a ceramic vase by the altar. It fell with a crash. She did not notice this at all. She slipped against the altar, gasping and choking, feeling her neck where fist-sized bruises were spreading around her glands, mandible and thyroid cartilage, already ripening from beetroot to purple. Gripping the tablecloth, she dragged herself up, quaking so badly it pulled off; its edges would be smudged maroon by morning. The torch lay on the floor, broken and forsaken. She tried to sprint. When she fell through the south aisle door into night air, she was still sobbing and shrieking. It will be nigh on dawn before she returns.

~

5:18 p.m., 24th of October. I am underground.

In front of me is a large circle of yellow torchlight ten feet in diameter, my field of view is a prisoner in its circumference. Outside of the circle is nothing. Inside it, the hollow outline of a wide doorway, high with a segmental arch decorated in stone carvings. This is the Hall.

A step forward. My shoe pierces the hush with a crusty scrape, a blasphemous disturbance. The atmosphere presses down on me like a clamp, holding me in place; my limbs have locked again. Woodwork and glass glint at me from a sleeping

239

city of sullen shapes beyond, framed in the archway.

It's freezing.

Inside the Hall. My guiding beam moves over the interior. I'm not alone; the face of the coffin-maker's clock stands aghast, every number a separate eye, fixing me. We contemplate each other a moment. The clock is the dominant figure here, taller than anything. Wherever I walk its face follows me. *What do you think you're* doing *here, girl?* Tick. Tick. Oranges and lemons.

Countdown. Here comes a candle, Rona.

I turn a full three hundred and sixty degrees. Crazy, no life could ever have graced this chamber, it's inconceivable. The grand piano stands by me, indifferent as the rest, and beyond the columns, small rooms drift in and out of the torch beam like oubliettes, immune to the light, revealing nothing. *They're not here.*

At the T-junction.

Looking straight down the east passage, contracting and expanding into nowhere. The walls shrivel inward, so tapered I cannot tell if it finishes in a dead end or a vanishing point. This optical illusion transfigures the route into a constricted channel of deceptive height.

I face this entity of a passage, separate from the rest and malevolent, and am at a loss. It seemed doable above ground, the plan was simple; *here*, sensory confusion switches coherence off-on, off-on. Was the note in my pocket a last resort or not? Do I actually have a note? Do I remember? I do remember Serge's tacit touch, his helpful gesture gliding on this uncharted ground. I can do it. They know you, remember that! They know you, this should be easy, long as I remember how to breathe.

Walking east, conjuring an imaginary permissive hand not unlike his, willing it to push me forward.

How far have I walked? Thirty-something feet? Amazing. I'm far beyond the trapdoor now. Heaven help me, I'm appraising myself. Each step I trespass here is a new victory for Rona, fuelling a chain reaction of more steps, and is this dreaded passage narrowing as it threatened to? It isn't! It's making way.

Found something. Two or three other rooms on either side, both wanting for doors, filled with sheeted objects and bones. Skimming my torch … There's nobody here.

Torchlight's wavering. Can't be, I replaced the batteries this morning. Getting my bearings with a flick of the wrist, a wave of nausea sways me as the torch leaps around convulsively, swinging me with it. Floor, walls, ceiling, everywhere cartwheels, stomach lurching, disoriented! About-turn, Rona. Where are we? How far from the T-junction?

The archway to the Hall is microscopic.

I'm deeper into the vaults than I have ever been. This passage, it has me. It's a personality unto itself. It was forbidding and coaxing me from the very beginning. Now I'm in its mouth.

Stop! I can see the end. You see it? There's an opening, more of a slit in the far right corner, two feet wide at most. I don't even know where I'm going, I *am* looking for Them, aren't I?

'Hello?'

A fail. My voice won't work. It sucked all breath from me with that single try.

'Serge? Edith? Hello?'

Sound tears overhead and I jump. Above, a rumble followed by another. The traffic! That jolts me onward; the proximity of Delfour Road is too alarming.

The dead end is very close now. *You've done well, Rona.* But my legs keep stopping. They're fighting me, pins and needles; I feel like I'm walking against a wind. I should still be able to see the Hall from here. I can't. Torch isn't finding it. I've been rolled downhill.

I'm there. I made it.

The dead end isn't much, a strip of coarse sandstone. This slit in the corner opens into an ancient section, too severe, slanting into a man-sized burrow.

Come on, torch, stop blinking. Hold out for me!

There is no brickwork in there, it's carved directly out of the bedrock, you can see the chisel marks. Soon as I'm in there I'll stop and call again, promise. Taking one more breath, tasting sand and ice. Oh God, I don't know ... I'm in.

Can't hear a thing. Atmosphere so dense my ears are closing up. The smell is fetid, metallic chalkiness, like their breath, thick with it. God, it's a cave of their lungs.

Get out of here.

Okay, yes-yes-right-okay, turning round, Rona Dean, don't think, just walk, we're leaving. (*Help me*) Yes, good, that's it, go, faster please, no ask me later, just go, *go*, good, that's it, oh God, please, nearly, keep-moving-keep-moving. Rocky sides jabbing my ankles, prickly gooseflesh, breathing shallow –

Everything just went black. Someone has taken my torch.

It darted and snatched me, quick as a cat. I have been lifted clean off the floor and restrained against the cave wall. The torch clatters and clicks back on.

What glares back is the most horrific thing I will ever see in my life.

You want to know what it looks like. You expect words. You think they will do? Maybe for you. Not me. I was there. How do you describe a colour without reference? How do you express a musical note in words? Human language is impotent here. I can only offer you features, and they on their own, insult. Because to see it, you go mad. There is no cure.

The face, was animal rage. The eyes, ebony fire. The mouth ... The mouth was a fury, a promise of death, the last thing you see before you die. Its top lip curled far back. The upper jaw casually dislocated from its skull and thrust forward like a shark's. From inside its upper gum, like extra teeth, two long, perfect, retractable sickle fangs slid out.

The noise that roared forth was a stretched, demonic rasp.

'*BAAAAAAAAAAD!*'

It was Serge. And he showed me.

What's the most frightened you have ever been? How did you react? I mean your *real* reaction, your automatic reaction, the kind that takes your dignity away.

Say night transforms your cosy household objects into creeping gnomes with triangular canines. The light switch dies, you are terrorised by noises, whispering, scratching, an inhuman shriek of laughter. Your nerves spasm, you look in the mirror – something unnameable with no face heaves you on through the glass.

You discover the body of your soulmate in the street and hope they wake up. You kneel. The crows have taken the trouble to remove their spectacles, leaving tendrils trailing from the optic nerves that loved you at first sight.

You watch a horror film at home, alone. Hardly recovering afterwards, you open the bedroom door to a festering zombie, leaking pus, sighing triumphantly down your gullet, '*Haaaaah …*'

In movies, those who scream die. Heroic survivors grasp a weapon or have the sense to duck. I'll bet you imagine yourself doing the same.

I did, too. I thought I'd be braver. I believed I was tougher. The jump of your heart, alert call of the great ape Hominidae: your scream, the deciding factor of your death in that room. Do you think you can conquer that evolutionary trait faster than the millionth of a second it takes to conquer you?

I am quite sure that October day was the worst of my young life. That day I was stripped down to the core. The brave new me, my every stitch of so-called armour pieced together weeks in the making – was a lie. I'm going to describe to you how

Young Rona was effectively murdered that day, and would never return.

The abomination held her off the floor by the neck. She thought she knew them well, thought herself above screaming like the primate she was. She died there, her dehumanising screams spewing forth like a dam, loud and shrill. She could not believe she was screaming, could not believe it. Her dying thought.

The figures of Edith and Hector materialised from an unseen vent not far away. I did not know them, their faces as misshapen as the demon pinning me. My feet scrambled to support my weight off the floor as he crushed my throat.

The creature blazed an exultant scowl.

'Look what the earwigs dragged in!'

It revelled in my screams, restraining me with an arm strong as a girder.

'Couldn't resist, could she? Little Miss Gothic thinks she's best friends with us now?!'

The monster's face breathed into mine. Pure outrage shone from his orbs.

'Who do you think you are?' he smouldered. 'Hmm? What do you think you are? Where the fuck does she think she is? How about it, Eddie, what does scurrying beastie think she is? Oh, but she must be *soooooo* special! What a valiant thing! Is she valiant, Heck?'

'Not!' yelled Hector.

'Why don't we find out?' said Edith.

Serge tightened his vice grip on my throat, blocking my cries. My thrumming pulse stood out on my forehead.

'What do scurrying beasties like her do to smaller beasties on her bed?' he called.

'They squish them!' crowed Edith and Hector.

Serge's free hand moved out of view and returned pinching a bulbous spider over my face. The arachnid fought, pedalling the air with eight spindly brown legs. Serge's thumb and finger squeeeeezed … My eyes closed.

Plssssssh! Thick liquid squirted. I wheezed pitifully as it congealed on my eyebrow in sticky blue strings.

Edith shook her head regretfully. 'Why must they scurry about?'

'Because they know no better,' Hector growled.

Serge's pupils were dilated to full-on black irises, and they did not leave me once. 'Just a matter of time, wasn't it?'

He leaned in close. Intimately close. I was powerless, couldn't draw away. With searching eyes, his voice dropped to an awful dragon's purr.

'What do you want? Hmm? Want me to fuck you, is that it? Convert you? Join the gang? Get yourself tongued? Is that what she wants? C'mon then!'

With this, he made a ferocious charade of demonstrating the insinuation. I could only move one thing, and that was my head. Side to side I jerked it, tears running, trying to escape his lips invading mine; the only reason I dodged him by millimetres was because he let me. His vindictive grin bobbed left and right with me, following my mouth, making a farce of it.

Right – 'Where is she?' – Left – 'Where is she?' – Right – 'Where's she gone?'

For however long this agony went on, Edith and Hector raised an uproarious cheer of savage caterwauling, applauding, laughing and howling malicious shrieks.

'Hahaha! Yes! Go on! Go on, Serge! Go on, Rona! Haha! She's there! Go on, fuck her! Haha! Get her! She wants it! Catch her! Fuck her! Aww! She's over there! Go on, Rona! Ahahahahahaha!'

The humiliation sliced me down the middle with a guillotine. What happened next, Serge could have done whenever he liked; the professional predator knew how to prolong psychological torture before the physical.

'Where is she? Where is sheeee …? *There* she is!'

There. His mouth lunged for my lower lip and snatched it between his, detonating an explosive cheer from Edith and Hector in the background. Serge sucked and squeezed until I thought he would tear off the chunk down to my chin. The more I struggled the more it hurt. Then –

God!

Two red-hot stabbing needles. I heard my flesh pop. Punching pain set off fresh tears like a tap, rivers of metal flooding my palate as fire erupted across my mouth. My pulse found a new place and thudded protest against his sickle fangs lodged in my meaty lip. Warm blood caked my chin. *Not happening. Can't be happening to me!*

My squirming became wild hysteria when I felt his tongue careen into my mouth, caressing where his hooks snagged and pulled me like fish bait. He lapped. Lapped and swallowed. *He's tasting me!* I lost all sense of reality then, my body descended into writhing delirium, arms flailing, thrashing and kicking aimlessly. Pushing Serge was like trying to push a redwood, I was a wriggling fly.

As I heaved desperately for air, the blood pooling in my salivary ducts gargled its way to my windpipe and I spluttered, drowning in my fluids. A dribble of regurgitated blood bubbled from my nostril. I couldn't breathe at all now and the applause from Edith and Hector was dissipating, sinking away as foamy light-headedness took over. Soon I would have lost consciousness.

I didn't know he had released me until after my knees hit the ground; if I had broken a bone and noticed, it would have been a miracle. I crawled onto all fours, grovelling like a dog, reconciling with my lungs, my shocked diaphragm slowly remembering how to function. A neat cluster of droplets spattered from my chin to the floor in a bloody fairy ring, drip-drip-drip. Edith and Hector were silent.

Next thing I knew I was being hoisted up by the scruff like a scarecrow and the torch being stuffed into my pocket. A voice hissed in my ear: 'Soon past your bedtime.'

This unearthly voice I knew. It had taught me that secrets age the heart. It had told me stories. It had talked about stained glass windows. It had never hurt me before. I was beaten and bled, but it was this, hearing this voice I thought I knew, that broke my heart, that broke *me*.

I was shoved out of their tunnel.

Physically incapable of running yet, I doubled over, stripped of pride until the jammed oxygen could pass my tubes.

All I thought I was made of, my strength, my integrity, disintegrated around me, and in front of those three it was more than I could bear. Each blubbering sob symbolised Failure, thus triggering the next, and the next until my tears were irrepressible. I awaited more abuse from them. Mock the trampled schoolgirl on full display to pillory, everyone, aim your crossbows.

Incidentally they could not have been calmer. Motionless in there, detached as owls in trees, jaws and fangs retracted. Serge pressed his palms on both sides of the passage, sagging idly forward, his lips and jowls bright with blood, my blood. Jesus Christ, that's my blood.

'As everyone's ostensibly awake now,' he said, '*is* there anything to which we owe this profound displeasure?'

To hear his vocal cords sound through that creature, as if it were miming a tape recorder – Impossible! It pushed me over the edge. *Oh no, please, that can't be your voice. No, Serge, that's* your *voice coming from that thing no I can't handle that I can't* process *that!*

'I …' My vocals were phlegm. I touched my unrecognisable throat. 'It … it, to warn –' I coughed, spraying the floor red. '… the road.'

'Pardon?' he blasted.

My nostrils were clogged with bloody mucus and speaking put knives in my tonsils. I couldn't find my breath, couldn't talk without pulling for air, and whenever I did, another rising sob competed with it, lurching my body up and down in gasps.

'The … radar, Delfour, they're using ground rad–'

No use, another coughing fit took me. Besides, my cause for being there, any cause in the world, seemed too preposterous now.

'That's *all*?' Serge exclaimed. 'Thank you, Professor, and when I need to learn my A-B-Cs I'll drop everything.'

He shooed me out with a scathing wave of disgust.

I ran.

I ran and ran and ran. Maybe I fell several times, I don't know; I think I vomited at one point. No idea where I was running or for how long, no remembrance of wherever I sheltered that night. I had no money, no plan; sooner or later I would have to crawl back, but for now I was running, running from undead snakes and the miserable wretch that was me. And from Falkirk, from his words. I tried to outrun it, I promise; his voice was faster than me. I stupidly hoped my boots hammering on the pavement might drown it out, ghosts careering at my tail, grasping my shirt, booming in my ears, all copies of Falkirk, Falkirk, Falkirk! – pulling at my wrists in a tug of war, pushing me on and off the curb. The pounding of his voice, it wouldn't leave me alone, it chased me through streets, through parks, through hills of autumn leaves, through housing estates and gutters; called from alleyways, from car horns, belted foul spittle, beat me with wicker canes, brayed behind my eyes, grabbed me in dreams and pulled me to its skinned, red skull.

'*You have no idea how brutal he is!*'

No idea how brutal he is!

No idea how brutal he is!

No idea how brutal he is!

Part One

Nighty-night, Rona.

PART TWO

It gifts the bearer with acutest sight
But clouds all other eyes with thickest night

Marbodus, 1060

Chapter One

Dawn.

I remember crouching, hugging my legs on a fallen gravestone in the churchyard. The streets were lifeless, not a cloud in the baby-blue sky save for clumps of muddy lavender on the horizon, while Venus, your morning star, strained through daybreak for her departing peep. Dawn is a secretive gift to witness; it carries the comfort of feeling you are the last person in the world. The air was pristine at this hour o'clock and flimsy dead leaves carpeted damp grass around the headstones, reviving my senses with earthen aromas.

Clear sky intensified the autumn chill; I hunkered in a nonstop shiver. Out all night without suitable attire, I had tried every trick imaginable: curling into a ball, walking briskly, rubbing my hands, breathing on them and tucking them into my sleeves. But it was hours before I'd truly registered the chill, and even then it couldn't push through the storm in my mind without a fight.

My inflamed lip hung out, as swollen and raw as I felt inside, bare and fluttering in the open, battered down to numbness. If you had seen me you would think me a corpse; bleeding, blanched and unresponsive, newly crawled up from the soil. My eyes would not blink at you. Shock, terror and betrayal scraped all human solicitude from me with a steel file. Whatever I saw I did not see, I was incapable of speech, no thread of logical cohesion ran through my brain. I was wiped away. The existence of Past or Future being unbearable, I clung on to the indispensable Present, the barricade of an eternal Here and Now, for survival. This is how I would see out the rest of the day.

I forgot about my day job; schedule and routine were fantasies. I sat in the graveyard, the vestry or nave, stiff, dumb, the rest of civilisation tactile as a television screen in a drab waiting room. They say that if someone or something hits you in the face, you reel in a punch of white light; for me, the shock wave of last night worm-holed into a purgatorial plasma and enveloped me in it, a stranger to myself.

The abyss I strayed into was bottomless, and when you're in permanent freefall the world is forever changed. Ironically, falling both imprisons and elevates you: only *I* was tangible today; people passed me, congregations came and went, voices laughed, heels clipped, birds flew overhead, bench legs squeaked, aeroplanes grumbled, car engines started, ringtones chirruped. Plasma, all of it. Empty plasma.

Did Falkirk spot my facial makeover? Of course he did. Did he say anything? No words from him, good or bad, could have baited me in this aftermath. It was his lack of words, that did.

Lunchtime. 'Rona. Kettle, will you?'

I rose from the vestry table. Kettle, water, teacup, spoon. What comes next? Sweetener. Only two teabags left, no coffee. Unopened litre of milk. The grumpy kettle gargling into life.

In keeping with our ill-spent camaraderie, Falkirk's attention, vocal and visual, had so far lived up to its daily habit, that is to say negligible. Naturally, callous fate made today the exception. I was fingers and thumbs with the teabags, breaking one, not concentrating, not noticing Falkirk peer at me from two feet away.

The kettle declared its chore done with an aggressive trill. I reached for the handle and saw him. Caught gawking, he hadn't the decency to recoil, but went on gawking, taking in the free freak show of my purple throat and puffed lip at his absolute leisure. Falkirk's slant-eyes and neck sticking forward like a taxidermy pigeon made him explicitly revolting. He lapped up the scene with more sessile vigour than Serge's tongue. Yes, look, uh-huh, there he gawks at my brutalised neck, taking in my butchered lip. Seen enough yet, Falky? Oh, no, there he goes again! Down and up, peering even closer. No discretion, is there? Not a shred. Christ, he's about to smile.

'Sugar or sweetener?' I said stonily. You wouldn't have recognised me, it would be a day or two before my crushed voice box recovered. What Falkirk heard was the grating of an old crone.

'Sorry?' he said, addled.

His eyes made an overdue trip north and caught mine: what he saw there wiped the beginnings of his toxic little smirk right off the plate. He took a frightened step back. Wise idea.

'Er, er, sugar, one sugar,' said the halfwit.

'Too late,' I said, trapping him in my gaze, holding up a substitute. It was my turn to smile, as slowly and savagely as I fucking liked. 'We've only got sweetener!'

Falkirk moved away as if I were possessed. Perhaps I was.

Yessss, go on, Falky. Hope you enjoyed the show. Think you can crack me in your victory? Think I care how accurate your warnings were? Does that mean I have to start liking you, Minister? Go. Get out of here.

He went. I spat in his teacup and poured the kettle.

Falkirk had nothing to say about any bloody palm prints on doors or tablecloths, because interestingly there were none to see. Some hygienic gremlin appeared to have saved me the chore.

A message awaited me on the altar.

Rona,

River Street, 8pm & Dover Street, 4am.

Check on Derek, he's ill.

E

Taxi instructions, full stop. No hint of reproach. Business as usual. They would find their orders carried out by a frosty recipient; anything from a scribbled hi–bye to a foghorn would have had equal effect. A thicker shell grew on this hollow watchdog, the girl of yesterday was a hundred years ago.

Ghoul. A fucking ghoul, that's what I am.

I knew no one, I understood no one, nor had I any inclination to. To hell with them. It didn't matter, little if anything did. I functioned mechanically, booking their taxis and phoning Derek. No answer, so I left him a message.

St Patrick's was locked up by 7 p.m. after a church meeting with the local charity group. Instead of tidying their communal chairs and biscuit trays away, I sat at the altar writing a reply to Edith, a line or two about phoning Derek, short and less than sweet. I planned to leave it there, hibernate in the gallery, smoke with a bottle of wine and sleep the world away.

My plans were to be delayed.

I heard it and stiffened. No other oak door in the world made a sifting noise like that. The sound had rooted through to my bone marrow since August, locking and unlocking, patrolling my dreams as a permanent earworm. Some nights I woke up with a start, unsure if I'd heard it or dreamt it. I'll hear it for-ever.

Cli-klick-sifffffffft

I hunched over the table, pretending to be busy, pointless as it was.

Here came his bright footsteps, brisk and springy with life, dressed in his usual casual trousers and business jacket that curiously always married well. The nave echoed his entrance as if to jump up and applaud, happy to see him, followed by the demure Edith and Hector.

To my utter dismay the star of the show immediately fetched a chair and made straight for the chancel. I saw he intended to sit opposite me, transforming the altar into a temporary office.

'Hiya,' he said, in a playful fashion that could only be Serge's.

I remained hunched and downcast. *Go away. Leave me alone.* I think I muttered something about the taxis and leaving a message for Derek.

'Thanks,' he said, clearly uninterested.

He made himself comfortable in the seat, coughed, and re-clined.

'Okay. Rona,' he began, very business-like, 'I don't think you're right for this job.'

I looked up.

He said it. Just like that. Hardly a hello, forewarning or in-troduction.

'What?' I said.

He slowly shook his head.

And that, right there, Reader, is what broke the ice once and for all; the way he shook his head, the pretentiousness. My anger quivered like an earthquake.

How dare he? After all this time … All this time! How fuck-ing dare *he?*

You'd think I'd be delighted, wouldn't you? Escape! Any

earlier and I might have sung to high heaven for joy, but to have this, *this*, thrown in my face after everything I'd been through, everything that had changed me. My face said it all: I keep my mouth shut and my head down for you three; my life revolves around you; I let you wire your way into me with your gifts, your dancing, your books, your charm. I forsake my humanity covering up your nightly bloodbaths; I bleed an old man; I get beaten up, bullied, humiliated, mocked. And attacked. I take it all on the fucking chin. Now you have the nerve to sit over there in your smart outfit and tell me … tell me *what*?

I could have left, couldn't I? Found a hostel somewhere, ventured forth into the so-called real world. Are you aware though, Reader, that *my* blood was now on this church too, bound from childhood, knotted with the present? It was not a question of shelter. When you leave a piece of yourself some-where, it's like losing a limb. I was scarred irreparably, but despite this I had ploughed through gauntlets. And now, now after all that, to hear his words, it was still crushing.

Before I knew it, I was steadily rising from my seat, sim-mering, slowly tearing up the note, polite timidity a thing of the past.

'You patronising … Oh no, I wouldn't be right. Ha! Last nail in the coffin of my humiliation, natural-born loser lives with three monsters and even they reject her! It would only be me, wouldn't it?! I don't belong anywhere, I –'

Serge lolled his head back and raised his hands theatrically. 'Oh God, the *drama*!'

Not quite enough to shut me up. His stinger of an opening line, 'I don't think you're right for this', was a grenade and the blast hadn't settled yet.

'Oh, don't mind me, Serge!' I retorted, all sarcasm, gather-ing up the shredded note. 'You've made up your minds, fifty steps ahead as usual! I'm Rona, remember? I'm supposed to be pathetic, no –'

Serge raised his voice like a parent, slicing a firm hand through the air for emphasis.

'Can you – just – let – me finish, please!'

He pointed to my chair, compelling me to sit.

'You see, Rona,' he said, playing with his fingers, 'when I asked weeks ago if you could handle this, I was thinking out loud. We've been debating this for a while. This isn't about yesterday, forget that.'

Forget that. Forget about that? I glared fresh venom at him.

'And you can pack that in!' he reacted, unyielding as an austere schoolmaster. 'You have no idea how lucky you are it was I who found you last night. Had it been Edith or Hector, by now whatever's left of you would be down that old well with the others.'

I whitened.

'Oh yes, Rona!' he said. 'And you couldn't blame them either, they'd only be acting on instinct to protect themselves. Fortunately for you, I'm more experienced.' He leaned forward, louring at me with a resentful hiss. 'And that's very … *very* … hard-earned, my lady!'

'Listen to him, Rona,' came Edith's cutting voice, arms folded, resting against the cupboard.

Serge reclined and continued. 'What we're trying to explain here is, over time this will fade you out. I've seen it, not only with Falkirk.'

I shook my head with a degraded smile.

'Oh, no, no, no. Please do not compare me to that man. Not Falkirk. Just don't, okay?'

'Oh?' he said, cool as ever.

'No. You can't compare us. Don't do that to me as well, Serge. Not someone I loathe so much.'

'Do you?'

'Yes.'

'Why?'

'You know why!'

'Really?'

'Yes …' I was going to say more. A portcullis fell. *Shit.*

'Really?' he repeated, saying what I knew he would. 'Are you two such chalk and cheese? He was twenty-five once, or hadn't you noticed?'

I walked into that, a resolute rabbit in headlights of my own ignition. I searched my mental list of reasons for hating Falkirk. In my confusion it handed me a blank sheet.

Serge's acumen was written all over him. He relaxed, locking his hands behind his head, elbows out. 'Is it sinking in yet?'

'He stole their drugs and got me into trouble,' I said.

'No, he didn't.'

The penny dropped. Oh … Rona, numbskull, I should have known!

'We did. Naturally!' he confirmed, smiling. 'Down the hatch. Or water well in this case.'

They sniggered.

Falkirk's triumph soared. The sky reflecting off Gaz's switchblade, Falkirk's smugness when I accused him, the fool they'd made of me.

My rising fumes smouldered. If I had to look at Serge's self-satisfaction a moment longer I don't know what I would have done. It was all I could do to keep a lid on my outrage by fidgeting; my hands twisted into tight fists, squeezing waxy shreds of the note still caught in the webbing between my fingers.

'Why do that,' I breathed, clamping my temper, 'may I ask?'

'We warned Falks to keep them out. He didn't. The evening after they assailed you with – what was it, a bottle? – Falkirk took an overdose.'

Edith joined in. 'He accurately predicted an angry visit from us. It was Serge who found him, Serge who rang the ambulance.'

No sooner had Edith spoken, something extraordinary happened. I heard Falkirk's voice. Clear as crystal, nearly startling me from my seat, his exact intonation and inflection syllable for syllable. A comparison springs to mind here: how much do you know about ravens? *Corvus corax*, the most intelligent birds on the planet. Are you aware, by any chance, that they have miniature tape recorders for voice boxes, more than a mimic, almost a carbon copy?

Well, I saw no Falkirk in the church with us, and if not for Serge's mouth, you have my permission to conclude a raven was hiding under the altar table.

'Ambulance. I have a history of-of ca-cardiac arrhythmia, c-can't breathe, can't get up, verapamil and amiodarone, took too much, feel sick …' For the finale of Serge's performance, I was treated to an inarguable impression of Falkirk's vomiting noises, delivered with minimal effort.

'Then,' Edith continued, 'we did the necessary with their cocaine, or heroin, whatever it is.'

'Wait,' I said, head in my hands. 'Why put *me* in Gaz's firing line?'

'Chance,' Serge answered. 'You get torn jeans and a scratched neck. Cry us a river. I told you what your attacker is. I never guess blindly. I've had enough injuries to dismember me, but' – he threw a frivolous wave – 'ahoy! Here I sit. They shan't be using the church again, which benefits us either way.'

I cupped my temples and gathered my thoughts, pacing from the trees to see the wood. 'You rigged this,' I said. 'You know Falkirk needs me, and you're trying to sack me?'

Serge commanded that mundane chair like a new throne.

'That man you claim to hate so much, recommended you, not yours truly. Which,' he royally crossed his legs, 'brings us full circle back to the point. This job will scour you out until you fold. Don't kid yourself that watchdogs with passable intelligence and no morals aren't our preference. Now, that gets tricky in a Daniels situation, but no riskier than someone,' he raised a damning finger at me, 'out of their depth. Yes, we know you're deep, we know you're sensitive, well done, lovely. But you're *too* deep, you're *too* sensitive. Everything affects you, you absorb it like a sponge, and frankly we're getting sick of playing gentle with you. The three of us are battered, scarred and, I dare say, survivors of wars that would fuck you catatonic. Serious watchdogs know to expect that.

'Rona, what if chance drew a policeman, nice buck with a wife and family, to our gate? Three guesses on what it'd be your job, as our trusty watchdog, to do? … No, I didn't think so. What good are you to us,' he gestured vehemently at the front portal, 'if they walked out of that door alive? Even Falkirk could deal with it sooner than you – What? What's *that* look for? That's why your pride hurts worse than your lip. You've played polite with us for England, but this place will turn your essence to powder like the underground dust; most of what you tread around our vaults is pulverised bone fragments, didn't you know that?'

My mind's eye saw the fairy circle of drops I'd left in the sandy floor of their cave, tears and blood.

'Do you understand me?' he demanded, frowning.

I nodded. How else could I answer that damning lecture? Sitting there taking arrow after arrow fired through my tender bosom of crippled pride.

'So what can you do to persuade us to keep you?' he dug. 'Sit down and write out *I Will Not Trespass* a hundred times?'

Another missile. I looked from Hector, to Edith, to my introspective inquisitor. Deciding what to say next was tiptoeing across a minefield of atom bombs. I took a breath between each sentence, treading carefully.

'You say the "serious" watchdogs. Have I not done all I'm asked? Have you no faith in that I'm different? That you're the only souls close to me?'

'Well, you've seen for yourself the teething issues.'

'You said to forget about last night.'

He lunged forward over the table again. 'But what about the future, Rona? Sorry to flatten your ego but if you think we're having this conversation for your benefit you're *so* far out of your depth you may as well pack up and leave this church *now*.'

Edith interposed. 'Serge just acknowledged your sensitivity. Ergo sooner or later we wake up and you're gone. What happens then?'

'I know better than to bolt!' I protested, cross-examined on the witness stand. 'I'm too far removed now.'

I felt tiny. They have seen so much, so many eras, so many Ronas, what could I do? Nice one minute, sadistic the next; how the hell can anyone imagine what sort of personality is born out of hundreds of years? It spoke through them. Try competing with that!

Serge twiddled my pen, tapping it on the tablecloth. In the stillness of the church it was a hammer.

'So?' he said. 'What's to do?'

'Serge, I ran out. But I came back. Though my lip looks like a fish, thank you –'

'You're welcome.'

'– I still came back. Dammit, I …' I trailed off.

'We know.' He sighed mournfully.

There was a long pause. Serge confounded me. He was not angry, so what was he? His reticence formed an impenetrable cap over another emotion. I tried guessing what.

Okay, Serge, you win.

Unable to tiptoe any longer, hurting, I snatched the pen from him and set to work on a fresh sheet of the notepad.

They're going to drop me. I don't know where I'll end up, spending the rest of my life questioning what they're doing and where they are. I won't have the heart to come near my church again. I won't go out at night, no street is safe, I know what hunts the hunter. Will I be a part of the herd now? Your live-stock? Fair game? Potential prey? Am I off the privileged list? Why did I bother arguing with you, Serge? I'm out of ideas.

I finished writing, ripped off the sheet, dumped my watch-dog keys on the paper and slid the lot across the table. *There you go, Serge, little bye-bye present. Keep it, throw it down the well, frame it on your wall, whatever. For better or worse.*

He looked at the paper, then at me.

I WILL NOT TRESPASS 100 TIMES

An almost indiscernible change drifted over him. The way he sat there like a Renaissance portrait, inert, serious, cloudy. We studied each other with an exchange of solemn rumination, communicating I know not what, but if I urged him to keep me at all during that interview, if there was a gulf traversed or some soft, congenial click – it was then, without words; any-thing said beforehand was a clunky prop; Edith and Hector had no part in it. I honestly believe that during those silences he couldn't read me. I think he chose not to. What was it he didn't want to find out?

At length I repeated myself, silently mouthing the words.

'I came back.'

Serge saw. He whispered, in the voice that used to flow through me like warm silk; I would never trust it again, though this time it carried an elusive trace of sadness.

'Do you want to stay?'

'Yes,' I said, barely louder than he.

Instantly he stood.

Switch, here rebounds his officious mask. 'The gate needs oiling. Use up what's left in the can.'

It was like snapping out of a trance, Serge heading out with the others, adjusting his jacket.

'Cheery-bye,' he said. 'Don't dream.'

They left.

Don't dream. What an odd thing to say. I got up to clear away the chairs, lost in thought.

I doubt Serge was done in his assessment of me. The cornerstone of his lethal charm was to mask those cogwheels with childish cheekiness, yet like any atmosphere, his had weather: clouds and snow, sunshine and storms. Make no mistake, Serge was a button-pusher through and through. Except for his tone a minute ago, '*Do you want to stay?*' ...That was new.

I paused suddenly, a chair under my arm.

That *was* new. That was a Serge I hadn't seen before, a million times as old as it was young. Like wind breathing through an untouched forest in winter. Just how many layers were in that man?

I reclaimed my keys to the cupboard and gate, still lying on the altar. Keys he had not repossessed. What he *had* taken, was my note.

Chapter Two

The week that followed was a lonely stretch of drizzle and drear. The weather sent in daily curtains of surly cloud and misty mornings while the afternoon winds transformed diagonal rain into pesky spikes, nailing me with pins. Rain became sleet. Sleet became hail. Halloween arrived.

Having no willpower to relive my childhood days by kicking up autumn leaves, I carved a pumpkin. I carved one every October, a personal tradition of mine, hence a comfort; it took more than faces on vegetables or witches on broomsticks to frighten me. The pumpkin was enormous this year. I cut two cruel pie wedges for eyes, pointing inwards, a triangular nose and a mouth of jagged teeth. Madness, I hear you say. It didn't upset me; my annual friend for a night was to its jaded artist a pathetic pussycat. I'd always personified him, too, he had his own name, *Michael* if you please. People usually commented on how scary he was. A year ago I would have agreed with them.

Routine continued. I rarely saw them, received no verdict on our meeting, and as for Delfour Road, they could stick it. *I* certainly had no plans to reopen the subject.

All Hallows Eve. A fittingly inclement night. Gusts whistled and stormed the church in circles. An elder tree, buffeted by wind, took out its ordeal on the chancel window, battering and scratching it in bitter lament. I switched off the lights and set my pumpkin on the altar. He beamed at me, his role reprised. *Hello again, Rona! How are you? And my, what a year since!* His fiery wedges flickered fervently as they explored the church around me, and soon his projected face was Brobdingnagian, pic wedge eyes swallowing up the aisles, his sharp nose hitting the ceiling, and over my church gallery an enormous set of zig-zagged jaws seemed to open, pulsating like a trapped nerve just above the balcony. My hollowed companion. For years I had sculpted the same design, we knew each other well.

What a year.

My smile failed. I stared at him, through him until my corneas stung in his tea-light pupils. My carving was off, the pie wedges were too slanted and mournful, or was it me? I allowed the tea candle to draw a tear. What a year. Where are you, Rona, where have you gone?

Michael carried on his ignited laughter, happy just to be there, the dying reminder of an innocent me. I wanted them to see it.

What a torpor I must have fallen into, to ignore the sound of their door opening. Michael's flame announced them for me. I didn't move.

Three distorted shadows curved and oscillated with the restless glow as they gathered behind me. No one spoke, more to humour me than in homage, though no less appropriate. Eventually they passed. 'Happy Samhain,' said Hector.

Serge lagged at my side, observing the pumpkin with me. It lit his face gold, concealing his eyes in a rim of shadow under his brow.

'Yours?' he asked.

I nodded cheerlessly, refusing to shift my eyes in his direction.

Sensing this, he regarded me with an inquisitive furrow. I

must have looked so haggard in Michael's light, feeling Serge watch me, almost daring me to look at him. Not a fortnight ago I would have later wasted hours wondering if his concern was feigned or not, such was his dual nature. It didn't matter now. At length, his furrow morphed into amusement at my stubbornness. Look carefully – if he smiles, above his top incisors you should see two incredibly fine points, protruding almost imperceptibly if you're lucky. Or extremely unlucky.

I turned my face away, desiring solitude, his stare burning more than my pumpkin's crisping flesh. The delicious cooking cupped us in a bittersweet glow, cutting us off from the tomb-like atmosphere.

'Nice smell, isn't it?' said Serge.

I nodded again with great effort. I had no desire for chat.

The tea-light burned out soon after I went to bed. You'll never guess what happened later.

Go on, guess.

Very well then.

I hadn't slept long. The lamp was abruptly switched on. Someone was shaking me.

'Oi. Pssst. Rona!'

I stirred and squinted, nothing registering yet, certain I was dreaming. The owner of an anxious face framed in dark bedraggled hair knelt over me, dripping rainwater onto my quilt.

'Trick or treat!' Alice announced.

I shot up like a catapult, nearly head-butting her.

'Jesus fucking Christ! What the fuck? What the *hell* are you doing he–?'

'Shhh! Chill. I need to crash here.'

'Are you out of your mind?' I shouted, rubbing sleep from my lashes, hardly able to believe the new dilemma. 'No. No! Get out!'

'Cut the shit and have a heart,' she whined, as if I was skipping my turn to make the afternoon tea or something.

'You can't stay here!'

'Why not?'

'Cos I said so.'

'Fuck off, it's a bed. Sort of.'

'*My* bed!'

'All the better. Now budge up.'

It was mind-boggling; the tomboy was actually pushing me aside to climb in! Had she no filter at all? It would be hilarious if not so exasperating.

'Wha–? Look, you ca–.' I stopped her. 'How'd you get in? Were you hiding?'

'Nah. I picked the side lock.'

My brain exploded. 'You *what*?'

'Wasn't the hardest in the world.'

This was the limit. I would have to follow Serge's example now and buy a padlock.

'Hang on,' I said. 'Why did you want my key if you can pick locks?'

'That fucking cupboard's a bastard. Was telling Gaz it wouldn't work the day you came out with granddad. Gave us a heart attack, you did.'

'I see.' Ask a stupid question, Rona. What's more, those doors were too heavy to be simple oak. I personally suspected their tame wooden casing covered reinforced titanium, that's not including Serge's rocket scientist locksmith skills.

'Gaz kicked me out, fellow hobo,' said Alice. 'It's just for a while. Cool pumpkin, by the way. Here,' she blithely held up a miniature Halloween-themed chocolate bar, 'have a choc Frankenstein.'

'Have a choc Fffff ...? Fuck!' I threw aside the quilt and sat level with her, fierce as Beowulf. 'Look, the last thing I need is you inflicting your shitty life on me. Find somewhere else.'

'Like where? A hostel? Get a grip, I'd catch rabies. *Fuck*, what's with your lip?'

'Fuck the lip,' I flustered, covering it. Not an ideal choice of words, Rona.

Alice smiled. She had the cheekiest smile you ever saw. 'Make it too easy for me, dontcha? Please, c'mon. Just for tonight?'

'Just tonight, then what? Beg you to leave tomorrow? I'd never be rid of you. Have a heart, you say? Says the one who watched that fuckhead beat me up.'

'Hey, s'cuse me, that's Gaz. What did you expect me to do? My ear's been ringing where he boxed it.'

I spotted an additional graze on her chin, too, a recent punch. Inconvenience aside, I inwardly questioned who was really being the unreasonable party here. The weather blew drizzly gale outside, her hair dripped with it and her pearly complexion shone luminous with rainwater. But if they discovered her!

'I told you it's not my problem,' I said.

'Boo-fucking-hoo, so Gaz knifed your oyster. He tries poking me for real. Now stop being a picky bitch and shift!' She made to push in by me again.

Then I heard something, a whistle and violent *thwack*.

Lightning adrenaline bolted me forward, slamming my hand over her mouth and grabbing her head to keep her still, listening. Alice froze with me, seeing my whites flash with fear.

The sound came again.

We stayed like this for a minute, rigid. Nothing. Then a gust. Another thwack. The wind. The goddamn wind and that frigging tree!

I dropped onto the mattress. 'Fucking gusts!'

Alice smiled thoughtfully. 'Jumpy, aren't ya?'

I lay in a recovering facepalm while she climbed over, muddy boots and all, to the other side of the mattress.

'Want a hug to keep the ghosties away?' she said, removing her soaked jacket. 'I have to stay now, don't I? Hehe.'

Her heel dragged trails of wet soil and a dead leaf along the quilt. If my aunts had ever found my bed like this they would have made me change my name by deed poll.

'Get your boots off my sheets,' I moaned.

'I am, I am!' she snapped, removing her sodden boots and socks. 'Zip it.'

Okay, where's the camera? You would think she slept here as often as I did.

'How am I supposed to sleep with you here?' I asked wearily.

She winked. 'I'll show you how, be patient.'

'God spare me.' I reached for my cigarettes.

'Oh, thank fuck, I'm dying for a smoke!'

I boldly withheld the packet from her. Not boldly enough; she snatched it all the same.

'Hey!'

'Trust!' she asserted, digging out two cigarettes with a comedic headshake. 'Can't even offer people a choc Frankenstein these days.'

This tom-bird was already making an ashtray of the floor.

She isn't going anywhere, is she?

'Listen,' I said, putting a decent glass ashtray between us. 'I have nowhere else to live and Falkirk will never let you stay, I'm sorry.'

Alice, her dainty wrist marked with extra bruises, likewise saw the patches around my throat, pesto-green today.

She drew and inhaled. 'Looks like this Falkirk and Gaz should be drinking buddies.'

My gaze fell. Apart from having to wear a concealing polo neck every day, lately scores of nightmares painted my sleep, my appetite was non-existent, my features drawn and worn. St Patrick's daytime cadaver. When Serge, Edith and Hector emerged this evening they were looking healthier than I.

'It was your pal, Gaz,' I fibbed, 'not Falkirk.'

'Uh-uh,' she corrected, examining my throat, 'too fresh-ish, baby. I'm the bruise guru. Christ, I should be a fuckin' nurse.'

She examined my green neck, stroking it from the jugular, down to the notch, to the other side, almost scientifically. I had forgotten what such sympathetic treatment felt like. So taken in was I, I let her thumb wander to where an inhuman snake had snacked from my face. *And lapped, Rona, don't forget lapped.*

I trembled. 'Stop. Tickles.'

'Does it?' she said, a nurturing tease, stroking my mouth.

'Yes. Hey, come on.' I withdrew from her suggestive caress.

With some disappointment, she plopped onto the bed. 'Woo, I'm tired! You okay?'

'Not really.'

'Sorry, hon.'

'It's not you.'

I saw the craving in her expression, looking up at me, guile-less as a doe-eyed pup. Alice was not kidding in her flirtations. Had I never met her before, if she had never made me laugh, I would have pushed this intruder arse-over-tit right over the balcony, but as it happens, I was not uncomfortable with her. Alice's quirkiness manifested in her wild honesty; whatever mood you were in, she could literally shock you into light-heartedness, never a dull moment with this tomboy. Her breeze of fresh air was exhausting me again, though not in a bad way when, in truth, I exhausted myself. It was getting harder and harder to say no to her.

'I'll just have to figure out a way to get rid of you later,' I said, smoking.

'If you meant to call the police you would've by now,' she yawned.

'Maybe. You're not going home to that thug, are you?' I asked, remembering the horrid way Gaz had nearly boxed her off her feet and squeezed her neck.

'No, mummy!' she smiled, poking my side. 'Let me stay,

then. You're weird, that's what I like about you.'

I puffed the cigarette, unable to face her. If she actually *were* a boy this could be a lot easier, I wouldn't feel so ... conflicted? Why did you have to resemble a handsome boy, Androgynous Alice?

'Likewise,' I said. 'You're a pain in the arse, mind.'

She may have sensed my conflict better than I did, though I was far more anxious about certain predators picking up her scent than either of our sexualities. I extinguished the cigarette and put the ashtray aside.

'I'm going to sleep,' I said, pulling up the quilt. 'You can stay until the rain stops but promise you'll be gone before dawn. I mean it!'

'No kiss goodnight, then?'

'Don't push your luck.'

Alice moved closer to me. 'If I pushed it I wouldn't be in here with you.' She dove in and planted a quick kiss on my mouth, smiling her pixie grin, a grin too funny to annoy me.

'How about a deal?' she said, propped up on her elbows. 'I leave early and turn in Gaz if you turn in the cunt who hurt you. What d'you think?'

'No deal.'

'Why?'

I popped. 'I said I'm not talking about it, so don't ask me!'

Alice sat up. 'The fuck you having a go for? Don't lecture *me* when you're playing the fat-lipped doormat!'

A doormat. Great. Well done, Alice, so true. Anyone else want to fire reproofs in my direction this week? More folk queuing to stamp me to a pulp? It was too much. I dug my face into the edge of the single pillow we shared.

'Let me sleep. Don't leave the lamp on.'

A few seconds passed.

Secrets clawed inside me with no outlet, for there was no telling Alice, not on her life, mine, or theirs. For however much

I hated them now, the three revenants and I had a history, cemented by an arcane thread binding me to them of my own volition, wrapping me in chains.

Meanwhile, I felt Alice lie back down, no questions or nagging this time.

About thirty minutes later (I remember from the bedside clock), just when I thought Alice had nodded off, she kissed my shoulder.

'Promise I won't take advantage of you till you pass out,' she said. 'Or what are you afraid of? Bible rules?

'No.'

I heard her sit up, there was a pulling and rustling of cloth. Alice took off her top and tossed it aside, bra-less again. *You've got to be kidding me!*

'What is this,' I yelped, 'a striptease?'

'Yes.' She lay topless, facing me sideways. 'What did happen to your mouth? You been giving blowjobs to staplers or something?'

'An accident. And get your tits out of my face, I'm not gay.'

'That's not stopping you so far.'

'How d'you mean?'

Here came her mischievous smile. 'I mean you're still looking.'

Oops. I really couldn't decipher precisely how or what I was feeling; her flattering advances in this uncharted territory were too unexpected for me to recognise I was in the early stages of sexual arousal.

'Yeah, whatever,' I said, turning from her, blocking it.

The tree thwacked on the window a few more times. It sounded like the moors outside, oddly soothing, lulling me.

I was about to doze off when Alice touched my elbow. Then my hip. I nudged her away. She did it again and I nudged her off again. When she did it a third time, subtly holding me, I lay still. It was either that or cry. Far too many gormless bed bangers underestimate what it is to be held, the weight of an arm over your side, or the prolonged deprivation of any human contact, what that does to a person. A minute later a change occurred: her hand on my hip travelled south.

'Why are you doing this?' I asked, not budging. 'Seriously.'

'Cos you're not stopping me.'

Yes, please stop, this doesn't feel as dreadful as I want it to!

A warmth I had not asked for circulated my body as the twinge came, that kind of twinge you fear explaining to your prepubescent kids after they accidentally discover it for themselves. *What the hell am I doing?*

I jerked up. 'Look, I'm not sure ... I mean ... Wait, Alice!'

Alice wasted no time. The weightless sprite bestrode me, sitting upright, her spine sinusoidal. I wrestled her poorly; she was stronger than she looked. I covered my face.

'Why this?' I said. 'Why you? I don't know, Alice.'

Alice's voice was cotton, not forceful.

'I don't want to get beaten up any more either,' she said.

She started moving her pelvis.

'I don't understand why now,' I said. 'I'm not like this.'

'Not like what?' she toyed, moving rhythmically.

'You know what.' I spoke through my palms, afraid of myself, and more than anything afraid of not being afraid.

'Your nips have gone hard,' she hinted. 'No one said you have to be gay. Tell me to stop then, if you want.'

Her hips moved faster, the zip of her denims massaging directly on that magic spot under my pyjamas at the top of my legs. My breathing changed with it; soon it would be too late to want to stop her.

She caressed my mouth again, telling me to relax, softly ...

What can I say? Adults. Obviously it made no sense, I made no sense. I am not in the habit of being attracted to girls, then or now, but what difference could it make when I was already unrecognisable to myself? That's why I let her do it, this tomboy,

275

this anomaly. She removed the last of what we were wearing, opened my legs and straddled the space in between.

Halloween on that confined mattress. The vaults and its nightmares were a distant dream, if only for a few hours.

~

Something has woken me.

How often do you feel the compelling need to look behind you when logic dictates there should be nothing there, the timorous prickling of breath on your nape from a vacant space *too* vacant to be ignored?

My weighty lids opened. There were my boxes, standing where they always did, the fading print, 'Marston Packers Ltd', bidding me good morning. I was teetering on the edge of a mattress wholly unsuited for two, a meagre portion of the quilt flapping over my leg and ribs. Alice hogged most of it.

What woke me? Possibly the tree's percussion outside; not much, though, the gusts were lessening. My clock said 7:20 a.m.

I edged sideways, trying not to crush Alice, albeit partake of my fair share of quilt. I was naked as the day I was born, but the bed was less chilly with two.

Alice breathed steadily, lying like a disrobed broken doll. I wondered how she could sleep like that and be comfortable, halfway off the bed too, an arm lopsided over her head, a leg skew-whiff on the floor. Five or six healing scars from cigarette burns dotted her thigh in an offensive line; in her open-mouthed slumber she looked a decade older. I had just had sex with a girl. Of all the random things that could possibly happen in my unheard-of lifestyle! Where the heck did this funny scarred thing come from, this tomboy who dropped out of the sky?

Reaching across her for my cigarettes, a small, rough object scratched my shin under the covers. The piece of chocolate she had offered me, in foil, melted and squashed inedible, the green monster's clueless mug flat as a pancake. *'Feed My Frankenstein', Rona. Happy Samhain.*

I sat upright, lit a fag and awaited the obligatory shame and self-disgust. Out of everything that had happened this year, shag a girl? Yeah, I'd probably have thought of that next, sure! Cigarette in one hand, gawking bemusedly at Frankenstein's monster in the other, instead of feeling guilt, I could only laugh, laugh until I gagged on smoke.

A complaining mumble came from Alice.

'Sorry,' I said, stubbing the cigarette out. 'Go to sleep.' I covered up, still drowsy after a somewhat *wakeful* night.

I couldn't doze off yet. Something was wrong.

Save my uninvited bed guest, nothing seemed out of place, but … something niggled me. It hung in the air like a shadow without an owner. I half-expected to see again the spectre of my mother from childhood, or what I'd thought was her; the memory of that apparition's face was growing more into mine every year.

The gallery, including the balcony, was too small for anyone to hide. The balcony – why would I think that? No one in their right mind messed around on the balustrade, unless they desired a deadly fall into the nave.

I lazily assessed the situation as sleep crept back. *The wind woke me, no one's here, it's practically daylight, they came in hours ago while we were asleep and inconspicuous, no harm done, shouldn't need to worry.*

I was too somnolent and drugged-up with post-coital endorphins, *to* worry.

Chapter Three

'All right, one more smoke, just one! Then I have to spray the place.'

'Fucking nag, you,' said Alice, half-dressed and cross-legged on my bed.

I shook the canister of air freshener as per morning ritual, chemical lavender today, to kill off the odour of cigarettes, as if that worked. Falkirk had no qualms about smoking in church either, so it put nothing on my conscience.

It was after nine o'clock when the south aisle door opened and shut. Enter our you-know-who.

Alice and I exchanged a look. I had wanted to ask him for the day off. It would cost me a day's pay, which I could cope with.

'There he is,' I said gloomily. 'Put that fag out. Hurry, for fuck sake.'

'What's happnin'?'

'Not sure,' I said. 'I can't stand the thought of going down there. It's weird, I'm an atheist but I like this church and hate its people, hate them all.'

Alice giggled. 'Should we jump up and flash 'em?'

'Shoosh.'

I went to the balcony. Falkirk stood pale and gaunt; since

the spa respite his weight had plummeted and his ruddiness faded.

'Where the devil have you been?' he yapped. 'Who's up there?'

'Nobody, Daddy Falkirk,' I said sweetly. 'Oooh, don't wear out the fallen angel's name in vain, you'll tempt Fate.'

'I heard someone!' he blared. 'What are you up to?'

'What's it to you, really, Minister?'

Neither of us got the next word in. Alice, crazy misfit, jumped up by me.

'We're up to here!' she yelled, and flung up her top with extravagant force, flashing him a full frontal. Falkirk's jaw hit the floor. So did mine, for that matter.

Do you think that's funny? Sorry, no. Jovial as her clumsy gesture was, I'd rather she hadn't. This was not her quarrel. She was an outsider; the three of us – Falkirk, I and St Patrick's church – had memories, ours for the keeping. Call me territorial. My inevitable distancing from Alice started its course at that point.

I motioned her away.

Falkirk blackened, his nose wrinkling into lines of contempt. 'You ... carnal wretch,' he gasped. 'You dare. You dare! In my church!'

I cocked my head with a bitchy half-smile.

'You know something, Donald Falkirk? I don't think you have the pox of a leg to stand on.'

He stormed away. I called after him, 'I never take a day off. Today will be the exception. Don't worry, I'll eat less without a day's pay if that's any consolation.'

Relishing his sulky thunder, I finished getting dressed.

A few minutes passed while I tied my bootlaces, feeling a glow of confidence, if not for the phantom of a grandfather clock ticking from somewhere. *Countdown. Here comes a chopper. Run, Rona!*

I shuddered. The church radiators were on, so the sly sprinkling of goose pimples up my forearms did not add up.

I still hear what came next to this day.

Not in a million years would I have believed dusky old Falkirk could lower his voice to so satisfied, so frightening a chill. Never. His serpentine sound waves found their way from chancel to gallery in smooth vibrations of sheer poison.

'*Roooooona?*'

It was a knowing voice. A diabolically gleeful, sordid, coiling voice. It communicated everything. There was no need to ask, I knew exactly what it meant. I knew immediately.

My blood went cold. Everything changed, a darkness fell over me. Like a ghost, I rose from my bootlaces.

'Gimme a minute,' I told Alice.

She may have responded, she may not have, I didn't hear either way as I drifted down the python stair to where Falkirk awaited me.

Our minister stood within a few feet of the chancel, glancing from me to the altar table with an air of fresh satisfaction. He used the lectern for services, the chancel he seldom acknowledged; checking the altar, that was my job, first thing in the mornings. Today he had purposefully beaten me to it. With a glint of triumphant malice, he departed and left me to it, twenty feet from the table. I could see the note from here.

One note. Square. White paper. In the centre, same place they always penned chores and travel requirements.

I had felt them. I can't say precisely what told me this or how I perceived it. An instinctive link, germinated from every second spent with them, every piercing gaze, every unspoken vibe, tied into a cord of two-way intuition. He was in *here*, in my head, had sneakily set up shop in there and rooted himself, enough for me to sense his soundless malice in my sleep, enough for me to know the tyrant had stood right there on that balustrade looking at us, at me. Rona, you really are the world's greatest dunce. Hide an intruder? Did you really think that would work? No, I had chosen to ignore it whilst luxuriating in a companionable break. Are we awake yet, Rona?

I got it over with. I marched, almost ran, to the altar. The handwriting was no forgery of Falkirk's; there is only one soul with that penmanship.

… Right.

The feeling of liberation after last night's minor rebellion hadn't quite burnt out, not yet, dear, and instead of being subdued into servitude, here it surfaced for its final battle, armed and loaded as my pupils burned two holes through the paper in my hand. In a fizzing rage born out of months of fear and manipulation, I crunched up the note and prepared to throw it back through their iron gate – much like the litter a dutiful Rona so attentively cleared from their domain once upon a time in 'far away'.

A minute later: change of plan.

On the vestry table, I flattened out the scrunched ball of crease marks and scribbled my reply under their message.

Choose. Or I decide

NO. YOU WILL NOT TRESPASS
100 TIMES.

Go to hell.

I could have written more. Pages worth! Folding the amended correspondence into a paper aeroplane, I quickly slipped inside the cupboard, without a torch, and felt my way to the gate.

I touched rusted iron, seeking a gap in the bars, trying – for my pride – to breathe normally. If two animal retinas were in there, I had no light to give their glinting irises away. It could be crouching within nipping distance of my fingernails, patiently holding its breath, smiling snake's fangs and shark's jaws, ready to spring. Squeezing the note through, I poised. Ready. Aim. Fire! I waited for it to land.

I heard nothing.

Electric shock in my chest! My insides lurched into a tight ball.

From somewhere far off in pitch blackness came a faint scraping of paper where it brushed the edge of a step, fell, and hit another. All the breath dropped out of me as I staggered against the gate with relief, damn trickery of acoustics!

I wish I could say it made me feel better instead of crystallising my inability to rewind the past twelve hours. Barely a week after their interview, Rona breaks a golden rule last night. They warn her and what does she do? Reignites the sparks by shouting back. People do a lot of things when they're angry. Irredeemable things.

I've just provoked them.

It was done. Where I wanted a boosting sense of justice as I relocked the cupboard, there were sinking blocks of lead in my stomach.

Alice was perched cross-legged on the mattress, bright-eyed and bushy-tailed, rolling a cigarette with my spare tobacco. 'Say, if I had my water pistol I'd make that minister look like he peed his pants,' she said, hearing me approach. 'Got a good aim from here. Did it to Gaz and Annie once, he bruised my tits for that. Don't ever get yourself punched in the tits, by the way … Hey, holy *fuck*, what's happened?'

My pallor was a deathly chalk, as chalky as the underground. I tasted it, walking through a mist to the bed, ready to faint. Somewhere in all this I think Alice stood up, dumbfounded.

Part Two

'Oh my God, oh my God, stop that, will ya! That look's scaring the crap out of me, and I don't get scared.'

I sat on the edge of the mattress, loosely hugging my shins.

'Roll me one,' I said, like a zombie. Alice handed me the cigarette she had rolled for herself.

'Alice,' I said gravely, 'you know you can't stay here. You're in terrible danger here, and me, if you do.'

Her brow furrowed. 'That Falkirk bloke threaten you?'

'It isn't him.' I sounded ninety years old.

'What, then?'

No answer from me. She shook my arm.

'Don't take the piss! You're freaking me fuckless, Rona.'

I saw her. I almost didn't recognise her. Who's that? What's she doing in my gallery?

'I'm going to tell you this much and only once,' I said. 'There are more unimaginably dangerous things than Gaz.'

'Who? They know Gaz or Annie?'

I told her no.

'Bitch-face,' she said, 'I come from the *crème de la crap*. I've seen fuckers get their heads split open, run over, all sorts of shit – and I've never seen anyone scared as you. Why're you staying here? Pot kettle black.'

'I'm required here.'

'What the fuck for, sweeping floors?'

I swivelled in her direction, my eyes a lost, dreamy film.

'I … I'm a ghoul.'

'And I'm Lady Gaga.'

What else could I tell her? I was back in that hellish plasma, Alice was a speck on the horizon.

'It's true,' I said, reanimating with the beginnings of a deranged smile. 'I am.'

I sank, drowned, senseless, and submitted to the whirlpool; it consumed me. I plummeted in a swoon, vomiting sick laughter into my palms.

'I do fucking laundry! Oh my God, I do their fucking laundry!'

It was a frightening laugh, no sound I remember from Rona before, a cackle of maddened delirium. I writhed on that mattress and gave myself up completely.

'A ghoul does laundry!' I howled. '*Ghoul! Ghoul does the motherfuckers' laundry.*'

Alice, stunned to silence, watched the breakdown run its course until I yowled so that hard my voice broke, lying there, floating in the middle of nowhere.

I heard the mattress springs creak as she sat, cautiously, beside me.

'Who are they?' she asked, sounding surprisingly grown up for her.

Seeing the change in her, I sat upright. 'If I told you, either we both die or you definitely never see me alive again.'

Alice steepled her fingers under her chin, thinking, and asked an infinitely terrible question, the worst question in the world.

'What's down that gate?'

I turned to solid stone and lit a cigarette; let the congregation smell it. 'What gate?'

'Cut the fuckery. Gaz kicked it shitless. It wouldn't give.'

'I'll bet he did.'

'Where does it go?'

'Nowhere,' I said, emotional as an android, staring blankly ahead, tears drying on my red cheeks. 'Rock. Blocked off for centuries.'

Alice tutted and bit her knuckles in frustration, at a loss. 'Okay, um … maybe just better get out of here for the day.' Typical famous last words of a defeated witness.

To me it was suggestion of the year. Suddenly energised, like a light switching on I sprang into life and grabbed her arm. She flinched at my wildness.

'Yes, let's get out of here!' I said. 'Let's go. Right now!'

I wanted to run away, the wind was at my back and I did not care where I went, I would gallop a thousand miles without stopping to get the hell out of there. Such was my folly in proving Edith's prophetic warning: *One evening we wake up and you're gone. What happens then?*

~

I absorbed an urban panorama from the summit of Ashley Hill, the highest and greenest place in Bronmeg. The ants' nest of miniaturised roads and moving vehicles below reminded me of the blood cells you see rushing through veins under a microscope. Ashley Hill was deserted today, a weekday; the kiddies were in classrooms learning how to be society's puppets, while Joe and Jane Public were at their office jobs. Secure, boring, stable lives. Just don't go out at night, guys, think I spotted your brother's shoe down a well.

I needed a place to think, somewhere secluded to decide what to do next. I would have to leave town somehow, catch an intercity coach? Already I fought vigilantly against regretting my impulsiveness, swearing I had slept my last night in the gallery and that, no matter what, Rona was on the run.

Not so my reluctant companion. The drug addict repeatedly complained of 'needing a hit' and 'gasping for a snort', whining non-stop about being limited to my tobacco without any weed. By about midday, when at last she grew unmanageable, I told her to for heaven's sake go where she pleased and that I didn't mind.

'When you going back?' she asked.

Not a question I wanted, especially since she asked 'when', not 'if'. Perhaps she planned on lodging in the gallery after all. *Too bad, Alice. My immediate priority is not your shelter.*

'I'm not,' I answered.

Alice seemed amazed. 'You gonna turn Falkirk in?' she

asked, rather less enthusiastic with the idea than she was last night. Yep, the little hypocrite definitely wanted to squat.

'No,' I said stiffly. 'I simply cannot go back. I couldn't in a million years.'

Hearing my intentions spoken out loud made it harder to believe them. I had to force my dwindling conviction through my brain with increasing friction, trying to outshout instinct. I felt loose, alien, outside of myself like the fugitive I was, without a damn clue what I was doing.

'Where you heading then?' Alice grilled.

Another unattractive question. She may as well have asked *Where do you see yourself ten years from now?*

'Fuck knows,' I replied.

Alice hugged her cheap jacket about her and bounced impatiently in the chill. The increasingly wintry weather, having deemed blue morning sky overly generous, now proceeded to eat it up with heavy turquoise clouds. A tell-tale raindrop hit my lashes.

'You head off,' I told her gently. 'I need to find my way elsewhere, and I have to think.'

Alice sighed. 'You're a fanny.'

Nothing was to stop Alice getting her 'hit' and she insisted I tag along with her, giving me some story about her brother's ex-girlfriend having a sofa bed. I was loath to follow but the deteriorating weather hastened me.

My legs were tired, I hadn't eaten and I dreaded not reaching a safe distance in what was so far a pretty damp squib of an escape. Had I the money I would have boarded the coach to London hours ago, feeling just as empty as I did now.

Alice's energy was boundless. Spurred on by her incessant hunger for narcotics, she traipsed me over six miles across town to an area of multi-storey council flats, flanking both sides of meandering roads like the towers of abandoned power stations, blotched with grime and peeling paint, many windows board-ed up. *Rockbank* seemed to be the predominant street name here, as in Rockbank Crescent, Rockbank Road, or Rockbank Terrace. You couldn't walk thirty feet without tiptoeing around mounds of dog excrement on lanes probably unknown to community service since their day of construction.

We passed gardens of trampled grass, shops and homes choked with graffiti; scrawled profanities, phalluses and any number of tags you like. None of the bus shelters were spared a signature, their acrylic sheets either smashed or missing completely, and some with what appeared to be bullet holes.

Two or three children, no more than seven or eight years old, not in school (surprise, surprise), ran by us on a crusade of sorts, their language and manners no better than thugs who may throw the odd beer bottle at you. A vicious Rottweiler leapt and barked at us from behind a fence, making us both jump. I stepped over lager cans, countless fragments of shattered glass and puddles of creamy vomit, not to mention the occasional – and to me, unmistakable – raspberry spatter of blood on asphalt from a late-night skirmish. Indecisive rainfall accentuated the misery; whenever storm clouds took a breather, the overpower-ing stench of dog faeces filled the streets and I gagged.

I heard more locals than I saw, for which I was glad; judg-ing by their vocabulary, they were the pavements with a voice. Then, paradoxically in all this, a harmless pensioner would pass us, trailing a shopping trolley behind them. What were they doing living in such a place?

As far as I was concerned, this was Hell. How certain 'aforementioned parties' across town would laugh at me! I blamed poor Alice for bringing me. On she went, talking bab-ble; to her this cesspit was home sweet home. I gathered I was narrow-minded, straining to understand how a remotely nice person like her could emerge from an upbringing in this Shan-gri-La. *Then again, Rona, are you exactly the same as those who raised you?*

Alice stopped at various flats. I declined to follow and smoked outside, pretending to ignore looks from gormless locals with impolite bull terriers.

When the barking of one such dog startled a kit of pigeons from a rooftop, with an eruption of wings they flew overhead, outlined against the overcast. I craned up at them in a useless beg. *Yes, fly away. Too damn easy for you, isn't it? A pair of wings, that's all it takes. What I would give for one pair of wings! You could fly up there until this town is a molecule. How superior and powerful it must feel up there. You could fly all the way to the sea.* In jams like this, throughout my life the sky always caused me heartache: the land has limits, fires and shorelines; the ocean spans the earth's surface but not all of it; the sky – the sky can take you anywhere. The sky is three-dimensional. The sky is freedom, even the doorway to outer space if you're able. The sky takes you anywhere. Anywhere.

I was ready to wring Alice's neck with the time she took, leaving me out here alone. What in God's name was she doing up there?

At length, she finally stumbled from the building, nostrils inflamed, pupils haywire and glassy-eyed, higher than the pigeons. Clearly having forgotten me, she leapt into my arms with a cry.

'Aaaaaah, that's better!' she squealed.

Restraining my disgust, I worried we were now on a wild goose chase for this friend's house. We had walked for miles, it was after 4 p.m., getting late, and the light was …

'This friend of yours,' I demanded, steadying her. 'Where? I'm knackered.'

'Aww!' The diseased firecracker slumped against me in an attempted hug.

I shook her. 'Where? Or I swear I'm fucking off!'

'Steady on!' she yapped.

I seriously foresaw myself giving up, stomping off and leaving her there, assuming sober reasoning would get me nowhere. Instead, with a sulk and unnatural strength for her size, Alice took my hand and hauled me onward through more lanes of dog faeces, glass shards and pavement gum.

The woman whom Alice claimed to be her brother's ex, Claire, moved about in a kind of semi-conscious sleepwalk, a hash joint dangling between her fake orange nails. Our hostess was a rather buxom woman in her thirties with unwashed blonde hair, puffy eyes and a vest exposing syringe tracks where her veins should be.

No passably breathable air circulated the tiny flat and its four rooms reeked of that wet stink you're afraid to find at the bottom of communal bins. Mercifully, Claire left us alone.

'It's all right,' said Alice. 'She's too fucked to do shit. Sleeps all day.'

My companion led me to a lounge and began unfolding the sofa bed.

'Can I open a window?' I asked.

Alice shrugged.

We sat on the bed smoking for a while, not speaking much while Alice cracked open beer cans from Claire's fridge and sat forward, elbows over her knees, deep in distant thought. She was annoyed with me, I saw it. I had spoiled her church-squatting plans, thrown a nutter's fit and done a runner. Now with the tables thus turned, I don't think she quite knew what to do with me.

Despite the rickety bed and unsanitary duvet stinking of many past Claires, Annies and Gazes, my head swam, persuading me onto the pillow, a day of walking, no food and broken sleep to make up for.

'You know Cromards?' she asked, pulling me from a doze.

'Er, I think so.'

'We'll have a piss-up there tonight then,' she said joylessly, puffing on a joint. 'You got money?'

Hearing her doubtfulness, I told her yes. I hated being the object of her resentment! Alice wants the gallery? Fine, she can sweep Falkirk's floor! Or no, maybe not.

I blinked, the shadows were lengthening again. Try to imagine how that made me feel. Night creeps out of locked doors: twenty-four hours ago, I was carving a pumpkin in Falkirk's vestry; less than twenty hours ago, someone's face shone in its golden tea-light.

Early evening beckoned outside. I turned away from the lounge window, not wanting to know, denying its existence, wishing time would come to a standstill. Wait, one more vital chore to do: I switched off my phone and chucked away my wrist-watch, anything to avoid seeing the minutes tick away from me. I lay there, butterflies in my gut, stranded in a foul flat, far from all I once held dear, a castaway. I remember-remember the first of November.

When I woke up the main light was on. The lounge window revealed nothing but a reflection of the room: TV, used tea cups, lampshade, a table packed with garbage, the sofa bed, and the dominant ashtray – Claire's carpet. It was full night.

By now they know.

Alice yawned at my side, not long awake herself and somewhat refreshed.

'Hey,' she greeted, swinging over the sofa bed for her shoes. 'You were talking in your sleep.'

'Really?' I recollected no dreams. 'What was I saying?'

'Dunno,' she said, tying her laces. 'Mumbling blah, blah. "Sage" or "show". Heard the word "sky". You coming to Cromards with us or what?'

Tagging along with that crowd sounded like being a sparrow among buzzards, but it was better than pacing in here. Through the paper-thin walls music boomed, neighbours crashed about like elephants and bickered for Britain; if they left me here alone I would drive myself crazy or leap from the window. My boots were on in a twinkling.

Less than an hour later, after catching a lonesome bus to Cain Road on the west end of town, I remembered that Cromards was a bar–nightclub. Ah, nightclubs, bane of my youth, the bang-bang of loudspeakers mashing my brain until it leaked from my earlobes in their mission to spread airborne tinnitus. Walking down Cain Road, however, not a church in sight, this blast-from-the-past reality was overwhelming. Busy streets, party goers everywhere, music pounding from pubs and cars, as if I'd spent the last few months locked in a cinema screen room: the film ends, the doors open, bright light as the non-fictional world blasts its way into your out-of-tune senses, recalibrating you at its leisure. When was the last time I'd walked through this at night, through society? I had to laugh, it was amusing, it was ludicrous! Average civilisation where there are no such things as monsters. You'd never know, would you? You would never know!

Here we are at Cromards. The stifling nightclub was basically a large room on the ground floor of a dated building, centred by a single bar with chairs and tables hugging all sides to make way for a cramped dancefloor. All seats were taken, naturally, and most revellers stood with vodka mixers and pints, half on, half off the dancefloor. You had zero chance of any free space unless you fancied the abandoned band practice area, hidden in a choked corridor beyond the toilets. A bored skin-head bouncer, in a better mood than I, nodded his good evenings to crowds leaving and entering as I sheepishly followed Claire and Alice inside, the square nail being hammered into a round hole once again.

Unreasonably loud music punched me the moment I walked in, while the heat of a thousand inebriated bodies instantly drew a clammy sweat from my brow under the low ceiling. Put me in this suffocating nightclub a year ago and I would have simply been uncomfortable; in here tonight, I wished the last twenty-four hours were a dream. Now I had bitten into thorny reality, it was more than I could chew.

I downed lemonade and vodka in greedy gulps, then ordered another, and another. Frosty weather outdoors had punished my lower lip by opening a scab, it burned and fizzed in the alcohol, painting it red, and though the booze should have helped, the only thing it numbed was my fear of searching for a seat and being separated from Alice.

She wandered off, chatting to people and sneaking into the loo, probably to 'powder her nose'. At length she re-emerged, lit up with that far-off glow and trippy bounce, flung an arm around me, kissed me and skipped off to see Cromards' more regular clientele, male and female copies of Gaz and Annie, who themselves were blessedly absent.

I watched her. She was doing the rounds, flitting from crowd to crowd, so childlike in her stature, no more than a merry street urchin from a Dickens novel. As I caught glimpses of pills and packets of powder changing hands and jacket pockets, the true character of Alice became clearer. She was a begging little bumblebee of the drugs world. She rarely had money so she squatted, skipping from dealer to dealer and flat to flat, taking the punches, the fisticuffs, anything, it didn't matter, long as she got her hits. It dawned on me that Gaz could not take all the blame for her bruises; that girl had been beaten and bounced off the rafters so often, she spring-heeled under an elastic skin, not to mention picking locks *and* pockets – I'd entered the club with thirty pounds and spent twenty on vodka, so why am I left with only fifty pence since you put your arm round me, Alice, hmm? To how many dodgy people did she owe money? How many gangs or homophobes would smash her up on sight? She lived a dangerous life; if an overdose or a knifing didn't kill her first, she would end up in prison. Tut-tut.

Out of cash for a refill, I sipped the last sad drop of vodka and procrastinated until the craving for a cigarette decided me.

What a pure thing night air is. What a breath of pearly clarity. It washes over you like a waterfall. The forgiving coolness cleansed my clammy forehead as I stepped outside and anchored my heel against the wall alongside my fellow comrades of the black lung brigade, the only sober-looking people in the street.

My tobacco was running low; this was a big problem. I had closed my bank account weeks ago and thanks to Alice my pockets fared no better. I despaired at the thought of searching for her and Claire in there, worse still, returning to that rank sofa bed. Well done, Rona, you have marooned yourself.

I exhaled, watching my plume of silky grey smoke join the clouds from other puffers, rising into a night sky tainted biscotti by light pollution. A drunken group argued over boarding a taxi; a hostile band of football fanatics hollered nonsense to the stars; smokers texted; under-age teens shouted at the doorman; car horns beeped; a streetlamp flickered.

This particular streetlamp, in fact, was flickering across the road, illuminating the brickwork of a sharp turn, on and off. I thought nothing of it. It flickered again, and I saw it lit the mouth of an alleyway opposite, so narrow that extra lighting was hardly worth the money, and so dark it may as well be disappearing into the ground.

A figure hovered there in the darkness. Male, barely outlined in the weakened light, reasonably tall. They stood very still. I could not help staring. This person, aiming to be inconspicuous, was to me the *most* conspicuous thing on Cain Road; they drew my attention like a magnet. Blame my nocturnal perception, sir, ha, I've had too much practice you see, watchdo–

For an instant my heart stopped beating.

The figure moved, zipped his fly and minced into the lamplight. A man, just a man, human, gone for a piss in the alley like a zillion other drinkers before him, no one – or, no one I recognised. My shoulders relaxed and my heart rate settled. Then it increased. They're awake. Heart beating faster. It's night time. And faster. They're out. Faster-faster than rabbit feet on churchyard grass. Fasterfasterfaster*faster* –

That is when all perspective flipped.

I pressed myself into the wall, as if that would help, and the whole world pointed at me as the veil fell and everything took on a terrible damning lucidity, slapping me awake. *Fully* awake.

Frantically I scanned and rescanned the street, left to right, up and down. Did I not name this outdoor environment 'reality' a short while ago? *Oh my God, Rona. Rona, oh my* God.

The full implications of my folly erupted as if it had been waiting, squatting down there, chuckling to itself, ready to pounce and douse me in scalding absoluteness. Reality? Yes, Rona, and welcome to it. Here you are! You know things this herd don't, things nobody in this walking larder, this farmyard, knows. Night. You remember what that means, don't you? Good evening.

I'm out. Ran away. I'm here, blowing in the wind on their hunting ground, which is everywhere, and they, they could be anywhere. *Anywhere*!

I drew in a slicing gasp, losing air as I cascaded into a full-blown panic attack, doubling over against the wall, balancing myself with one hand and biting my knuckles on the other, hard. Repulsed viewers either hurried by or asked if I was okay; they were invisible.

Fraught with senseless panic and the irrepressible need to run, I trotted up the street in a cold sweat, fighting the urge to break into a race, everything out of focus, desperate to sprint. I blindly crashed into the gang of football fans, cried out … and that was it. – Ignoring their laughter, I swerved and ran back in the opposite direction, careering into more people, losing direction. Reality, the *real* reality, the worst kind of reality with unspeakable shapes scratching beneath, ricocheted me, hyperventilating, racing in circles, up and down the surrounding streets and back to Cain Road, out of breath, out of my wits.

Nowhere is safe! They could be in any corner! Oh God! Don't you people know? Don't you *know*? *NONE of you are safe!*

Not a single shadow was harmless, not a nook in the world unoccupied, oh I knew, I knew, I knew, I knew! The church … The church had been the safest place. Now I was out, a traitor, on *their* hunting ground! I'm out with the livestock in the killing fields! Try deflecting those meteors now!

Running … Panting … *Nowhere, nowhere is safe! Nowhere! NOWHERE!*

Cromards. Strobe lighting. Can't see straight. Loudspeakers bombard. Stumbling over people. Heads turn, they're all Hector, they're all Edith, all Serge. Alice pops up, 'Where the fuck you been? Was looking everywhere! What's wrong?'

Shoving Alice off. Head's grinding. Running past crowded toilets. A fire exit.

Another door to the right, featureless, an 'Out of Order' sign. I pound against it. It is stiff but gives. I collapse my way inside.

I punched on a light switch and slammed the door. The room was bare but for a pile of crates and a tired, overused drum kit. The band practice room, stuffy with a whiff of leather, weed and gum. The club music blissfully dimmed.

I had found a hideout. No other doors, no windows, nowhere to surprise me from.

Touching my sternal notch to steady my breathing, I felt a prominent lump under my shirt. Something dangled and shimmered. I lifted the small, smooth sphere. It sat there pleasingly in the centre of my palm as I stroked and turned it over.

My birthday gift. Their gift. To me.

I lost the power of my legs. Down I slid. My face fell into my hands and hot tears flowed into them, filling the crevices with a network of rivers. Why? Why am I crying?

Their gift. Their entrusted gift …

I had grown too used to them. No, I was *accustomed* to them. Would I take Alice's world instead? Never.

Fear gave way to confusion. Confusion gave way to nostalgia. My shoulders shook, pumping up a sob. A bout of fresh tears replenished the salty rivers streaming down my wrists and sleeves, more followed.

Ran away from home. They were dangerous, they were monsters, Edith, Hector, and a young yet so very ancient relic with grey-blue eyes, always lingering behind mine, always with me wherever I went. I hated him. I breathed him.

'I'm sorry,' I mumbled.

"Sorry", same words as on my maiden voyage to their underworld; Hector scaring me, Serge catching the lamp on the stair, and waiting there for me.

'I'm sorry, sorry …'

I switched my phone into life. The time: 01:18 hours. Missed calls or texts: zero.

As sure as ivy penetrates ruins, like it or not they were a part of me. Whatever they thought of Rona, their pet human, I hadn't altogether missed the world I'd shunned for them. And here I'd done the stupidest thing, sacrificed my safety by walking out on St Patrick's.

Go home.

Home. Their home? Go back? I'd have abject hell to pay! What now? What now?

I curled on the floor in a foetal position. Alice and her mutants can search out there, I don't care, I can stay here forever, me and that disabled drum kit. Hello, drum kit.

It was never confirmed whether or not Alice had spiked my drink that November evening, so many years ago. I wouldn't put it past her, though it is irrelevant. The carpet was spongy and accommodated me, my tears blurred the drum kit, the room whirred, alcohol coated my throat and grievous exhaustion rendered my muscles dead weights. Like the formidable turquoise clouds creeping over Ashley Hill, the fog rolled in.

Chapter Four

Gradually, I was stirred awake by my own heartbeat.

A delightful softness moulds itself around my cheek. On this side the ocean waves break in thick foam upon the rocks, not striking sharply; they wash over, churn under, then rise again in succession. They do this with punctual regularity, swirling and washing me under without drowning me. I see them, submerged in a turbulent sea like a bug in a car wash. I dream, kicking to reach the surface, but am entombed.

There is the faintest *pad-pad-pad* under my ear where waves bounce off the pillow like a patter of insect feet. Moth wings flutter where my eyelashes meet the fabric in a rustle of inoffensive intimacy. The water solidifies to a hammering fist in my cranium; if I could only crack open my skull with a mallet and let all the badness pour out.

I do a foolish thing – I turn over. Ocean, waves and pain swish to my left temple like thick syrup and rebound, bouncing boulders back and forth through brain to scalp. I let out a subconscious groan.

My head weighs a fine tonnage, yet how comfortable my body is, how soft the sheets, cushioning my frame! A ruptured spring prods my knee; it is familiar in a somehow valuable way. I move and the cover moves with me, stroking my arms and legs, indicating they are bare. No nasty smells assault me, no detestable music or taxis or voices, every sound is gone. Only the waves persevere.

My lids are too heavy to open yet. I understand I'm in a bed, enclosed by the sheet and micro-climate of my own body. If I unwrap from this chrysalis a chill will cake me. I am warm. I am safe.

I rose and fell in and out of sleep. Minutes were years. My pulse beat on my eardrums with a low-pitched whine while the sea bashed about in between. Eventually, with an inexplicable reluctance, the exterior sensations of sound, touch and smell caught up with one another and sluggishly coalesced into one. All it omitted was sight, that could wait.

I am in a bed, that's certain. I know this bed, the firm base, the weight of the quilt. I must have been dreaming, for nothing has changed. Like a science fiction character I have side-stepped out of the parallel dimension of yesterday, stepped out free and untarnished. I must have! Everything is so unspoiled, unaltered, none of yesterday happened.

It was a reassuring interval, that semi-conscious stage, and too brief. At some point my eyelids lost their weight and I could put it off no further.

Marston Packaging Ltd. Good morning.

Same pillow cover, same mattress, no need to ask about the quilt. Early morning light. There sits my unassuming alarm clock where I see it every morning. Nothing is different.

Except everything. How did I get here?

With utmost care, the waves threatening tsunamis, I lifted myself onto my elbows.

Yes, the gallery. I have been undressed to my underwear, vest and socks; was that me? I searched for some clue.

Marston Packaging answered for me. There draped my jacket over the boxes, a small pile of clothes on top, my handbag at the foot of the mattress. It was not my custom to place them so.

What's the last thing I remember? Crying. A spongy carpet dotted with trodden gum. Vodka. The stale taste still basted my tongue. Alice, Cromards, strobe lights.

I winced as something snagged a mole on my neck; the silver chain of my beloved pendant was caught in my hair. I righted it, the opal glimmered. What am I doing here? Both the hangover and questions exasperated each other and neither would be shushed.

There *was* an answer to this, an unutterably unwelcome sibling to my premonition of being watched yesterday, it loomed like a hatch provocatively ajar, waiting to be opened. I shunned it, lying in bed, propped sideways on my elbows to bide time, wishing I hadn't woken up. The only feasible plan being to focus, I ran down a very biased list of options.

Safe Logical Rona spoke up: I was so drunk I don't remember getting here myself.

Alone? You had no money for a bus and certainly none for a taxi.

Well then, I was taken here.

Yes, I rather gathered that, dear. By? How?

Alice and her friends, duh.

And where is she, milady? Not here. Or maybe I need my eyes tested?

No, she was not. Not a sign of her. She must have stayed elsewhere. Yes, that could work. She dropped me off here.

Really? (The condescension was morphing painfully into His voice.) *Alice would bugger off after planning to squat here, then go all the way across town for a shit-eating sofa bed?*

Okay, In-Denial-Logical Rona chimed; she left earlier, then!

That's positively funny. Look at the time, Rona. Go on, look, you chickenshit goose! 7:40 a.m. *You had to kick her out of bed at nine yesterday. And correct me if I'm wrong, but where's that whiff of cannabis that chases her everywhere like the flies?*

Fuck off, says Scared-Logical Rona. Fuck off! Maybe yesterday was a dream after all.

… Blankness.

I languished with my inconclusive thoughts, hoping sleep would reclaim me. Failing that, I grappled with a growing awareness of thirst. My throat was sandpaper. The idea of moving or dressing equally unfavourable. I must have passed a full hour in this mental–physical stand-off before deciding that if I made it downstairs for water, I could sleep; that way headache, thirst and sore throat are cancelled out.

Even just rising from bed, never mind dressing, was torturous. The waves surged until I wanted to keel. I moved like an elderly woman, resting intermittently, clasping the railing of the python stair, unflattering squelch noises coming from my stomach; my blood sugar must have been a disgrace.

At the base of the stair, I drew the burgundy curtain, bulkier than normal this morning, autopilot directing me eastward – to the chancel.

All motion ceased.

If the Bogie Man happens upon you in, say, a car park instead of jumping from your closet, it is so misplaced that your brain cannot select an emotion until it computes. You may simply go into screensaver mode, you may not feel anything, you may simply stand there, as I did.

Cautiously, stealthily, my feet worked east, lifting and landing, taking me closer. Not by willpower. I was driven by a shady entity still in its infancy, conceived over weeks of blood-stains, coffin-maker's clocks and loose jawbones, beetles scuttling from keyholes and dripping wells. You might argue an independent shade of Rona left its physical body standing by the burgundy curtain.

I am unsure if that shade, whose words you see here, was ever restored to its original owner, Reader; the owner may yet stand where that curtain hung in the present-day ruins of St Patrick's church. There were three human heads on the altar.

Three. Left, centre, right. The mind fills in gaps when you don't quite accept what you see: three odd shapes, what's to write home about that? The altar could otherwise be normal; the tablecloth, the decorative crucifix, the vases waiting to be refilled.

Separate pools of crimson laced the tablecloth, dripping having ceased hours ago. Jowls sagged in bags of greyish-yellow, in the early stages of decay. The dead look artificial, I have told you this before; the fact is they seemed too unrealistic not to be real.

In the head on the far right, an eyelid remained partially open over its sclera, lazily questioning something beyond my shoulder; the other lid drooped, tar-like bristles of a fake eyelash swinging in some indefinite wind like a dead insect. Claire's lip drooped sideways with her jaw, obeying gravity, a straggle of her bleach-blonde hair glued to her teeth. Where I expected to see ears, were two ruby holes.

The head was mounted on a tall brass candlestick, as was the one far left, a picturesque statement. No blood trail led to the altar. I calculated its engineering by the patterns of spillage: the designer had removed the candles, fished out the head, held it by the temples and borne *down*, chipping bits of vertebrae, crunching the neck deep until brass filled it from trachea to tonsils, perhaps giving that extra press on the crown, squeezing out the last of their juices. I could see the designer making adjustments, ensuring the position was secure. We don't want it falling off and spoiling the show, do we? I pictured them nudging it a bit this way, a bit that way, standing back to gauge it. Does that look squint? Never mind, it'll balance.

The brass holders were dyed barn red.

Most surreal were the mouths, or what was in them. The

cheeks bulged, horribly like a failed attempt at amateur taxidermy, their mouths transformed into ashtrays and waste paper bins overflowing with cigarette butts; plain ones, brown ones, filters smudged with tar and lipstick; chocolate wrappings, crisp packets, used bus tickets, jam-packed full. For a truly certifiable moment I had the temptation to laugh. They were a morbid cartoon of human hamsters, pouches stuffed to bursting.

The other head on the far left. Tatty fair hair, a face crumpled in agony, crow's feet spiking, Annie had died shutting out the sight of her executioner. Same mouth treatment, with an addition: under a biscuit wrapper stuck between her front teeth, her tongue flopped out too far to still be attached.

I did not notice it myself, but you might have seen me swaying absently in the chancel. The only other thing moving in St Patrick's was Claire's dangling eyelash. What am I looking at? Is it real?

Cue centre stage.

Mike? Is that you?

My pumpkin, the largest I had bought in years. Michael was back, complete with stalk cap, his spoiling face indented, gradually caving in. When my knife sawed through that golden flesh two days ago, his chunky jaws were ripe, succulent and tough. Today his canines celebrated no more; they curled inward, slick with pasty rims, forming the toothless snarl of an evil old codger. Falkirk threw Michael out yesterday, someone had retrieved him especially. He stank of sweet rot.

Nice smell, isn't it? Yes, Serge.

Something was inside it. I saw the milky layer peeping through a pie-wedge eye. Michael was possessed of a devil in his afterlife, winking a dead scalp at me; he had new masters now. Two nights ago he was rejoicing with me, his childhood pal, shining his naughty visage around our new home. Michael greets me this morning, transfigured into a shrivelled whore of Hell chuckling defiant triumph in my face, freed, liberated, finally in his true element. Another slice of me severed, gone forever. The stalk cap was a light lift away.

I couldn't. I knew what was in there. It is her, isn't it? They corrected her, too. It is. It's my fault.

I could not imagine her in there. I saw only her mischievous smile and boyish sparkle, not her jaw lapsed to one side, not her mouth yellowing in a deathly gape. *Cool pumpkin, by the way. Have a choc Frankenstein.* Three unwise monkeys on the altar: hear no evil, speak no evil … See none? Alice didn't deserve that!

Incensed, I lunged and punched the pumpkin's caved-in mug with all my strength. The cap toppled away, rolling on the tip of its stalk. Michael, my Pumpkin King, split in two.

Ta-daaaaa!

Oh.

Quite unaware of what I was doing, I bowed over the rotting vegetation.

Such a surprise. A carefully orchestrated provocation of my overlords' making with expert forethought. I had reacted exactly how they'd wanted me to. What a gag!

A sallow, egg-shaped countenance slopped on its side. Both eyelids had been torn open in two ragged lines. The orbital cavities were slushy pouches, still moist, literally bitten out.

They showed you, too, didn't they, Gaz? Been there, my dear, got the T-shirt. Showed you the last thing you would ever see, two viper sickles coming for your eyes. I saw them too; I screamed too. You got off on the wrong foot. No handshakes for you, no waves, no 'Yoo-hoos', straight down to business.

They had deliberately left his mouth alone, wanting me to see his scream and plainly visible tongue slumped across his teeth like a lecherous slug.

I surveyed the exhibition, took in the whole display. I can virtually see myself as I was, Rona standing there in her socks and yesterday's clothes, seeing the altar, her eyes moving robotically, side to side like a machine. What does that remind me of? Got it.

Dray Beach. My aunts' summer destination every year during my primary school holidays.

The funfair was their annual treat. They bought me ice lollies, paid for donkey rides, the ghost train and carousel. Aunt Pam gambled on the fruit machines in Happy Harry's Amusements Arcade while I rode the coin-operated green dragon outside, safely out of the way, inhaling the luscious vapours of hot dogs and candy floss, obsessively fixed on the coin slot as the dragon rocked me in stationary circles, not looking up. I was afraid to look up in case Harry caught me.

Dominating the arcade entrance towered a twelve-foot humanoid ice cream machine, Happy Harry the Ice Cream Clown, a chilling figure painted in a stripy sailor's shirt. He ran on a constant motor, drowning out the carousel music with a clunking, dead *hummmmmm*. My aunts told me not to be so silly, it can't hurt you, et cetera. I did not believe them. His eyes were alive, they constantly moooooved, swivelling slooowly, side to side, moving away from me (*Where is she?*), coming for me (*Where's she gone?*), coming …

I detested it. It was malignant. It was a monster.

(*Where is sheeee …? There she is!*)

I am looking at three decapitations. I am as still as a rotating ice cream machine, as alive as a stripy sailor clown. Shouldn't I be feeling something, doing something? There was nothing to feel, yet conformity says otherwise, so I noted this advice and analysed the altar for help. What trouble the designer–executioner went to, I thought; how ridiculous the thugs looked, in life and in death. I thought about how *I* looked.

I have brought Happy Harry to life. And he is laughing, laughing through my larynx, no Rona here, she's on holiday at Dray Beach, gone away, would you like to leave her a post-it?

Exterior noise Number One: a door opened and closed from

the south aisle, clippety-clop.

Exterior sound Number Two: 'What's so funny?' Good morning, Minister Falkirk.

Exterior noise Number Three: quite a din as his books, belongings, whatever, fall to the floor. For that matter I think he has fallen to the floor. Oh, wait, no, he's colliding with the pew benches, that sounds like his soles sliding sideways on the tiles. I'll have to wax them again, sigh. There goes another toppled bench. Better take a look.

I turned to him, almost hearing Happy Harry's mechanical *hummmmmm* enabling my neck.

Falkirk swooned, paler than the altar décor, attempting exclamations. 'Gah!' and 'God!' escaped, not much else. I'll give him his space, would be rude not to. He really does seem to be having trouble with that swoon though, doesn't he? He is not being clever, tick-tock, morning service soon, better float over to remind him.

Hickory dickory dock, the mouse ran up the grandfather clock. The clock struck nine, mouse called the time. Hickory dickory –

'What did you *do*?' He exploded from the knees up, the church shook with it and the organ pipes resonated, stopping me in my tracks.

That did it. Rona the Ice Cream Clown was exorcised. Now I woke up properly.

I gaped at him as he repeated the damnation, supporting himself on a pillar, hobbling to his feet. His cannonball shouts struck the ocean of my headache, restarting the tidal waves like a fire alarm and for a second they deafened me, sloshing in and out of the crater.

'What did *I* do?' I echoed, wounded.

'You caused this! You set this off! Dear God, help us!' he cried to the skies. 'Damn this accursed house!'

He was having a meltdown. Morning service started in half

an hour. Dray Beach was replaced by a sick awareness of the altar behind me. If I faced it sober I might go the same way as Falkirk. Grim, I was a grim thing and he a maggot, but the congregation would be here soon and no number of martyrs or ice cream clowns was going to stop the tick-tocks, Falky, ask any coffin-maker. Bugger his noise, is he still blubbing?

Falkirk wept in the aisle, wringing his hands, grunting and cursing. Morning service? What a joke, look at him!

No. No-no-no-no-no, that would not do; he made too much noise. I could not carry the raging waves, the altar and his ravings all at once.

'Stop it,' I said.

He cried on.

'Stop it.'

He would not.

The waves charged, steering towards me. I seized myself. It was my chance; I had a job to do; if I did not act without reflection or feeling we would both have infinitely more to panic about. I went to Falkirk and smacked him.

'*Stop it!*'

The minister careered into a pillar and sprawled, subjugated, nursing his assaulted jaw as I set the benches upright. When I approached him he retreated as if I were last night's assassin.

'Change your underwear later and listen,' I said, a voice of stainless steel. 'Bring the bin bags and gloves from under the sink. I'll get the air freshener and spare cloth. Move fast or by fuck I'll make work of you. And *shut up*! You've seen as bad. We both have.'

Falkirk brought what I asked for then slipped away, leaving me to attach a notice outside the front portal: 'No morning service due to sickness', with his apologies. Falkirk could deal with things sooner than I, Serge? Believe everything Serge says and you will sooner or later pay. Disbelieve anything he says and you'll pay before your next toilet break.

I removed the crucifix and vases, remarkably unstained; next I folded up each corner of the tablecloth, covering the exhibit like a ghostly shroud.

The altar. Three clothed mounds more terrifying when hidden, already zombies daring me to uncover them. From an unbidden compartment in my subconscious, that which produces nightmares so twisted you worry what unspeakable part of your brain conjured them up, a vicious imp muttered secretively, *What if you lifted the cloth, Rona? Oh! What if their lopsided jaws tried moving? What if their eyes open? Lift it and find out, Rona. Claire's winking at you under there, I swear, winking her dangly insect lash. They'll spit at you, Rona. They'll try talking through the crap in their mouths, 'Gllrrrrullz!' then POW, like popping a crisp packet, ashtrays and bin gobs blowing straight into yours. You'll choke on it. 'And then you'll never shut us up, Rona! We'll yell and yell and yell, no matter where you bury us! You'll never get any sleep up in that gallery ever again! EVER AGAIN!' Egg Face wants to know why he never found Derek on Delfour Road. He deserves an answer, ooooh, you fibber!*

I tasted stomach acid and succumbed to it, my retches repeating with nothing in me to vomit up. It took four glasses of water to compromise the nausea while I double-bagged everything, hauled it to the Menzies crypt and dumped the burden.

Brass holders hit the stone floor with a piercing clank, jutting out in all directions like an odious set of bagpipes. Gaz's head could be lying on its side in there, seeing me better without eyes, his screaming lips pressing a big 'O' through the tarry plastic. I practically ran out, bolted the door and relocked it five times. Five times.

Just like riding a bicycle, my job. I changed the cloth and scrubbed the floor. In feverish need of a shower, I spent fifteen minutes knocking on Falkirk's door before he poked his snout through the lounge curtains. We spoke no more that day.

The hours passed. I kept outdoors. I visited Fergus Green, the riverbank, the streets, the churchyard and Fergus Green again. If people saw me walking in circles, sod them.

I *must* stay outdoors, there are ghosts inside.

Chapter Five

The sun set before five. I climbed St Patrick's bell tower to watch it through a peak window, as far from the gallery as its prisoner could reach indoors.

Church towers invoke all manner of romantic ideals and Gothic enchantments; unfortunately this tower was not grand, a sixteenth-century structure no higher than sixty-something feet, its stairwell too narrow to fit more than one person. Fine by me, I needed the seclusion. A crisp twilight breeze soared high above Bronmeg's car pollution and blew in through the window. I might have been watching the clouds from a hill-top, browsing the horizon for birds in flight, imagining I might transpose my spirit onto their backs; some wild geese perhaps, it was their time for migration. I loved listening to skeins hulla-baloo at each other from hundreds of feet high, you could hear them coming miles away; comical when waddling on webbed toes, then when they flew over you they were sky gods, air-borne soldiers. Sadly, no geese tonight, not even a pigeon.

The peak window was not vista-friendly or adjustable. By rights I should have been able to climb out onto the ledge like Notre Dame's gargoyles, they fitted my mood. Metal blinds restricted my view of a spectacular stratosphere streaked with lashings of gold and plum, the sun dropping until the west was ablaze with a rippling sheet of fiery cloud; brush your palm on its underside and you feel the feathered belly of a red swan, hot as a searing furnace. It was Helios' chariot of fire.

No such beauty exists to last. Fire cooled to aubergine, fading to silver as the stratosphere gave a final encore of magenta, then died. I had to leave this hilltop, there were no excuses left for being here.

Nearly five o'clock. What awaited me? How right you are to ask. I gave up hypothesising however they'd managed to track me to Cromards' band room and bring me home. And I *was* home, things were back in place (I wished). They had even gone to the trouble of leaving me tokens, employing Michael as their personal messenger. Gaz would bother me no more. Summoned by three mutilations, a tornado at my heels could not have impelled me harder, a gesture as specific as Serge's snapping knuckles, this time *commanding* me to sit! Sit right there and wait for them.

Was I afraid? Quite so. What would your choice have been? I had two legs, I could have bolted again if I were the world's greatest fool. I stayed, rigged by their psychological fetters until the hour arrived.

Which is now, by the way.

Fear being a perfectly acceptable escort, I let it accompany me as it pleased. Why not take a book with your tobacco and go sit in the pews, Rona? Have a sip of nostalgia and reclaim St Patrick's as your reading room for old times' sake? Certainly, I'll do that. So, I took my ashtray, left the church lights on and – what was I reading, let me see … a Thomas Hardy novel, yes, six days since I'd bookmarked my page; I was having trouble getting into it. Anything might happen tonight, who knows, maybe I'll die. You should have chosen a more interesting book for your final hours, Rona, what are you like?

This is how I drifted through the minutes, losing my mind by conscious decision before anybody else got the chance to do it for me, because it's all very well having Fear sit by you, but to have it jump on my lap? – that would finish me. I propped my feet up on the pews and fooled myself I was reading, tottering on some fine purgatorial line between hysteria and fainting.

Three trembling cigarettes later: 5:35 p.m. and no company yet. My burning bladder gave the next orders. Washing my hands in the sink afterwards, a fleeting glance in the toilet's oval mirror revealed a very thin girl. My eye sockets were hovels, and with the assistance of lipstick I might have auditioned for an anorexic Snow White. Speaking of lips, at least my lower one was healing.

The toilet door swung to as I re-entered the aisle, still devoid of company. It was horribly quiet. Not even the routine hum of rush hour traffic outside, a rarity, as I started back for my seat. I suddenly stopped dead.

The wonders of peripheral vision. It tapped on my shoulder with invisible shaky fingers, a voice of elusive precognition, more afraid than I, hissing a whisper out of nowhere.

Rona. Rona! To the left.

No, not there, further left.

Rona, look *up*!

They were standing on the balcony, looking at me.

Hector, Serge, Edith, standing straight and solid as three caryatids in a Greek temple. Not in the balcony – *on* it, twenty-five feet high on a balustrade less than ten centimetres wide; you or I would fall. Nobody spoke, nobody moved.

Then they jumped.

In perfect synch, they jumped. Their shoes hit the floor, releasing a singular echo which died instantaneously as, placidly, they proceeded towards me, no rush, taking their time, Edith buttoning her cashmere, Hector coughing in his usual offbeat manner. Edith's impersonal heels clipped along, leading them to our habitual rendezvous point at the chancel, where she greeted me with a voice of liquid mercury.

'Good evening, Rona.'

'Good evening,' I said.

'What's the matter?'

I had no willpower for constructing word-perfect answers. 'No quarrel from me,' I replied.

'Well, that's always nice.' She shrugged, unfurling a posh chiffon scarf. 'Looking a tad underweight though, aren't we?'

'Am I?'

'How are your eating habits?' she asked, fastening a pair of leather gloves.

'I don't keep track.'

'Do we have to cook for you again?' she joshed. 'No matter, we will anyway. Taxi, Clemensworth Street at four a.m., please.'

'Very good.' I nodded woodenly.

'And come to us at six tomorrow evening,' she instructed, wrapping the chiffon about her shoulders.

I locked my hands behind my back; there was nothing else to grip on to. 'May I enquire as to my dues, please?'

'Your dues,' she echoed mockingly.

'My AWOL.'

Silence.

'The assumed punishment,' I said, humiliated at having to spell it out. *Get on with it, punish me, get it over with!*

Edith rewarded my naked submission with a predatory grin.

'Open the window for a moth and what does it do? Flies back to the flame! Why do you think we didn't tear off its wings and impale it in the entomology cabinet?'

'I'd rather you tell me.'

'Because we're not idiots. People *will* fuck.'

She and Hector laughed out loud. I waited until they finished their gratified snigger.

'Did you kill her?'

I had finally asked, as morosely as I looked. *Was there*

313

enough left of her to throw down the well? I wanted to shout it, but if I shouted I wouldn't stop, I'd get louder, I would holler this fucking house of God down. That would cause problems. Be smart if you can't be kind. Besides, I assumed it was a redundant question; Alice was dead and gone.

'Hmmm, no,' Edith replied, picking haughtily at her gloves, 'but I wouldn't expect to see her.' She clipped her petite handbag shut, yawning. 'Nor will the elfin locksmith be picking at doors any time soon. Excuse the yawn but noteworthy topics don't wear out so quickly. Did it look like rain outside? No, no, put your phone away, we're in the mood for exercise. The Taurids meteor shower is due, did you know this?'

Obviously not if I thought I could deflect meteors, Edith.

'No rain,' I answered. 'Clear forecast.'

'Ta. See you later. Oh, and don't trouble yourself contacting Derek again. He's deteriorating. G'night.'

The south exit was closed and locked from the outside. I looked stupidly at my book.

What did you make of that? Brief, was it not? No punishment, no lecturing, no impaling, and here I am booking their taxi. Do you reckon I escaped that encounter without chastisement?

There was chastisement. Or it was due. It simmered through their pleasant greeting like acid, and though I could deal with Edith and Hector laughing at me, never had the deadliest vibe been so sugar-coated. I ask again, what did you make of it? What did you notice?

While Edith did the talking and flaunted her chiffon scarf, while Hector ambled and laughed along with her, there was a third party, leaning on the altar: arms folded, head cocked sideways, staring the entire time, void of expression or emotion. It coated the chancel with serrated frost.

He – had – not – said – a word.

~

The usual monotony of duster and brush ensued after morning service. The most tedious part was sweeping under the rows of pew benches, a favourite place for shoe marks and a job I put off, transepts and aisles being easier to deal with.

The day was bright for November and granted the stained glass its full glory. At this hour the sun penetrated most windows in the south aisle, dabbing me in multi-coloured rays. I slouched on my brush, watching the minute specks of dust glide in lazy motion. In this meditation, I secretly questioned if sunbeams could sing like wind chimes. As a child, I once tried sitting on a sunbeam and earned a bruised posterior for my efforts. Today, with Falkirk avoiding me like a sewer, in this isolation I wanted St Patrick's to feel like mine again, building of my childhood, dappled in rods of sunlight from arched windows. And it never would be. It never was. *No, Rona*, it corrected; *you're mine.*

I was raising my brush to chop a sunbeam in half when the policeman walked in through the front portal.

I remember him perfectly. You always do.

He sauntered boldly down the nave, imposing in his suit and well-combed hair. His shoes were as expensive as his attire, chestnut-brown, good leather, contrasting with his watery eyes. A clicky-top pen sat neatly in his pocket as if sewn in there. He strode to and fro with practised nonchalance and addressed me with the plod of a polished cogwheel, very professional, not above a bit of vanity. In his six-foot build I saw years of physical training and gym workouts, so three-dimensionally alive, so in one piece, such a normal day for him. So alive.

'Hello, there,' he said. 'I was looking for the minister, please?'

'He's out at lunch,' I said. He never answers his door either, mate.

'Oh.' He fumbled in his breast pocket and took out a folded leather wallet. 'Maybe you can help me.' The man showed identification.

Voilà. Detective Inspector, CID.

'D. I. Matthews,' he said. 'I'm investigating an attack that occurred on Cain Road a couple of nights ago.' Out came his tiny ringed pad and tiny biro attached by a tiny string. 'I'll just take your name, please?'

He took my name. It felt like giving my body away. The church refused to echo me.

'Are you acquainted with a Miss Alice Peiper –'

(*'Did you kill her?'* – *'I wouldn't expect to see her.'*)

'– by any chance?'

My circulation turned to porridge. 'Afraid not.'

There he goes, fishing into his breast pocket again. Oh, Jesus Christ, it's a photograph … She looks so young! Stop showing it, please, put that sprite's smile away!

It was unforgivable of me to flush at that moment. Cops are trained to read everyone; the bastard pushed that photo further in my face.

'You're sure? You don't know this girl?'

I shook my head.

Matthews' tone changed. 'No, you're not sure, or no, you don't?'

I slipped, badly. 'Cain Road? Was that girl hurt?' I almost bit a chunk from my tongue at the blunder. Shit, no, Rona! Zip it!

On went the light bulb above Matthews' head. 'You just said you didn't know her.'

'I don't recognise her.'

'Hmm.' D. I. Matthews was good at his job and I had already fucked up, because he took up his dinky stringed biro again. 'I'll just grab your date of birth, thanks.'

Great, my personal details in the belly of the beast by the

powers that suppose themselves to be. That's just great. If I had my lighter I would have ignited his notepad.

'So, working here,' he pursued, adding a lilt of expert inflection to rile or trip me, 'you see a lot of people going in and out of this church, correct?'

This was becoming a masked interrogation. The blood rushed to my forehead; knowing he caught a scent, the tiniest mistake on my part could explode the keg.

I answered him, 'Yes,' at which he baited the next question.

'Well, all we've got out of Miss Peiper in hospital is the name of this church. Have you seen this man, perhaps?'

What did he say? Hospital? Matthews was now waving a photograph of Gaz, which I did not need to see. *Hospital. Is he speaking in past or present tense? Dead or not? You three manipulative ... calculating ... pit vipers!*

I am sure Matthews read my distraction, immediately triggering a bigger problem.

'Mind if I have a quick wander round while I wait for the minister?' he asked decisively.

'Of course not,' I said. 'Go ahead.'

What else was I supposed to say? The inspector had no intention of forgetting me yet and ... and he's already wandering towards the python stair.

Lava plumed beneath my brow, hearing my mental voice shout in depraved affiliation with Falkirk's: *Don't you know it's private, Inspector? No access!*

This thought was answered by another.

Ronaaa?

I knew where it came from, too. *Choose or we decide. What good are you to us, Rona, if –?*

D.I. Matthews was drawing the burgundy curtain.

Mechanically, inhumanly, I propped the brush and duster against the altar, bent, legs trembling, and picked up my usual torch. The keys were in my jeans pocket.

Ronaaaaaaaa?

I hear you. Yes, I know. I hear you. I hear you.

Cli-klick-siffffffft

Detective Inspector Matthews wheels around.

'What's that?' he blurts.

He would have been blind to overlook my key jittering, me detaching the fake base of the cupboard, feeling extremely sick. There was nothing else to do. *Rona, what if chance brought a policeman to our gate?* How surprisingly easy to push the exact button it intended. Dear me, I remember that cop so well.

'This?' I said, giving my body language one hundred percent permission to give its skittish self away, hideously simple, no acting required. 'It leads into the Menzies sepulchre. I, er, must, er, change the mouse traps or they breed throughout the building.'

D. I. Matthews' desired attention brought his chestnut soles further and further away from the world, directly towards me.

Come on, moth; incriminating evidence, isn't that what you want? This is incriminating, your bread and butter, you see how scared I am. Why don't I humour you, Inspector, help you out? Help me, Derek!

'Mind if I …?' Matthews assumed control of the torch, plucking it from me.

Surfing on nerves filled me with a bizarre kind of quavering energy as I held the door for him. I thought my bowels might liquefy.

'I really don't have to reset the traps now, you know,' I pleaded. 'I can do this later.'

'No, it's okay. After you,' he ordered.

After me, in case I lock him in, no doubt, and he's left the cupboard doors wide open, too. How predictably sensible. He'll smell Gaz, Claire and Annie very soon.

Matthews commanded the scene, swinging my torch in thick hands that had arrested drug dealers, thieves and maybe reduced the toughest of psychopaths to tears in the interview room. This is your bag, Matthews, you could wrestle me, no contest. I see him following me in there, his tie of speckled puce, his dimple, his wedding band, an oblong mole on his neck. Escape, D. I. Matthews. I'm begging you flee from here now.

'The, er …' I said, diverting him without trying too hard. The cautious Matthews did not walk far, not that it was necessary; I make the tiniest tweak on his strings and bingo, he is ready. Mark how in control he thinks he is.

Matthews, distracted by the smell of dead meat and ashtrays, followed it into the sepulchre, specifically where he thought I didn't want him to go. I stayed out of his way, hands behind my back, unfastening by feel, by experience, too easily, the secret latch with feather-light touches. In about two seconds Matthews would discover three heads.

'So,' says Mister CID, sniffing suspiciously, 'where are those mouse traps?'

A piercing creak! Matthews spun to see the iron gate, agape and ready with all the patience of a Venus fly trap.

'I'm sorry, Inspector,' said my silhouette in the cupboard doorway. 'You're in it.'

I will always hear that oak casing slam and lock twenty times louder than the day Daniels died.

The next thing I remember was bursting from the south exit and crashing into the façade, plugging my ear holes until my cuticles filled with blood to stab out every other possible sensation. *Eyes, clamp! Ears, ring and bleed! Scream and scream only inside, see, hear and speak no evil while you do it all.* And nothing I did seemed to block the vibration of Matthews' borrowed heartbeats coming through the stone walls. The building murmured and rippled with him.

Happy? Are you three leeches happy now? I just died a sec-

ond time. Are you not fucking happy?

The church was so freakishly still you could have made a dent in the air with your fingertip.

My lonely brush and shovel waited for me in the chancel nearly an hour, just visible through a gap I made in the south aisle door. I could not stay outside forever. There they were, my brush and shovel propped up against the wall, a snapshot from a more innocent time, aeons ago, still cloaked in the acidic whiff of Matthews' insistent aftershave. Temples burning, moving stiffly, I collected the cleaning utensils, keeping my head down and shoulders hunched, which was probably why I got no chance to register the cupboard doors flying open behind me.

Two clumps of snow landed over my eyes as Matthews' voice speared my eardrums like two knitting needles.

'*So!* Where are those mouse traps?'

I whistled a scream as my body arched, squirming round.

Stepping forward, Serge raised what appeared to be a brand new phone to his mouth from which sprang no voice of his own: Matthews' vocals, intonation to rhythm, replayed with sublime fluidity.

'Dave? Matthews here … Dead end at Clayburn. I'll follow up a lead on Rockbank Street and report back tonight … You're on, see ya!'

Quoth the raven. Perfect mimicry.

Tap. Off. Throw. Smash! A few hundred shards of Matthews' phone exploded off the nearest pillar and showered the pews.

The maniac was not through. For next I saw what cannot be imagined, what Falkirk had promised me could never happen, never-never, not ever, not in daylight! – He took another step forward.

Dazzling sunbeams were instantly transformed into murdering swords, they affected him immediately.

But he can't. The sun. He can't!

He appeared to take no notice; first, his colour extinguished to transparent gypsum until every underlying vein and tendon, red, pink, blue, turning black, made a hideous roadmap of his face, out-shining his eyes, nose and mouth. Then, rapidly, he degenerated from broad-chested man, to a decrepit. His limbs atrophied to brittle sticks as he hulked over, his joints ready to snap off like plywood, and *still*, shuffling like a broken marionette, the eroding cadaver was coming for me, glaring victoriously!

'Runaway will run away!' declared a voice of gravel. 'Leaving us, without this?'

Raising a twisted tree branch of an arm, he shook a keyless car remote system under my nose. Matthews' car. I'd forgotten his car.

The radiation sent off dry showers of exfoliation from him in appalling vapours, mixing with the sunbeams. When he groped for me, whether to attack, for support, or both, I wrestled, brushing his dishevelled face – it rubbed off as powder on my sleeve. He was crumbling! His skin! Every second worsened him.

Smiling senseless excruciation, Serge seized and shook me off my feet like a rag doll as his temper finally exploded full blast.

'Look what she makes me do!' he shouted, pressing the keyless remote into my hand. 'Haha! What will Runaway do? Drive into the sunset, or her job? What will she do?'

The sun was destroying him. His muscles imploded, his veins blazed crooked lightning across his body, throughout which the tragic creature laughed like a manic child, as if oblivious to what was happening to him.

He's insane! Is he actually daring me to watch him die in my arms?

'Jesus, why!' I screamed. 'Stop it, Serge! What are you *doing*?'

Serge yanked me to him, his nails slipping off.

'What she makes me!' he answered. 'Haha, oh, anything for the Dean! Yes, the sun works fast, doesn't it? Didn't your aunties tell you never to play with dead wasps? Aww, look, Falkirk, we're worrying Rona!'

How long Falkirk had been there I don't know. He materialised, standing in the opposite aisle like a cardboard cut-out, gripping some books at his navel, dour as a nameless gravestone. 'If you answer to God in his light of your own accord,' he told Serge, 'so be it.'

'Which god, Minister?' Serge brayed. 'Shall I answer to them alphabetically?'

I, worm in the middle, past caring if I hated him or not, was trying to push the immovable beast to the cupboard, trying to replace a mislaid card when the whole deck was capsizing.

Serge did not look like Serge anymore. The thing was film over a skull; his nose cartilage collapsed to an indented triangle; bone powder spilled from his mouth; the sunlight bleached away his grey-blue irises. No! I would not be guilt-tripped into seeing this manipulator disintegrate like an unwrapped mummy, not for his spite!

'No, Serge!' I shouted. 'Damn you, stop. Stop this!'

From inside the passage came a thin, withering, human wail.

Serge grinned maniacally, the indent where his nose used to be almost touching mine. 'Fee fie foe fum.'

This was the last blur I saw of him before flinging myself against the closing cupboard and slithering down the woodwork, soundproof woodwork through which no phone signal, screams, nor Serge's laughter should penetrate. Yet I heard it. In my pores I heard him, as did St Patrick's, its delayed reaction buffeting off the timber beams. Echoes are ghosts in their own right.

Disturbed sunbeams spiralled dizzily in the aftermath. They did not sing.

Lesson learned. Predict no beast; a dead wasp is just as dangerous as a live one, day or night. I squatted, suspended in some paralysed inertia until the world re-formed into recognisable shapes, much like the cry-baby at choir rehearsal, same place, same position many times since infancy.

Rona? Rona, can you hear me? Look at her, all grown up!

Uncanny to think fourteen years ago I sat here on a sorry Sunday before high school, my last day off before six infinite years of cowering from bitchy cliques in gymnasium corners and being ostracised in classrooms; six years of name-calling, of no life, of prison. Aunts Pam and Alison were so proud of my new high school uniform, showing me off to their churchy pals. The hard pews were intolerable that Sunday. I kept fidgeting; my lower back was unusually tender, as if someone had kicked me in my sleep, and my insides tingled with sharp pins. The only physical relief I'd found was this cupboard, its sturdy oak providing the heavenly support I needed. I'd stayed there awhile. Later on my aunts would freak out, bitching, 'Goodness sake, oh, you've ruined your new uniform! Why didn't you tell us?' A damp scarlet smear stained my school skirt. Fourteen years ago I unwittingly left a drop of my first woman's blood on this floor, where I am crouched now, 'all grown up'.

Falkirk was still there. See him, Reader, his gloating outline in the opposite aisle, his eyes meeting mine, not a crease of feeling in him.

I got up, locked the cupboard, scooped up the pulverised phone, and did my job.

This may not work, I thought; if I simply drop a match into the gasoline, it'll puff out.

Desolate Rockbank Landfill, a block from Rockbank Street, was a twenty-minute drive from Clayburn Avenue. The keyless remote system made it blessedly easy to locate Matthews' BMW, which stood out from the residents' vehicles anyway. No desert is more sinister than a landfill; they are the ultimate in man-made graveyards, mountains of dead waste like the festering bodies of leviathans that can't decompose. Taking the four-pint container of my lamp fuel, this amateur arsonist haphazardly drenched the interior, the boot and inside of the bonnet in gasoline, stuffed scrap paper into the cap and – keeping an anxious distance – ignited it, threw it into the BMW and ran for all I was worth.

Nothing happened. No flames. It hadn't worked.

Now what? I can't stay or leave! Nothing's hap–

I grabbed my temples as the heat waves knocked me. Flames swam between melting metal in the rear and passenger windows, spewing fumes and burning oil. Next the fuel tank blew, sending a vertical column of smoke above the leviathan hills. This impressive mushroom of fire seemed to carry a percipience I'd never encountered before; it rose like an angry soul over the blazing wreck, seeking me out, searching for me.

He was so alive. I locked him in.

It was crying my name in many voices. Can fire have a voice? (*I locked him in.*) My name! I heard my aunts, my aunts' friends, my school teachers; I heard Alice; I heard a seven-year-old running from the burning car, she's wearing that dress she hated, wasn't fair, they made her wear it every Sunday, she is running, coming for me. You locked him in.

Her hair was ablaze. She was screaming at me.

I fled, pelted, faster than her. I hope I did. Don't let her catch me.

You locked him in you locked him in locked him in locked him in

Occasionally I still see her. It happens only to us. Kills never haunt us, only our own ghosts, always unannounced.

Chapter Six

Edith and Hector were early.

'To hell with six o'clock,' Edith said. 'You're coming now.'

It was pointless asking why, Edith wanted none of my apprehensions tonight. Halfway down their stairs I nearly tripped over a shoe, chestnut leather, posh, lying on its side. It tumbled down the abyss in a series of jumps ahead of us.

'You'll be working down here every night for the time being,' she said militantly. 'Through the night.'

'But … my day job.'

'What of it?'

'It's what I'm paid for.'

'That's unfortunate.'

'How will I eat?'

She answered me with a threatening look, all but deleting my argument.

Underground at the T-junction, she turned in a semicircle and I was hauled, hostage to Edith, along a route I never expected to travel again in my lifetime.

'No. Edith, no!'

I almost saw her, the shred of a girl crudely resembling me, running past us in and out of my torchlight, her face raw with tears, dripping a red beard from lip to sternum, blue spider blood drying on her eyebrow, gaining distance. The cries waned, growing fainter and fainter until her sobbing phantom dissolved into the dark, gone. She was gone.

And with it, the spell of the east passage was likewise broken. The geometry presented itself, unapologetically vapid, meeting in a triangular vanishing point at who cares how far away.

We were getting worryingly close to their tunnel at the end, the fairy ring of my blood and tears probably still in there, dried to a neat circle in their carpet of so-called pulverised bone fragments. I would have fought the Devil himself if they meant to drag me in.

'Where are you taking me? Edith? *Edith!*'

No sympathy from her. My torch looped in a dramatic arc as she thrust me sideways through the doorway of a new vault. I landed in no fairy ring but on muslin, lots of it, shrouds and sheets blanketing an uneven landscape of objects.

'All this must be moved,' Edith commanded. 'All of it.'

'Moved where?'

'The Hall.'

To coincide with her answer, a rumble of traffic resonated from above, joined by a siren, too close. Delfour Road.

I made the mistake of thinking out loud. 'The roadworks.'

Edith nodded.

Good heavens, I was right. Why else would they move the vaults? My old concerns rebounded. What were they to do? Moving possessions is one thing, concealing themselves another. *I was right, I was right!* Given Edith's present indignation, I decided there and then to save my questions for Hector, not her.

Tough luck, watchdoggy; Queenie sensed your self-satisfaction before you did. She approached me, sophisticated, slender and saturnine, her contours hard and stern, she wanted to kill me.

'Do you like jelly, Rona?' she said. 'Ever make it at home,

kiddies' cooking crafts, lapping cake mixes off your aunties'
wooden spoon?'

'What? I don't know.'

'Ever not set it properly, let it turn to semi-gush?'

She moved closer. I had nowhere to retreat.

'Edith ...'

'Because that's what eyeballs feel like, Rona. And if you
so much as dream in your sleep of congratulating yourself, I'll
pick yours out in baby scoops with my fingernails. Fleas can
jump further ahead than you. We know everything about you,
and every strigoi in the county knows of here. And of Delfour
Road. Your game is our dice. Here, have another throw, on us.'
She threw off a muslin sheet.

Met with a new type of treasury, my jaw fell like a rock. It
was beautiful, and sad.

Gilded brass pommels, knuckle bows and grips in a pile
of nine or ten worn sheaths. An intricate basket hilt, once
gleaming proudly in the sun on its day of forging, lay flinty
and knotted with rust. A pile of longswords, rapiers, sabres and
cutlasses rested on a mound of plates measured for the biceps
of heavyset men.

Away flew more muslin sheets.

Here lies a hill of dented breast armour, armets and coifs,
pauldrons, gauntlets, tassets, pieces of joint, foot, elbow discs
and other plates I couldn't name, none glamorous or particularly romantic; the shine was gone, chipped and eaten by dirt.
Others showed signs of traumatic impact: a hounskull bascinet,
split across the snout as if by an axe; a piece of chainmail,
smashed breast to waist by a lance or a spiked mace. This
was no commercialised expo in a museum cabinet, no bullshit
here – this was men bleeding, this was marching through fields
of bog and gory mud. Minute clangs of uncovered steel sent
twinges up my sides.

I knelt, breathing in every detail. I had never handled a

sword in my life and would not presume to insult its memory now. Stroking a coned pommel, it guided me to the welded ribbons of an apple-shaped hilt. Where my imagination predicted smoothness, it found none; age had devoured the design to gnarled knots. Who had the guts to fight with swords in today's age of guns and smart bombs? Survival is survival, but I asked myself who really trained the hardest, the swordsmen of extinct generations or the gunmen of today?

'Save your romantics for later,' Edith scowled. 'I'm not in the mood. Pick those up. No, not like that!'

She pushed me aside and wrapped the weapons in muslin, more intentionally belittling than instructive, throwing the pile of armour and weaponry, a starter for dozens, into my arms. I buckled under the weight.

'Stop that, Runaway,' she said. 'You caused enough trouble today!'

'Today?' I retaliated. 'I didn't invite that cop or your deranged master into the sun!'

That was very stupid, Rona.

With stately grace, Edith reached into the muslin sheet, drew out a rusted, formidable rapier and, wielding it with the skill of a veteran, pressed the tip to my mouth.

'A reminder for imprudence,' she said. 'On behalf of Serge, Hector and I, we three owe you an apology – for thinking we needn't inform you of the first rule in our service: there is no such thing as argument. When we say frog, you hop.'

No quarter was given. The blade parted my lips and entered my mouth.

The pile I held instantly reunited with the floor in a deafening tumult. Healing wounds reopened and I bled where the rapier scratched my upper palate. Edith restrained me with her free hand.

'Why are you not hopping?' she demanded.

I tried everything, pulling away, gripping the blunt weapon

and grazing my palms as she carried on forcing it as far into my throat as it would go.

'I said, frog! Hop, Froggy. Is it deaf?'

I made a crooked sort of jerk, gagging, eyes watering, my raspberry-ripple saliva running down the blade.

'Call that a hop? Frog, or ... jelly!'

She moved the rapier to my eyes. Now I really *did* jump.

'Edith, no more!' I cried, hating myself more than her for my succumbence. 'No more!'

Edith lost interest, settling for the spectacle of me nursing my throat in hacks, spits and heaves.

'And look what you've done!' she carped. 'Made a mess. Pick it up and walk. Or we'll kill you.'

Edith prodded me in the ribs. 'Don't forget this, silly,' she said, sliding her bloodied rapier home with the rest.

There was a tangible air of unrest in the Hall. Edith's demeanour was non-negotiable and Hector was harried, gathering bags and empty bottles, both of them preparing to go out. Serge was nowhere to be seen.

They spoke urgently, arguing in a mix of foreign dialects while Edith refastened her gloves and I stood there, straining under the weight of weaponry until Hector relieved me of it.

'Go up, Rona,' Edith said. 'He wants to talk to you.'

Wants to talk to you.

Wheezing with pain, I, Rona the Runaway, clambered through the trapdoor, preparing myself for worse chastisement in the church upstairs.

On my way to the stairwell, there came the most doleful of voices I think I've ever heard.

'Rona.'

I stopped. It came from the right. The jazz chamber, Derek's milking room.

'In here.'

I directed the torch.

What I saw … I forgot my lacerated palate.

A drawn, emaciated figure lay sprawled across the sofa, head lolling on an armrest, ankles over the other, polishing a humerus bone on his lap. A bottle of blood sat at his side, two swigs from finished. I had passed him twenty minutes ago without realising. Weakly, he beckoned me closer.

Oh dear, what a sight he was.

Very ill indeed. The clothes he always filled out hung off him. Two buried eyes moved deep inside what appeared to be the cut-out slits of a clay mask, not epidermis as I knew it, a crust inundated with a million criss-crossing cracks, the sort you find on smashed china or peeling paint. The most trivial movement exhausted him; I heard his bones grating like door jambs. He had no jowls or muscles to speak of, he was skeletal, worse than our introductions months ago. Though his nose had regained shape and his retinas swam with enigmatic fervour, they were albino and unable to reflect.

With excruciating effort, he made himself more perpendicular.

'Grab a seat,' he said. 'May as well turn up that lamp for yourself.'

For all my hypocritical principles, this was irreconcilable, what Serge had reduced to. I turned up the lamp and moved a chair over.

'Don't get up,' I said.

'I, er, did not plan to,' he said, ogling me sardonically as always. 'I'm indoors tonight. Edith and Hector will be doubly busy. Full recovery will ta–,' he paused, breathless, '– take a few nights.'

I adjusted the gas lamp, glancing at the humerus bone on his lap. It was dry and corroded but adorned with the beginnings of some elaborately carved figures or Celtic knots.

'Hector's work,' said Serge. 'Poor oaf wastes his time. This is too old, too porous.'

I was not listening. The gas lamp illuminated more of Serge than my torch. In sporadic patches on his face, neck and wrists bulged enormous chunky black blisters, some drying to crisped bubbles, others bloated and greasy like obese leeches, it was disgusting. My stomach squirmed.

'After-burns,' he explained. 'They'll fall off soon. Get the surgeon's case.'

'For what?' I asked, obeying.

'For nursing an old man. Come here.'

He pulled me to the chair, fishing out the tubes and needles.

'Sleeve up,' he commanded.

I see no Derek here, do you? Serge grabbed me by the wrist, preventing escape.

'What?' I cried. 'Oh, no.' I leapt off the seat, not that it helped me break free. 'No, Serge, wait, please!'

He thumped me into the chair. 'Hold still, ninny! You're not anaemic and I need the pint more than you.'

Even in this state there was no fighting his strength. He proceeded. To be fair, my wriggling made it more painful; Serge was not sloppy.

'*Ahh*-tsss!'

'Oh, shut up,' he said. 'There we go.'

There was nothing I could do. My own blood ran away from me with alarming enthusiasm, through the tube, directly into his mouth. I squirmed while he demanded I stay still, seeing him drink me like a straw. Nothing I could do! It is debilitating to see your true place on the food chain thus executed; Rona the piece of meat. Serge fed in long sips on and off, between breaths, reclined and tranquil.

I latched on to my seat, queasiness taking me.

'Or would you prefer the old-fashioned way,' Serge mocked, 'where I risk popping your radial artery?'

'I'll use the bottle instead,' I begged. 'Serge, let me use the bottle.'

'What for? I'm right here!' He licked a red drop from his lip. 'Ha, she doesn't trust me. That'll make this more fun.'

How fast was he draining me? How could I trust him? My feet pedalled the floor, I couldn't help it.

'I said stop that,' he husked. 'Waiting for those two won't speed my recovery. I stay topped up or I wither.'

'Recovery?'

'We're essentially dead bodies, Rona. At my age, you just ...' he squeezed the frangible head of the humerus: it exploded like a puffball, '... crumble away,' he finished, sprinkling the fragments in dreamy contemplation.

'And that's your bane of daylight?' I asked. 'It makes you crumble?'

Serge gradually glazed over until I wasn't there. He was zoning out, far off, seeing through me from somewhere I could never visit.

'It makes us rot,' he said.

What had the storytellers taught me about the undead in daylight? That they ignite or evaporate? No fictional account did justice to what I had seen today.

'Then why jog its knife edge?' I asked him.

'I told you my experience was hard-earned. You were very funny. Here,' he sipped, 'get used to it. We're beautiful.'

Leisurely, purposefully, Serge showed me again.

A snake's fangs, and yet they were not. Nor hollow like a viper's. A retractable pair of robust, two-inch sickles ending in the sharpest possible needle-points designed for precision, designed to pierce. They were *extra* teeth, in the gum above his incisors, nothing like the modified, spontaneously-elongating canines in your books and films. Fully bared, each fang pulled on a thin outer layer of gum, its base pink near the root, sudsy with spittle. By some muscular mechanism he controlled the length and speed of retraction from steady to super-fast.

Again, I cannot compare the disfiguration of his upper jaw to anything other than a shark's, thrusting forward so the fangs get a better aim and avoid piercing his lip. It terrifies and humbles you, but it also hypnotises, the same way a majestic tornado or volcano will transfix you to the spot until there's no time left to run. Then gobble you up. You may think you are bold as brass; you must believe me, you're not.

'And yet you live under a church,' I observed.

Serge sipped watchfully, gulped and subtly smacked his lips together. 'We're older than Christianity, madam.'

There goes another storyteller's myth, deleted by his flinty tone.

'Rockbank Landfill,' he said. 'I smell it on you.'

'Is this,' I touched the tubing, 'my dues?'

Serge sipped and swallowed.

Finally he asked, 'Did you like our decorating?'

Decorating? *Decorating.* A nudge here, a nudge there, bingo, it balances on the brass holder. Without trial, judge or jury, the concepts of right or wrong knew no place in this room; just nature's barest face. I had no choices or filters left. They were banished.

'It reminded me of the altar roses,' I said. 'People pick flowers for decoration to watch them die. You can only display them for so long before they brown and dry out.'

'A pity.'

'Thank you anyway,' I said, losing focus as light-headedness set in.

'Do you think it a waste?' he asked.

'Of what?'

'The roses.'

'Yes. I never saw the point.'

'You should've taken a photo for remembrance.'

'Of roses?'

'No.'

The game of metaphors over, Serge removed the needle. 'Done.'

'You're still angry with me,' I said, pressing cotton wool on the spot. How he restrained himself from draining me dead I'll never know.

Instead of answering, Serge reached and lifted my pendent.

'*Patronus forum*,' he said, rolling the opal between his thumb and index finger. 'The patron of thieves. "It gifts the bearer with acutest sight, but clouds all other eyes with thickest night." Marbodus, Bishop of Rennes, 1060. According to him, they granted the power of invisibility. If a bearer dies, its tints dim without their body heat, hence people feared them as harbingers of death. The spectra, they shine over your heart.'

Where did the next few minutes go? I had plateaued, and I don't mind telling you it was easier to bear than the quicksand of humanity's conscience, infinitely easier than grieving for a murdered policeman with a wedding band who walked into St Patrick's alive today. I had found myself a real dragon. Happy Harry would be so proud of me.

The other two returned. Serge's animalistic pupils announced it.

'Here comes the cavalry,' he said.

Edith and Hector passed the vault without acknowledging us while I packed up the surgeon's case.

'Where do you think you're going?' Serge growled.

'I thought we were done.'

'Unless my memory fared worse than my good looks, you were specifically instructed to grace us with your presence tonight. You have work to do.'

Serge picked at a carbonised blister on his neck, causing it to rupture and crack inward. Ebony flakes fell into a cavern of salmon-pink tissue beneath. Fourth degree burns. Perhaps not all storytellers were inaccurate.

Very soon Hector came in, a suspicious stain on the corner

of his mouth, and lifted Serge from the sofa, half-carrying him to the Hall.

Until I started walking, I thought I would be okay. Whatever you drained, Serge, you took more than a pint!

I picked up the lamp. It weighed a ton. I almost dropped it, aqua-green with nausea, my lobes throbbing in pins. My legs went numb and my vision swam, multiplying the trapdoor into three-and-a-half trapdoors, causing me to stoop in dizzy spasms. I saw the latch cut my thumb and felt no pain; the digits might have belonged to someone else's body.

By the time I caught up with them in the Hall my brain was frothing to my ankles. I crumpled to the floor, swaddled in a spherule of lamplight, three beings passing through it. It would be categorically impossible to carry out Edith's instructions tonight, or make it to the gallery for that matter.

Hector eased his master into the Byzantine chair with an undeniable devotion that quite amazed me, fussing over him and feeding him from more green bottles. Hector's assistance had unwittingly dislocated the left side of Serge's jaw, twisting his face skew-whiff like a melting waxwork. I have to admit it sickened me. Seeing me blench, Serge self-consciously touched his chin – and the jaw lapsed entirely, slumping unnaturally to his collar.

Viperous Edith stepped in front of them, obstructing my view. 'What are *you* looking at?' she snapped defensively.

The semblance of a voice, no more than a wisp, came from an otherwise comatose Serge.

'Edith. Give her the tissues from my pocket.'

I had forgotten about the bloody drool around my mouth.

'Edith,' I panted, ready for unconsciousness if she brandished another sword, 'the armoury … I've no strength.'

'Good,' she said, delivering the hankies, 'now you're at least one-tenth as weak as *he* is!'

Judging by the sense of urgency, and not least by Edith's happy mood, she and Hector were in for no respite tonight either, readying themselves for another excursion. Serge was seriously ill and typically it was all Rona's fault. On their way out, their supposedly slumbering master abruptly lunged forward in his chair at them.

'Wipe your *mouth*, Hector!'

I worked my way despairingly through the hankies, my pockets filling up with the rags, and flumped, weak as a kitten, facing the ceiling.

Serge, meanwhile, of all things, was whistling, also facing the ceiling. He swigged another blood bottle of emerald green glass, a flutter of renewed energy in his flippant voice.

'I keep meaning to find a swivel chair for this Hall,' he said. 'One of my favourite inventions, those, spinning round and round to kingdom come. It's those random snippets of absurdity that keep the world alive, isn't it? These fatuous spurts between the rush hour traffic of functionality. Come to think, that's your job, my girl! Buy one, will you?'

Lost in the ceiling, semi-conscious, I pictured him spinning in such a chair as he spoke, clockwise here and anticlockwise there in his smug delight.

'What colour?' I said.

'Ummmm … Purplish? You like indigo, I think.'

'Fine.'

'Ro-na?'

'What.'

'I'm over here.'

Or as my headmistress would have said, look at me when I talk to you, young lady. Serge pointed and whistled at a jumbled mountain of furniture-cum-scrap for disposal. All I wanted to do was sleep; antiques, bottles, chairs, the Hall were slipping away.

'You know I can't,' I murmured, too frail to speak any louder.

'Cinderella Dean,' he mused. 'Does she realise her greatest weakness is her mightiest force? Would you live as a clown or die for dignity? If everyone got what they deserved, there'd be no deserving people left. This is why happy people get so tiresome. Nothing comes free; every joy is someone else's misery. Rona Elcanor. She may make a wise ape yet.'

I remember no more before passing out.

Chapter Seven

You always remember where you were and what you were doing when something profound or life-changing happens. I suppose that's why I recall my inaugural months as watchdog so well. Memory is a plane of alternating landmarks varying in height like a bar chart, where specific conversations, actions and places stand out as staples. The spell between early November and the next six weeks was a series of such landmarks, and though I cannot say with certainty in exactly what order they occurred, I can name highlights.

Ever since a front-page headline, 'Appeal For Missing CID Agent', jumped out at me, I entered the newsagent with one eye closed to shut out the newspaper stand. Whether the press eventually forgot about Matthews or not, my imagination printed copies of his face on every front page of every newspaper, every day in every shop in England.

Hence I welcomed the following distractions.

To start with, this period was a major moving event of three vaults from the east passage to the Great Hall. My main assistant in this was Hector. An illuminating experience, since I saw a side to his personality he'd either previously withheld or I had ignored. He would usually help me for an hour or so, lagging behind while the other two were out before leaving himself. It is deceptively reassuring, how congenial conversation in relaxed settings makes you forget what you are speaking to, although you're punching gusts of wind if there is no solid answer. I gave up trying to categorise them. Good and Evil? In the end there is only Perception. Play the cards you're dealt.

For instance, I learned that not only was Hector the mildest of the three, but the youngest. Three hundred and eight years, two months old. Encouraged by his openness in our privacy, I chanced to ask how he met them.

'What you mean is, how was I Changed,' he retorted. Note their subtle choice of phraseology: 'Changed'.

Hector was no less than the son of former watchdog Charles Embaldt – Lord Menzies' valet and maker of grandfather clocks. By the hazy outline he provided, I sensed a tragedy. Embaldt's role, unsurprisingly, forbade him marriage and fatherhood, a rule he ultimately disobeyed, keeping Hector at a safe distance for many years. The fact that Hector was Changed just days before Embaldt's death in September 1706, suggests things spiralled into acrimony, and we shall have to make do with that, because Hector spoke no more on the subject.

We were lifting a mountainous load of dented plates and worn daggers from the armoury when I remembered something else.

'Hector, Edith mentioned the word "strigoi". What does it mean?'

'Edith's phraseology,' he replied. 'Romanian. To some it means "scream", or Latin or Greek for "witch". I don't know about that, except that she means us.'

'Ah.'

'And don't go throwing the word "strigoi" around when Serge is here,' he added. 'Or any other labels you've heard. It's disrespectful. Edith wouldn't dare.'

'Falkirk warned me as much. Why?'

'If *we* don't believe half the myths about us, why should

we use tacky names passed down by your like? Serge's native language, when he wasn't Serge, is long extinct. No records survive, no current civilisation remembers it. So if he has his own name for us, I don't know that either.'

'Hector,' I asked with caution, 'would you be permitted to tell me his age?'

This question caught him unawares. He set down the load he was carrying, thinking. 'Older than his chair,' he said nervously. 'The answer's no, even if I knew. Neither does Edith. Rona, these daggers are scrap metal, dispose of them.'

Hector's angst at such a basic enquiry brought home to me Serge's sphere of influence, not to mention an untold reign of fear affecting even Edith. I thought of the petty verbal duels I had flippantly exchanged with Serge – what was I messing with? The trouble with, and perhaps strength of, obsequious Hector was that he was impermeable: his depth would go so far, then regain shallowness like a lava lamp. Hector would protect me with his life if ordered. He would slaughter me if ordered. To him, his master was a demigod.

Their collections were the most jumbled, nettling cocktail, many leftover artefacts not originally acquired by them. The armoury, for instance, had been dumped centuries earlier, already in bad condition, and left to deteriorate. When I asked why they let it go to waste, Serge shrugged. He, Edith and Hector being antiquarian artefacts in themselves, to them these relics were average everyday possessions. You would be amazed by their casual attitude. A modern historian would be beside himself.

I don't think I ever got used to that twisted east passage. I think it got used to me. After we finished the armoury, two remaining vaults awaited us, vaults I had overlooked, almost directly opposite the no-go fissure of their private tunnel.

Hector eagerly escorted me into the nearest.

I entered what was essentially another communal crypt, with a big difference. Where bodies should occupy the nich-

340

es, disassembled skeletons were neatly stacked according to limb, specific slots for skulls, femurs, fibulas, tibias, ribs, collar bones, pelvises and vertebrae, all commanding one side of the vault. The opposite side made a startling contrast.

Hector saw my reaction and beamed, one of the rare occasions I ever saw him smile.

'This is my workshop,' he announced.

Hector was a craftsman. The interment spaces on the opposite, or 'display' side – what else to call it? – were reserved for his finished designs, filled with them. Heaven knows how long it took, but it was obvious Hector passed an inordinate number of hours carving and chiselling patterns into countless human bones; some, I realised with guarded anxiety, too small to be adult. This carved army of the dead lined the wall in droves, each a polished masterpiece of Celtic, Aztec, Baroque, Eastern or Western designs, including serpents, stars, moons and suns, gods and goddesses, runes and Phoenician symbols, sculpting mundane calcium carbonate into unique works of art.

Not only human. In a separate corner were stacked oxen, stags, horses, cow bones, even cats and dogs, dominated by the centrepiece skull of a Nile crocodile, immortalised with a Cyclops eye. Moving the lantern over row upon row of sculpted death, truth be told, I found it breathtaking.

Music broke out in the tomb. I spun to see Hector playing the same Galician cantiga from my birthday, ringing sweetly through the underground like a desert oasis from a humerus bone flute tipped with a carved dragon's head. The artist keenly exhibited another instrument; I could not solve how he had engineered it: the thick hindquarter of a bison, lined with anaconda ribs and gut strings for dual synchronisation. The wind and string instrument sung like a didgeridoo and ghostly clarinet combined.

'This is all your work?' I asked.

'And Serge's,' Hector said, setting the instrument down.

'He taught me. Here! He wanted you to have this. The polish set recently.'

With a child's enthusiasm Hector placed the millionth skull of that evening into my hands.

The species, human. The detail, hard to believe. Not a centimetre of space was spared; you could scan it a hundred times without seeing the same thing twice. I saw animals, maps, eyes, Solomon's knots, the Sicilian three-legged gorgon of Trinacria, Hercules knots, round Minoan labyrinths inside the orbits, the Assyrian sun wheel Seal of Shamash, myriads of Pictish symbols and the wrath of a Phoenix, every gap packed with tripled Neolithic spirals, polished a golden bronze. Judge it how you will, the skill and patience for such work was unparalleled.

'You made this?' I stammered, flattered, if wary of my obligation to accept it.

'No,' said Hector with sober awe. 'That's His.'

Flattery gave way to suspicion. 'He made this? For me?'

'Yes.'

I tightened with goose bumps. Serge does not present gifts for your health; he commits no act of kindness without a sting in the tail, or so I believed. Whom might you be, Mister or Miss Carved Death? Annie, Claire, Gaz or Daniels? Alice? Isn't it enough I have to mop up their blood without your trophies at my bedside? No thanks, Serge!

In a slip of convenient forgetfulness, I may have inconspicuously left Serge's gift in the workshop.

The final vault to clear contained a heap of artwork, paintings, sculptures and busts, carpets and rotting tapestries I was loath to unfurl, given whatever invertebrates nested inside.

'Are they valuable?' I asked.

'Maybe once,' Hector said. 'Serge would discard them. He's only a critic when it suits him. Edith takes convincing, she's the collector.'

A roar of traffic penetrated the ever-thinning layers overhead.

'Please can I ask you, Hector, about Delfour Road?'

'Serge knows what to do.'

'Yes, but do you have to abandon this east wing forever?'

'Correct.'

He offered no more information; that there was a plan, was all they hinted.

Oh, and somewhere in those six weeks I got fired. Yep, Falkirk gave me the shaft.

Put in the inescapable situation of working night shifts, I did my best to fight tiredness during the day via catnaps, which unfortunately accumulated until they merged. After a couple of weeks it became a losing battle.

The nightly clear-outs were a cumbersome, bitty, drawn-out operation, if not also a compelling history lesson acquired literally in bits and pieces. As in the library, not only did it involve moving hundreds of items from A to B, I was charged with their sorting, storage and disposal, *including* everything in their burned antiques warehouse of a Hall. In fact, the Hall became the central hubbub of this chaos. What was not fed to the water well, I sneaked to external dumping sites and bonfires on Guy Fawkes Night.

Speaking of the well, their flow of overnight guests, whose phones and fluids I usually swept up, dropped off to virtually nil, sparing me the underground stench. Don't say we do nothing for you, Miss Dean.

Meantime, my dozy eyes ached in the lamplight, debating over what to divide between treasuries, artwork, furniture, armoury, what to keep and chuck – What the hell is this? Too precious to throw away? It cost me lots of criticism from Edith and Hector, along the lines of, 'No! Don't get rid of that', or 'What are you keeping that for?'

Serge was the only sentinel not to ridicule my nescience,

responding with a temperate nod, a headshake, or by discreetly taking problem items from me.

At noon, I would wake up in the gallery with no memory of getting there. These topsy-turvy sleeping patterns did not escape Falkirk's attention, and though I asked to reschedule my daytime duties, eventually the day came when his boot kicked me awake in the gallery.

'Tired, are you?' Falkirk said. 'Am I working you too hard?'

'No,' I answered, smelling the oncoming fumes.

'No?'

'I've been helping downstairs.' I sat up, still dressed.

'Helping? That's good of you, isn't it?'

'No. It's my job.'

'Oh, I see! Your job.'

'I'll be up in a minute.'

'In a minute.' He nodded sarcastically. 'Hmmm.'

'Yes. Give me time.'

'To what end? It's the afternoon. Stay in bed as long as you like!'

'I couldn't help it. If I don't sleep I can't do what they want.'

'Oh dear, we can't have that. How could you possibly work? Oh, but I forgot, down *there* is your job!'

'A job you nominated me for!'

'How correct of you,' he concurred with dreadful spice. 'Well, I believe I already paid you for last week. As your duties were kindly covered by a volunteer while you rested your weary head, and as you've just intimated you prefer working for free, I think I'll keep my forty pounds pocketed, thank you. Furthermore, under such circumstances I don't take kindly to squatters on the property. This, for instance,' he kicked my boxes by the bed, knocking one over. 'You will kindly remove yourself and your belongings from my gallery at once.'

This should not have surprised me. I am sorry to admit it did.

'You're sacking me.'

'Otherwise,' he went on, 'by tomorrow your junk will be in the front window of a charity shop. This mattress will be in a skip by sundown. Sleep it off until then; you can *dream* upon your sins.'

Without waiting for a reply, he pranced downstairs to greet the congregation in his best phoney Christian voice. Falkirk could not have sounded more pleased with himself. He had been waiting for this day, to squeeze me into the crunch, and now I had to fend for myself. Why did he hate me so much? Forty pounds a fucking week and he sacked me.

Well, that was that then! Devoid of an income, meaning no food and no bed, there was only one alternative. My boxes wound up in the Menzies sepulchre.

In a rage, quilt over my shoulders, I let the trapdoor crash.

'Smile, dear!' called Serge as I thundered into the Hall. 'The night is long and the winter young.'

'I don't care, Serge,' I shouted, tossing my quilt onto the French sofa. 'I'm unemployed, fucking starving and I'm out of cigarettes!'

The three laughed, as they would.

'Well you can't stay here,' he said, retrieving the quilt and throwing it over my head.

'What do you think I've been doing?' I burst. 'I've conked out on that sofa a dozen times.'

'And we've had to carry you up to the gallery a dozen times.'

'I see, I'm to sleep up there with the sarcophagus like a fucking necrophile?'

Serge assumed his wry pose, rocking heel to toe. After letting me stew a moment, he said, 'Walkies.'

And so I was led, all the way to the nightmare end of the east wing and my brush with death. Serge said nothing, which spoke for itself. I mentally marked the spot where I'd choked on tears while they'd watched from inside.

345

I stopped there. I would not walk a yard further.

The things you will do when afraid. Adrenaline is a powerful form of possession; though it may occur in short bursts, for the briefest instant it alters your entire personality. Who would dare defy Serge? Try adrenaline. He indicated the man-size slit in the end corner, dark beyond, clean and dry as a surgeon's gash. When Serge tells you to do something (*Hop, Froggy!*) there is no discussion. You do it.

Me? I muttered at him to forget it. I shook my head and gripped the wall, as if there was anything to grip on to! I don't know if events leave their mark on places like a parallel dimension, but my lip swelled again with pain. I forgot how to breathe and saliva congealed in my throat where invisible claws strangled me once more. I couldn't swallow. Hector had almost taken me this far, and foolishly I had settled into a false sense of security, thinking I'd be spared this walk on hot coals. Surely they wouldn't haul me back here. Not there. Not in there!

Serge's perceptiveness needs no introduction. He took me by the elbow. 'How it taxes you, my Rona.' He pulled sharply, walking me in.

'Why here?' I protested, resisting.

'You're hurting my feelings, monkey.'

It was like being dipped in Arctic water, re-entering the stagnant climate of this cave.

'I make no apologies, Rona,' he said calmly, leading me. 'I have a responsibility to Edith and Hector. They didn't need another fright like that so soon after Daniels. We've lost too many to do-gooders with torches and pitchforks.'

I opened my eyes. We were in their old den. Good gracious, how plain and unremarkable it was; not exactly a cave, more a corridor chopped out of the bedrock, part brick, part sediment. It curved as jaggedly as I remembered, no wider than three feet, same for the rank smell and memorable jarring at my ankle bones. My scarred lip pulsed. The tunnel magnified Serge's height.

'The traffic above,' he said. 'It's waking us up now. Watch your feet here.'

Just as I wondered how this hugging shell could lead anywhere, it ended abruptly. The ceiling was higher than I expected and roughly arched. I subconsciously compared the hugging surroundings to a medieval Venetian wine cellar. Other than this, the passage was quite featureless and divided into a fork of two pathways which, though sizeable, were very crudely burrowed out. He stopped me here.

'Tour it while you can,' he said. 'The foundations are coming down. These chambers are bare now. We've moved to vaults in the Hall, that's why you can't sleep there anymore – not so near us.'

'I knew you'd slept here.'

'No coffins,' Serge replied. 'I trust that doesn't disappoint.'

He allowed me to wander through a miniature warren of empty barrel-vaulted rooms, this place I had demonised. Bland, bare, bleak. As if in a mark of respect, the atmosphere commanded that we whisper.

'In March, 1020 A.D.,' Serge explained, 'a monk stood where you are right now, overseeing the foundations of his new monastery for the first time. Stobell, his name was. He belched ale into the architect's face and thanked him with his blessings. Then, when Stobell held back the payments, I reached in behind his tonsils, pulled, and snapped the brother's head from his spinal cord. I let him keep his tongue. It fluttered as if still alive, drumming on his lower palate. The whole east wing stank of his ale after that. And his excrement.'

Reanimated dust rose and danced in the heat of my torchlight, which cast a hundred shadows on his face.

'Now it's all going,' he said, gazing around. 'Strange to think. But so few places outlive us. Become attached to things at your own expense. Have you any fear of death, Rona?'

'That depends.'

'On what?'

'On how.'

'Correct answer. Know why?'

'You're only allowed to tell me if I don't have to write an essay, Professor.'

'Tut. The truth is, death – for which you have countless books, an inordinate number of hobgoblins, scythes, spooks, tap-dancing skeletons and charlatan psychics in its name – is nothing. Death is endured, mystified and coined over by the living. Hence death, as you think you know it, is in fact life. Real death, actual death, is the light going out, *you* going out, eternal unconsciousness with no dreams. Ghouls and ghost stories, phantoms and *memento mori* created by the living, now, that's exciting! Death? – is boring.'

Above, traffic zoomed over us, setting off a discomforting tremor. Serge followed my gaze upward.

'Next week you'll hear a huge explosion from Delfour Road,' he said. 'We're detonating their dig.'

'Could that not expose you?'

'No. It'll block them off for good by levelling the whole section to an impenetrable plug of nondescript rubble. Their GPR hasn't reached us. Yet. When sniffers are about, eliminate their target if you can't save it.'

'What total damage will it cause?'

'A third of the vaults may be salvaged. The west end will be habitable. Either way our humble abode will shrink and that's just too bad. It'll be a dangerous time. We'll have to vacate the vaults for a spell until they stabilise. Out you go, wave goodbye to it.'

He ushered me out.

'Meantime,' he added, 'when Delfour's night arrives, be on guard.'

'On guard where? Sleeping in the damn churchyard?'

'Shut up.'

Edith and Hector were waiting for us at the trapdoor, coats buttoned. I asked where we were going.

Later, when I dropped into bed – that's right, a bed: not a mattress, not a sofa; a proper bed! – while the rest of the country yawned, showered, breakfasted and clocked in to work, I lay on a pillow, convulsing in such a fit of giggles it hurt.

Rewind a few hours.

I blindly went along with it; they wanted me to tail them out.

Not taking their usual route, we went around the churchyard, following the façade through soggy grass, wetness soaking into my socks. Now and then they communicated with each other in a mixture of Spanish, Latin and French. I lost sight of them more than once, skipping to keep up until they snatched and guided me.

The first to leap over the façade, graceful as gazelles, were Serge and Edith. Then, without warning, Hector's great arm wrapped around my waist like a harness and I was as good as airborne, dangling under him. Familiar lit windows rose into view from the other side, then shot upwards as we fell with a mighty thump in Falkirk's rear garden. Hector shifted me in front of him to keep me in sight. With a lump in my throat I watched Serge kick in Falkirk's back door, followed by a pitiful cry and voices.

When we joined them in the lounge, Serge stood quite cordially, hands in his pockets, Falkirk cowering against a bookcase like a cornered fox.

'Just saying to Falks here,' Serge began, 'we're occupying this property until further notice. He's fine with it. He'll oblige us, of course.'

Falkirk shook his panicked head. 'Too short notice!' he

wailed. 'Where for me? You creatures gave me no time!'

'You know precisely where,' said Edith. 'Rona found her quarters quite homely. Didn't you, Rona?'

'Uh … yes,' I replied, though I must have looked about as stunned as Falkirk.

'There you go,' Serge said. 'Gather whatever you need, toothbrush, et cetera. And be quick about it, we haven't all night.'

'Leave my house?' Falkirk shouted. 'To sleep in the church?'

A bottle of whisky, a quarter full, sat by his plate of oven chips on his low coffee table. I wondered if Falkirk would dare shout at Serge like that when sober.

'Yes,' Serge answered him.

'There's nowhere to sleep!' Falkirk cried. 'The mattress is in the skip!'

'Better scurry on and get it, then.'

'From a skip?'

'Yes.'

'*Now?*'

'Yes.'

Hector unceremoniously raked Falkirk's pockets and took his house keys, passing them to Serge while the minister hovered pathetically, on the verge of tears. Their plan made sense; if they needed to temporarily vacate the vaults, Falkirk's house was the safest bet.

'Why are you staying here?' Falkirk belted. 'Explain this!'

Serge, Edith and Hector laughed so wickedly that I almost pitied the man. *What the hell are you doing, Falkirk? Have you a death wish? Don't question them, for Christ's sake! Are you stupid?*

Serge took two, slow, threatening steps towards him.

Scared as he was, Falkirk muttered something incoherent. If I heard him correctly, it was: 'Your promise …'

Promise?

'Look at you,' Serge hissed. 'You bitter, used grub of a man. Rona, did he take your aisle keys?'

'He did.'

Serge opened his palm in chilling demand. Copies for the portal and south aisle were hurriedly retrieved and delivered to me whilst Serge stood examining Falkirk's house keys.

'Thank you. Out!'

Minutes later Falkirk was tripping through his front door with a badly packed suitcase. I hadn't the heart to watch him go, locking the door while the others went to explore various rooms upstairs. In the messy lounge a wind blew in from the broken rear door, a cigarette burned in the ashtray and a game show blared away on the muted television set. *What the hell just happened?*

I wandered into the kitchen. It was a repugnant tip again, a mound of dishes God knows how many days old filled the sink under cabinets spattered with globules of chip fat, spilled sauce and lumps of jam solidified to the floor, opened tins and crap everywhere.

'Rona?' Serge called from the landing.

I went to meet him. It was somehow tremendously relieving to see Serge up there, commanding the top of Falkirk's stairs with his hands on the banisters, new lord of the manor. It made the place feel more like home.

'Take any room facing south, not north,' he ordered. 'The windows have shutters but gather us all the curtains you can find.'

'All right.'

I set about disrobing the lounge windows. Bedrooms with north-facing windows were instantly bagsied; no direct sunlight, you see.

'We'll deliver food to you later,' he yelled after me. 'I smell his morgue of a kitchen from here.'

My role as housekeeper over the next three weeks began.

Chapter Eight

The weather fell chilly with moody skies as we entered December.

Housekeeper above ground and janitor below, my indoor rhythms jogged in tandem to their long winter nights, up to twelve-hour outings per evening, though I secretly rejoiced in the occasional hour of actual sunlight through the window.

Technically unemployed, you may ask how I fed myself. Simple. Serge, Edith and Hector were never short of money. Furthermore, you recall the impromptu meal they prepared for me on my birthday? This transpired to not be an isolated event. Approximately three times a week I purchased beef or pork from a local butcher, initially cooking for myself, before things took a funny turn …

Menstruation pains are fickle things; benign one month, sadistic the next. During our second week in Falkirk's house, menstrual fish hooks lodged in my lumbar and dragged me down to China Town while an elephant kicked me in the ovaries. On top of all this I caught the flu, lodging bricks in my nose and a fever in my limbs. Add cramps to this and you found me abed for days, only to be astounded by the smell of them cooking my food as a rare favour, thus spilling over into erratic habit during my illness.

I digress.

Mid-December, and I had failed to move everything from the fated east wing. The Hall was packed and the library swam in Hector's bone sculptures. 'No matter,' they said. 'Leave it.'

They would not permit me anywhere near Delfour Road on the big night, street cameras being a major reason, so I cannot describe the scene in detail and Serge grew cagey on the subject. Edith proved the most informative. The weapon of choice, she told me, was, of all things, good old-fashioned dynamite.

'Old school cliché, you agree?' she said. 'Sadly, it will work.'

Many sticks of sawdust, nitro-glycerine and sodium carbonate were planted in the roadworks, along with as many explosives in the east wing directly below. It would be devastating. I was no arsonist but I knew that detonating that many explosives necessitated multiple pairs of hands and a swift getaway.

'Edith, how the shit are you detonating them?'

'Fire. The rubble will choke it.'

Another fire. I asked who would be carrying out this deed. Edith said she and Hector were to be above ground, Serge below ground, with 'the others'.

'Others?'

'The suppliers,' she said.

That evening, the night of the event itself, we were to expect visitors.

The knocking came soon after midnight. Wednesday, a week-night, when the streets were desolate and we were home.

When I opened the door I was in for a shock, more so than the guest. From one servant to another, I cannot say either of us felt particularly thrilled to meet again. The man from behind the counter of Cole's Medical Supplies on Sanders Avenue, the same gum-chewer who had called me a stupid bitch and told me to piss off, when I was a different Rona. So, so long ago that seemed now.

Physically he was much improved, brawny and very full of himself, coming up in the world, evidently gaining favour with his own mysterious boss since we met in his shabby shop. It embittered me that he likewise saw how I had changed, a stone lighter, careworn and pallid. Were he less obnoxious I might have seized the chance to make a friend outside my present circle.

Besides Alice, Rona?

If that mental voice had a neck I would have broken it.

Cole stomped past me into the house without any hellos. They had specifically told me he would arrive by the rear door, but for this top-secret operation he'd entered by the front, on a public street. They would be furious. The lounge was empty where the four of us sat seconds ago. Bad sign. I wisely stayed put in the hallway.

Cole sauntered about the lounge and eyed me derisively.

'Tell your boss I'm here,' he said, assuming himself my boss for the present. 'Tell them my benefactor's outside in –'

Hector appeared from the dining room behind him, serenely lifted the boy's index finger to his mouth, and bit it off.

Lights, camera, action! Cole proceeded to howl and dance about the lounge, nursing his gushing digit while Serge emerged from shadows I didn't know were there. Without missing a beat, he inserted his index and middle finger into Cole's nostrils, and *yanked*, thrusting the boy backwards with measured violence into a perfect horseshoe. Any harder and the visitor would be irreparably paralysed – I heard his spine grate. Hector looked on blankly and chewed away, fingernail, bone and all, crunching between his molars.

How Serge balanced Cole in that U-shape was sickeningly masterful. The fellow watchdog arched way below Serge's waistline and in substantial agony.

'Does my friend not teach you anything on Sanders Avenue?' Serge asked my counterpart. 'If you think he's languishing outside in the car, you're more stupid than you are underbred. Rona, open the garden door for our actual guest please – not this fly on the wall, in case you were wondering.'

I made a beeline as instructed for Falkirk's back door, recently reattached, its frosted film window brightly lit by the hallway. What I saw in it halted me. Despite having no choice in the matter, I didn't want to touch the door handle.

A long, white face and pointed chin leered at me through the blurry glass. The figure it belonged to was tall and oval. It didn't knock. Even without moving or speaking, this new presence exuded a foreboding hitherto unknown to me, opening a fear of different dimensions. I had to work against all my instincts granting entry to the newcomer. Was it this way when I first met Serge in August? Really, was it the same? The months had moulded and hardened me beyond redemption, true, so why did I feel thrown back to square one?

The winter blew in with him as I opened the door and stood aside, eyes firmly to the floor, defenceless against his palpable observance running over my body the way melting hailstones trickle under your collar.

The cries of his servant continued from the lounge, to which he turned his attention, and as he strode in I got a better look at him. He wore an expensive winter coat of charcoal grey, longer than Serge's (who is more your midnight blue type), gelled hair clung to his scalp in severely combed mats, and by appearances you would think him about two decades older than Serge, but that meant nothing; he could be of any age, because even for a watchdog of a mere five months, I knew another master on a par with Serge when I saw one. Edith and Hector couldn't hold a candle to their presence. You might also be forgiven for labelling our guest the more handsome when, unlike Serge's vulpine lines, this master fitted the bill of a debonair model. His features were perfectly placed. And odious.

I worried what he would have to say about the treatment of his abused watchdog, but damned if I didn't hear a pleasant exchange of greetings instead! I skulked outside the lounge, feeling somewhat misplaced.

Cole, a finger short and bleeding from both nostrils, was curled over a chair, spurned to the sidelines whilst Serge and guest shook hands, conversing in a baffling mix of dialects. So multilingual were this lot that they flowed in and out of languages like rivers, blending and stirring them like milk in tea. Our guest spoke through incredibly soft vocal cords with a perpendicular resonance that made me uneasy and an accent no less confusing, an elegant blend of English–Irish–Italian. And he was breezy, *too* breezy.

I averted my eyes for dear life; it felt criminal to look at him. Every sentence and move he made smelled artificial, and despite his cheer, he was also acidulously prissy, moseying over to his now nine-fingered servant.

'You *will* receive my subjects in your usual fashion, won't you, Serge,' he chuckled, patting Cole's shoulder.

'You will insist to train them in *yours*, Goddard,' Serge retorted, more phlegmatic than usual even for him.

This Goddard straightened and scrutinised me, his deep brown eyes pinching like needles. 'And how does your wild mouse here fight in a corner, if she can?'

Edith intervened. 'Rona, stop loitering like bird shit in a vacuum and see to Goddard's man. He has to drive him home, you know.'

I tried helping Cole from the chair. He shoved me off.

Goddard furrowed at Serge, oozing condescension.

'Correct me if I still detect no sign of a vehicle in your possession, my lord. Or do you keep that safe and snug in your precious crypts too? Does your dogsbody,' he nudged Hector, 'dismantle it at dawn and reassemble it at dusk especially?'

'If you have no car you have no identity,' Serge, King of

Poker Faces, replied. 'And not *my* vaults, milord. Ours.'

'Ah, beg your pardon.' Goddard sniffed, openly glib. 'One might too easily miscalculate the growth of that padlocked Treasury of *ours* via charged admission to our domain. *Cui bono?* Tell me, what does your mouse' – he made a prurient gesture at my pendant – 'exchange for the concession?'

Yes, I know I was supposed to keep my gob shut, until that brattish stab of his poked a hot cinder.

'My name's Rona,' I blurted, 'like they said.'

Goddard twisted around in amused surprise. Serge's pupils shone jet from me to Edith, who promptly tugged me away with Cole, jabbing my funny bone.

'Now there, see, Cole?' Goddard sneered. 'She has introduced herself and you have not. Your manners baffle me tonight!'

The boy stuttered, 'C– Col–'

'Be quiet!' snapped his master. 'The girl has ears.'

Edith pushed us out to the foot of the staircase.

'Sir Goddard, Esquire,' she muttered, 'amongst other titles. Bandage the boy, keep out and both your voice boxes muted or we'll surgically remove them.'

Cole wanted none of my help with the first aid, fine by me, and while he did a rotten job of bandaging himself in the bathroom, I sat on the stairs and listened, trying to decipher what went on.

Seeing these two masters together was a sobering realisation of the niche I had earned for myself: we were servants, Cole and I, their pet ghouls and, especially in this tense rendezvous, wholly dependent on them. If I were put in danger or threatened here, Serge was my sole advocate and protector. Now, that made him no white knight, it merely cemented the inferiority of my position. Look at them! Look how aged and powerful they are, as familiar as an oak with the earth it's rooted in. Oldest of allies. Or adversaries. Perhaps both. What was it Derek had told me? – There are fair leaders and there are backstabbing leaders, but the leaders who *endure*, who last, they tread somewhere in between.

Serge and Goddard were the principle spokesmen, and though most of their dialogue was foreign, snippets of English invaded. The plan, as it panned out, was that Goddard, Cole, Edith and Hector would detonate above ground, while a separate team led by Serge took their chances detonating below.

'I would not presume to nostalgia and outstay our welcome so soon,' Goddard slithered. '*Carpe noctem!*'

Despite Goddard's passive enmity, protecting the vaults was ultimately in all their interests, and Serge played him carefully. The destruction of their landmark was a historic event for their network, and certainly the imminent, irreversible damage justified Edith's recent mood swings to a degree. All things considered, it honestly irritated me to be excluded from their plans when Cole had free rein to go where he pleased, but then again, Goddard clearly encouraged brasher tactics with his own minions. When I asked to help, Edith and Hector dismissed me like perfunctory parents. Serge took me aside.

'Stay here,' he said, explaining that four of Goddard's drones – hot-headed young strigoi, I believe – had invited themselves to view the fated underground wing as a treat. I smelled a rat, as did Serge; Goddard liked caveats in exchange for his services.

'Can you trust them?' I asked. 'He keeps going on about the Treasury.'

'Who do you think you're speaking to?' Serge chided. '*Our* vaults means his too. He knows he's free to dip in when he likes. I don't care *who* they serve: stuck underground with me, they'll sooner die than test my wrong side. Let them spy away for all I care.'

'Are you safe?' I asked, meaning it.

Serge smiled, and proceeded to warn that if I moved from

the house tonight he would flay me alive.

'It's a good way for live ones to bleed out,' he said. 'We'll lick you dry like a hanging lollipop.'

Serge was in no mood for joking, you would not have laughed.

~

Two hours later.

Boom.

The roadworks were over a block away. The house shook, dogs barked, car alarms went off, sirens sang their songs, woken neighbours stood on doorsteps in dressing gowns, called through windows and crossed the street in their slippers to catch the war zone via phone cameras. All I could do was wait.

No one came back.

I paced and paced the kitchen. I went through eight cups of coffee, and when that ran out I started on the teabags, finished my tobacco and made second-hand smokes from dog ends. A headache was punishing me and I needed sleep, but fought it off, my mind too hyperactive.

A fat plume of dirty smoke, radiant in the street lamps, burned until dawn. Dawn. And still no one came back! *This is ridiculous. Have I missed them?* No, their bedroom doors were open. No sense waiting in broad daylight, exhausting every possible morbid scenario, only a pet ghoul would worry about the welfare of gruesome monsters; so be it, at least I still had all my fingers.

Out of options, I carried myself to bed at nine in the morning, patriotic lights still rotating from police cars and fire engines on Delfour Road.

~

'Don't you want to see?'

A male voice woke me. He was smiling.

Edith stood in the doorway, the landing light bulb framing her like an aura with an eldritch veil of statically charged hair.

There was not a scratch on him. His clothes were unblemished, hardly any burns or fragmentation, indeed he looked very well. They both did.

'The others are gone?' I asked.

'What do you think?' Serge chaffed.

After the explosion, Serge had extended his hospitality to Goddard's cubs by sending them off, overburdened under the weight of as many souvenirs as they could carry, with additional tokens from the Treasury for Goddard with his host's gratuitous compliments. 'It's French for piss off,' Edith said.

Underground, the debris had settled to fine puffs of stone powder bouncing in my corneas per footstep. The vaults were coated in it. Uprooted masonry bled a suffocating odour of earthen grit and great chunks of brick petered out at the former T-junction, where we found Hector kicking them aside for us. I bit the bullet and circled to view the devastation.

Fuck.

The east wing, that endless mirage I thought I abhorred, was completely gone. It was just *gone*. The T-junction was now demonstrably L-shaped, and from where I had experienced the worst day of my life there bulged a massive wall of disjointed rubble and boulders. The route was annihilated, blocked, filling every crypt and foot of the passage as if it had never existed. Incredible, how it takes so long to build something and mere seconds to destroy it, you wouldn't have believed this was the same underground. Likewise, the hole in Delfour Road, surrounded by traffic cones twenty-four hours ago, today clogged up by an immovable pool of rock. Their home had reduced, oh very much so.

Obedient Hector behaved no differently and Serge betrayed no sentimentality; he could not afford to. Whereas in Edith I saw traces of tears. As she drifted into the Hall, Serge briefly put his arm around her.

It would be another week before they reoccupied the underground and I the gallery, a period Serge spread out solely to aggravate Falkirk. The mad Delfour rush at an end, this was a leisurely phase where I came and went in my own time to the plod of my recovering flu. Notwithstanding Serge's previous proximity warnings, we developed a system in that house, treading water in a tentative equilibrium of scribbled memos on the kettle and weekly wads of pocket money; here, Watchdoggy, buy yourself something nice. Not to mention the gas and electricity bills I left on the altar for ostracised Falkirk, a sweet and sour chore I wickedly enjoyed. They brought no bodies to the villa.

Thus went the blur of those six weeks: clearing out, getting fired, commandeering Falkirk's house, dynamite, and meeting Goddard. Reader, I would happily have continued with the lull of peace that followed; the home I made of Falkirk's villa became my own, but you already know things change, it's just a matter of when the tide comes in. Something was tipping slowly off balance. I could feel the water rising about my ankles, I just declined to look down yet.

On the eve of quitting Falkirk's house, I found it.

Chapter Nine

It started after my flu.

The lazy interlude of coughing and sneezing saw a good deal of unwashed dishes and refuse pile up, namely bin bags, loose and stinking. The process of gathering them up was a lousy job dead set against me. A tear ripped the undersides, sending packets, teabags and cartons over the linoleum I'd swept only minutes ago, no quelling for my temper.

Fizzing, I kicked the emptied rubbish about, releasing a more disgraceful stench. In this angry fit, something caught my eye. I could so easily have missed it.

Between an empty milk carton and a tin of beans – a squishy lump, wrapped in clear polythene.

The transparent packaging was unopened, its contents tawny fuchsia. Next to it, another polythene splodge, also unopened, both bearing similar sealing labels. I knew what they were, but they could not be, it was a mistake.

Donning Marigold gloves, I picked them up. Bulky. I recognised the labels whether I liked it or not.

Wait a minute.

In one hand were the beef cutlets I had purchased from the butcher on Monday for a medieval casserole recipe Edith told me about, since cooked and eaten by me. In my other hand, the lamb shanks from Wednesday, lamb I had fried, eaten and digested. Yet, lo and behold, here they were, unopened, uncooked, uneaten.

But I know they were cooked. I ate them! They specifically ...

The room, the very air, darkened about me. The tide at my ankles swelled, spilled and overflowed.

I reopened the second bin bag, racking my brain to remember recent meals. Let's see ... Beef last Monday, the uncooked beef I just found; Wednesday, the lamb shanks, yes, we know that, too. What else? The civet of hare! The stew with hare's blood, rosemary and sage. And they definitely started cooking the venison on Friday, too, leaving me to finish it, berries and frumenty. Makes no sense, this can't be right, no sense!

An overpowering fetor of rot poured from the bag. Holding my breath, I put my arm in and searched, unwilling to accept the conundrum, feeling among unattractive shapes and sizes inside. *Ten seconds*, I thought, *I'll give myself ten more seconds and if there's nothing in here ...*

Nausea feels like somebody inflating a scum-filled balloon in your belly. The piece of polythene crinkled over a distinct texture, sludgy. I withdrew a putrefying cube.

No.

Puce globs squelched inside viscous puddles of green, the candid label in impersonal Courier font:

VENISON FILLETS, 5.2lb. Bronmeg Butchers Inc.

No!

I had eaten that venison. I remembered it. I saw the son-of-a-bitch throw it on the hob, chop and fry it in the pan; the date on that fucking label confirmed it! A label on unopened packaging. This decomposing grocery I cupped had cooked and sizzled and gone straight into my mouth and through my system, like the civet of hare's blood. Blood.

No. No no no no nonononononono.

I got the hell out of that kitchen.

I ran to the bathroom, lurched over the sink, splashed my face, gurgled, spat, and lurched again, awaiting vomit. When nothing happened I splashed repeatedly, nearly hitting myself. Then all I did *was* hit myself.

On either side of these bathroom walls, beyond the shower and towel rails, locked bedrooms protected sleeping inhabitants indulged with the heaviest possible curtains and closed window shutters. Their culinary generosity, their passive insistence … Fool. Fool! Who could be such a fool?

A grisly, dripping ghoul unknown to Rona Eleanor Dean raised its head with mine and introduced itself in the bathroom mirror over the sink, aesthetically no more human than I was.

Weeks, weeks of this charade, the sycophantic ghoul eagerly devours leftover scraps from the lord and master's table for faithful service. For birthday treats! They have taught me so much, free rides in their time portal of an underground, sparing me the burden of bodies in this villa, trailing me on a leash deep into their world while they laughed at me. Oh so, so, *so* laughed at me! This is their reward.

I imagined them guffawing, laughing forever and ever, the three of them, peeping into the kitchen as I scrambled through the bags, roaring heartily at their sham. I almost heard Derek laughing, too. 'They like to plaaay, Rona!'

'You bastards.'

The baggy-eyed ghoul breathed steam onto the mirror, gripping the sink white-knuckled, tap water dripping from its rat-tailed hair into the basin.

They have stamped out the last pimple of softness in me. The deception. The sick, sick, malicious deceit!

The ghoul listened intently, a creeping smile kinking the corners of its mouth.

Yesss, got you good, didn't they?

'Yes, they sure did.'

So, how's Rona feeling?

'How can you ask?'

By answering you. You seem passable to me. Where's the cry baby today? I see your posture, you can't even vomit!

The ghoul is accurate, I cannot.

For the first time in my life I could not recall a single solitary minute of my existence outside of this house, this bathroom, this mirror. Through drops of tap water on my lashes I saw the scarecrow in my clothes punch through the mirror, lodge its phalanges knuckle-deep into my orbits, and wrench me on through the glass, out of existence. Rona's going mad, she thought, observing the smashed remains of Falkirk's mirror on the tiled floor, its ghoul triumphantly multiplied to twenty, piercing her with china-doll pupils.

'You son-of-a-bitch. You bastard. You … absolute … bastard.'

There was nothing good on TV, or if so it escaped me. The clock ticked from midday through to 3 p.m., me on the couch, thinking.

Fortunate that I made the discovery during daylight; it averted any humiliating knee-jerk reactions, such as presenting the uneaten spoils to Serge, dropping them at his feet in a grand entrance or exit, a fashionably dramatic reveal, strike a pose and take a bow, Rona! I mentally scripted and choreographed every disingenuous vice of confrontation feasible, from exhibitions of silent treatment to declaring vegetarianism. Of those ideas I turned over and over, none satisfied the ghoul I'd met in the mirror that morning, its wiry voice maturing by the hour.

Fool rhymes with tool! They pull strings, the puppet will dance – that's you, by the way, Rona. What in the name of all the ages can you *possibly do to rile them? Don't make me laugh!*

True, they were shit ideas.

Besides, Rona, you're stronger than that.

Twilight had faded to cobalt navy when I arrived at my decision.

They have been laughing at me too long. They want me to crack, to slide in pusillanimous despair. I won't. Upon my life, I will not give them that. You're not getting the satisfaction, milord. Not this time.

'How can you be so heartless, Rona?' Serge joked. 'Making the minister waste away in that mite's nest you've the temerity to call a gallery.'

'Architectural terminology, not my problem,' I replied, sangfroid, brewing an Earl Grey.

'Hoity toity. Listen to this, Edith. Rona's trying to be clever!'

'You're out of touch, milord. Any idiot can make a cup of tea.'

'Take the teabags with you. They'll go to waste.'

I instantly forgot about the Earl Grey.

Serge nodded. 'Your luxuriating is over. Unless you think shacking up with Falkirk's worth a trial.'

We were to leave the next night. He asked if I was hungry.

Another directed trip to the butcher. If memory serves, the fillets, this time tossed onto the hob by Hector, masqueraded as pork in the typical drill – they start, I finish, sizzle-sizzle in the pan, a candy-sweet steam too similar to bacon or veal. Soon as Hector walked out I lifted the kitchen bin lid. Sure as sunset, my purchase, dumped fresh and unopened in Bronmeg Butcher's tatty Courier label, PORK CUTLETS, 4.3lb, and there it stayed. I had a plan.

They were passing me hither and thither while I positioned myself on the couch in front of the square coffee table, buttoning their coats and getting ready to leave, yet present, which gave me time. If he thinks me a wimp, let him put his money where my mouth is if he wants to see what I'm really made of, or, more certainly, what they've made of me.

Taking the deepest of breaths, I sucked in my navel, picked up my knife and fork ... and scoffed the spicy sautéed remains with deliberately excessive, exaggerated, gluttonous, indelicate, immodest, staged relish. I put on the best performance of my life.

I spat messy words of innocent praise and sauce, stabbing my fork, ploughing through it, the whole cannibalistic thing.

My peripheral vision detected him; I must have missed Edith and Hector. I went on, barely breathing through my nose to avoid an unbearable dose of the full taste. I chomped, vocally praising the culinary artist non-stop, then chomped more, gagging shallowly.

How desperate was I for it to be over! Chunks of tenderised meat swimming in juice melted in my mouth, burned my tonsils and tumbled to my stomach where they formed a gaseous block of indigestible concrete and squeezed, begging me to slice my guts open and empty it out. I craned over the low table with my fork, smiling vindictive deception, slaughtering every natural-born human instinct to hurl the plate at him and regurgitate projectile long pig across Falkirk's wallpaper. It was the hardest thing I had ever done.

Nonetheless, once the hauteur presents, it must persevere, and here emerged an unforeseen catch to calling his bluff: the more I consumed, the stronger grew my spirit. My heated defiance expanded from budding coals to an inferno, building by the minute until I was raking through the mouthfuls like a warrior. With every bite I grew bolder and angrier. *Fuck you, Serge. Fuck you. Just watch me.*

'I never thanked you properly for this,' I said, teeth coated in carmine sauce. 'My reward, is it? Part of my wages? What I deserve? *Do* I?'

From the rear garden an oblivious Edith and Hector called impatiently to Serge. Where was he? Not listening to them.

Serge was standing against the opposite bookcase ten feet away, his top half bathed in shadow, cutting him in half at the torso like one of the broken headstones outside, the coat he was fastening a minute ago now dangling over his folded arms. His countenance was a vacant nothingness, worse than rage, more threatening than any snarl.

It was working.

I did not falter; to do so would discredit the objective. I ate, chewed, gulped, ate. Serge threw his own dice in, playing along without a sound or a flinch.

Mute vibes of ice and flame fired across that room in winds of turbulence. If my fire did not melt Serge's ice, his snowstorm would extinguish mine. This was a game I couldn't win – nor lend to his victory, for as long as fearlessness was on my side I'd claw my way to stalemate if it was the last thing I did.

'As I said,' I chomped, 'thank you, lordship. So good at this, aren't you?' Final mouthful, swallow. '*So* good!' I finished, wiping my scarred lip spitefully.

He stood very still.

His shaded profile had the dull luminosity of an opaque spirit, lit by two tiny shining points of light where his retinas reflected the table lamp, the only sign of life about him. He would stand there for hours if he wanted, waiting me out; he would win, too. An electrifying sense of victory tingled: I, inferior Rona, have succeeded in genuinely surprising him. Serge, Earth's champion of sagacity! It should have felt triumphant.

It did not, for now the fear crept in.

The others called to him again. Again he ignored them, his terrifying unresponsiveness part of the game, plunging the lounge into deep-freeze. I wanted to call it, draw a line under this degrading scene so we could both go about our business, but that would also make him the winner.

Serge charged into the light.

I held my ground on the couch. *Don't scream, Rona.*

He crossed the room, put his nose in my hair, wrinkled his features and inhaled sharply, a harsh *sniff.*

'Monkey meat,' simmered an evil voice. 'I forgot to tell you. How you tasted. No two are alike. Some taste of perfume, some of fruit, oil, slime, sugar or spice. You? You taste of stone and tears. Your alveoli are popping bubbles. Your bronchus, swinging on inky cartilage. I see it in there,' his fingertip stroked my breastplate, his lips moving against my temple, 'swinging like our clock pendulum, ticking out. Your piquancy is of dead leaves, d'you know that? Your haemoglobin's weighted with carbon dioxide. You, you're just … *ash!*'

Serge rose, giving me a conflicted, tortured frown; whatever my fearlessness had hit, it hit deep. Jesus wept, has he the actual nerve to try making me feel guilty? Don't you dare, milord!

'What in the hell is wrong with you, Serge?' I said, steadily. 'Legendary leader or not, this mercurial, brattish temper's nought to do with your damn species. Edith and Hector aren't like that. It's you, as a person. I don't care how timeless you are!'

Serge contemplated me, sighed, spat on a napkin and wiped the sticky sauce from my chin. 'Spoil you rotten, don't we?'

The other two appeared. Before Edith could complain about the delay, Serge beamed at her.

'There you have it!' he announced. 'That's two hundred quid British Sterling, Lady Edith Deveroux, by a nose! I understand you're due me the same, Heck?'

'Oh, what?' Edith cried, crestfallen.

'Yes, chefs, I told you she would. Come then, cough up, cough up, no excuses!'

They begrudgingly submitted their forfeits and walked out, leaving me on the couch while Serge fastened his coat.

'Oh, and thank you, racehorse,' he said, waving the wad of money. 'Thought you'd never tweak it.'

'You're welcome for winning your bet,' I said, sour as milk.

Serge pulled up his collar. 'Don't forget to lick your plate clean.'

Chapter Ten

'Coat, Rona. We're going out.'

Serge stood over my dingy mattress at 5 p.m., an uninvited optical illusion striking the ceiling. His stoical intonation set a burner under my heels as I rummaged for extra clothes to bundle up; it was perishing outside. Once ready to leave, I automatically inclined towards the coiled python stair, an erroneous reflex in this case, because Serge arrested me. I saw what he intended to do.

'Hold tight,' he said.

At his mercy, he took me by the waist, lifted me over the balcony and put my arms about his neck as he leapt onto the ledge … off the ledge.

The bludgeoning *jolt!* upon landing rebounded to my head; it rattled him no more than a beach ball. He may as well have bounced.

Ah, Rona, Rona.

I would shortly kick myself for not having appreciated basic routine prior to the roadworks fiasco, the clearing out, and what lay in store.

Ever since they 'showed' me in October, it had unfolded that no sooner was I recovering from the latest hurdle or a fresh

371

defacing, another plopped in to replace it. These hurdles were about to landslide until I was in freefall, affording me no time to compromise or adjust. Their agenda was set, cunningly orchestrated to disable any refusal. I could only act and obey, they wanted none of my smart-arse antics and there was no slowing down. As I have mentioned, nothing tests you like adrenaline driving the bus, their exact plan.

A quick update before we proceed.

Minus a demolished east wing, their sleeping quarters were relocated to secondary chambers in the Hall beyond the arcades, zones off-limits to the likes of me.

Serge and the others were my abiding source of income and willing to prolong this arrangement, but with my laborious night shifts over, what was I to do with my days? Chinwag with the minister? My relations with Falkirk were as toxic as they could be. The future seemed worryingly uncertain.

Recurring dreams invaded my sleep too: Serge was targeting me from Falkirk's bookcase, arms folded, two points of light in his luminous death mask. Within days of that meal, the sensation of being watched stalked me everywhere like an itchy flea bite, a haunting need to compulsively look over my shoulder. I had set something in motion when I threw down that cannibalistic gauntlet; something was off and waiting to snap.

Those were my thoughts as they ushered me into the taxi, Edith boarding ahead of me, the other two holding the door for us.

I have narrated thus far to you, and you in your patience did bear with me, to arrive at my very first outing with them – three members of a species that escaped Linnaean classification, but hadn't fooled whatever roots in your DNA still demand you fear the dark.

~

You would think four cramped in a taxi should stifle the winter's breath. It invaded by whatever crevasse, from the radiator to the driver's outrageously open window. Edith sat on a fold-out seat, her legs elegantly crossed under her lengthy cashmere apparel, applying lipstick and a smacking of powder.

The taxi was large and oppressive with an enclosing scent of leather. Were taxis always this oppressive at night? The only interior lights were a couple of tubes above the windows.

Sinking into this seat, being wedged between Serge and Hector did not denote a great sense of trust on their part, though when I shivered a third time, Serge took a loose cotton scarf from his neck and draped me with it. There was no talking for several miles as the vehicle gained distance from Bronmeg, the street lights dwindling into a poorly lit minor road.

The leather, heavy atmosphere and speed of the drive lulled me into a daze, transforming the passenger area into an eighteenth-century coach ride. I envisaged the clip-clopping of horses' hooves carrying us, their snorting breath steaming up the hackney cab lamps, swaying and jerking with the trot. I was so tempted to nod off in this temporary illusion, if not for my anxiety.

'Where are we going?' I asked.

'Various places,' they said, very reserved. I got no more information from them. It was not a scene for chatting.

To be driven through unfamiliar streets is maze enough; to journey them at night was a hopeless mirror, especially when the windows revealed no more than our reflections and I gave up searching for a friendly landmark. Mile after mile we covered. I was lost. Surely we were in another borough by now?

As the number of street lights gradually doubled and we approached some form of civilisation, I despaired at the tell-tale signs of an uncouth neighbourhood not unlike the type of hellhole Alice called Home. *Try not to think of her, Rona!*

My alertness spiked during a short verbal exchange between Edith and Hector in French. All I interpreted was '… after travelling …', '… two or more …', and '… going'. My mind wandered. 'Serge', a French name despite his blatantly English accent. *Serge, hmm. Serge, Serge … 'Servant', that was the translation!* Servant? I bit my inner cheek to stop an ill-befitting snigger. And of what did those devils I loved and hated converse under my nose?

'Are you French?' I asked Serge.

'Not inherently.'

Conversation over. The taxi was coming to a stop.

The woods at night a whole other world, aren't they? Every twig under your sole is a thousand times louder per footstep on what you hope against hope to be a path. If a break in the oaks, birches and elders exposes you, arrows of a winter gust seek you out, delaying your judgement. Now and then you hear an upstart or a scampering, a mammal or bird sensing your presence up to fifty feet away, shooting off for safety like a bullet.

With your superficial senses demoted by evolution since mankind quit the jungle, you cannot gauge the dimensions of tree trunks or the space between path and shrub because your depth perception is blocked. An owl hoots from straight ahead, then repeats from behind – how did it get there so fast? In this befuddlement, a fir branch juts out of the void, scratching you with needle-like spines; you utter a childish cry and jump, making noise, blowing your cover.

Unpractised apes like you generally opt out. Or you may pause to stand in this world you thought yourself so well-acquainted with by day, trying to get your bearings and develop a third eye. It is then that you feel the true flavour of night sink in: every smell is magnified purity, the flora, the bark, the air; if you wait a while and listen, it is bewitching. Night does not suffocate and bombard as daylight does; it caresses you, opening an organic freshness found nowhere else on the clock, and the coolness drags out new scents, energising you with earthy perfume. It is freeing, exciting even. Love it or loathe it, everything feels poised, including its waking beasts that, like all competent hunters, are compelled to wait.

The woods boasted no grand expanse, but at this hour they were vast, and through an ever-changing myriad of vegetation I spotted house lights about a mile off, possibly less. I wrapped Serge's scarf tighter around me.

We stopped and started. This seemed to be taking hours. I longed to see my wrist-watch but clouds obscured the moon. I begged leave for a cigarette.

'Later,' they replied.

They said nothing else, not to each other, not to me; I was an imprisoned bystander, with one of them (I don't know who) tailing me, keeping guard. I am sure we followed no established footpath; the surface was untamed with bumps, logs, stones, the occasional soda can, thorns tugging my jeans and I whacked my shin walking into a massive obstruction which my guides seemingly glided through. By feel I think it was a fallen tree. A strict fist pulled me onward and I raised my knees, stepping over several feet of thin air before certain I was clear.

Finally, we stopped.

Where is not worth guessing, except that the lights were closer now and a pleasant trickle of water sang from nearby. I was restless and, despite the company, felt so alone. No one would talk to me, no one would debrief me, I had all my wits tied taut as string. I knew to shut up, that they wanted no questions, but oh, what I would have given for an arm around my shoulders, I would have buried my face in their coat.

The cans I tripped over to get here (some still emptying liquid) were, as it turned out, no accident. If in daylight, I would see this so-called forest for what it truly was – a large copse of trees on the edge of a cheap council estate separated by an abandoned building site, a failed investment reclaimed by weeds and faded 'Keep Out' signs.

The woods were no *au naturel* haven either, I'm afraid. Carrier bags and used condoms fluttered in place of leaves on the younger trees, the undergrowth pebbled with more. The river did no better if you discounted the upturned shopping trolley, rusted brown. A local sewer connected to the water via pipeline, and should you fancy picnicking here on a sunny afternoon, good luck ignoring the sudsy foam decorating the riverbank with chemical phlegm.

Enough! Here is what happened.

My guides chose their spot with calculated care. A dell. In the absolute stillness I attempted likewise, embarrassed to breathe, and for a terrifying moment thought I was left there, hearing nothing and seeing much less. They, incidentally, heard or saw *something*, for their ears pricked up with their noses like a trio of composed wolves.

I don't remember where I heard the story of the cyclist attacked out of nowhere by a cougar, whether from my science teachers or the TV, but its narrator said, 'A bear or wolf gives chase. You see it, you run. If a big cat's stalking you, you never want to know, because once you do, it's during the last second of your life.' Memorable words, soon to resurface. I was about to witness an ambush.

Pow! The hush was punched by a beating of wings, wood pigeons frightened from their nests. Edith dug her nails into my biceps – an unwary lot were stomping our way, raucous voices signalling a band of four male youths, passing very close.

The predators side-stepped away from me.

The youths slurred and yammered yards away at the edge of the woods by the derelict building site. I clung to the scarf, my dear comforter in this spider's web.

How does a spider hunt? How do wolves and cougars hunt? Serge, Edith and Hector walked straight up to them.

No running or pouncing, no need; they walked in plain

view. Outlined by distant orange streets, the seven in total were nameless characters in a shadow puppetry act. I squinted, losing focus, who was who?

Too late to tell. Curtain.

I had never seen them kill, and even here I heard more than I saw. I wish I had a better description to offer you than seven puppets merging or blending into one another. Somebody whipped out a knife, next came a soprano squeal followed by an ear-splitting *crack* and two grassy thumps.

Not only was it too dark, the puppets were too fast; strain with an infrared camera and you'll miss it; try searchlights and you'll miss it; my mind couldn't replay it. But the speed! Nothing can move that fast, and they did. A gushing shatter. Sound like a hose. Somebody fell and – *am I seeing this?* – an attacker embraced and lifted the attacked, a pair of hapless feet tap-dancing the air.

Five excruciatingly unrevealing seconds it took to ambush and kill four males bigger than me.

I kneeled in a foetal ball and shielded my head with the scarf, banishing my front-row view of the performance, unmindful of the thorns cutting my jeans. Safely enshrouded in there, the only things in existence were the evergreens and the ceaseless, trickling river.

After an age in this ether, a voice reached through the vacuum.

'Come here, Rona.'

Dear God, will nothing make sense? What manner of tone is that? What the hell can they mean by such benign enunciation? Nevertheless, 'Little Miss Gothic' is no best friend, no bosom buddy: she is a ghoul; she does as they bid. I got up.

The puppet show was over. Backstage spread the riverbank, where chemical sewage assumed spectral clouds of methane in gassy pockets blowing rebelliously perpendicular to the water flow, moving with an uncanny appetite towards four human bodies. Serge stood alert as a vulture, waiting for me.

'Listen carefully,' he said.

Edith and Hector were at work with two of the victims. The last you and I will ever hear of those boys, bones scattered, sanded and buried under river sediment years ago, are a couple of splashes. And that was all, chucked and forgotten, reclaimed by nature while Serge lectured, presenting the scene.

'Wildlife photographers say nine out of ten hunts are unsuccessful,' he said, 'but gazelles don't go moaning to the ungulate police force when leopards attack. Imagine if they did. No such thing as acceptable risk. It's do or don't. Hector, show her that one. If she hesitates, drag her. I won't have her going squeamish on us now.'

I did not wait to be dragged, thanks; I didn't want to be touched with so much as a feather. Hector held up an unconscious boy who appeared to be urinating into a bottle held by Edith, his shoes twitching, tiring of the tap dance.

'There's the trick, Rona,' Serge explained. 'Stab wounds. These neighbourhoods are a buffet of muggings, gangs, shootings, rapes. If he's found, what's another knife fight?'

It was pissing out of the boy all right, but squirting from a deep fissure in the side of his abdomen, anatomically incorrect place for a bladder. I heard the high-speed *chsssssshhhhhhh* as it hit the glass base, followed by the hollow gurgle of the bottle filling up.

'What's wrong?' Serge derided. 'Not clichéd enough for you? Practicality is key.'

Splash. Third body dispatched.

Serge hauled up the fourth victim. Ah, there it is, your classic sign. To be honest, the tidy bite marks were barely discernible out here.

'This,' Serge continued. 'We can't leave him like this. Where's the cause of death? Puncture marks in the carotid? Monsters only belong in stories, Watchdog!'

Serge's head disappeared into the youth's throat. My hands automatically went to mine. There was a wet ripping noise.

Like a handful of bird feed, Serge flung him to where I had crouched minutes ago. Thank you, clouds, for blocking the moon and helping me believe that rubbery, segmented thing trailing over the youth's T-shirt was a loose bow tie, not an unreasonable guess when it came from what – I think – used to be his neck, flapping open like a sandwich.

'The foxes will help themselves,' Serge added. 'A skulk followed us through the woods. You were sitting on their den, you dope. We won't keep them waiting.'

'The taxi she booked for Cruickshank Terrace is in under an hour,' Edith announced.

'Good. Stroll on.'

In these cases, your best coping mechanism is to completely close up inside. I managed to walk, though my legs felt like artificial limbs, and I forbade myself from betraying a speck of emotion. This may sound simplistic, but the only logic you can count on in this situation is tunnel vision – *Do as I'm told, do as I'm told, do as I'm told* – if you want to be alive tomorrow.

Serge led us away from the housing estate through a clearing in the trees before reaching a hilltop overlooking another road. From this vantage point it forked, winding into the village of Krellingsgait and our next stop at Cruickshank Terrace, a mile's detour. Our alpha, Serge, kept a few metres ahead.

Hector muttered to me, 'Krellingsgait is haunted.'

'Everywhere is, Hector,' Edith scoffed. 'See that she keeps up.'

'I will,' I said irritably. For anyone as wired as I was right then, unwanted attention distracts the solid bubble of your self-preservation; whether by touch or by talking, it sparks you off like a grenade. 'Stop it,' I grouched. 'I'll be all right!'

'Course she is!' Serge called gaily to the skies. 'Don't baby her, Edith.'

So, this is where my aunts used to live. The village they quit for the sake of adopting a bastard orphaned by its mother's aneurysm.

The end of the trek found us standing in the middle of Cruickshank Terrace on a public bench by a war memorial near Krellingsgait High Street, too cobbled and narrow for its daily onslaught of cars and buses. At this time of night, the antique village was a ghost town; you wouldn't think anyone lived here or that the traffic lights blinked red and green after sunset. A weathered market cross centred the square in front of an eighteenth-century community hall covered with overdue scaffolding, and the youngest buildings were at least two hundred years old despite retail conversions.

There was a strange odour. In fact the whole vicinity held an undercurrent of clamminess and unseen overgrowth, as if it should be in ruins. Shut your eyes, open them, and weeds should be crawling up between every cobble, roof slate and crevice; open sewers should be drying in the gutters and the buildings crumbling shells interspersed with mounds of rubble. An unsavoury humidity, atypical for December, slinked past us in a vaporous miasma. I blinked and nearly saw it, grey slivers and wisps slinking over, in and out of the imagined ruins of this old settlement.

Under the eave of a closed tavern, The Fisher Will, a drain spout dripped fist-sized blobs of green scum. I wanted to believe that was the source of the smell … Wishful thinking. It was everywhere! In the ground, in the buildings, in the weather, and *under* everything – in the present, the past and the future, overshadowing us like a fifth dimension.

I did not like Krellingsgait, the village felt poisoned. Hector may be right, and why shouldn't he be, after all? Here was no gang-ridden housing estate of ugly flats, druggies or muggers, true, but the place felt somehow ill, unwholesome. I lit a reassuring cigarette.

Edith and Hector, naturally fearless, flanked me on the bench. This stupid taxi was late. Serge stood against a lamp post, keeping watch, his sandy-brown hair blowing soft and bushy. Past caring for being flanked, I wandered over and leant on the other side of the lamp with him.

'Haunted?' I asked.

'On and off,' he replied, eyes to the road.

'By what?'

'Just a sad soul. They typically are. Sadness breeds anger. Anger is hungry. Rage is tasty. Leave it long enough and it stews until self-sustaining. That's why she would devour you.'

'She?'

'A girl died in the pond not far from here. Long, long ago. People still go there, chiefly because their instincts are toast. Cigarette out.'

A welcome sight of fogged-out taxi headlights veered into the market square, searching for us. I was glad to leave.

More fool me.

'No! Actually, sorry, could you double back on that left and take the next left at the crossroads? I've changed my mind.'

The taxi had not long steered us clear of Krellingsgait while Serge sat, stroking his chin thoughtfully, a mischievous grin creeping over him, and now he was leaning forward, excitedly instructing the driver to alter our journey. My insides instinctively hardened. All I wanted was to throw my coat over the boxes in the gallery and lie with a pillow over my head.

'Oh?' said Edith. 'What happened to the Warwick tour?'

'Rona is curious!' Serge replied, sitting back down. 'I don't see why we should waste the opportunity. Compose yourself there, Hector; you're a big boy now. He grew up in this district, Rona, he knows its ups and downs of old.' Serge slapped Hector's knee approvingly.

Hector had visibly tensed. Passive glumness being his

general profile, you would think any genuine scowl from him should go unnoticed. Not so. Though the youngest, he was no less the predator, so to read signs of actual fear on him … None of this boded well. Edith nudged Hector, egging him on. Uh-uh, he shook his head. Our eyes met, mine silently questioning him. He averted me and grumbled.

The taxi headlights found a crossroads, scarcely lit, and next came a turnoff into a suburban lane dividing into several cul-de-sacs of dark windows and drawn curtains, nobody awake. We stopped here. They paid the driver.

I was last to climb out, oozing disdain and hugging myself in the inclemency.

Where Cruickshank Terrace felt unwholesome, this area was desolate. A line of semi-detached blocks, more tombstones than homes, fringed the lane regimentally on both sides, cars in driveways, conservative gardens, names on letterboxes – and still I could not imagine them lived in. There was not a dot of colour anywhere. It was a suburban mortuary. Whoever lived here cowed behind drawn curtains at night, and by day pretended to be either dead or on holiday.

We were on the very cliff edge of the village. Beyond it was a rural expanse, every back window overlooking a valley reaching to what may as well have been the black rim of the earth, not a single lamp in sight. The gusts boasted bolder out here, and a roaring wind swept up and over a hinterland of fields behind the houses; *I'm coming for you!* it seemed to rave. I wanted to run from it, run for my life. No chance: a mighty hand of air targeted and punished me with a slapping blow. Edith doggedly pulled me on. Her touch, however, was not cruel, not tonight.

Serge waltzed his usual insouciant swagger. 'Lead the way if you like, Heck.'

Hector, impervious Hector, overtook us, so hunched with stress that his neck disappeared.

Between two end-terrace houses, a pavement of speckled asphalt tapered away into a footpath of soft soil, bordered by low fences of lopsided wooden stakes and bent steel wires. Wild tufts of grass, blonde as lions' manes, waved at us through the fences like sentinels.

The path steepened downhill into farmland, on our left a row of feeble, soulless trees, to the right a cheerless, grassy field used for nothing. Down we walked, further and further from the lonesome bunkers, their unlit windows looking on solemnly, watching us go as if sorry to see the last of us but grateful not to be in our shoes. I had to fight the urge to look back myself. Soon the open plain howled with armies of angry winds, swirling and dive-bombing us. At least the vandalised woods of our earlier trip, owls, glass and all, had provided cover and a sense of life. Here … I don't know. Here was bare and exposed, even the vegetation seemed a ruse to disguise its true form beneath, alien to what I had taken for granted to be the natural world. I could not shake off a vibe that we were being watched.

Farmers' fields are supposed to be loamy and fruitful, isn't that the idea? I saw no country haven here, its soul was barren: shut your eyes again and this time you're in some parallel universe of rocky wasteland, a death zone of grey scarps bleak as abandoned quarries far as the eye can see. We were descending into the badlands.

'Why are we here?' I asked Edith.

At which Serge jeered, 'Don't you want to meet your namesake? "Dean", meaning "Dene", as in the Old English "denu", for "valley". This valley.'

And how far did this depraved path lead? As the slope became gentler and the valley levelled out, I stuffed my pride and held on to Edith – the smell was back. In fact, it was thickening. Serge intended to usher us straight to its stronghold.

'Tell me what you see, Edith,' I asked her, blind beyond a

few metres.

'The hill is a smooth slope,' she said dispassionately. 'When it flattens out, wild grassland and trees take over. A bird sanctuary. Every few decades, the birds inexplicably,' she pinched me for emphasis, 'flee. They decamp. They high-tail it. Absent for years. No explanation for the poor ornithologists. It drives them crazy.'

'That's invariably when people start dying,' said Hector, marching on.

'Disappearing, Hector,' Serge corrected. 'They disappear.'

Edith continued. 'At the very bottom is deciduous woodland, quite big.'

'Then what?' I pressed.

'You asked for what I see. That is what *you'd* see. It is clever, well-hidden.'

It. Hidden. Clever. Ugh, that smell!

You like the smell of cut grass, don't you? After rainfall? Most do. What would put you off? Basting the lawn with countless worm guts? Mashing the stems to a purée with maggots? Adding sewage, pus, or the dead? That clump of pipe slime circulated my mind; the painted sign of The Fisher Will, above it the clogged drainage spout, algal and saturated with mucus; the greasy blob slides, drooping over the edge, elongating, dropping … The stink! It splats, but does not spit green. It is laced with streaks of blood.

Rotting vegetation, that's what it was. I smelled the bottom of a diseased swamp. Yes, definitely that, a thousand impure weeds and moss, but not so simple or earthen; more mephitic, with an overtone of stale meat.

I held on to Edith's cashmere all the way to the woods, through them, to the source of Hector's fear.

At length Serge strode off at a sharp angle, pumped with upbeat enthusiasm. I think it sometimes troubled Edith the way his volatile moods switched polarities like that. Me too. Earth-quakes are more predictable, and he knew it.

'Let's wake up the warden,' he asserted. 'Very rude to grace the maiden's threshold without an offering, I should gather, Hector? Or this tedious expedition has been a damp squib if she gives us the slip.'

Sparsely distributed timber signs, reading 'Car Park', 'Pic-nic Area', 'Boathouse' and 'All Dogs Must Be On A Leash', said we were in a recreational public park. It seemed legitimate and, like most else in Krellingsgait, a sick joke.

The painted signs were peeling. The public right of way, formerly a pretty track of red sand lined with boulders, was shabbily overgrown under a free-for-all of browntop shoots, nettles, meadow-grass, tail grass, brambles and a melee of oth-er weeds. No, this park was not frequented, not lately.

Krellingsgait is uneasy. Its populace is uneasy. They are afraid and they don't know why, in a slump. An intelligent malignity holds sway for now and it *will* have its way, it *will* run its course, until done. Then once the smell recedes, people will timidly unbolt their doors, start walking their dogs, bring sandwiches and trample out the weeds with their jogging shoes and bicycle tyres. After an ambitious local asks the warden for keys to the boathouse, within weeks the pond – wherever it is in this accursed valley or dene – will be teeming with boats of sunburned families and competitive beer guts showing off their brand-new fishing poles.

But not today, not tonight, and not tomorrow.

A warden? How could there possibly be a warden on duty? What's the point? In December!

Serge's detour took us to a cottage bordered by a high wall. A brass plate was nailed to the patio gate: 'Mr R. J. Templeton. Park Warden. PRIVATE. No Parking.'

How we scaled the boundary to invade Mr Templeton's gar-den should need no introduction. A ceramic gnome guarded his doorstep, an apple tree overlooked us and rock gardens cushioned the patio with knee-high firs, very homely, very harmless. Edith policed me while Serge and Hector approached the front door, locked and bolted of course. The outer doormat said 'Welcome' in threadbare saffron, I never forgot that.

They cannot cross a threshold without being invited.

Myth or not? Decide for yourself. They busted down the entrance like a sheet of cardboard. Sorry, folks. Nor was I spared the pleasure of accompanying them inside.

I hated it.

I hated that the warden was clearly no violent thug or conveniently forgettable gang member. I hated the lovingly-kept garden, the welcoming living room, the framed photographs of adorable children, nieces, nephews and possibly late wife on the mantelpiece. I hated the sleepiness of his embroidered furniture with the lights out, the cosiness of the décor, his comfy cushions. I hated his coarse rugs, the recently used coffee mug on his dinky table, his velvet curtains, his vacuumed carpet, the ceramic plate of painted ducks hanging above his television. I hated the TV magazine open at today's date on his bouncy couch. I hated the house, the floral wallpaper, his immaculate book shelves, his golfing cap and coat on the hat stand (still damp with today's rain). I hated the polished surfaces, his fucking tea cosy, his homely harmless doormat, his homely harmless bowl of fruit on the homely harmless dining table. Homely, harmless, homely, home, harmless, harmless, a harmless man! I hated the innocence. I hated the warden for being himself. I hated seeing it. I hated being here, I hated right now and I hated being me! 'Welcome'-welcome-*welcome*!

This was an average tip-your-hat Joe, defenceless and minding his own business, whose mother had kissed him goodnight as a boy, promising him that spooky film on the telly was only make-believe. 'Just stories, darling. See, I'll show you, no beasties under your bed, no monsters in your closet, though I wish you'd tidy it up, young man! Now be a good lad and turn that light out, and remember, no monsters.' – 'Yes, Mam.' – 'That's a brave soldier. Goodnight, sleep tight, don't let the bedbugs bite. Mwah!'

Bedbugs bite. The middle-aged warden lived alone, snug in bed, moulded by Mam's advice. Sorry, Mr Templeton, the bed bugs waited, they came unannounced without knocking, into your house with the dripping fangs and shiny eyes you grew out of believing in, and killed you. They came in the night, as promised. You betrayed your mother, you let them bite.

I heard him screaming.

Edith babysat me while they were busy upstairs, holding the end of my coat as I covered my ears. All Watchdogs Must Be Kept On A Leash.

Step out of this page a moment and listen to me. Just listen. What excuse did I have for that? None. I knew I was a hypocrite. So are you if you harbour any admiration for a predator then denounce them for surviving within their means when you witness a snapshot of gritty reality. Do you think a lion discriminates? Do you think it can afford to select antelope from the herd via personality tests? This is not a hobby! I've seen their pastimes: Serge is an accomplished engineer, architect and sculptor; Edith is a linguist and art historian; Hector is a skilled carpenter and blacksmith; and they are all musicians. What about you? Is eating your hobby? I was young.

Edith watched me, shaking her head, ashamed of me.

They rejoined us. Hector entered carrying a life-sized dummy under his arm, its bare feet swinging from pyjamas, bland except for bedbug stains where the arteries would be – if a real person, that is, which it wasn't, not a real man who drank from that unwashed coffee cup earlier today, oh no! A nasty gang met their death in the woods tonight, okay, fine, shit happens. This? No, this cottage is a doll's house and Hector carries a dummy.

Serge hurled something across the room to me. I caught a packet of cigarettes, eighteen smokes inside, ready for a new owner, from the warden's bedside I'll bet. Serge had spotted it there and automatically thought of me. Fuck the smell of swamp slime, I needed to get outside, I couldn't stay in here! Why were they procrastinating? What were they doing?

Serge, Edith and Hector, those legendary, mysterious, supernatural beings of the night, were scavenging the warden's belongings like common thieves. Hector discovered a wallet, ignored the credit cards and pocketed Templeton's paper money. The money didn't surprise me, but I hadn't foreseen this level of ruthlessness, and I should have; their gloved hands ravaged his coat and pockets, opened cupboards, drawers, bags, even his dresser. I thought of their big fat shiny safe, Sam their Treasury, the jewellery, the opal around my neck.

My revulsion must have shown, because Hector saw me.

'Why not?' he asked. 'It's common sense.'

Edith concurred. 'How do you think we're feeding you lately, madam? If it bothers you that much, go have another relaxing cigarette we paid for.'

'*They* paid for,' I replied, sounding nothing like Rona.

'Starve with your cravings then,' she retorted.

Hector accordingly swiped the cigarette packet from me. Be my guest! I slunk defiantly to the vestibule and produced a pouch of tobacco I (ahem) 'paid for' yesterday. I should have known better than to try on that attitude in front of Serge, he tolerates no nonsense.

'Get out!' he barked at me. 'Now!'

Body in tow, I was followed into the garden, mumbling to myself.

'What's that?' queried the mordacious bunch.

'I … I said so much for no entry without an invite.'

'We're hungry. You're immeasurably unsafe the longer we wait, have you figured that out yet?'

The track disappeared into a thicket. About ten minutes in, the woods thinned and Hector halted while Serge overtook him and sniffed about. Without going any further, he motioned to us to join him.

Out of nowhere, all too suddenly, flat as black glass. Krellingsgait Pond.

It spread in a wide U-shape almost four hundred metres across; on both sides the woodland continued. Edith was right: most people would find this place purely by accident. It presented itself, stagnant and portentous, the rotting smell having suspiciously dissipated, lifted from detection by a wintry updraft.

Serge walked to the edge of the slippery bank, gave the site a final browse in a heedful mark of respect, and placed the warden on soggy moss. A light kick set the poor man afloat.

Without any gloves, my fingers were too numb to bend properly or fasten my coat buttons. I tucked them under my sleeves and huddled, shuffling and restless, temporarily obsessed with averting an onset of hypothermia.

We waited and waited. There was no wind or movement from anywhere, like being trapped in some impregnable sphere. *Is this how it feels to be deaf?* I thought. *Nowhere should be this soundless.* More sensitised than I realised, my perception answered me:

It's the water. The slime is in there.

When day broke, whatever the weather, the pond would be irresistible, I was sure of it. A secret tranquillity, a fisherman's dream. The surface would break noiselessly under a pair of rowing oars, fishing boats swimming through seductive ripples like syrup, and so restful that no bird sings, the visitors insensible to this critical warning of something dreadfully wrong here. The water … the water did not reflect. In a single burp the fisherman would be under, consumed in a belly of toothed mud. Deception, the whole place! The scummy glob outside the tavern, the meaty vegetation, the smell – this pond was its mother.

We were not alone, I sensed it. I felt far too conspicuous. Next to these three corpses my warm blood and living flesh would light me up like a Christmas tree; any predator with night vision might see me a mile away. Nor could I tear my eyes from the pond, and though my five senses had nothing substantial to report, I perceived it sensing me right back. Why? Because I was better attuned than you are – I lived with worse.

A cloud uncovered the moon and I saw the shape of Templeton, a carcass, a person no more, floating on between some reeds.

'Maybe she isn't interested,' said Edith.

I edged nearer. Serge was the most pensive I had seen him, watchful as a hawk.

'Hmmm, no, it isn't that,' he told her. 'I don't think she appreciates being fed like a goldfish.'

'Oh, well. We waited. She probably won't play tonight.'

'We'll give it a few more minutes,' he said. 'She'd sooner wait us out. If no-show, we'll crack on.'

An agitated Hector lingered furthest away, practically in the woods. 'It'll be tiring of us,' he protested, refusing to genderise the uncooperative inhabitant.

'What say you?' Edith asked me. 'Are we hurting its ego, Ro–?'

A split second.

A Goliathan thrust of Serge's arm – me flying twenty feet backwards – in the background, a splash – a call of alarm from Edith.

Disabling pain as my body hit damp terrain. I was not seriously injured apart from some contusions and scratches, still I groaned when Hector arrived at my aid and I begged him not to move me, mewling in pain as he sat me upright. The others were coming to view the invalid, I heard them, muttering soberly under their breath:

'Edith, if I tell you to watch our charge I expect you to be doing exactly that.'

'Apologies, Serge.'

'It's all right.'

They stood over me, a happier distance from the bank.

'Uh-huh, there we are!' Serge proclaimed. 'Let that be a lesson in heedlessness. She went straight for you.'

'I saw nothing!' I said.

'Nor would you. It only takes a micro-second. I saw her hand on your foot.'

'It was dragging you in,' Hector said, ashen, helping me up. I wanted to be sick, my legs refused to support me.

Then! – An explosion of water from the pond.

We all went to see, Hector carrying me, Edith splitting with excitement. Serge cautioned her.

The body was gone. A patch of disturbed water rippled outwards in its place. Edith and Hector tried to speak and Serge shut them both up, concentrating. After a moment of anticipation, he raised a finger, pointing to the centre of the pond.

'There.'

Bubbles.

Minuscule, short-lived ones. Then larger, more numerous. Now a flood of them, fizzing like champagne. For several minutes, they persisted in a boiling fury.

As they diminished and fizzed out, a cluster of small shapes bobbed to the surface, large and small, reflecting the moon off amorphous chunks in shreds of lily cloth, same cloth as Templeton's pyjamas. I had seen enough.

I squirmed in Hector's arms like a troublesome kitten, ready to bolt and find my own taxi. He shook and shushed me. Travelling clouds blotted out the moon again, which is why I didn't see what came next, but whatever it was it made Serge ecstatic.

'Oh-ah, oh-ho-ho-hereshecomes!' he shouted. Edith leapt.

A bomb of water erupted at the very edge of the bank and sprayed us all. I stopped fighting Hector and clung to him, my nose in his jacket, certain that she, it, would be there, a bedraggled water nymph hag dripping with pondweed, her pruned hand anchored to the mossy bank, wet strands of long black hair caught in her fingernails; it would be every bit as sewage-green as the slime it breathed. Oh, I really thought she would be there!

But no. Show's over, tourists, go home and don't feed the animals.

Serge, soaked, was staggering backward, doubled up with laughter. Edith seemed less impressed by the fright.

'Do you plan to antagonise her or seduce her, Serge?!'

Serge straightened, his laughter dying down, and glossed over us with a caustic sneer.

'Look at my little army! Old as the world and perceptive as a rock! We'll quit this circus big top, Rona. Meantime, don't look at us until I deem them worthy. Make Hector carry you.'

'*You're* very quiet,' Serge commented.

I shrugged. Taking that as the extent of my conversation, they returned to gazing vacantly through the taxi windows at road paint whipping by in a stream of yellow wands, shrinking and shrinking until my sleepiness locked it out.

I woke from a doze to find my head resting on Serge's shoulder. I jerked up, mortified, how long had I been lying on him like that? Otherwise they were incomprehensibly relaxed, Edith reading from a newspaper and Hector toying with a Rubik's cube. Serge was away in his own world.

'Why tutor me this way?' I asked them. 'Why bring me? What good will it do?'

'Well, we wouldn't want you to get bored!' Edith quipped.

Serge intervened. 'A necessary heads-up that the Earth has more curiosities than us. Your general ignorance was our responsibility too and had to be dealt with. You're floored and scared, so stop pretending you're not.'

'Do me a favour, then,' I said. 'Remind me why I'm still alive.'

Edith opened her mouth to reply. I think Serge's gander stopped her.

'Because introverts are either spectacularly trustworthy or the polar opposite,' he replied. 'Anything else?'

'Do you think Falkirk trustworthy?'

'You've just answered your own question.'

'Pray, which millionth one?'

Serge leant in until my breath skimmed his hair.

'Watch him,' he said.

We sped on, Serge humming to himself, a habit of his when in thought. I, meanwhile, thought of the night they kicked Falkirk from his villa, and was about to ask what Falkirk meant by 'Your promise', when Serge swung his arm around me.

'*Pray*', he jived, echoing me, 'whatever happened to that spinning purple-slash-indigo chair I requested?'

Chair? Oh. The chair, eh? Requested on that demeaning night Serge and his plastic tubes left me practically anaemic; a chair for spinning the world like he spun me.

'Oops?' I said cynically, immune to any hackneyed displays of idle coquetry, despite his electrifying nearness.

'Poor show!' he japed. 'How to punish her tardiness?'

'Send her to bed,' said Edith. 'She's tired, Serge.'

'As you say, milady.'

He conversed with the driver. Under the circumstances I should have been wide awake. I was not tired; I was exhausted. Our taxi passed a Thai takeaway, followed by a familiar chip shop and, if I was correct, a cash machine and bus stop should come next? They did, a couple of blocks from Delfour Road. We were going home.

Chapter Eleven

The next day.

I was still drying my hair when I got the news. I kept spare keys to Falkirk's house, agreed purely on discreet terms of using his shower (I had to wash myself *somehow*) at specific times. He would rather I'd stood in the December rain with a shampoo bottle, but consented in case tattle-tale here went off telling her bosses to pay him another disgruntled visit.

Derek had died.

The bearer of this news was a stout community nurse dressed in uniform, clearly on a goodwill errand taking up her lunch break, clogging into the church while I rubbed a towel over my head in the gallery. Service over, the weather was sleet. Falkirk habitually shunned me and kept to his house whenever he could, plus I refused to scrub the church without a wage and there was nothing he could do about it. Therefore, this nurse and I were the only souls in the echo-rich building, making for an appropriately funereal setting.

'Hello there,' she called up. 'I'm looking for a *Rhon*da?'

Close enough. I must say this somewhat startled me, because who on the outside knew me these days? She was possibly in her forties, too young to be in my late aunts' social circle, and I am not clairvoyant but I wouldn't place her in Goddard's rabble either. She smelled of hospital floors and cheap cherry perfume, pouted like a codfish and her eyelids were as beefy as her neck fat, nor did she strike me as the sharpest in the toolbox. I pondered her with caution before responding.

'That's me,' I answered, going to meet her. 'What can I do for you?'

'Oh, okay, hello. I'm Phoebe. I nursed someone who claimed they were a friend of yours.'

Were a friend. Past tense. Pondering diminished. I knew. I knew before she continued.

I hadn't known him too well; he *was* a friend, though, wasn't he? The only friend in cahoots besides me. My ally. Our meetings were too short, his exaggerated stutter, his kind and weary gaze. Derek, how often had I thought of you lately? Not at all.

I'll spare you the blow-by-blow account of her babbling, biding her time to stay out of the sleet, twiddling her pink umbrella. In short, his influenza had progressed to pneumonia, worsening him. He refused hospital, was medicated, cared for, and refused hospital again, which typically ran out of ward beds anyway. His cremation happened over a week ago, said Nursey, over-the-top certain he died peacefully and is with his heavenly maker, yadda-blah-de-blah-yadda. I don't care how long this impersonal female cared for him, she did not know him. You deserved better, Derek.

'He mentioned you to me a few weeks ago and said he had a letter for you. He was pretty adamant about it, and too ill, poor dear, to go out. Quite forgot where he was as he deteriorated. An orderly found the letter on his dresser when clearing out his room. Sheltered housing, you see.'

She presented a vanilla envelope, saturated and crimpled with rain; she had not even taken the trouble to avoid that. The writing in blue biro was nearly washed out.

> RONA DEAN
> St Patricks Church, Clayburn Ave
> **URGENT**

Urgent.

'I was caring for another patient and they just lumbered me with it,' Nursey blabbed, throwing up her chubby palms. 'Oh, well!'

I held the sodden paper, watching it flop over my fingers.

'Lumbered,' I echoed. 'Lumbered, you say.'

'Well, yes!' she said airily. 'Just doing my bit.'

'Your bit.' I nodded, darkening by the second. 'Um-hmm. Just your bit. Not your *job*.'

'Sorry?' she stammered. 'What?'

'A few weeks ago. He wrote and left this for me weeks ago, "adamant", if I remember you correctly. An orderly finds it instead. After he died. *After* his ashes were in the dirt!'

'Uh, hold on, am just helping here! There's no need to get –'

'I think I hear the sleet easing up. You can go now.'

How old was Derek? A lifetime of going through more than this Phoebe could have stomached, and what respect is he granted in his dying moments? Not even his parting wishes while he still had his marbles. I have to be told by this negligent, double-crossing fish-face who can't even pronounce the name Rona properly, not even when it's written on the bloody envelope she ruined. I may be an accomplice to slaughter, Derek too, that doesn't change the fact he was a friend. I entered adulthood with a revulsion towards the elderly; Derek had changed that for me. Fuck you, World, if you undermine the wisest when they're too weak to shout it!

This Phoebe would not dare retaliate, not with the scowl *I* was giving her. I saw fear in her. I was not like this. No Rona of mine spoke to strangers this way; *this* Rona was proving me wrong.

The nurse waddled out. Yes, go. Go, Phoebes. Lucky escape you had. Derek killed female puffer fish like you, ya know. Oh, and don't forget to re-open your brolly, sweetheart, cos I lied!

Hallo. Is that you, *Rona?*

'Yes. Apparently now, it is.'

I inspected the pathetic envelope written in his dying hand, its blue ink spread like aeroplane trails, the paper inside probably stuck together with moisture. That nurse was fortunate she left before I found out if the contents inside were ruined too! I rushed it to a radiator in the vestry and resolved to hope for the best. Hang in there, Derek, I'm sorry.

Edith and Hector emerged at 4 p.m. I was waiting for them specifically, inexpressive and stonier than their vaults, Derek's crinkled (and salvaged) letter safely hidden in my jeans pocket.

'Edith, Hector,' I said, 'what did Falkirk mean the night you kicked him out? He said you promised him something.'

I was answered by Serge, if you can call it an answer.

'Wait up for us tonight,' he ordered, briskly locking the cupboard. 'We shan't be long.'

In passing me, Serge did something unprecedented, something I wouldn't have predicted in a thousand years. He kissed my cheek. With deliberation, he kissed it. Cool and lacy as a rogue raindrop.

I watched them go, each unrecognisably healthier since August. Winter nights fed them well. I soullessly called once more.

'Serge?'

He paused, holding the door for Edith as she went out.

'Derek's dead.'

There came a curious standstill. Serge took longer to respond than I had expected, the way he stood in the open doorway, studying me, seemingly more interested in my tone than my news.

'Thanks for letting me know,' he said.

I re-read Derek's words a fifth time, questioning for the umpteenth time why Falkirk hated me so much. *What exactly did you promise our minister, Serge?*

Rona,

I once told you they made me an offer I refused. You remember? I saw how he watches you. He never treated Daniels that way.

They're grooming you. Run.

If you leave at dawn and go far enough, you have a 50% chance at most. I served the British Intelligence in WW2 – its radar is no competition. I wish I could promise you better. They are patient.

Stay and your services will end one of two ways:

– You die. Unimaginably so.

– You watch everyone else around you die forever.

I leave you all soon. For the love of Jesus burn this note, dear.

May God have mercy on us.

Your friend, Derek

~

Serge did not exaggerate; they were home abnormally early, 11:30 p.m. By then my stolen cigarettes were finished, chain-smoked to the filters by me in the gallery, lost in thought and a soupy veil of smoke.

Latches clicked. Here we are. In they come.

I count one, two, three …

Four. Five.

What's that cackling? Someone's happy, it seems. Make that two happy someones. Oh, what ho! Two happy girls. Two very happy, very *attractive* young girls. I see. Serge – you remember, that man in the coat who delivered that exquisite kiss on my cheek? – they seem to like him, oh yes they seem to like him very much! So much they're thrilled to bits about it aren't they, drunk as they can be, fondling him either side. They can't keep their paws off him. (*He has his arms around them.*) He's plucked himself a pair of groupies, well, how couldn't he? See how obviously perfect they are? How well-dressed, shimmering with lipstick, eyeshadow and styled hair; the most I ever do with my hair is wash and brush it. Yes, yes, they've miniskirts under tops over bulging tits, lots of flesh showing; how on Earth have they the stamina for being practically naked on December nights, girls like that? They must be ectothermic like lizards! (*He has his arms around them both.*) I don't even have clothes like that for July. And heels! I might've known there'd be heels, tall ones. Blimey, they're happy all right – and loud, falling about and snuggling into him. How much have they had to drink? Is that you admiring the place? You, the blonde on his left, you like the church? What's that you say? Oh, no, sorry, we don't stock kinky nuns' outfits here; I'll remind the minister so we're ready for you next time, that okay? (*His arms are wrapped around them.*) What about you on his right, you with the red hair? Speaking of hair, you sure like his, don't you, the way you keep stroking it. Yes, I know, soft, isn't it? Extraordinarily soft. Heartbreakingly soft. Sandy-brown. He's well-fed these days, you see. Did I ask who the hell either of you ARE, by the way? Yes, *you*, the two he has wrapped in his fucking arms. Pardon? Who am I? Well, incidentally I live here. Yes, I see you thinking what's that ugly brunette baggage in jeans and cardigan doing in the gallery? Fuck off, Serge; if it's that sort of mind game we're playing, I'm not the one who'll bite. Do they have cigarettes? Good. Leave them on the altar when you're done. Well, if there's nothing else, I'll politely fuck off. Have fun, see if I care.

'Ahahahaaaa!' the blonde guffawed, at what, your guess is as good as mine.

Edith beamed upon them, impressed as a doting stepmother.

'Whoozaaah?' enquired the redhead, pointing a redder press-on nail at me like target practice. I've seen less fascinated visitors at zoos. I almost checked behind me to see what spectacle I was missing out on.

'Up there?' cheered the harem master. 'That's our Rona! What are you doing up there, Rona? Come on down!'

'Bless her,' Edith mocked, nice and loud. 'She's shy!'

The girls giggled madly, groping Serge about the hips, in his pockets, in his hair. I was trying to remember how much tobacco I had left.

'Ooooh, a church!' oozed Redhead. 'Nice. I'm still freezin' though!'

Serge hugged her to his side like a seedy Santa Claus. 'Aww. *Is* she?'

'Me too!' Blondie cried. The fact that they were dressed in serviettes for skirts in December was apparently no excuse for winter's lack of consideration.

'You too?' cried Serge, pulling them both so close to him their busts fused. 'What to do about that? I may need help warming them, Hector!'

The sniggering girls slobbered all over him, undoing the top buttons of his shirt and snaking their fake talons under there, onto his bare chest.

'No, haha, we're fine here,' they drooled. 'Hehehe!'

Fine there. I'll bet you are, girls.

I, meanwhile, banished myself to the quilt, the kind owned by elderly ladies, not girls in their twenties who are supposed to concentrate on dyeing their hair, wearing serviettes and snaking their coils down men's shirts.

Serge walked them to the chancel.

'Where's Rona?' he teased. 'Why is our Rona not here?'

Edith, merry, frivolous and loving every minute of it, yelped up at me. 'There's a party here, choir girl! Don't you know what parties are?'

They all sounded too similar to every school bully I'd ever had.

While Blondie's drunken speech was indecipherable, Redhead bounced her dainty posterior onto Falkirk's altar where three severed heads had dripped not many moons ago, swinging her heels.

'We got this place to ourselves?' she squealed.

'Ourselves,' Serge replied, lasciviously prodding her fishnet legs, 'and more! Do we have to go up there and drag her down, Eddie?'

'No, no,' Edith, his lookout, answered. 'She'll come down.'

I did not need this. Leave me out of this, I get the hint! I wanted to block them out; I'd listen to angry metal music on my headphones at full volume on replay a hundred times if I had to.

I chanced a quick hi-bye appearance on the balcony. 'I have my headphones and I'm tired,' I said thinly. 'I'll be fine.'

Serge wheeled around – I ducked out of view.

'Headphones?' he belted upward. 'I'll *hang* you by your headphones!' He turned to Redhead, grabbing her waist, challenging her. 'Isn't that the latest craze these days? Asphyxiated fucking? Can you do that?'

Intimidated and excited, she shifted uneasily. Perhaps even drunken strumpets can sense a rabid tiger.

'Oh, I dunno!' she cheeped.

Serge moved to giggly Blondie.

'What about you?' he crooned. 'Can you?'

These girls really had no idea, did they – I saw it as he neared her – not the faintest of what waited under there, dripping salivation. Edith and Hector were busy taking the girls' coats. Kiss your belongings goodbye, ladies, hope you enjoyed them, you ain't getting them back.

'Oh go fetch her, Heck,' said Edith, getting bored.

What the hell do they want *me* for? Leave the coats, if that's the help you need. I'll deal with their phones and other crap once you bugger off downstairs! I stayed hidden, fuck this.

'No!' Serge corrected Edith, a bubble of temper popping from his magma chamber. 'No, she's going to come down direct.'

I really did not like the obdurate tone of Serge's insistence. What's he up to? I'm a trained ghoul now, why are they punishing me? I passed their frigging tests! What the fuck do they want from me now? (*They're grooming you. Run.*) No. No, I don't know what you mean, Derek, nor do I want to. I *am* groomed; they think me too inferior for much else, can't you tell? Huh! They take the piss like you said, Derek, that's all.

So I refused to move. Donning my headphones, though? Maybe not. That would be pushing it, and stressed or not I knew better than to antagonise. It is a cliché to say, but I truly had a bad feeling – I really *was* supposed to be down there. They give orders, not offers, and they were calling me, my determination was being tested. Serge is a flawless actor, had all his wits … and his voice was rising the longer I stayed up here, meaning my resistance was lighting the fuse of a ticking time bomb. If I didn't comply soon I could be in serious trouble.

Serge called up. 'Don't you want this?'

By the clink of glass and jostling liquid, I heard him jiggling a bottle. He knew the brand of wine I liked.

Blondie and Redhead treated the nave like a toddler's crèche, kicking off their heels and parading on the pews, loud as hell. One (I'm not sure which) squawked at me, 'Who's sheeee?'

'Someone who could learn a lot from you,' said Serge.

'Oooh, gimme a drink of that!'

Edith laughed and yelled, 'Uh-oh, now they have your wine, Rona!'

'Finders keepers! Hehe!' glugged either Blondie or Redhead.

Edith performed her role well. 'Shall we all call her?'

Drunk-as-skunk Blondie was the loudest by far. 'Who cares?' she said. 'Mmmmmm, you're so waaarm!'

She had her tentacles fastened around Serge, I could tell. I heard slurping noises that could only be kissing …

I did not want to feel what I felt next.

Only foolish girls would react, I told myself. You're too old to be so foolish, Rona. Did you actually get excited by a peck on the cheek from him? A pathetic peck on the cheek? Please don't tell me you did! Please don't! This is not a man, remember. Don't fall for it, Rona! Whether he gives a shit or not is irrelevant, don't give him the goddamn satisfaction of giving a shit yourself and … Oh shit! I should bear snide humiliation with indifference for the sake of my dignity, I will not have it turn my world inside out.

It did, though. It flushed me in a fountain of murdering flame.

Edith insisted on rubbing salt into the wound.

'Let's call her!' she repeated. 'Why not? Ro-*na*! Ro-*na*! Ro-*na*! Ro-*na*! Ro-*na*! Ro-*na*!'

It was too deliberate. How remarkable that picking on Rona

should be such a high priority, surely you're not that bored, Edith?

What started as she and Hector became four chanting, clapping wild dogs. Note, four.

'Ro-*na*! Ro-*na*! Ro-*na*! Ro-*na*! Ro-*na*!'

I wanted to cry, kneeling on the mattress, hands shaking with fear or jealousy or both as I fumbled for my tobacco pouch, feeling as ugly and decried as Quasimodo. I found the pouch. Picked it up. Dropped it. Hands not working, shaking, shaking, shaking!

'… Ro-*na*! Ro-*na*! Ro-*na*! …'

I couldn't roll the cigarette. Could not roll it. *Oh no. No, no, Rona, don't you dare, don't you* dare *cry! Don't cry, don't!*

I squeezed my lids shut against tears, clenching them to stop a spasm of waterworks.

The girls slurred, jabbering drunken banter as the chanting lessened. Suddenly, Serge broke. He stepped forward and bellowed up at me savagely, blasting the joke away and giving them quite a scare.

'*YOU EITHER GET DOWN HERE RIGHT NOW OR I'LL BE* REALLY *ANNOYED DO YOU HEAR ME!*'

The girls shut up, I felt their recoil from here.

You would think an asteroid had hit. His outburst slapped the shit out of the air and thumped me in the chest. The tobacco pouch slipped from my hands.

It had stained the atmosphere a shade darker. The girls muttered awkwardly between themselves, trying to recover from that out-of-character bit of weirdness; after all, they had had a good night, it was gonna be okay, wasn't it?

I admit he gave me a fright too. Seconds ago I had sworn to take Derek's advice and be out of there by morning, for a petty reason, a girlish reason unworthy of me, confident I'd never speak to Serge again even if he begged, resolute and decided upon it; he could go groom someone else! Then that bellow … It was a five-second hurricane, smacking me into reality like an immature adolescent.

No options. I snatched up my tobacco, papers, filters and a lighter, clutching them close, my sole friends right now, and headed for the stairs, pressing myself to the wall for inconspicuousness, tail between my legs. You couldn't have hurt me more if you'd hit me with a boxing mitt.

My efforts at camouflage were useless: a jeering cacophony hit the ceiling from the chancel and even the girls cried delight, relieved at the cheery revival.

I reached them to find Serge doing anything but cheering; leaning vacuously against the altar, head hung, an arm loosely around each girl either side. He eyed me poisonously.

'Don't you ever do that again,' he hissed.

His damning leer belonged to an uncompromising, denigrated brat; anyone would think *him* the injured party! The nerve. I wanted to kill him for that, and made sure he saw this exact thought in my face.

Yep, he saw it. It didn't move him in the slightest.

That is when Redhead threw up. A lovely, copious torrent of beige custard washing the floorboards. Great.

'Ugh, gimme watah!' she cried, spitting out offensive clots from the back of her throat.

'Some water for the guest, Rona?' Edith requested.

I did not move a millimetre. Serge nodded at Hector, who fulfilled the task while Blondie tripped about, torn between searching for her high heels and chuckling at her phone. Texting? Texting! That was bad. Imagine it: 'Hey guess wot we're in a church & dis guyz fit wanna see his pic lol!' It would only take a Send button to blow St Patrick's out of the water.

On impulse, I went to rake it from her and she pulled away angrily, shouting, 'Hey! What *she* want?'

No, thank Christ, she was not texting, just scrolling down her phone's music list. Serge was faster, and subtler.

'What's that song you were playing in the taxi, jingle-jugs?' he said. 'Hand your phone over here.'

The trusting Blondie surrendered it without question while Edith and Hector unlocked the cupboard.

Finally, now fuck the hell off, all of you! Don't forget to leave the cigarettes. Keep the Merlot, it was in her gob before you were.

Serge the walking museum piece knew his way around modern technology no problem, and after a few scrolls, the track he sought rang out in curly twangs of electric guitar chords. I recognised it: Puddle of Mudd's *She Hates Me*, an old favourite of mine I was about to be robbed of permanently. Then, like a glorious stage exit, Serge flung out his arms to reclaim Blondie and Redhead. 'Without further ado,' he announced, 'let's give them the tour!'

'Yes!' cheered Edith and Hector.

Serge escorted the girls, happier than ever to be entwined about him again, to their grand finale as I looked on dismally, wishing I had changed my mind about the wine they took, and guess who'll be mopping up the vomit too? The song went with them, fading as they passed through the fake cupboard.

That's weird. Edith and Hector were waiting outside the doors, as if expecting me.

What? *What?* What are you two gloating at? Go on, piss off. No thanks to you I have extra work to do and oh my Jeezuz it stinks!

They exchanged a look. Before I knew what was happening, in a matter of seconds Hector had charged, seized, pulled and forced me through their hole in the wall, sealing it and moving us onwards. Torchlight danced from below, the song reverberating.

'How did you find out about Derek?' Edith asked.

'His nurse came in, said he'd mentioned me.'

To them, nurse means outsider, a risky red light.

'Go on,' Edith said.

'That's all there is. She was passing on the news. He died weeks ago. Edith, let me go to bed, and I have that crap to wipe up.'

'Her name, please.' Edith was balancing me on the stair; the threesome ahead had hogged my torches.

'Phoebe,' I answered. 'I didn't catch a surname. She was clueless, really.'

'I believe you.'

I asked again to be excused, what the idea here was, et cetera. Edith's responses digressed no further than to mind my footing.

We were in their lair now, and the girls went from singing to whining about the dirt, the low ceilings and temperature drop; Serge must be showing them the Great Hall. I recollected my first impressions of that Hall: my elation, the fascination, its feast of detail a visual orgasm and how, if mine, I'd take pride in presenting it to even the lowest of the low – and all these girls could do was complain about not getting a signal on their phones. *If their phone disposal is my reason for being here, you're on. I know exactly where to find the fifteenth-century mace and chain.*

Can you imagine these two girls in the Hall? I thought by rights such an offensive misplacement should make them disappear in a puff of smoke. Or can you imagine how it felt to see Serge allowing Blondie, semi-conscious, to slump in his one-thousand-five-hundred-year-old Byzantine chair? He just *let* her! A game, you realise, the girls had seen their last birthdays, but … the sting of it. The sting!

'Fucking hell, Kirsty,' said Redhead, hopping off the edge of their grand table. 'A bit creepy, innit? What're we doing here? Where's my coat? Am freezing and I need a piss!'

Nobody answered her. Edith was removing her own coat and gloves, checking her handbag while Hector straightened the tablecloth.

Redhead frowned at them. 'Hey!'

Nobody answered her.

Having vomited some alcohol from her system, she was sobering up, and in stark contrast to Blondie, who slumbered in dreamland, Redhead's protestations doubled until she was babbling misgivings like an obstreperous parrot, her head darting in all directions: 'Oi, I said what's going on?'

Why shouldn't they ignore her? No persuasion needed anymore, she was on the plate.

And here comes the cutlery.

Hector opened the surgeon's case. Out came the long piece of tubing, pale as a roundworm when clean, this time ending in a small razor blade of stainless steel securely wedged into the plastic, so fine it was invisible side-on. Edith casually arranged a row of empty bottles on the table accordingly. I had to scowl, somewhat confused; it seemed an absurdly bourgeois method of killing, drinking via straws when their fangs did a quicker job. The use of tubes and blades made no sense down here; they were home, so the hell what if they left traces galore?

Serge reappeared from an arcade with a candelabrum, candles and two pewter goblets, humming along with Puddle of Mudd, stopping to ask, 'Might I trouble you for your lighter, Rona?' I threw it at him. He tapped Blondie's phone and put the song on replay. He would do this, replay it over and over, for the next thirty-something minutes, mincing about dubiously, now and then humming or whistling with the same bloody track.

Redhead noted all of the above with rising agitation. 'What the fuck!' she shouted. 'Why's nobody answering me?'

No help from them. It was when she saw the gaunt, careworn, hollow-eyed ghoulie shivering as far away as possible in the Hall doorway, that things changed. Woman to woman, silent body language communicated a terrible intelligence between us.

Redhead's mouth clacked shut.

To see her countenance fall, to watch her slowly fill with realisation … I had to watch that. It cut an open wound through me that would never completely close.

You're dead. You're not getting out. Sorry.

The intuition, the hurt innocence dawning behind her eyes, asking, *But why?* Redhead was no strumpet or mindless tart then; Redhead became a person, a woman like me. She had a mother and father and a home where she'd dressed for partying, willing to accept a hangover tomorrow. She had perceptions and loves and hates like me; she was a student, I saw the university sticker on her handbag; she had ambitions and a life ahead; she'd just wanted a fun night out, nothing like me and every bit as human as me. Now here she is, absorbing grim knowledge in the final minutes of her life. She sees me, she is starting to understand.

We were equals in that moment, bare humanity. My apologies for hating you, Redhead, whatever your name was.

Paling, Redhead bolted around and shook her friend.

'Kirsty? Kirsty! Wake the fuck up.'

This Blondie-Kirsty groaned, snoozing, out for the drunken count in Serge's chair.

'Wake up!' Redhead rasped, genuine fear nibbling at her now. 'Fuck! Right … Okay …' She straightened, looking this way and that, the song playing, Serge, Edith and Hector watching, ready. 'I, er, I need to go outside a minute,' she said, feigning ignorance. 'I'm getting no phone signal in here, I need to check a text.' She hurried to me.

Oh no, please don't ask me for help! Please don't ask me. I can't bear it.

'Wanna show me the way out, what's ya name, er, Rona?'

Goodnight, Redhead.

Hector seized her by the arms, lifted and threw her ten feet across the room to Edith. Redhead grunted, the wind knocked from her before kicking and shrieking in Edith's death grip.

Serge, who had been humming on the other side of the big table, now purposefully bent across it to give our fretful guest a good one-hundred percent, no-filters, three-dimensional view of him, the three of them. Their pupils are dilating to black dinner plates, an automatic reflex when they feel peckish and suitable hunting tactic; imagine your nocturnal vision with pupils that size. The song is blaring at full volume, drums and electric guitars are letting rip, Serge sings along.

In time with the lyrics, the unimaginable animal from October, the demon who found me in the east wing and saved my life from Edith and Hector, resurfaced.

Three pairs of falcate fangs almost two inches long, showed her. Redhead is being 'shown'. So few survive to know what that means. Her rational world and the fabric that wound it together are forever gone. She hasn't screamed yet; she will, though.

She does.

Serge moved around the table and tacitly motioned me over. 'Rona?'

'No.'

'Why?'

There were a million reasons why. To my disbelief, the well-trained watchdog moved forward, walking under water.

'Here,' Edith said, placing the razor-tipped tube in my hand.

They mean for me to kill her. So that's why. *That's* the premeditated climax of this whole hellfire of a house party. That's the tubes, the bottles, no quick-fix biting; that was them bellowing me down from the gallery.

Edith silenced Redhead by pinching her airway as Hector covered her mouth. The song restarted.

'You've seen us,' Edith said. 'Now let's see what you learned from last night. Exsanguination.'

Edith grasped my wrist and impelled it, driving the blade to Redhead's neck. Though I hadn't the physical strength to pull away, in my resistance I shut my eyes and hit off-target, slicing the girl clumsily, my arm muscles going flaccid as Edith forced me twice, thrice, and each time I kept missing, the quivering blade cutting zigzags across Redhead's collar bone.

Edith and Hector had had enough: the militant drilling commenced. Like sergeant majors, they puffed up and let me have it, shouting atom bombs into my ears.

'Get on with it!' 'Do it!' 'Get on with it!' 'Hold still!' 'Don't you dare!' 'Hurry up!' 'Do it, incompetent bitch!' 'Do it, watch-doggy!' 'Dooooo it!'

Edith's agonising grip crippled my wrist, making my digits bulge, but she cunningly waited until I chanced to open my eyes before tugging me harder, and she wasted no time: my eyelids opened to see the blade plunging. The next thing I heard was the elastic snap of something imploding in Redhead's neck. I had severed a tendon. Thick, deep crimson ebbed and rushed, rushed so fast, swimming over her breast and squelching between my fingers, drenching the slippery tube until it slid away from me. I dropped it. I was yelled at.

Edith, no mercy in her, repeated the action, pressing so hard that my digits disappeared under Redhead's skin. Warm, wet velvet texture pushed.

Then it sprayed.

They shouted louder and closer, close enough for their fangs to cut my earlobe.

'DO IT!' 'DO IT!' 'DO IT!' 'LISTEN TO HER!' 'DO IT!' 'COME ON, RONA!' 'WHAT ARE YOU CRYING FOR?' '*NOW!*' 'HUMBUG!' 'PATHETIC!' 'FASTER!' 'GET ON WITH IT!' 'FASTER!' 'NOW NOW NOW!' 'I SAID GET ON WITH IT!' 'HUMBUG, SOBBY POLTROON!'

Those two had laughed and cheered when Serge mauled me; Edith had once attacked me with a sword; Hector had never harmed me but would if commanded to … Neither of them had ever treated me like this. Not like this. This, killed me. Their shouting overlapped until my rattling brain ricocheted with incoherent roaring, which didn't matter, because I couldn't hear that song, or Serge humming, or myself screaming back at them through the shaking and the sweating and the blood and the tears.

'Stop it! *Stop shouting at me!*'

Cruel? Yes. Did they shout with contempt or passion? None. Not a bit. Just determined, tactical noise for old-fashioned textbook drilling, during which Hector used my free hand to fill and replace bottle after bottle where the tube emptied in a visible rhythm – PumpPumpPumpPumpPumpPump – in time with her waning heart. The pressure decreased as her complexion changed to alabaster, and I knew she was dying when urine gushed down her fishnet tights and pooled on the floor, mingling with arterial blood into the hue of petroleum, forming a network of tributaries running between cracks in the stone slabs.

The din soon roused Blondie-Kirsty from her sleepy inebriation, mumbling, before her eyes, bluer than Serge's, ballooned and her fake nails dug into the wood of his priceless throne. Edith and Hector made way to provide a full-on view of her slain pal. Nothing happened for a moment, we were like a photograph while her phone's music app strummed the slaughter's soundtrack on and on.

She, Blondie, could have died so easily, far less painfully. Her mistake was to notice – hence run from – the new faces of her three hosts who, minutes ago, to the best of her knowledge were acceptably human. She cried out, piercingly.

Blondie's speed was impressive for a sleepy girl so recently sobered. She scrambled from Serge's chair, fake nails breaking off as she half-ran, half-crawled for the passageway, and was nearly there when Hector yanked her by the hair and firmly lodged his fangs into her forehead. In desperation she jumped forward, another mistake: a shredding sound ardently competed with Puddle of Mudd as a huge section of her scalp tore away along the hairline. Watch surgeons perform facelifts: skin is highly malleable; the ease with which Blondie's scalp peeled off, it might have been a wig if not for that underside of veinous meat, flapping up and down like a flag as she ran out, losing a high heel, hobbling and sobbing.

'Oh, dear,' Serge mocked drily, leaning against a pillar. 'She's getting away, Rona. Better go fetch.'

'You fucking do it,' I said. 'I'm the ghoul.'

In an act of macabre surrealism, Edith, laughing joyously, resumed charge of my wrist and jogged me out, her strength leaving me no choice. 'Come on!' she laughed. 'Hehehe! Come on, Rona!' She skipped heartily, running us hand in hand like two fairy tale children through an enchanted forest. 'Come on, Rona! Hahaha!'

I heard Blondie, crying and lost in the passage.

Amazingly, our scalped guest was actually reaching the trapdoor. Blondie clambered, reptilian, on the steps, pushing it up with all her might as she cried and shoved, cried and shoved in despair. Quite a hefty chunk of iron for a girl her size; it jammed easily, I had chronic cramps in my lumbar and hips to prove it. They usually left it open for me accordingly.

Such was her motivation, the wicked piece of metal dealt the cruellest hand in the game – it temporarily relented to her efforts. Not rising all the way, just far enough to give her a parting smidgeon of hope in her young life, room to get most of her body through. That iron trapdoor is not a device you leave semi-open. It is not! You do not do that. You either open it completely or close it flat. She paid for it. Oh, she paid for it.

With her flopping blood hood, cuts and grazes galore, wheezing and bawling she crawled through, the trapdoor hung three-quarters of the way open.

There it goes.

Crash.

'*AAAAAAAAAAAAAGGGGGGHHHH!*'

I needed no torch or candle to know her head was flung back in wailing agony. Her ribs would be busted, more than a single vertebra shattered. Spasmodic in the trap, she was the enlarged picture of an unfinished bug or housefly. You have seen it yourself, in childhood, when you or a friend valiantly proved their gusto by executing a small insect in the garden or playground: hero of the day stamps on or smashes it with the newspaper, but not always successfully; sometimes you miss, or maybe you didn't hit it quite hard enough. Lift the weapon of choice and you find what Blondie has become here, a poor insect virtually cut in half, glued to the ground by its squished innards, top and bottom ends pedalling, still trying to escape, pickling in its own juices. Her legs beat in a rabid paroxysm, her arms aimlessly breast-stroking the air; she's calling for help, calling from a soundproof underground with no one here but us.

Edith snapped her knuckles in my face.

'Do you plan on leaving her there till Springtime?'

'You're the fucking strigoi,' I growled. 'Not me.' Ah, but then in my young feeble-mindedness, I covered my ears.

'End it, Edith! Shut her up!'

'*You* shut up,' Edith quite rightly said. 'Squeamishness is one thing, hypocrisy another.'

As she lifted the trapdoor, took Blondie by the flapping scalp and began dragging her back to the Hall, the volume of Blondie's screeches now competed with a new, soggy ripping noise too much like a dish cloth tearing in half.

'No. No. *No!* Naaaaaa-oooooooow! *Naaaaa*-oooooow!' Blondie's last words.

God knows how many spider-webs I destroyed, clawing into the passage wall behind me, subconsciously digging myself a hiding place by the time Hector arrived to see what kept us. He observed me, waited and, after Edith had passed, did a phenomenal thing: he gave me the most harmless smile in the world, and softly patted my shoulder.

'There, there,' he said. 'Come on, silly.'

Chum-like, he wrapped his huge arm about me, coaxing me from my hideaway. Hector, what a piece of work. Not a day in his life did he patronise, it was not on his radar, rarely speaking unless he needed to, and I don't think he could tell a lie. You won't appreciate this yet, but he was an unsung gem.

'It doesn't have to be this complicated,' he said. 'There are no accidents with us, especially Serge.'

Speaking of which, from the Hall his master called. 'Best wrap this up soon. Come on, for heaven's sake!'

Re-entering, I saw a woman redder than Redhead, redder than Redhead's nails, plop by her dead friend.

'You complain at us for shouting?' Edith lectured me. 'Look. And look well.' She pointed to the hairless, broken, dripping victim. In dragging her, Edith had shredded the rest of Blondi–, okay, *Kirsty's* scalp so ruthlessly it was now attached to her nape by a few pathetic threads. I would never visualise the term strawberry blonde the same way again.

'That,' Edith preached, 'is why when you don't do as we say, *you're* the one making it worse! The result? A big mess!'

Serge concurred from his throne, slouching idly over the table. 'We're hunters, not sadists, Rona.'

Loyal Hector prepared another razor-edged tube and passed it to me. Due another round of hell, I held it dumbly, which exasperated Edith.

She straightened and swigged from a fresh bottle.

'*Must* we bother, Serge?' she sighed.

'Same motions,' Serge ordered, moving to the piano.

'We'll be here all night!'

'Rubbish,' he said, playing the background song on the keys. 'Moaning is beneath you, Eddie. Have some faith.'

Would he never stop playing that fucking song?

Mangled Kirsty troubled us with no resistance. *Let this end. Help me help you, Kirsty. Pass out. Pass out! It's all I can do for you. Why did you come here? What sort of idiot are you, getting into taxis with strangers?*

Edith and Hector reassembled. 'Now, come on, Rona!'

No, you will not, you two will not smash me through concrete again. Hey, guess what? To hell with you!

This time I shouted at them; I would do it and do it fast, they wouldn't gain ground and pummel me to swill for Round Two. I can do this, I can, I can do it because I already have, don't get into taxis with strangers, Kirsty.

'Fucking shut up!' I yelled, raising the weapon, eyes red raw. 'Shut your mouths!'

Damn that song! I burst her artery.

Blood jetted, Blondie didn't fight. *I-want-her-to-die-want-it-be-over-I-never-ever-want-to-hear-her-scream-again!*

Kirsty's body began to convulse. Excrement spilled between her legs.

Serge coughed, signalling the okay to conclude this exercise, at which point Edith and Hector released me, discarding tubes and blades for the real tools. On my knees, on the floor, I watched fresh rivers of fluid cut a new course, zig-zagging under the table before slowing down once the flow was blocked, and redirected, at its source.

She took so long to die. I thought it would be quicker. She took so long. Would you believe me if I told you that after all the screaming, the running, struggling and crying, seeing them feed was the easiest part? That it looked peaceful? Edith and Hector latched on, everything went mute and the heaviest stillness fell over the Hall. I hadn't expected that. Nor did I expect a sight more horrific than Templeton's 'Welcome' doormat, more animal than Kirsty wriggling under the trapdoor: Edith and Hector's pink cheeks, working, dimpled, no louder than a baby breastfeeding, in-out, in-out, in-out, in-out, in-out. It'll be over soon, soon be over, soon over …

The song finished.

In the Hall. They're moving about. No music. They chat. Sentences bump into me, Latin, Greek, Russian, English, Edith saying, 'Well, *that* certainly took longer than it should have,' Hector saying, 'Leave them. We'll deal with it later.' An odour of defecation, someone saying, 'Don't shit where we eat, I wish.'

I wiped my hands together. It didn't help. Blood dries so fast, and smeared across both palms it highlights every looping fingerprint in dried maroon and paints crusty red lines under your nails. I was light as a feather.

An invading noise said, 'Here.' Serge in front of me, reaching into his pocket, and I knew exactly what was coming next – the wet wipes, his omnipresent supply of tissues. Tissues! Half a year of them, coming to a head, the way he stood there, unscathed.

I forgot to be afraid and slapped him, hard as I could.

Serge didn't move, possibly the only reason Edith and Hector kept a circumspect distance.

I hit him again. Why not, what did I care for repercussions?

'Rona,' he said.

I struck him a third time, losing my balance and stumbling into a Renaissance desk.

'Rona.'

Serge got me to my feet, made sure I was steady, and went to the table for the two goblets, filling one with bottled blood and the other with the red Merlot. He gently passed me the wine, got into position and raised his goblet, facing me.

'To Derek,' he said sombrely.

We stood there, the rims of our goblets touching, I, stricken. Very delicately, he tilted his cup, the tiniest portion of blood dribbling into mine, a couple of drops landing on my shoe. In my goblet, a red lagoon reflected my face and its two pupils glimmering in the candlelight.

'Derek,' I echoed.

Serge clinked the cups, and wouldn't leave my side until I drank the entire measure, which I did, in one. The rest of the evening is indistinct, their outlines came and went, nobody bothered me, my vision swam and sound became fuzz. I found a sofa and finished the Merlot.

Chapter Twelve

Auntie Alison is dead.

The church is full. It's winter. The candles are burning, cooking my hair. Wreaths everywhere, lining the aisles, the nave and chancel swamped in them, also bunches of pink, blue and yellow posies on people's laps. This many flowers must be normal, the dream says so, and I cannot be dreaming because this is real. I am here, ergo I am not dreaming. The church looks Christmassy, what with the candles and green decorations. I was mistaken, Alison must have died this December and not six summers ago. I was mistaken because I'm here, the dream says so.

Her coffin sits on the altar.

Everyone's looking at me, the lovely niece; they'd all said so. (Shh, Rona, it's okay, they don't know, they don't know.) They're looking at me funny, something must be amiss. None of them offer consoling nods. None are welcoming, like I'm a convict entering a courtroom.

The coffin's getting closer. Am I walking? I'm too close to this coffin, can see the chinks in the lid and handles. I'd rather not, thank you. It's getting too close. Fifteen feet. Fourteen feet. No. Why? Hey, hey! I've no willpower over my feet. I'm sliding to it and can't stop. Coffin getting larger. I don't want to go near it, it's bad, a BAD thing, that feeling, that shapeless doom that lurks only in nightmares; the thing you never see in full form, not far behind you in the woods, and when you wake up the dim ripples in your curtains look too much like the trees, something lurking, something bad.

('Baaaaaaaad.') Serge? Oh Serge, are you here?

He isn't, he can't help me. It's them, the world of my aunts, their crowd. The coffin, they want to feed me to it. Help me, Serge, make it stop! This is a bad place, not the church I love, not our church, Serge.

I think I have flowers in my hand. It's why I'm here, to put them on her coffin. Please, Auntie, no. Can't stop moving, it's pushing me.

I don't want to touch that coffin. I know what's going to happen.

I'm speaking, trying to shout. It takes humungous effort to issue sound from my immoveable lips. The strain! Can't speak.

They know, these people. Auntie Alison told them. I did those things. Nicer Auntie Pam didn't win the argument this time. They know now. They know I've been bad. Can't they just leave me alone?

Help!

Alison is angry.

EEEEEETCHU, RONA! EETCHU EETCHU EETCHU!

Please, Auntie, I just wanted to give you these roses. It's your ceremony, let me do that, I was a good girl, nonononon-ononononononononono …

Pushed by an evil wind to the altar.

EEEEEET, EEEEET, eet-eet-eet-eet-eet-eet-eet-eet-eet-eet-eet-eet-eet-eet-eet-eet-eet-eet

The coffin lid flies open.

Alison's limestone face is in there. Red lipstick. Dyed fair hair with grey flecks at the roots.

Auntie swivels her head. Her mouth explodes open, filled

*with jagged shark's teeth. She opens a pair of orange eyes rid-
dled with red veins and yowls at me. She's going to kill me.
She intends to rip me apart, yowling a high-pitched, visceral
'HAAAAAAAAAAAAAAAAAAAAAAH!'*
  Help me!
'DON'T!'

I jerk awake on my elbows, thrashing.
  Where am I?

It is pitch.
  Pitch and glacial. I lift my arm, crimpling with goose pimples, to feel space inches ahead. I touch bodiless iciness. Sitting
up is hard work, the blankets are too heavy, sheets of them,
layers of textile sediment solid as a lid. This is a bed.
  I stop, motionless.
  Where … am I?
  A very narrow tunnel made of orbiting dust particles, level
with my hip, opens to the right, its endpoint a pinhead of light,
a spot of fire, but getting brighter. Friend or foe? Apprehension
stiffens me, but I need the light and must watch it grow.
  The tunnel expands and dissipates into surfaces and objects,
taking shape, tainted various shades of amber from the weak
gas lamp: the edge of the bed, its wooden legs, stones in the
wall, a low stool, the sleeve of a shirt, a cuff around the wrist
adjusting the flame. A feathery tuft of sandy-brown hair stirs in
the lamp's heat.
  He is lying atop the covers, fully dressed like me, propped
up against a very tall headboard, a large book open on his lap,
its paper patched with age.
  The bed is large and framed in strong oak, its four corners
accentuated with columnar head and foot posts without an
overhanging tester. Once upon a time it might have had curtains, grand hangings of velvet with frilled borders. Four or

five lonely wooden rings hang from the rails, jobless, draped in a wool of long-abandoned cobwebs. The ornate headboard is panelled, Tudor in design and, for want of a polish, in surprisingly good condition.

To be tenderly tucked in bed under a nest of blankets secure as animal hide next to the architect of recent events … The contrast was outrageous and, in that sense, ironically comforting: last night had scoured a cave of emptiness to my core; these blankets were rough and moth-eaten, and yet they took care of me. The room being Arctic, I submitted to the bedding cocoon; he must have removed my cardigan.

And then there was Serge, in repose in his private quarters. His swaggering masks, feral menace and volatile sarcasm, had no use here. I detected no trace of them. He lay there, more unassuming than I had ever seen him, as subdued as the atmosphere, and when we spoke, it was softly, as if not to disturb the ennobled solicitude encapsulating this chamber. It is alluring, how hushed tones come naturally in restful, close settings; your vocals take on new dimensions with textures of smooth pearl and whiskered fur, so delicate, so intimate. Serge's attitude, lying by me in his room, encompassed this.

'I told you not to dream,' he murmured.

'What is this? Why am I here?' Though sensibility told me to get up, physically I was at rest. I felt involuntarily safe here.

'You had a lot to digest last night,' he said. 'Go back to sleep.'

'Why am I here?'

'It's all right,' he said, returning to his book. 'Besides, your shoes are down the well, along with your cardigan. The blood stains on them were permanent, wouldn't do. Put your head back, make yourself at home.'

I beheld the room. I took everything in. He had his own personal library, books unknown to me, stacked on a cabinet and floor. A medieval vielle lay in the corner, by it a spectacular armillary nautical sphere globe of gilded brass and dizzying rim alignments of ancient gnomon style engraved with astronomical symbols. The battered jigsaw of armour I'd transferred from the crypts had been fully articulated and reassembled into a standing knight, seven feet tall. There was a massive bureau, more books, modern science journals – engineering, mainly – and some unsorted engravings. Though his possessions boasted no distinct opulence, I gained the impression they were very personal to him if kept so near; *his* finds, and precious ones, each with their secret tuppence-worth of priceless history. Serge's room. Simplicity, not a damning castle of obsidian atop a misty mountain, no extravagance or grandeur, just his. Serge had a smell, always on him, most prominent here: a musky scent of aged wood and cloth, mingled with a natural perfume like daybreak across a dewy meadow. If you don't understand what I mean, wake up ahead of the eastern sun, walk outside where tall grass absorbs the breeze, make sure lots of sky is visible – I promise you, dawn has a sacred fragrance.

It was no good, taking all this in, I was soon wide awake.

'I can't,' I said. 'I can't sleep.'

'Daydream, then.'

'It's daytime?'

'It's gone seven in the morning,' he said, downcast, reading.

So different and self-effacing in his own environment. I realised this was a desperately rare glimpse of the unmasked Serge. The organic, hidden Serge who once asked me, 'Do you want to stay?'

He's sad. Why?

'Don't you sleep, Serge?'

'Generally. I'm a reader. Chronic habit, I'm afraid. I won't sleep without it.'

I hesitated. 'Can I ask what you're reading?'

'*Bestia deus profectiones* by Culmacio. Traveller's account of animal deities, 988 A.D. People know infinitely more today and they're still just as stupid. That's why books like this never get old.'

The handwritten page was open at a barrage of paragraphs surrounding a central drawing of two long-haired companions, a woman and a bearded man commanding a childlike rendition of a stormy ocean. From the waists down, they balanced on bouncy lines of water with two scaly fish flukes, while on the horizon a masted war ship sank to its maritime fate. The image brimmed with guiltless naïveté and was not without a spark of endearing simplicity. I heard waves drowning the mast and saw fish scales glisten in the spray; the cry of a gull and salty whiff of tempests sifted through the page. Unfortunately, the Latin text was lost on me.

'Oh.'

'I can translate, if you're interested,' he said. 'Do you want to hear?'

'Okay, then.'

I was not truly interested, but saw no point in declining. Besides, he was in an odd, taciturn mood: he refused to look at me. As he read aloud I prepared for it to wash over me without listening. The opposite happened. Serge's rhythmic narration was caressing. I fell into it and found myself paragliding on each sentence.

' "Traveller's tales of half-bird, half-sea nymph conflict and coalesce. The sailor aboard our ship regales that maidens transform between both. They may sing like birds to break a man's heart, then morph and swim to fill your lungs with water. They are as talented, says he, in the knotting of seaweed for throttling as we with our rigging. They lure by stealth and strategy: the pod splits in two, from the rocks and sky they sing to us in winged voices. The men cry, their souls bleed, the flying sirens reach for them in sweet songs of deepest longing. He tells me the distraught sailors and even the Captain reach for them, forgetting their vessel steers against the wind. The west wind, their forgotten friend, protests without vice or power to counter their yearning. The other half of the pod waits below until the vessel overrides them, their ravenous mouths agape. The fish maidens assail the keel, climb and unbalance the vessel until a briny void digests our crew. As we reached the Gulf, the crew were ordered to be safe from the threat of nymphs by force of restraint to the mast or by plugging ears with wax" when I yelled at you last night.'

A strained moment. I waited for him to speak again. No. He was waiting for me.

I finished his ad lib, tasting renewed bitterness:

'For ignoring you from the gallery.'

From somewhere I heard the grandfather clock's *tick-ticking*, very faint. It seemed to punctuate our discourse.

'Ignoring me is not what I meant,' he replied, still not looking at me. 'It's why you were.'

'So? Why was I?'

Tick

Serge sighed, turning a page. 'This book's harder to translate than you.' He read on to himself.

Slotted in the book cover, I saw his bookmark. A piece of paper. The paper was crimped, the familiar handwriting smeared and blotted, written in blue ink, biro. It was recent.

I slowly pulled the blanket over my face. It did not matter how he had found it, he'd found it.

'Serge. Please. It wasn't my fault. I only got his letter yesterday.'

'I know,' he said forlornly, reading, or pretending to. 'If earlier, I'd have known too.'

Tick

'It wasn't my fault.'

'None of it was your fault. The past five months haven't been your fault.'

What he did next. What he did. Stroked my head, gently

425

smoothed the back of his hand over my face, and rested it there. *Now* he was looking at me, exploring me as if new to it. The sincerest *sotto voce* nestled the fragile quietude, embracing me inside-out.

'You were very drunk. A lot of vodka. A piece of gum from that rotten carpet was stuck in your hair. I had to snip it out or I'd have woken you. Your face, so puffy and red. You were still crying when I saw you on that green carpet, crying and unconscious. The opal was in your hand; I loved you for that. You were too senseless to remember, but you opened your eyes, opened your eyes and looked at me. What would have happened if we hadn't found you that night, Rona?'

Tick

'No,' I answered softly. 'Set something free and if it comes back it's yours. I'll never tell you.'

A beat pulsed.

'I'm glad Daniels was scum,' he said. 'I mean that. You're the reason I'm glad he's gone. I speak for Edith and Hector also.'

'Thank you.'

Tick

'Thank you.'

Tick

He read more, not moving his hand from my face.

' "More than a hundred sons of Oceanus are the Potamoi, Lords and captives of rivers. They present as man and horned bull and water snake. Away from shore they guard to embody that which breathes the water of life into our fields …" '

His deliciously palpable narrative seeped into every corner of me, soothing me. It washed into an ocean. I was lying in a boat, being rocked by the sea. I would have let him touch me. I am looking up at cotton clouds in a rich mazarine sky, sailing away.

He read me to sleep.

Part Two

Cushioning waves break harmlessly around the rowing boat frame; it is small and fits my body, the sea gigantic. There is only me. I'm free. The waves tell me this is so; they raise and lower me as if I'm lying on an infinite, breathing torso. There are wild animals in this sea, flesh-eating animals, but the water is blue. They won't hurt me. All is blue.

All is right and all is wrong. It is not December, it's a sweltering summer's day. The sun and sky are hot, and I am so, so cold.

Chapter Thirteen

Shhhh. He's asleep.

Who would think? Serge at his most vulnerable. He probably knows I'm watching. I've been watching him for some time.

The sound of water dripping from a tap into a sink, *thud … thud … thud*, a series of rhythmic, muffled booms, gently, steadily rousing me.

My position in bed was largely unaltered, lying on my right side, wrapped chin to toe in protective blankets. His position, fully clothed above the covers, *had* altered; when I woke he was facing me, as inert as death could make him, my breath a moist layer of condensation on his face. My body heat gyrated in a pod of space between us, sealed by his frame and mine, and by the way he had oriented himself, I think my body was warming him. His circulation was a tired, lethargic tread, the *thud*, wait for it … *thud* … coming … *thuds*, his own unique, part-human heartbeat.

Serge. His exanimate contours of porcelain, his vulnerability here, hurt. In sleep the beast was an evocative tomb effigy, and mournful. But I had to get up; the wine had left my throat searing with thirst. I was restive and ready, my muscles ached and I needed to move, not that I wanted to. I procrastinated, watching him incessantly. Is he breathing?

Serge, I don't know what's worse, your brutality or this cruelty. I was scared to accept what this could mean. I admit I had fantasised moments like this, you already know that. Now that it was unexpectedly here, I couldn't judge the wisest thing to feel. I was enraptured. I was benumbed. I was confused.

At any rate, there I am minutes later, relieved of the covers and sitting on his bed, watching him still.

A meagre glow of light came from somewhere, indicating a meandering passage leading out of the chamber, guiding me to a snippet of the Hall framed in a Gothic archway. The grandfather clock was a distant matchstick. By it, tall chapel candles had been relit to show the way, some paper money left for me on the table, their custom.

A final glance at Serge? It was a new side of this monstrosity, seeing him asleep, upturned on the covers. He had changed position.

He read you to sleep. He took your shoes.

I went. By subconscious inaction I would not change my clothes that day; they smelt of him.

Morning service been and gone, I sneaked into an empty church. My watch said 10:40 a.m.; Falkirk would brain me, having arrived this morning to a puddle of vomit to mop up. Tough. I had forgotten my tobacco underground, though. Bugger. Oh well, thank goodness for pocket money.

I felt fine. How funny, I thought; the more horrors they put me through, the more I emerge as if from a dream, learning to recover faster.

They're grooming you.

Oh? By milking you, Derek? No, to this day I don't think so, Derek; you were a chore.

Run.

429

Hmm, no thanks, I'm fine. I'm fine, Derek, honest! Don't you worry your dear old head. Serge found your message, by the way. Sorry about that. Not my fault, soldier; any problems, see him. Besides, I won't get too far without my shoes today, will I? Hah!

No, you won't! Derek's voice reproached.

He is right, I won't, and truth be told, I'd felt scared to tarry underground this morning. Rona, excuse me, but who are you? There's dried blood on your hands, smell it.

Oh, so there is. Into the vestry. Sink. Soap. Coffee.

'Rona!'

Falkirk. Here we go.

'Get out of my church.'

'Fuck you, Falky,' I said, head down, toneless, calmly washing my hands under the vestry tap.

'What did you say?'

'I said fuck you, Falky. Or would you prefer "Minister"?'

'I want you out during the day! All day. Every day! I've taken your keys to my house. Find your own means of showering. You were responsible for the mess this morning! If your eviction angers them, they'll blame you! They need me more.'

'You do fuck-all for them,' I said, unperturbed, scrubbing under my nails. Acne bubbles ran off the soap bar and swirled anticlockwise around the plughole.

'You are a fool, Rona Dean. No, less than that. Don't you know how expendable you are? I'm the staple in their secrecy. Delete me or delete you? You are the go-between with no bank account, no address, no job. Anyone can replace you. You're the weakest link!'

I scrubbed away. 'What did they promise you, old man?'

'What did you sa–?'

'Are you deaf?'

'I said, get out of my church!'

Enraged at my outlandish coolness, he shoved in and twist-

430

ed off the tap. I had not finished with the soap; it remained in the silver basin, destined to dry marshmallow-pink.

I raised an eyebrow. '*Your* church, hmm? Or what?'

'Or I'll call the police. You laugh? Try that when they arrest you for the cocaine in your bag and belongings. What's wrong? No one needs keys to the gallery! Do you think I'm stupid, girl?'

He would do it. I see him, the ruddiness, he's getting fat again, and high. He's in the game. He would. Falkirk would set me up.

'There are lots of potential candidates to replace you, child,' he fizzed. 'I've a man lined up as we speak, wanted by the police and more than grateful for the mattress up there. He's a phone call away. You or him? Are you so thick to think it makes any difference to Them? That they'd care?'

He crossed his arms, thoroughly impressed with himself. 'Maybe you should broaden your horizons, go find a real job, call the DWP for a zero hours contract, stack some Tesco shelves, sell the Big Issue, grab a food bank voucher.'

I could have washed his mouth out with the bloodied soap.

'I think it imprudent you make these decisions without consulting our superiors,' I said, drying my hands with white paper towels, soon to be raspberry-ripple.

'Are *you* deaf?' Falkirk shouted. 'They don't care. You, you were *my* foolish choice.'

'No.'

'Sorry?'

'You locked me in on my first night for them to kill me.'

Falkirk did not respond.

'You thought I'd never figure that out? I was a witness, a loose end to trim. You didn't think me their type, and you're too pathetic to fill Daniels' shoes.'

I dropped the towels in a bin.

Falkirk thought. 'Yes,' he said. 'So are you. Daniels could've killed that Detective Matthews himself.'

We faced each other in morbid stalemate for a minute, my arms folded.

'Why do I offend you, Falkirk? How does someone like Daniels manage years when I get ousted within months?'

'You're reckless.'

I shook my head. 'Less reckless than your lies. What's this spite really about? What were you promised?'

A very long beat.

'No one knows them better than I. Get out, Rona.' Falkirk was buggering off.

'Shall I tell you, Falkirk?'

'Get out!'

'Shall I tell you what I think they promised you?!'

~

My raggedy spare trainers had holes in the rubber. Not much a girl can do when they're the only extra pair she has, so with two hundred pounds Christmas shopping dosh, courtesy of hunters, I owed myself some new shoes, maybe a cigarette too, missus.

I stopped at a newsagent, queueing behind some local office workers and a traffic warden buying their lunchtime sandwiches and crisps. Eating for me was out of the question. It took this outdoor breather to gauge the magnitude of the last twenty-four hours; any of those customers in the queue could be next.

Do you remember, Reader, what you were like as a five- or ten-year-old, the state of mind you were in? How many years or decades ago is that for you? I couldn't remember the Rona I was less than a year ago, and that's why it was getting increasingly difficult to miss her. She'd forced herself to be numb; I had to force myself not to be. The deeper you wound, the tougher the scar tissue, which is technically not even skin.

The newsagent was a stone's throw from Delfour Road.

Delfour. The name rose like an adversarial shrine in my mind. Lately I avoided the roadworks, or, I should say, former roadworks. Mezdon's ambitious plans were indefinitely castrated; an army of fallen and upright traffic cones surrounded a nondescript infill of new cement, collapsed paving and shattered pieces of tarmac bearing swabs of yellow parking lines like the aftermath of a miniature earthquake. I turned from it to savour the busy street and crisp December day.

The weather had changed its mood. Without wind or rain it was grey and stark, the chill held sway but allowed for the hustle and bustle of festive shoppers. On busier streets the annual decorations were up, bland and meaningless as the overhanging sky when unlit. What an Achilles heel, I thought, to rely solely on electricity for Christmas cheer when a century ago the ever-present holly, berries, gold-painted bells and stripy sugar canes were the required given, day and night. Even snow, the father of winter in this hemisphere, was a rare visitor now, and street decorations don't really count until nightfall.

What did I care? Christmas, a time for peace and love, so children are raised to believe. Dickens instructs this in no uncertain terms. A time for family. He obviously never met *my* family. My aunts and cousins, since deceased or moved to America, were a pistols-at-dawn waiting to happen. You should not put people of their generation and feudal opinions in the same room. Free presents, though! As a child that made Christmas for me; a kid gets toys, everyone's happy. A kid grows up, they get boring clothes, stationery sets and calendars, hence we kid ourselves with the ideological happy family substitute. My happy family? That option hit redundancy before I was ten.

Christmas. Bah. No humbug. No hallelujahs either. Let them shop away.

The boots I purchased, like everything in this season of giving, were shamelessly extortionate, as were the gloves I sorely needed, poor quality too. The weather nipped my fingertips ivory and dyed my nails mauve. All I had was my coat.

And Serge's scarf.

Lengthy, of Victorian wool embroidered with Celtic knots in willow brown and fir green.

I blew into my palms, dodging a ladder where two civil servants climbed to fix a busted bulb in the road-width decorations. *I killed two girls yesterday.* I folded both ends of the scarf around my hands, stuffed them into my pockets and walked down the pavement of frozen puddles in my new boots, going I could not say where, his scent wrapped around my neck.

It took me a while to register it was a Saturday. I was losing track. A few blocks later and crowds swamped the centre of Bronmeg. A lone saxophone player in a Santa hat and stone-wash jeans told me to have myself a merry little Christmas. I had no shopping and carried no more than my cigarettes; everyone else was loaded down with Christmassy trademark carrier bags and lethal cylinders of wrapping paper that whacked my knees. Many shopped in pairs or groups. I was alone. This reality breathed rough as the weather. *You really don't know* anyone*, do you, Rona? You have no friends. But that's okay. Or do you?*

It was on this thought that I did a double take at a shop window. What I saw inside somehow cheered me up. No friends?

I bought it without hesitation, though they sold none in purple, sadly. The fabric was cushioned and the backrest high, you could have rolled your head back and snoozed in it. A random detour to make, I seldom shopped on impulse, yet to do so here and now was strangely invigorating. It just felt right, plus they would deliver it to St Patrick's within hours. I gave my delivery name as 'R. Dean, et al ', lest Falkirk supposed Santa was paying him an early visit and kept it for himself. *Try that, Fuckirk, I dare you!*

Banished from the church, condemned to wandering streets by day in the depth of winter like this was not going to work.

Part Two

It couldn't go on. Judging by the recent weeks and Falkirk's ultimatum this morning, things were speeding up. Something was about to happen. Even the weather seemed to know this, halting its stormy performance in favour of a weird calm, as if observing, waiting.

At 5:50 p.m. I entered the church much fatigued, brewed myself a coffee and scoffed the rest of the biscuits without switching on any lights. Lights off meant no Falkirk, and I could have navigated St Patrick's blindfolded.

Plus, here's a rewarding sight. The swivel chair, blue, newly delivered and cloaked in packaging, wheeled into the north transept. I pictured a flummoxed Falkirk yapping at the unexpected delivery men. 'Oh, er, um, ju-just leave it over there!'

I sniggered and produced some notepaper.

From Santa, etc.

P.S. No indigos in stock, sorry.

I reflected on whether it was worth mentioning my recent argument with Falkirk, then thought better of it. A standard watchdog must possess the initiative to take responsibility for him- or herself, anything less is incompetence and hell mend you if you try milking it, I won't be sorry for you. Any benevolence on Serge, Edith or Hector's part is insurance purely for their benefit, not mine.

The day of wintry malingering equipped me for an early night.

I awoke the next morning to a Christmas rose on my pillow. A white hellebore. Never a vain or exuberant bloom; a modest, simple thing, prepossessing in its boldness. Like a star.

Said hellebore came with an attachment, its long stem inserted through the orbital cavity of a miraculously sculpted skull. I had forgotten about it. The gift I left to its fate in Hector's workshop, a paragon chiselled by his master specifically for me. Its placement spoke more than words.

A beautiful start to the ugliest day of my last days: the 20th of December 2014 A.D.

Chapter Fourteen

Let us skip the unimportant details of my second lousy day banned from St Patrick's under the petty threat of a drugs bust. After three in the afternoon I could bear near-hypothermia no longer. I was crazed with it, my knuckles rattled inside the disappointing new gloves, my teeth chattered, and I could have auditioned for Rudolph at Santa's Grotto. Maybe Falkirk wouldn't notice if I dashed upstairs and kept out of sight.

He did notice. Nor was he alone.

A man, wiry in a khaki T-shirt, stood with him in a private chinwag. Assuredly private! They both shut up with resentful looks when they saw me. I wish I could forget the particulars of this newcomer, this ratty jackal of a man, but seeing as we're here … I would have wagered my cigarettes his sooty hair went unwashed for weeks, greasy with neglect, avaricious peanuts for eyes, nose beaked, unshaven muzzle, his mouth small and pruned. He was a drug addict, I saw that straight away, the circles under his eyes, his twitchiness, a sickly pallor and irascibility towards everyone and no one in particular. Also, I recognised him from somewhere.

I made for the curtain and python stair, my pulse tickling in my wrists. The presence of Mister Jackal-Rat set something very off-key, a maladjustment like blocked ears with altitude, because a real sense of disdain seeped from them. Their furtive hush-hush made me so nervous I kept my coat on.

Their muttering ceased abruptly, and as soon as I thought it safe to light a cigarette, Falkirk ascended to the gallery. I held my ground, senses wired, as the minister strode to me, holding out his hand, proud as a peacock.

'Keys for the cupboard,' he demanded.

What fresh hell is *this* display of boldness? Falkirk is dirt, but this stupid? A terrible deadness sat in his pupils like a robot.

'May I recommend you write to Santa?' I replied. 'Who knows? He may hurt you less.'

'Now,' he ordered, as if warning a spoiled four-year-old.

'First lesson they taught me,' I said, rising militantly to my feet, 'never take instructions from anyone else in their name. I surrender those keys to no one, man or beast.'

To my bafflement, Falkirk snorted, amused.

'In their name,' he simpered. 'Very well, then. The gentleman downstairs requires storage space, a mutual favour I needn't disclose. I will answer to Serge and explain, I promise. I know the potential ramifications better than you. I do possess *some* faculties. You and I dislike one another; you'll happily run to them declaring what a naughty boy I am. Whatever. You won't get the reaction you're hoping for. So, a minute of your notoriously invaluable time …?' He gestured, making way for me.

I didn't like this, but I was tired. I got up to be rid of Falkirk, to get this shit out of the way.

The north transept. The pair of doors getting closer and closer, peripheral vision going fuzzy. The image stays with me as I remember escorting a nameless man to the cupboard. Yesterday's blue swivel chair had disappeared.

Jackal-Rat walked a few paces behind, though he may as well have been breathing down my neck. His aftershave was nocuous.

Part Two

As I held the doors for him, the departing sun bled a towering stained glass reflection across the pews, towards the purples and Prussian blues of my St Hannah. And the red angel, favourite window of a friend of mine. *Funny, I hadn't realised they were opposing windows. In the bleak midwinter the red angel wrestles Jacob, softly wind made moan, Rona.*

'Whaz wrong?' said the man, breaking me from my muse.

'Nothing.'

My torch flickered. The batteries needed changing. Falkirk, who was supposed to be preparing St Patrick's for its annual Junior Christmas Choir, was anomalously absent.

We went inside.

I *had* seen this man before!

Millennia ago, in this very church, a gang of four thugs, him included, threw a bottle at me. Rewind to November and perhaps the irony of his missing friends' heads, rotting in a bin liner a metre away, would have unbalanced me. A month here does a lot to a person. It crossed my mind to ask him about Alice. No, bad idea, hush.

Jackal-Rat knew his way, heading for the sepulchre automatically. Might this be your candidate for my replacement, Falky? Believe this if nothing else, Reader, I cringe to think of the consequences if he had taken my torch.

This ensued.

Jackal-Rat ambled into the tomb, took a measly bag of dope from his pocket and dropped it on the sarcophagus, job done. I waited for him to move.

He did nothing. He just stood there, dormant, foreboding, facing away. I should have listened to my instincts.

Instead I called, 'Hey!'

Stupid mistake, Rona, stepping into the crypt with him. That was when he flew at me with the knife.

A knife he cleverly concealed under his sleeve. Forget Gaz's dinky switchblade, this was the Real McCoy hand-to-hand Bowie combat weapon, complete with chunky wooden handle fit for a bear's fist and a curved edge, shining in the torch beam, a giant shark's tooth. In that foggiest flash I heard my aunt yowl her vengeance again, not seeing my reflection in the blade, but hers, the judgemental Alison, orange light, orange eyes, the hungry mouth of a great white shark in her great white face, rows upon rows of hagfish teeth. She was coming for me.

He was slick and agile. I had no lethal weapon. I am not sure how I managed to match his speed, deflecting his aim by smashing my torch on the knife spine. He had specifically targeted my branched iliac artery at the waist; I would have bled out, probably not made it to the cupboard, he would have taken my keys.

Scorching pain down my side as the deflected knife tore into my hip. A shocking flood of wet warmth dredged my jeans. I veered sideways, twisting in the dirt, and fell on something hard with a smart *clink* – one of the brass candlestick holders, broken through the bin bag.

The torch lay out of reach, impersonal by the coffin, overseeing us like an insensitive eyewitness with a camera, illuminating a pair of legs and his rising arm. He would slash my throat in a single sweep.

I dived for the brass holder and bashed it on his shins as he swiped the blade, missing me and slipping. Not waiting for him to grunt, while I had the chance I beat the holder on his kneecap.

Gaz's mummified head rolled out of the bag.

Jackal-Rat dropped to his knees. I swung again, knocking him in the face. And here came my big break. His hands shot to his split nose, blood pouring between his fingers. The knife was lost.

My gashed hip cried with me as I tried crawling out of his way, not soon enough to see his fist slicing the air, executing a club strike on my head. Stone, torchlight, coffin, ceiling and floor whirled and landed me on my stomach. It was all I could do to reach for the torch before he jumped on me.

The moment of greatest terror – he locked his arm around my neck until the crook of his elbow squeezed my windpipe. I couldn't breathe; I had no control; he was snarling, 'Bitch! Bitch!' My eyes bulged from their sockets, capillaries rupturing, they wanted to pop out. I opened my mouth for oxygen and none came. My body panicked, my legs and boots danced a humiliating jig. The only thing I breathed was his hairy forearm.

I'm going to die in here.

With every – every! – ounce of energy in my being, I drew my lips as far over my teeth as they would go, and bit him. I tell you I clamped my jaw into him like a barbed vice. My incisors crunched. I tasted metal, a lot of it, latching on. Harder!

Aunt Alison's abominable noise became his. He pummelled me, trying to wrestle his arm away, and the more he shook, the deeper I bit, breaking into an unfamiliar texture. Biting through raw flesh is harder than you think. Muscle is stringy stuff, tough clumps of countless fibres, and all is connected in there, pulling on other tissues with it, and be prepared for the biting pressure; the roots of my teeth ached like hot coals. It *can* be reckoned with, if you dig and wrench.

It loosened. The assassin howled.

Pinched between my four incisors dripped a sizeable chunk of meat, and in his forearm wept an elliptical indent where his hairy flexor used to be. Another chance. I had to get him off me. The life-giving oxygen rushed to my lungs, granting me the energy to wrestle him sideways, thumping his head on the ground, slowing him.

Out of the blue he released me.

Completely! No questions asked. I wriggled away and staggered up with his flexor in my mouth.

Jackal-Rat, horrified, concussed and bleating, had not

counted on meeting his dead friend in here, face to decayed face. Hello, Gaz. Thank you.

Without thinking, I spat out his flesh, cursing, ranting, panting, 'Bastard. Bastard. *Bastard!*'

I had him. My God, I had him! Acting without delay I raised my foot, new boots, heavy soles, walkers' wear perfect for ice and winter. *Slam!* I stamped exactly where his legs met. I shit you not, I hammered the bastard right in his manhood, the blackest fury taking possession of me, devoid of mercy.

That knife. He tried to kill me. Tried to choke me. I'm caked in blood! Fucker, that piece of shit fucker! I can't believe it. Everything I endure with cunts like you in my life, now you come here to kill me? WHY? Why should I take this? Why did I always have to TAKE this?

The cone of Vesuvius blew. I shouted myself hoarse.

Everything I had ever hated and feared, all I had grovelled through with a whimper, a simper, an apology, a sob, a nod, an excuse, politeness, from a distance, from up close, from the classroom, from the vaults, from home, from the balcony, from my island since the day I was born – culminated and exploded. I was on fire. I became molten hell itself, the backdraught coming and coming and coming in pyroclastic torrents. Do not ask me if this Rona had always existed, had been awoken, or was created by the presence of fang and blade; she was here: Rage. Correct again, Serge; the want of rage is pain and suffering; rage itself, the release of fire, is sweetness!

He's mine. Mine! He came here to kill me. He came here to fucking kill me. I'm gushing blood! No, I've suffered enough. Nobody kills me.

'*No* one kills me!' I raved at the top of my lungs, stamping his groin. '*No one! Nobody! Nobody!*'

Unstoppable flight of fury. It was glorious. Oh, glorious rage. Pure unadulterated rage fills you with the strength of fifty. It seemed I was never going to stop, either. The eruption

442

billowed through me and I welcomed it, true fire made for me alone, and instead of burning I was flying. I wasn't stopping, exhausting myself, stamping him, bellowing on and on.

'Nobody! *Nobody!*'

Alongside this release, a tactical situation presented itself: he must be disposed of. He was deadly. Mashing genitals may kill a man but there was no trillion-percent guarantee.

The problem was, as it turned out, uncomplicated.

Feeling skittish, Dean? Can't move, something else has me pinned flat, the leathered sole of a giant holding my seven-year-old neck down. Must be a giant, for no person is this strong!

I moved my boot from his crotch to his exposed neck, lifted my knee high, and brought my full weight down.

No stamping necessary here. It was so incredibly simple. Quite leisurely I saaaank my boot, pressing downward, and kept it there, pressing and pushing, though in truth it required no extra energy.

There came a fractured crunching; his prominent Adam's apple split; blood spattered the torch in a couple of fat spurts, dyeing its orange beam vermilion. Jackal-Rat's legs jiggled.

For good measure I repeated the action, moving the ball of my foot from side to side. *Need to be sure, be sure, it pays to be sure.* A guttural spume, a splintering …

Then nothing.

My volcano wheezed its last.

The price of self-consuming rage is to wind down on fumes, it demands rest. *My side. I'm injured.* Awareness of my physical pain finally intensified until it claimed me and I wound down to the floor, breathless.

Let me breathe, please, please just let me breathe.

I wanted to be certain he was dead. It can't be this straightforward, can it, to get off so easily? Niggling paranoia reminded me I hadn't the stamina to fight him again if he moved, which he didn't. Under his chin some pearly ridges of cervical vertebrae poked through a sludge of tendon and cartilage. A minor eternity passed while I waited for his diaphragm to rise or sink. He would have identification, a phone, wallet, money, and don't forget his knife, Watchdog.

I know, I remember, but, sore throat, bleeding, breathe, please, please, give me time, time. Ow!

Moving hurt so much. The knife injury was a handsome wound, I must say, and would scar. It soaked me scarlet, hip to knee, and my clothes were already adhering to the gash. Undressing would be torture. I felt queasy. I needed first aid, bandages, maybe stitches, their surgeon's case, I needed it!

Palpitating with adrenaline, I destroyed Jackal-Rat's phone and searched him for what else, discovering three wallets and two fake IDs, not much money. I wiped his knife on his trousers, finding no reflections or sharks, dead aunts or amber eyes in the blade, not even a Rona. I had killed a man entirely on my own and I refused to think; in fact, I refused to think about not thinking. I just operated. If less faint, I might have heard the trapdoor opening at the bottom of the stair.

Need bandages, need them, need – I caught myself from tumbling down their steps – *No, have to move, move, going downstairs, don't fall, don't fall …*

The torch beam jerking all over the place, spiralling, disorientating me, vermilion, murky bricks above, steps, walls, steps, sliding, keep going Rona, stone, no, come on, focus, black, black, where's the torch? I'm upside down, battery fading … stone, bricks … keep moving, keep moving … steps, stumbling … dizzy … hurts … torch … shadows … *tapetum lucidum.*

'Hector,' I stammered, finding my voice between gasps. 'Here, wallets, I –, money, I think, this …'

The figure in front of me became two figures.

'Is … The bandages? He's fresh, Serge, but, no, the … No bottles, he's dead.'

444

Hector, puzzled, took the wallets from me.

Serge's expression betrayed no more than his percipience. He pointed up the way I'd come. 'Up there?'

'Had a knife,' I said. 'Look.'

Once I gave them the weapon, my gelatine legs subsided, sliding me onto my undamaged side. Serge took the knife, passed it to Hector and craned his neck, arms akimbo, eyes locked on the stairwell. I thought they would go and investigate. Serge, he just stood there.

'Get her the necessary,' he said, stock-still.

Hector was helping me to the trapdoor.

'Heck?' Serge added. 'Then bring Eddie and yourself.'

Minister Donald Falkirk's second attempt on my life.

'Hhh-*gaaahh*!'

My top peeled off the gash as painfully as I'd expected, under the academic scrutiny of Mistress Edith. The bandages had a separate section to themselves in the surgeon's case, spirals of shabby cloth feathered with age from the Cole's Medical Supplies package, never of use until now. Its complimentary bottled water, months old, was stale. I drank the lot. Swish and gargle as much water as you want; the flavour of blood lingers on your taste buds for ages, believe me.

Apart from Hector and Edith swapping mutters in Latin, they otherwise asked no questions. She wet her finger on my chin, sniffed and sipped Jackal-Rat's blood.

'Male,' she said, sniffing again. 'Heroin addict. Early thirties.'

'I could have told you that, Edith,' I said. 'Will it need stitches?'

'No.' Edith straightened. 'Mead or mulled for the invalid?'

'Both, please, nurse.'

I imparted the particulars of Falkirk's last confrontation and his threatening to frame me. The rest you know.

445

'We told you to watch him,' Edith replied. 'Your phone?'

'In the gallery. For taxis? I thought you were walking to-night.'

'Ah. In that case Serge has it by now.'

Edith and Hector donned their coats.

'You know where everything is,' she said. 'We shan't be long.'

They were longer than implied. My mind kept replaying the attack upstairs, seeing the Bowie knife coming for me. Amazing how I'd survived when months ago I couldn't have deflected a blow like that, I was stronger than I realised. Then again … Months of heaving their trapdoor, of shifting sculptures, armour, swords and furniture when tired, hungry, afraid or underweight. They knew what they were doing. In August they met an introverted, ignorant young woman recruited for an infinitely dangerous job – and trained her. Oh, they trained her! At least in Stage One. What's next? Guns? Fencing? Bows and arrows, for Christ's sake?

Hector returned alone and ventured out again shortly after, leaving me with a bottle of cherry brandy, Serge's prescription. No use arguing, although curse his wisdom if it wasn't a fair choice. The sugar was re-energising and the alcohol thawed me.

Concealed by killers from my would-be killer, scared and unsure of the future, I confided my fears in Hector.

His response? A big, hearty guffaw!

'I wish I could share your optimism, Hector,' I said, stumped. 'I'm afraid it doesn't help.'

'We had a meeting with Falkirk.'

'A meeting? You *spoke* to him?'

According to Hector, this was the gist of their consultation:

Serge had dialled Falkirk's house from my phone in the gallery.

'Ambitious man. Stop by, will you? You have thirty seconds.'

Falkirk found Serge and Hector sitting in the pews, Edith perched on the altar, and both cupboard doors open.

Falkirk griped, 'Well? What?'

Swigging bottled blood, Serge gesticulated at the Menzies crypt and waited for him. Falkirk didn't need long; he took a few eager steps in … followed by a single leap out. Hector described the scene like a film, Serge relaxing, cross-legged, hand dangling from his elbow over the pew bench.

'Wasn't me,' he told Falkirk.

'Nor me,' added Hector.

Falkirk looked at Edith, who scoffed disgustedly.

'A Bowie knife, Falkirk?' said Serge. 'Really? Another street rat? Truly?'

'Did you tell her?' Falkirk blustered. 'Our agreement?'

'Agreeeement,' Serge mocked.

'She pressed me about your promise!'

'Promises are words, Minister. *That*,' Serge pointed to the scene of my crime, 'was an action.'

Falkirk hardly knew where to look. Serge went on.

'Meantime, I'd brush up on your gentlemanly skills. I advise extreme caution from now on.'

Serge was infuriating Falkirk with his facetious composure.

'Caution?' Falkirk's nostrils flared, beads of sweat breaking out on his brow. 'I've lived and prayed caution under your thumbs for over thirty years!'

'Oh, I grant you with an open heart, Minister, it isn't *us* you're in danger from now.'

Falkirk paled, dumbstruck, and then, Hector told me, apparently proceeded to make quite the fool of himself in front of them, descending into an embarrassing tantrum of grovelling and weeping like a baby.

'No … You haven't. Her. You can't! No!'

This much Hector disclosed before leaving me to my brandy and cigarettes, underground.

Chapter Fifteen

It's the most underrated role in the underworld, watchdog for the undead. The servant. The human ghoul. The key-jangler with the lamp. People who don't mind that the world forgot them. The victim who survived. You'll find no better expert on the monsters under your bed, nightmares we must live with cheek by jowl. We're on more intimate terms with them than Beelzebub. We know them better than any Van Helsing. And have a care – if you stray too close to these nightmares, the monsters may not kill you, because they won't need to: the last human being you will ever see is locking the door behind you. I have to. I have a job to do. They trust me.

Even unpredictability gets predictable in this place after a while. Hmm. Only a watchdog understands that, you know; the way they operated, fair and unfair, an appraisal here then a reprimand there without reason. All on purpose, of course, very deliberate. It's nothing personal, they just want to see how you'll react. They need to know how loyal you're going to be, constantly testing your threshold to form a picture of you for themselves. It's all a test. Every single last tiny goddamn thing from the word go was a test. And once their picture of you is complete, they'll make some adjustments, tweak it to suit them via more, let's say, *exercises* designed to chip you away, moulding you until one day you wake to find yourself actually fitting into this new skin. That sub-monster you've both fought and become, gifts you with a kind of unbreakable outer casing, an energy, a solemn platform all of your own. Then, and only then, are you a true watchdog, and you won't feel the need to look in the mirror to remind yourself this time, I promise. There is no pride, no vanity, no rewards apart from your pulse and a roof over your head, what more do you want? Pick up your cleaning utensils and make sure you remind them not to miss their taxis again.

I accepted it, wholly and staidly. A servant, naught more, naught less, no matter how lovingly he once touched my face.

Here we are again, Rona, alone in their vaults, alone with the dead. I am alone with ghosts. This place doesn't scare me. The grandfather clock keeps watch like a real grandfather; he seems to be grandfather of every soul in here, all you relics. You, Embaldt the Elder, dead over three centuries and still their night watchman, resurrected in your own ticking sarcophagus, the Greek word for 'flesh-eating stone', ha! Embaldt, you're making me look bad!

The remnants of their generations surrounded me like a patient audience in an amphitheatre. I'm talking to myself. Lo and behold, Rona has just murdered someone and she talks to furniture. I laughed and swigged the brandy. Gah! Too sweet. I sipped it.

Drunker on wistful nostalgia than alcohol, I'm sitting amongst forgotten centuries. Try getting most locals around here to feel your unspoken tears, my faded threadbare friends, you didn't always smell this way, not that it's unpleasant; it's retired, not rotting.

Sunlight makes you crumble?

– It makes us rot.

'If you had voices, my audience of antiques, what would you say? I do believe I love you all, did you know that? I love my love for you; I hate my nostalgia for you! What stories can you tell me? How about you, coffin-maker's baby? Go on, tell us a story! I have a handful. Your owners have hundreds. Thousands! Did you know I love them too? They've destroyed and sewn me back together like that fucking patchwork quilt. In whose image, though? Not in God's, I promise you. Can they love? Have they the capacity? How many more knife-wielding thugs do I have to kill before I go numb?'

I was standing in front of the clock, challenging the hand-painted face, swinging the bottle in my hand.

'Is being numb good? How can there be any emotional punishment in feeling nothing if you feel nothing? Maybe I should follow your example and stand,' I clacked my tongue in a tick-tock-tick-tock chorus, 'and be made of wood. You do that and manage to stay beautiful!'

The latest addition to the Hall was Mister Blue Swivel Chair, still wrapped in transparent packaging, positioned at an angle by their table.

'All but you, Mister Blue. I'll give you a lesson on behalf of your new acquaintances here, from our generations to yours. Now,' I sipped the sweet cherry tipple, 'you're newer here than I – what a revelation – so tune in. If I could recite you a dirty limerick I would. Alas, I am no bard. A fact: don't fall in love with beauty. It's usually deader than you; it can't love or hate; it can't anything. You can hold it in your heart forever – knock yourself out. It'll never hold *you*. That's the trouble with beauty, too much of it around to love and you don't know it's a dirty trick till you reach out and realise you've spent your life living behind a pane of unbreakable glass. Love is Phylum Animalia's oldest narcotic and –, oh Jesus-fucking-tit, I'm talking to chairs! I'd park my arse on you if they wouldn't hand it to me for breaking the rules.'

The dying torch winked out.

'Bye-bye, batteries.'

I dished out my trusty lighter and lit the candles. Ah, much better. The empty goblets from two nights ago remained by the candelabra, and under the table, several floor slabs were outlined in yellow-brown, dried fluids from two dead girls.

There was something else there too, meandering into the Hall from outside, to the sofa, to the clock, to table, to candles, to swivel chair, double-taking here and there from furniture to table and from table to me. A trail of bloody boot prints. The medieval floor looked like a painted kiddies' track in an adventure park, gradually fading in sequence from thick marks to irregular crescents, dried blobs and smears. Brand new boots, too! It was horrendous. It was positively farcical. I followed its loop-the-loop course with a kind of dumbfounded wonder, delirious.

'Uh … aha … uh-ha-ha … hahaha … *ahahahahahaha* …!'

You would be forgiven for labelling me inebriated, though here's a thing, the brandy was so sweet I only managed two shots worth. I laughed until my bandaged side leaked, unable to contain myself; the more I looked at the prints the funnier they were. They would lead here all the way from Menzies' crypt! I burst another guffaw, nursing my slashed hip, gripping the table for support, tottering and landing in (where else?) their new swivel chair, of all places, the packaging crinkling aggressively.

The unused chair was very ready. Landing instantly spun me in several full circles without slowing, distorting the rest of the world until no world could catch me. Like cutting through space and time, it swaddles you in a private dimension while everything else slugs by; you are the constant, the outside is redundant and finite. If I could always manipulate the world this way! The rush of air on my brow, to lose myself in that spectacular revolving ceiling, spinning and spinning. Carry me away. The ceiling warped faster and faster into a soul-freeing funnel. The funnel spiralled into a maelstrom.

I switched directions and spun anticlockwise. The maelstrom morphed in reverse to a colourful kaleidoscope as three pairs of dots, brown, hazel and blue-grey, floated in and joined the eye of the hurricane. I sped up. The six dots conserved angular momentum by becoming sixty, whirring into a vortex of coruscating stars. I smiled up at them freely. An object materialised from this vortex: an index finger, a submarine through the waterspout, touched my forehead lightly, and stayed there. I understand, I am transformed into Rona the Spinning Top. I laugh. They laugh with me. Round and round and round and round and round … The blue-grey lights were last to fade out.

Edith eyed me winsomely.

'Look at her. How shall we entertain the angel on our Christmas tree over there? Hanukkah, Noel, Michaelmas, Yuletide, anything to mark the season for you, Rona? Any illuminating history lessons of the since-hijacked winter solstice?'

'Nope,' I said glumly, slumped against the table.

'Not even a ghost story?' said Serge, smiling slyly. He and Hector were busy restringing a lute, a vielle and a clarsach while Edith carried bundles of next week's laundry here and there, my offers of help having been shooed away. Unusual.

'I don't believe in ghosts,' I replied.

My irony amused them no end.

'Oh, Rona!' Serge sniggered. 'I think that deserves something.'

He spoke (in Spanish? Italian?) with them, at which Edith dropped what she was doing.

'Up, Rona,' she said, taking me by the elbow. 'Your clothes have had their day.'

True, they were cardboard with crusted blood. She took me to a small vault at the far-right end of the Hall, virtually hidden under the arcade, cut off from the reach of candlelight.

'Edith, I can't see. I'll get a candle.'

'No need,' she said stiffly. 'I shall choose.'

Indoors it is Edith's custom to wear embroidered slippers with thin leather soles; guiding me by sound, their padding scrapes were followed by the squealing latches of half a dozen closets. I had helped move them during the clear-out, they were a job to open and, though their resilience was mind-boggling, relented in a series of hinges busting painfully like thunderbolts, each dying a little every time. Their unseen contents filled the mini-vault with a stifling fustiness.

'I could go up for some clothes from the gallery if it's easier,' I said, grimacing at the noise.

Edith's voice came in the dark, a voice from nowhere.

'This is easier.'

Outside in the Hall: music, the piano, and a violin? No, Serge's vielle, the bridge of the instrument almost flat, allowing phrases to overlap in sumptuous harmonies. In here: black, sightless; shifty whispers of cloth on cloth, a movement of clothes pegs. An uneasy ambience befell us.

'Why are you still here, Rona? Why are you with us?'

'I chose to be.'

'That's the technicality, not the answer.'

The grimalkin had me where she wanted me, sightless in an interrogation chamber.

'You have no explanation?' she went on, sifting fabrics. 'No what, or who, keeping you awake on your mattress, dreaming before sleep?'

Oh, I see! She thinks I've forgotten Serge's sliver of benevolence is as fickle as his temperament, she thinks me an even greater fool than I spent months berating myself for.

'I won't give an answer to mockery paraded as a question, Edith,' I said. 'Push–pull, your ever-present tactic, the lot of you. I stamped a man to death today. I may be your watchdog, but I'm not your *dog*. Please don't insult my intelligence again.'

Never had I stood up to her so! I prepared for a retaliation.

Edith's reply was extraordinary, almost grateful.

'My apologies,' she said. 'Undress. This will suit you.'

I did as she said. I had to strip bare; the wound had bled to my underwear.

'Raise your arms.'

Over my head, fabric brushing my breast then swamping me in a curtain, Edith dressed me in three separate layers, starting with a loose undergarment like a chemise, reaching my shins. The next covered me completely in a thicker material, grainy with hard dust and, judging by its weighty texture, a main gown of creaky velvet. The sleeves were testing; I had to help Edith work them down my arms, past my wrists to my thumbnails, where she pulled the ends together firmly and fastened them in hooked clips, incidentally disabling the use of my thumbs like shackles. When I relaxed my position, the full tightness of the taut fit came home, pinching harshly into my armpits, hugging my ribs and squeezing the circulation in my buttoned hands. I thought the gown too long and fragile; my feet trod on the hem, I already sensed a tear or two per movement, and hissed in pain where it nipped my knife wound. At least it cushioned the bandage.

'They haven't been worn in a long while,' Edith said as I winced. 'Smell musty?'

'Reekingly so.'

The final garment came, much thinner, I hardly felt it over the gown. It had a very loose, wide skirt and no train, hanging over my shoulders like a sleeveless apron. Edith also gave me a pair of slippers, plainer than hers but equally robust. I worried about mothballs or mites; the psychosomatic need to scratch was maddening and the pinching in my armpits drove me crazy, I kept pulling at it. Strict Edith told me to leave it be, that I would get used to it, then abruptly shifted me round to run a wooden comb through my flowing hair.

'You are a maiden,' she characterized. 'They don't cover

their hair until wed.'

She took me to a mirror in the Hall. I saw myself.

Good Lord.

The top layer partially covered me in a surcoat of chestnut brown, charmingly deceptive in its humble modesty, baggy and shapeless without an owner, so feminine once adorned over the V-necked main gown of deep forest green. I had virtually stepped out of the fourteenth century. That I, Rona, was capable of looking like this! Edith had dressed me as she wanted me to be seen: not a lady of nobility; elegant plainness without extravagance, highlighting my pale face. I am not prone to self-flattery, nor by any means a fairy tale princess, there are much prettier fish in the sea, no competition. But this! My hair glowed autumnal auburn in the candlelight, complementing the gown's deciduous forest, green as my eyes. Green.

In the mirror stood another figure, further away by the candelabra, seeing me, wielding a crescent-shaped bow of birch and horsehair, the vielle set on his shoulder.

The spell dissolved. He laughed and poked Edith in the ribs. 'Ha, poor Rona. Your theatrics, Eddie!'

The music resumed. Edith sat at the piano, Hector tuned one of his many ornamented bone flutes, and for a while it seemed I was forgotten about, though it felt more entertaining than disheartening, watching them sail flawlessly through multiple tunes whilst conversing in multiple languages. Mesmerised by their duel concentration, soon I was quite happy to just sit, smoke with my brandy and listen, relaxed. Can you imagine that? Me safe in the vaults with Lucifer's leeches, so-named by Falkirk – the man who'd attempted to kill me twice; and the admittedly brutal, indiscriminate killer Serge, who had saved my life twice, in Krellingsgait and in the bygone east wing. I remembered this atmosphere, the same as on my birthday, the atmosphere when they were kind. Kind before they educated me properly. What was this then, another charade?

Part Two

Rona, shut up for now. Where do you think you're sitting? Where? Does that look like a sofa, box or a stool to you?

The implications hadn't sunk in yet. I consciously abstained from jumping to conclusions when it took enough psychological stamina to focus on the immediate present, in the oblique wisdom that if they really planned on keeping their promise to Falkirk, he'd be the one sitting in this new chair at their table.

Serge led them fluently in and out of medleys, a few of which I recognised, picking up some bars of *A Coventry Carol* and Renaissance melodies and *Pat-A-Pan*; the rest were a mystery. Though my hands starved for that piano and the vielle, I hadn't the heart to ask for tutoring. Quite a bittersweet cocktail, isn't it, to be both intoxicated and left out.

'Are we too dated for you?' Edith quipped.

'I don't judge,' I replied, hearing the tinge of envy in my voice. 'I just can't play.'

I transferred my cherry brandy to a goblet from which, ultimately, I would not get the chance to drink, because a few bars into the next song I nearly spilled the bottle. Leering audaciously with the vielle, Serge, the teasing Devil himself, was closing in on me. On impulse, I steered the chair wheels away and sprang up, albeit too slow. Cheetah-speed, Serge caught me from behind, raised the vielle over my head and anchored the chinrest to my collarbone, securing me to him. He playfully swayed me, left to right with the tempo.

Edith quit the piano to sit with a small clarsach harp propped on her lap, and as she struck the delicate stings, this next song I recognised. Don't say the church choir never taught me anything. A Yuletide carol, surviving since the fourteenth century, *Als I Lay on Yoolis Night,* in Old English.

Edith sang.

'Als I lay on Yoolis Night, alone in my longynge …'

Not my favourite, though it carries the lilt of a lullaby, enticing enough for me to stroke the vielle's moving bow, swaying, not free of Serge yet.

'Do you never think it sad?' I asked him. 'That someone's life, any life, so potent with its private internal universe, disappears forever once dead? Absorbed into the ether with the others. Worlds of feelings and possibilities, extinguished.'

Serge lowered his vielle.

'But look what they leave behind,' he said, placing the instrument on the table.

He did, and did not, dance with me. He didn't touch me. To the music, he approached and paced me, stepping me backwards, forwards, changing directions, sideways, walking me on the surreptitious precipice of a hands-off waltz.

'Are *you* not sad for killing a man?' he teased. 'How easy was it?'

'Ask your mind-reading self.'

Serge switched roles and reversed. I followed him.

'What if I choose not to?' he toyed. 'Your sincerity is valuable to us.'

'Vice versa.'

Serge changed the game, coming to a halt too soon so that I almost walked into him, his very intention. He lifted my hands, locked fingers and wheeled us in an impromptu non-stop circle, whirling me like a javelin thrower.

Edith was singing. 'Synge now, moder, saide the childe, wat schal to me befall …'

Serge's impaling pupils probed. 'What are you? Where do you live?'

'What do you mean?'

'What are we?'

'Strigoi.'

'A human's label,' he said. 'Try again. What are we?'

The Hall whizzed in a roulette wheel.

'Hunters,' I answered.

'What are you, human-person-woman?'

'I'm a watchdog.'

'That's your job, not what I asked. What are you?'

'I'm Rona.'

'*Another* human's label. What are you?'

'I don't know.' The truth.

Serge and music were the only solid things remaining.

'Why did you really leave university? Why did you never join the world? Where do you live? What did you want?'

I spoke without thinking. 'Freedom.'

He slowed us down. 'Rona?'

'Serge?'

'You're made of mazes in there. Enlighten *us* with a story if you don't want to hear one.'

They were not anticipating my reply. Neither was I; it slipped out. Wherefore the song lyrics or not, it pounced from a file of buried memories by sheer chance.

'If … If it's ghost stories you want, when I was kid, I think I saw a doppelgänger.'

Serge stopped.

I told them a true tale as the minstrels played.

'My aunts said she looked a lot like me before she died. I kept a photo of her in my bedroom drawer. My Aunt Pam criticised her, called her aloof. Well, if mother was like me, that's not true: why speak when every other mouth quacks like a motor duck so you don't get a word in or don't know what to say?

'It was an October Monday. I was fourteen and midterm break was over. I was walking to school. Terrible place, it made me worse. And something in me turned askew. I stopped at the traffic lights. I couldn't go in there. This Monday was our deadline for an English assignment on literary examples of Descartes' *Cogito ergo sum*, "I think, therefore I am". I'm not a dunce, but I dreaded the day because I hadn't done my homework. I had a block. I was struggling to get my head around the line because I too badly wanted the freedom to yell "I am, therefore I do", instead.'

Serge smiled ever so slightly.

'So I didn't go to school. I did a runner. I thought I'd run to kingdom come. I'd head for the Scottish bloody Highlands if I had to. Instead I wound up here.'

'Here?' Edith queried.

'Your transept. It's easy to hide there, my childhood spot. Nobody was about. The cupboard, I'd forgotten the keyhole had a draught, I … I tried the door handle. The draught, it was magnetic.'

I held up my palm for emphasis.

'Then I felt someone watching me.'

Hector's flute playing slowed down. Edith had stopped altogether.

'It wasn't Daniels in the gallery,' I said. 'I thought it was a ghost, up there, standing at the balcony, not a blink or a word. I thought it was her but I'm not so sure anymore.'

The Hall – you could have heard a pin drop. I noticed my listeners and lost track of my tale, stumped by their engrossment.

'Rona,' said Edith seriously, inclining forward, almost timidly. 'You're saying she looked like you, adult you?'

'Well …' I faltered, wishing I hadn't bothered bringing up a story I could barely remember anyway.

'How did she look?' Edith dug.

'She, er … Like her photo. Longer hair, though.'

'Like yours. What else?'

'There's nothing else. She was looking at me.'

Edith glanced at Serge. When I saw him I caught my breath.

A minute ago, his complexion was a healthy olive. Now it matched the colour of the floor. He was alarmingly detached, elsewhere.

Hector tuned in. 'How was she looking at you? In what way?'

'That's enough,' Serge suddenly snapped at them. 'Both of you!'

I was too busy trying to answer Hector. 'Er, she … Harsh. Sad. I couldn't really say. I don't remember, Hector. Falkirk came in and I dashed. It was all too fast, Edith. Zip-zap.'

No one spoke.

What an unsettling pause. I hadn't foreseen this, couldn't understand their reaction or why they were taking the story so seriously when for heaven's sake I'd even hammed it up a bit for them, so little did I believe it myself; they would know, wouldn't they, they see through fabrications! Clearly I was missing something here, Edith and Hector silently questioning Serge as if for help, he, whom they relied on for solidarity, so effortlessly in command, their safety net and rock for rebalancing mishaps.

Serge, no less aware of their uncertain faces, on this occasion regarded their reliance with an icy resentment, then me. I stood nonplussed, perceiving only that he wanted the damn subject abandoned and forgotten about.

'It's snowing outside,' he said.

My sympathies, Rona. I do apologise. You received no forewarning, no build-up, it happened instantly.

Serge's pupils were swelling, larger, larger. Two trickles of blood emerged at the corners of his mouth a split second before he seized and pulled me to him.

The force knocked me halfway to the ground, making me grab Serge's bicep for support as he yanked my head back by the hair, forcing a full-on view of his opening mouth. What I saw inside was a pool of burgundy blood, his, collecting in the palate and spilling over his lip, muffling his words.

He told me to open my mouth.

If he pulled any harder my neck would break. I arched, bending my legs, fighting for balance.

'Op-en,' repeated his liquid voice.

I glared hateful defiance at him, whatever this sadistic new game was. Seeing I would sooner risk a broken neck than comply, he returned my glare a hundredfold, using a sight he well knew I had never accepted: once again, the muscles under his cheekbones slowly twisted and contorted into the most unnatural disfigurement. With a near-audible cluck, parallel lines of solid bone rippled forward under his skin as the upper jaw detached from his mandible. Alien, repugnant. It looked like a separate animal squeezing out of his face, sucking and stretching his features like bubble gum. Inhuman blood dripped from his chin onto mine with the sluggish viscosity of tar, eating the heat from my face.

'Open!' he repeated, spattering the pronounced 'P' as he obstructed my breathing by holding my nose, leaving me no choice.

Damn him! My lips parted. Serge dropped his lower jaw, emptying the red pool in his palate.

Unearthly liquid gargled past my tongue and raped its way into my system, coating every crevice from my windpipe to my tonsils, causing me to cough and splutter as I fought Serge, who now stepped back, pressing his lips together.

'A taster,' he said, forgetting to wipe his mouth for a change. 'Nothing more.'

It was exactly that. A taster, no more than a tablespoonful. It felt like a barrelful.

The initial sensation was nausea; my body rejected the fluid, which, with an almost wilful intelligence, refused to be regurgitated, rendering me defenceless and unable to speak or cry for gagging. I doubled over, hand at my gullet. The taste was strange, extremely difficult to describe. I tried comparing it to the consistency of treacle with a rusty juiciness as it dissolved in my body heat. I realised with horror he had in fact spat a single runny clot down my throat, inadvertently revealing a bizarre aspect of their anatomy: they were paling somewhat, they hadn't been out yet, meaning the longer they went underfed, the more their circulation slowed and clotted into one combined mass.

It was a violation. His blood cells reached my stomach where they crystallised into countless sharp icicles, but these foreign cells were also osmotic; they immediately filtered through my stomach lining and disseminated, burning like acid before proceeding to attack my nerve endings: my joints stiffened, collapsed, stiffened, collapsed, stiffened, fell limp. I crashed into everything, the furniture, the table, the pillars. My only means of control was to grovel on my knuckles and knees. *If I stay like this, if I can just stay like this …* No such grace, child, your nose is bleeding, and hear that whining deep inside your ears? Serge's blood has circuited your arterial system and made headway for your brain.

A scorching bulb thrummed in the centre of my skull. What happened next, I thought would kill me.

Where his cells invaded, my human nervous system had to attack itself to win, causing a chain reaction that thwarted my senses, enhanced them, conflicted and blew them out of proportion into kamikaze as dormant buttons in my gene pool, inactive since pre-history, juddered on and off frantically. As a result, what I saw, heard, touched and smelled, was real, a hallucination, and every possible permutation in between.

The world you see – is not the world. Not truly. You know nothing of the world and its dimensions, you don't know what's hidden, you have no clue what's slapping you in the face as you read this page, what you can't see baying under your nose, what you can't hear! You see nothing, hear nothing. I did not see the Hall … I saw EVERYTHING.

I saw the snow falling, hundreds of feet up through the vaulted ceiling. I saw Edith and Hector, *glowing*, enveloped in light, their heads auras, their hearts – I saw it! – pumping b'dum-b'dum under ribcages above impossibly concave abdomens devoid of gut or intestine. There were ten Ediths and Hectors, then twenty of them, then five of them, copies scattered throughout the Hall.

Singing, there is singing, men's voices, a choir, tens of them, monks, a lonely, haunting gyration of voices. There's the very bottom of the well, over there! There are bodies, unnumbered bodies beneath this floor; this place is built on three plague pits; the two girls Blondie and Redhead are buried in the rubble out there, I smell them; they're in pieces, they took their heads. The ceiling, I'm on the ceiling, it's hitting me, wait, no, I'm falling, teetering from the stonework, trying to find it, can't reach, I'm going to fall! I'm scratching – what? My hands, my arms, where's my skin? I've no skin! I'm flayed, my veins are slurping worms and pulsing serpents! *Hsssssssssss.* Someone catches me; they're made of fire, their body, fire, crackling like a screeching hawk. *What's happening to me?*

There's Serge. That's not Serge. Serge is not his real name. He is crimson and ebony and purple and blue, there are hundreds of Serges in him, I see them all at once in the same man. There! A skeletal old man with silver hair so long it trails the floor to beyond the clock, his scalp is sediment, look, I swear, drenched with tears emptying from him in waterfalls. Jesus, what's happened to him? He's been wounded, bleeding everywhere! Other Serges are clawing from inside him like a glasshouse; a frightened young man, a desert, a scarp, an effigy, a temple, a youth, a never-ending forest, a child. Serge? No, it can't be. Oh my God it's terrified!

What's that noise, what's that noise? The drumming, my heart, their hearts, their vessels. Who's that? Wait, who's that, who *is* that? There's someone here. Who's broken in? No, there she goes! A kid wearing my hair, behind that pillar, she stole my dress, the dress my auntie bought me; she's afraid of me, trying to get out, wait, stop her! My heart, the heaviness, my chest, it's too much it's *beating too fast no I'm too hot!*

The figures on the Byzantine throne came to life and shouted, each individually carved figure pointing at me, at us, throwing things through their wooden encasement. I saw thousands of insects gnawing labyrinths through the stonework. I watched the candle smoke change to violet, green, luminous aqua and neon, rising higher and higher so it tickled the ceiling. There were energy waves, lines, grids of curvilinear interference patterns buzzing everywhere like swarms of bees going through the walls, turning them to water, racing in and out of the Hall. I fought them, trapped in their three-dimensional electromagnetic web like a fly, but it was useless, because my every move and breath generated more and more waves, humming and buzzing and sticking to everything like glue. They're sharp! They sting! Poison!

Shutting my eyes gave no peace. I only saw masses, clouds of blood cells cascading through capillaries in my lids: there was a war going on; my red, mortal cells versus the intruder – a very fine, muddy fog, smaller and infinitely more resilient cells than mine. Red battles the fog; cells implode; the fog divides into smaller islands in a battlefield strobe-lit by atom bombs flash-flash-flashing in time with my pulse, too bright! The heat! Oh God it's gouging my eyes out.

'My eyes are coming out!'

A voice, real or not, came through from another hemisphere:

'That's your neurons talking, caught in the crossfire. A taster, not a transfusion. Your system's fighting it, and has the advantage. For this round.'

Stop talking! Too much noise! My eardrums can't take it, they're ringing metal forks screeching down steel over grating static. Hurts! Aaagh!

I was wandering aimlessly in the passage, staggering with Serge's meaty treacle still lacing my teeth, and with every lick of it another dizzy spell levelled me. I clutched viciously at the cloth over my thundering heart as my native blood, at war with the 'taster', attacked my own canals until the vessels groaned and capillaries exploded in my cranium like an overheated battery. In my pain, I shredded the surcoat in two, thinking it was a scythe splitting my body in half, crown to crotch.

My system shut down. The internal Battle of Bloods required ammunition; wakefulness would only weaken its position. It had to shut down, consigning me to a state of semi-consciousness. When I came to, Serge was proven right, my body had won. 'For this round.'

~

The piano is reviving me. *In the bleak midwinter, frosty wind made moan.*

No children sing.

I stirred. Edith was at the piano, swinging side to side with the Hall. I was swinging with her, on the swivel chair, side to side.

No fire was burning me, no snow fell through the ceiling, no electromagnetic webs bound me, I was not skinned nor dying, nor anything other than human. The Hall was its normal self, as were my company, and I, sprawling in the new chair so far unclaimed. Serge, evil tyrant, angelic saint, the fey centre of everything, was sitting patiently on the edge of the table.

'Serge,' I said, 'who are you?'

He whispered. 'Genesis 32:29: "Why is it that you ask my name?" Alive, dead, if not a man then I don't know either.'

I whispered too, not quite *compos mentis* yet.

'Your war injuries. Stopped bleeding. Are they better now?'

Serge flinched, fazed for a moment, then, gathering himself, hopped off the table and signalled to the others. The piano music ceased at *Snow had fallen, snow on sn–*. Edith and Hector stood as Serge walked off in the direction of his chamber.

The atmosphere, how different. This large vault is listening.

Edith and Hector, there is something new in their stance, something in their reception of me. This is not routine, I have never seen them behave like this. They stand disciplined, almost regimental, and there is a pinch in the air, a vibe like the sweet breeze of reaching a summit, not a booming triumph, more an elevated and tired serenity. I have seen my way through trials, many, clawed my way here over miles and miles, without comprehending the journey. The events of half a year, from the moment I found smoke leaking into the transept, are culminating, here.

Their commander reappeared. Serge's demeanour was cloudy, the nearest you might dare put him to shyness, his eyes wide and cool. He carried an object in his hands, a bulky rectangle bound in brown paper and string, that quaint style you find on Victorian Yuletide cards.

'Early Christmas present,' he said.

He set it on the table and took up position in front of Edith and Hector, giving me space. This was not a gift, this was a ceremony.

I rose from the chair, my leather slippers disproportionately loud as I moved to the table. Gently peeling away the string and paper, I picked it up, gazing at the front cover of an old acquaintance I had not seen or thought of in months, years probably; I'd forgotten it existed. *They've been rummaging in my boxes.* I opened the front cover.

There I am. There's me. How can that be me? Ha, the ward band around my wrist says I weigh 6.5 pounds. My then-blue eyes are open, interested in the camera, my hands knotted into tiny, determined fists. My hair is quite abundant, a soft brown, satin layer. A fresh, untainted human being. Unbelievable. That was me.

I turned the page.

I am months older. Who's smiling? What was I so happy about? The infant's face beams, dressed in a yellow frock. I hated yellow, still do. And look at this other photo; I'm chewing on a pacifier with one end of my mouth and trying to munch an ice cream cone with the other.

I turn the leaf, and another. Pages of me.

She gets older and older. Her hair grows, her puppy fat wastes away, so young, she doesn't know anything; she has every reason to be happy, doesn't she, because she is so innocent. There she is rehearsing in the choir; ah, there, she is sad, detested that choir, but she escaped it. There I am in the church; Aunt Pam photographed me when I fell asleep in the pews, a typical result of hearing sermons; how it angered Aunt Alison! I was so bored that night at Christmas Mass. There's the transept cupboard; see anyone you know, Rona? No, this is not that kind of game. This is no game.

Annual school portrait photos. My smile gets phonier every year. The class photograph: there's Naomi, Stephanie and Jason, the trio who pasted gum into my textbooks, harangued me in the playground, put dead moths in my hair, name-called me out of the choir and found me in my hiding places, not all though. Later, someone found *them*. There's Chris, the class heartthrob. There's Mrs Collanger. There's a former friend, Karen, so protective, bless her, I passed her in the street a couple of years ago; she didn't know me.

More pages.

Me, wearing rubber boots dipped in mud, windswept hair on our holiday at Loch Assynt in Scotland, my best memory, and here we are in Banff, where my aunts were convinced they heard a ghostly bell tolling from the vacant tower of a ruined church; they were so frightened we quit the place early a couple of days later.

The album's final pages. The photos are catching up with m; I'm in my early twenties here, feeding the rooks in Fergus Green, lines starting on my face already, creases at the corners of my mouth and crow's feet; I have some white hairs, likely hundreds more in a decade. But there were several photo albums in my boxes, why did they only pick out this volume?

I turned the next page and saw why.

This album is incomplete. It can yet be filled. There are a good thirty-something blank leaves to go. Can I fill it?

Their early Christmas present began to make unutterable sense.

Can I fill it. I have the option. Fill it with what? Would I choose to?

The pendulum swung, ticking. It swung through many ticks as I stood, unresponsive over the empty pages. I flipped to Rona feeding the rooks; that Rona I recognised, not baby or toddler Rona, I didn't know who that was. But this Rona with the rooks, her expression, her sadness, she's thinning out inside. I flipped the next leaf forward to blankness.

They're showing you your life. What was I a year ago? Episodes of my life, planted out before me in chips and slices. Remember her? Do you know this girl? Do you want her back? Does she exist? Oh, Rona!

I wiped away a solitary tear.

This album wrapped in brown paper is not a gift. It's a choice. A taster is a taster, I could still say no.

The remainder of the album lay open at severe white sheets. I looked up at my family.

It is the finality.

They know it.

I know it.

Edith and Hector held their ceremonial silence. Only Serge, my unfathomable Serge, the being who will disarm you with a single look, addressed me.

'What are you? Where do you live?'

Tick … Tick … Tick … Tick

'Do you want to go back upstairs now?'

Tick … Tick

'Or are you staying down here?'

Without looking, my fingers moved over the candlelit paper to the leather binding, slipped under the thick volume, stroked the front cover. In that bleak midwinter, long before your time, in a rumpled sigh of leavened old plastic, the album closed.

To be continued...

ACKNOWLEDGEMENTS

Firstly, I am forever indebted to the staff at St Mary's Parish Kirk in Haddington, East Lothian, for so generously granting permission to include a detail from their windows in the cover design, and for sharing their wealth of information with me. Thank you also to the Historic Environment Scotland staff at Seton Collegiate Church in East Lothian, for being so helpful and accommodating.

There will never be enough thanks for my editor, Catherine Dunn, and publisher Chimaera Productions for this second edition. Their time and professionalism has been an absolute lifeline.

Immense gratitude to you my wonderful sister, Andrea Fisher de Cuba, to my lovely brother Rhys, and sister-in-law Nicki for your encouragement throughout, and to the following people for their invaluable feedback, tough love, and, most of all, for giving me hope.

Kat Hanlon, you have a massive heart and a great mind. I cannot overstress what a help you were when I needed it most. A special mention to authors Ian McKinney and C.W. Hawes for their truly extraordinary support, kind words and promotion. Not to mention a massive shout-out to the amazingly dedicated reviewer Leonard Tillerman, who helps so many authors every day.

Thank you forever and a day to my long-suffering, talented, closest friend, Ashley James Pryce, for being my critic, clown, hugger and rock.

And finally. Formal front page dedications aside:

This book is for the one who inspired the eyes. Not a word of it would not exist without them.